Also by Erica Waters
Ghost Wood Song

THE RIVER HAS TEETH

ERICA WATERS

HARPER TEEN
An Imprint of HarperCollins*Publishers*

HarperTeen is an imprint of HarperCollins Publishers.

The River Has Teeth
Copyright © 2021 by Erica Waters
All rights reserved. Printed in the United States of America.
No part of this book may be used or reproduced in any manner whatsoever
without written permission except in the case of brief quotations embodied
in critical articles and reviews. For information address HarperCollins
Children's Books, a division of HarperCollins Publishers, 195 Broadway,
New York, NY 10007.
www.epicreads.com

Library of Congress Control Number: 2021934290
ISBN 978-0-06-289425-0

Typography by Jenna Stempel-Lobell
21 22 23 24 25 PC/LSCH 10 9 8 7 6 5 4 3 2 1
❖
First Edition

For everyone who's been made to feel like prey,
and wished for sharper teeth

ONE
DELLA

The prison is always quiet but never still. A train's low rumble vibrates the cement walls, releasing ancient dust in ghostly breaths. Water drips. Mice scurry in the ruins. Starlings flutter in the rafters, all rattle and rasp. Wind moans through the narrow, broken windows.

Everyone in town thinks this old prison is haunted. They don't know how right they are.

"I'm here," I call. My voice echoes in the predawn darkness, making the starlings stop their chatter. I shine my flashlight over the path, watching for rubble that could trip me. If I fall, she might decide I'm prey. If I fall—

"Are you awake?" I ask, pushing away the fear before it can get its roots into me. I pause, listening for her slightest movement, a single breath. There's nothing.

The short, fine hairs at the back of my neck prickle, and I spin, ready to block a slap, a lunge, a bite. But her silhouette in the darkness is still. She's back in her human form now, only a slight, pale woman with long, dark hair and a smell like the river at flood time. I wait for her to move, wait for her to show today's mood. Will she be quiet and sly, or raging?

She steps into a shaft of weak light. Her hair is matted with dirt and something dark and wet. Her eyes are as shadowed as the forgotten corners of this derelict prison. A smear of dried blood turns her thin lips into a clown's crooked smile. She comes closer and reaches a bony hand toward my face.

Everything inside me wants to startle and back away, wants to bolt. But you can't show her any weakness, so I brace myself for her touch. Her hand is moist and cold and smells of earth. She caresses my cheek, her gaze almost gentle.

Some old blood instinct, some half-forgotten longing, rises in me. "Momma," I say, leaning into her touch. She smiles at the endearment.

And then her hand snarls in my hair and I'm flying across the room. I catch my balance just in time to keep from toppling into a brick wall. My fingers splay over the peeling white paint, knocking long flakes of it from the wall in my hurry to spin back around. A brick barely misses my face as I turn.

Momma cackles.

"Are you done now?" I ask after a beat, keeping my voice steady, almost indifferent. That's the way to handle my mother when she's in a mood like this. She's human now, but only just. By noon, she'll be more like her old self. But I'll be stocking shelves at the grocery store by then.

Momma shrugs, but I can tell she's already lost interest. She

wanders across the open room and pauses beneath the squawk-
ing starlings, gazing up at them. That must be where the blood
came from—a bird she caught in the night. At least I hope it
was a bird. I guess it could also be a rat or possum.

"I brought you some breakfast," I say, crossing the room
with my pack. Momma settles onto a clear place on the floor
and I sit across from her, pulling out a thermos of decaf coffee
and a fried-egg-and-cheese sandwich, which she regards with
deep skepticism.

She turns her eyes back to the starlings and begins to hum.
Her voice, even while humming, is eerily beautiful, especially
here, echoing in the stillness of the prison. The starlings stop
their chattering to listen. Maybe this is how she caught one last
night.

"What's that you're humming?" I ask, hoping to draw her
back to human thoughts.

She looks at me and smiles, the blood on her lips turning it
into a chilling expression. She sings, picking up where she left
off.

From ear to ear I slit her mouth,
And stabbed her in the head,
Till she, poor soul, did breathless lie,
Before her butcher bled.

I go as still as the birds, my eyes fixed on hers. Her expression turns troubled as she sings the next verse, but her voice
seems to caress the words.

And then I took her by the hair,
To cover the foul sin
And dragged her to the riverside,
And threw her body in.

"That's enough, Momma," I say. "Stop it." I shake myself, as if the movement can release me from her song and the memories it evokes: gray skin and sharp teeth, a curtain of hair like seaweed. The wildness in her green eyes as she pushed the body into the river.

I should have known better than to encourage Momma's singing. I used to love to hear her belt out these old ballads, songs carried to Tennessee by our ancestors. Sometimes she sang to draw the magic, and sometimes she sang just for the love of it. But now her beautiful voice is only a tool for the monster to use.

She stops talking and grabs the sandwich from the floor, raising it to her mouth. I grit my teeth as a sour taste rises up my throat at the thought of the last food that passed through her lips.

Once she finishes the final bite of sandwich, her eyes are clearer, less hungry. "Do you want to come home with me today?" I ask out of habit more than anything else. For some reason I also add, "I'm sure Da would like to see you."

She takes a cautious sip from the thermos and smirks as if to say, *If he wants to see me so bad, why's he not here?*

"He's busy," I lie. "Gathering ingredients. We've been getting more customers lately. The heat must be making everyone more bloodthirsty than usual."

It's only June, but already it feels like the middle of summer. The forest is like a wet, green mouth, oppressively hot by ten in the morning. This old prison is probably the coolest place for miles.

Momma starts humming again, but I cut her off. "Come home with me today. You can take a shower, see Da. Maybe help with some of the spell work."

Her eyes flash, and I know it's time to back down, but I'm so tired of leaving her alone here. "You're still human," I tell her. *For now*, I add to myself. She only changes at night, but every day, she becomes a little more monster than woman. "You're allowed to go home."

She only bares her teeth at me in response. Is it my imagination, or have her canines gone a little more pointed?

I sigh and gather my things, leaving behind some food. I always bring a full day's food and water with me. Every morning I offer to bring her home, and every morning she refuses. I don't know if it's because she's doing penance for Aunt Sage, she's angry at Da, or she just doesn't want to play at being human anymore.

"See you tomorrow, then," I say as I make my way over the broken floor, stepping carefully over piles of rubble and small animal bones. The sun is fully up now, and I can see the prison in all its decrepit glory. The high, grim windows, the lonely, empty cells. I let myself out the usual door, padlocking it behind me, then head toward a crumbling brick wall. I skirt through a body-sized hole, and then I'm under the barbed-wire fence and trudging to my truck, which I left parked on the shoulder of the road.

I pull onto the pavement, Momma's song still echoing horribly in my ears, louder than the train barreling down the tracks on the other side of the prison. Momma has barely had a lucid moment in months now. She's locked up inside herself, wandering the strange labyrinth our twisted magic has made within her. She's never been able—or maybe she's just not willing—to tell me what happened to her and Aunt Sage eleven months ago. I don't know how she feels or what she wants. These songs are the closest thing to sense I've gotten from her in weeks, but I think I like her silence better.

I leave behind the industrial area of the prison as I cross the bridge over the river, and then the nature park is on my right. Soon, my view is obscured by trees on either side. I wind my way up into the hills, breathing a little freer as I distance myself from Momma and her prison and the row of falling-down warehouses that line that side of the river.

Ten minutes later, my truck's engine whines as it strains up the steep, rutted driveway toward home. At the top of the hill, I glance into the rearview mirror for a final look at the forest that borders the road. Green fills my vision for one perfect moment before I look forward again and the house comes into view.

It's a big, rambling farmhouse from the 1800s that looks a little more abandoned every year. It used to bustle with the activity of five witches, but now it's just Da and me rattling around inside. Six months ago, someone set fire to the front porch, sending a column down and leaving the front door a blackened mess. It might've been kids playing pranks. More likely, it was someone who found himself at the receiving end of a Lloyd vengeance spell and wanted some revenge of his own.

I start to pull into my usual place by the dogwood tree, but an unfamiliar car is parked there, one of those sporty hatchback numbers suburban women drive, complete with a smiling stick family on the back windshield. The house looks even more broken-down next to the car's shining white paint and cheerful bumper stickers. This car says *wholesome, safe, happy*. Everything the Lloyds are not.

A bitter, noxious smell hits me before I even reach the porch, which means Soccer Mom is here to buy our brew for a cheating husband. Not so happy after all.

I make my way through the cluttered living room, down a dark hallway full of closed doors, and into the kitchen at the back of the house. The door creaks when I push it open, startling a petite, mousy white woman in yoga pants. Her eyes are wild, like those of all the women who come here. She's sad and angry and desperate—I can tell because that's what the brew simmering on the stove smells like: misery and rage. But right now, she's afraid. Afraid to be in a run-down house in hillbilly country, afraid of the dried plants that hang in bunches on hooks and of the jars of insects that line the shelves. Most of all, she's afraid of the short, stocky man who leans over the simmering pot, muttering in a harsh, heavily accented rasp.

My father stirs the pot one last time and then motions to the woman. "Come 'ere. Add those seeds I gave you, name your intention, and the brew'll be done."

The woman slowly opens her tightly clenched fist, revealing

a bright pink seed capsule with dangling red seeds. It's *Euony-mus americanus*, or bursting heart.

She might be small and scared, but this woman means business. She hisses something I can't hear and tosses the seed capsule into the brown, lumpy water, and Da stirs it in, whispering the final words of the spell.

I'm not sure anyone deserves what this brew will do to them, no matter how big a cheater. On its own, bursting heart is poisonous, causing severe diarrhea to anyone who ingests it. But when it's made into a vengeance spell, diarrhea takes on a whole new meaning. It's an old family recipe called Shits-His-Soul, so called because it hollows a man out, taking away his desire, his ambition, his personality, all he is. For six months, he becomes a shell of a man. And by the time a soul grows back, he's lost everything—including his mistress.

This spell killed someone only two months ago. Da said it was because the wife administered too much at once, but I think the magic just slipped out of bounds, the way it's been doing for the last year and a half, since before Momma was turned. Maybe I should feel guilty about that, but Momma taught me it's not our job to judge whether someone deserves vengeance—only to give our customers what they ask for. What happens after we hand over a spell is none of our business.

When the spell caused that man's death, I was worried the police would make it our business, but the wife kept her mouth shut, the spell's ingredients didn't turn up in a toxin screen, and the medical examiner ruled the man's death a heart attack. Still, I'm surprised Da's selling this brew again.

"Cash," he grunts, making the woman flinch. She pulls a leather wallet from her purse and tentatively places two crisp twenties on the scratched counter. Her hand hovers above her purse, which is always the sign to ask for more money.

"This spell's eighty," I say. "It's hard to get bursting heart this time of year." That's not strictly true, but this woman won't know. And who can say when another customer is going to come along. They've gotten rarer since our magic started going wrong—our Liquid Lies spell gave a man bleeding mouth ulcers instead of allowing him to deceive his boss; a brew that was supposed to make a woman's thirty-year-old son move out of her house sent him into a violent temper so extreme he smashed all the windows in their home before he left. A dozen more stories like that are floating around Fawney. So only the people who are angry or desperate enough to be reckless come now.

Like Soccer Mom. She pulls another forty dollars from her purse while Da pours the concoction through a mesh strainer into a small mason jar. The contents are as murky brown as the river that runs through this town. That's mostly owing to the handful of forest soil Da has started throwing into every brew he makes. He says the soil grounds the spells, making them homely and serviceable. I think that's more superstition than anything, same as having the customer add the final ingredient with their own hand. I'm not sure there's any measure we can take now to keep the magic under our control.

Da fastens the lid and holds the jar out to the woman. "Now listen carefully and do exactly what I say. You need to get it into his food or drink. A third today, a third tomorrow, a third the next day. Don't do anything differently. Exactly that, and you'll get what you came for. His new girl won't recognize him." Da gives the woman a contemptuous smile. "You understand?"

She snatches the jar and rushes for the back exit, leaving the kitchen's screen door banging in the wind in her hurry to get away. Soon, her car tears down the driveway.

"Poor bastard," Da mutters, shaking his head.

"Couldn't you have given her something else?" I ask.

Da snorts. "Uh-uh. That woman won't be satisfied till her cheating husband is limp and lifeless as an overboiled crawdad."

"Well, let's hope it's more limp than lifeless this time," I say. Da grunts in agreement.

I start helping Da clean up the mess scattered all over the kitchen—dried mushrooms on the table, drifts of dirt on the counter and floor, water dripping down the stove. We work in silence together, each of us content to keep to our own thoughts. I don't realize I've started humming Momma's murder ballad until Da swears and says my name. I nearly drop my broom.

"'The Bloody Miller,'" he murmurs. "That sort of morning, then?" He finishes washing out his brew pot and then tosses it under the kitchen sink, where it lands with a dull thunk. When I don't answer, Da sighs and leaves the kitchen. Soon, the busted old recliner in the living room groans with his weight. He turns on the TV, and the familiar, monotonous voice of anchorman Jerry Jones drifts down the hallway. I half listen for a few minutes as I rummage through the kitchen for something to eat. I take my bag of chips into the living room just as video footage of the road that runs past our house appears on the screen.

Jerry's face turns grim. "The hunt is still underway for local woman, twenty-one-year-old Rochelle Greymont, who went missing last week."

A posed photograph of a beautiful white girl with blond hair and perfect teeth appears on the screen behind the news anchor. "Authorities have located her car on the outskirts of Wood Thrush Nature Park, but—"

Da shuts off the TV, and we sit in silence, only the ticking of the clock over the fireplace making a sound. Worry unfurls in my gut like a fiddlehead uncurling from its bud. Another missing girl. The second one to go missing on the Bend— a four-mile stretch of land hugged on one side by the river, roughly approximating the borders of the nature park, though of course the Bend came first. The Bend has been the secret source of our family's magic for the last hundred years, whether it's been private farmland, unclaimed wasteland, or a state-funded nature park. The land has never belonged to the Lloyds, but that doesn't matter. The Bend is ours.

And now girls are going missing on it.

The first one, Samantha Parsons, had been out hiking with her boyfriend. He said he turned around and she was just gone. One girl missing, fine. But two?

My mind flits to the smear of blood on Momma's lips.

"Da," I say, but he interrupts.

"Don't even think that, Della. Your momma's locked up good now. She's been there every morning, hasn't she?"

"Yes," I whisper. *And singing about the murder of a blond girl.*

"She's not a killer."

"She killed Aunt Sage," I say.

Da flinches at my words. The memory is still as painful to him as it is to me.

Momma and Sage had gone out to try a new spell to heal the Bend's wayward magic. But something went horribly, unimaginably wrong. Da and I found them just in time to see the monster Momma had become push her sister's bloodied body into the river. I had to go home and tell my cousin Miles that his mother was dead and mine was to blame.

Da shakes his head. "That was different. She'd only just changed, and she didn't know her own strength. She wouldn't hurt those girls. I know she wouldn't."

I rub the sore spot on my scalp where she grabbed me by the hair this morning, but I don't say anything. Everything in me wants to believe that Da's right, that Momma is more than the monster who hides inside her by day and comes creeping out at night—the one I've begun to call the river siren.

After Aunt Sage, we locked Momma in the defunct Wilson J. Monroe Penitentiary, where she couldn't do any more harm.

But the closed-down prison is closed down for a reason: it's old and crumbling, with a dozen possible escape routes for someone cunning enough to find them. And my mother is nothing if not cunning.

My eyes wander to the framed pictures on the wall, all family snapshots. Momma and Aunt Sage with their arms around each other, Sage smiling like a sunflower while Momma looks at the camera with a mysterious smile. Miles and me as little kids, playing at spell work in the mud. And my favorite, of me and Momma and Da at the kitchen table, Momma blowing out the candles on her birthday cake. The difference between the mother in that photo and the half-feral woman I left behind in the prison this morning makes me want to weep.

Now this new girl, Rochelle Greymont, is missing, and her disappearance sits heavy as a weight in my gut.

But if Momma is escaping, if she's hurting people, what am I supposed to do? When she first turned, Da and I tried every brew we could think of to change her back, and nothing worked. After a while, he gave up. He visited her less and less, until one day he stopped going at all and left her to me. Miles was too angry and grieved to stay here; he took a cleaning job at Highland Rim University, saying he was done with magic. I lost my aunt, my mother, and my cousin in one go. Now I'm on my own, and I have no idea what to do.

I could shoot her, I guess, or I could lead the police to her and let them do it. But I know I'd kill a hundred park visitors myself before I'd let my momma die.

It's an ugly thought, but maybe the Bend makes monsters of us all.

Someone starts knocking on our front door the next morning before the sun is fully up. I'm brushing my teeth, so I wait for Da to wake up and answer it.

"What?" Da finally hollers, dragging himself down the hallway toward the front door.

The banging comes again.

It's too early in the morning for a customer. I've been up for half an hour, making Momma's breakfast and getting ready for the day, but Da never shows his face before nine if he can help it. Besides, customers don't bang like that. They are much more timid, afraid a witch is going to blast them at the threshold.

I peer out of the bathroom when Da opens the door. Two uniformed police officers stand there, a burly white man and a short white woman with blond hair. I walk softly down the hallway to see what's happening, toothbrush still in hand. I catch the end of the man's sentence.

". . . checking in with the neighbors, see if anyone heard anything or saw the girl."

Da keeps his hand on the door. "We didn't, and you might've noticed we don't have any neighbors. We're the only folks around here for a long ways."

"Yes, that's why it's so important for you to give us any information you might have," the man says patiently.

Da sighs, and I come to stand next to him before he can say anything too nasty. "We don't know anything about the missing girl," I say, meeting the female cop's eyes. She's kind of hot, but cops mean nothing but trouble for us. "If we did, we would've called already."

She raises her eyebrows like she doesn't believe me, and my heart starts to race. She cocks her head as if she can hear it beating in my chest. "Mind if we take a look around your property, just in case?"

"Actually, I do mind," Da says, but I step in front of him.

We can't give them any reason to look into us. We've got too much to hide.

"Feel free to check the yard and the shed," I say. "But we really don't know anything."

She looks to Da for permission, and he gives a terse nod.

The male cop looks over Da's head, trying to catch a look at the inside of the witches' house. I'm sure he's heard more than a few stories, probably seen the aftereffects of some of our brews, whether he knew it or not. "Only y'all live here? Nobody else?" he asks. "I thought the Lloyds were a big family."

I freeze, but Da answers. "My lazy wife got tired of looking after this 'un and hightailed it off to Memphis with her sorry sister. Just us two now."

"And that cat there," I add as the enormous orange tabby Aunt Sage named Sunny darts past the cops' ankles and into the house. The female cop meets my eyes again, as if checking to see I'm not banged up. I give her Da's patented disdainful smile and she looks away.

"Thank you for your cooperation," the man says. "We'll have a look around and be on our way. But if you hear anything, you give me a call." He places a card in Da's hand.

"Yes, sir," I say before Da closes the door in their faces.

"Shit," I whisper, leaning against the closed door. "Shit."

Da puts a gentle hand on my shoulder. "Ain't her, Della. I told you that. Them sniffing 'round here don't make a damn bit of difference."

"What if they ask more questions about where Momma and Aunt Sage are?" We never reported the death, and Sage didn't have anyone but Miles to wonder about her. Miles agreed to keep quiet about her murder for the family's sake, but if pressed by police, he might reveal something. "The lady cop seemed concerned about my lack of a mother," I add.

Da snorts. "They don't give two shits what happened to your momma. They'll see these girls going missing's got nothing to do with us and be on their way. Now, don't you have someplace to be?" He looks meaningfully at the old grandfather clock standing across the room. "You're gonna be late, and she'll think you've abandoned her for good."

"I'm not the one who's abandoned her," I mutter as I walk back to my room. Da picks up Sunny and strokes the cat's head, pretending not to hear what I said.

As I drive over to the prison, my mind starts churning through every possible escape route Momma could take. I picture her breaking through a window, scaling the high walls of the prison, and dropping to the dead grass below. I picture her racing across the road and into the forest, bounding on all fours, making for the river. But I don't let myself picture what might come after that. I don't let myself think about teeth and claws and blood. Not yet. Not until I have to. For now, I'll keep pretending, just like Da.

TWO
NATASHA

I've seen posters for missing people before—usually a little grainy, with MISSING splashed across the top in bold red letters. They always seemed like a relic to me, something left over from the 1970s. How could anyone go missing now with constant social media updates, cell phone towers, and facial recognition software?

Maybe that's why it doesn't feel quite real as I staple a poster with my sister's smiling face to an electric pole, just above an advertisement for a dog walker. I smooth a crease in the paper and stare at the words, which are starting to blur from the mix of sweat and tears in my eyes.

Rochelle Greymont

Age: 21

Race: Caucasian

Blond hair, blue eyes, 5'10"

Last seen—

"Nat," my best friend, Georgia Greer, calls from across the quad, pulling my attention from the poster. She shakes an empty canvas bag. "I'm all out. Do you have more?" She holds a staple gun at the ready.

I quickly wipe my eyes and reach into my bag, but there's only one poster left. I glance at the time on my cell phone. We've been papering Rochelle's college, Highland Rim University, for the last two hours. "I'm out too," I yell. "I guess we should head to fencing anyway."

Georgia jogs over, her long, thin braids tapping against her bare shoulders. "God, it's hot today," she says, fanning herself. Her dark brown skin is beaded with sweat same as mine. "Are you sure you want to go to fencing?" she asks when she gets close, probably noticing the traces of my tears. "We can skip if you want."

I bite my lip. It feels weird to go to fencing club like it's a normal day when my sister is missing, when she's been missing for over seventy-two hours. But right now it's better than going home, where I'll be sure to do nothing but pace and worry and go out of my mind with fear, just like my parents are doing. Where my brain will run through worst-case scenarios like one of those old-timey movie reels Georgia's got on display in her basement studio.

"No, let's go," I say. "Mom said I should stick to my routine as much as I can. She said it will help keep me calm."

"Well, your mom must've never noticed how terrifying you are with a saber in hand," Georgia says wryly.

"You're one to talk. You beat me in every single bout last week."

Georgia smirks. "I'm always telling you, short and compact girls make the best fencers—and the best lovers. That's why Odette can't resist me."

I snort, and Georgia's eyes flit up to me, her serious expression at odds with her banter. The joking is for my sake—to draw me out of myself. She's worried. She's been my friend long enough to tell that even though I look calm on the outside, a volcano is starting to rumble underneath.

Because as my sister's face stares out at me from every newly hung poster we pass, I feel my old anger—the anger I've worked hard in therapy to get under control—begin to boil and bubble up. And when I see a flyer advertising the live music at Papa's tonight, I know no amount of fencing will keep the volcano from erupting. I just need to make sure I unleash it on the right person.

I'm still sweaty and wired from fencing when I step into the dim, smoky atmosphere of Papa's. It's four in the afternoon, and outside the sun is still a burning yellow ball in the sky, but inside the bar, time has no meaning. There are only neon beer signs, sticky tables, and faded band posters from the early 2000s. Rochelle's boyfriend, Jake, stands in front of the stage, fiddling around with his sound equipment. There's no music playing, and Jake looks up at my entrance. The light from the window at the front of the bar throws him into shadow, so he's more of a silhouette than anything—the outline of broad shoulders and tousled hair.

"Hey," I say.

"Hey yourself." His voice sounds tired. When I get up close

to the stage, I see he looks tired too—he's got dark circles under his eyes and a haggard look about him. He's only twenty-two, but he could pass for thirty right now.

"Staying busy, I see." I try—and fail—to keep the judgment from my voice.

"Can I help you with something?" Jake asks, as if I'm some girl who's wandered in off the street, not anyone he knows or cares about.

"Wanted to know if you've heard from Rochelle," I say mildly. My dad, who's an attorney, taught me you can't go straight in for the attack; you've got to warm up the witness. It's not my style, but I'm trying. I want to be a lawyer too, so I guess this is my chance to practice Dad's methods.

"Nope," Jake says.

I sigh. "That's all you've got to say for yourself? Rochelle's been missing for three days. Everyone's running around trying to find her. And you're just here, dicking around with amplifiers." So much for warming up the witness.

Silence stretches between us, but I refuse to break it. I stare Jake down, waiting for a response. His expression is one of studied irritation, like I'm wasting his time. Or maybe he's high and having trouble focusing—you can never tell with Jake.

I pull out my last missing-person poster and toss it onto one of his amps. Rochelle's face stares up at the ceiling. Jake flinches when he sees it, but then he meets my eyes again.

"You know what she's like. She'll turn up," he finally says, looping some electrical cords over his arm. "This is classic Rochelle. She gets pissed off at me and disappears for a few days. She's done it plenty of times before." He gazes across the bar, clenching his jaw. A muscle in his cheek ticks, revealing the strain he's trying to hide behind the nonchalance.

"Rochelle doesn't disappear," I say. "She's never done that to me."

Jake laughs. "Ask Margo. They had a fight last month and Rochelle didn't talk to her for a week straight, even made me pretend not to be home when Margo came by."

Margo Yoon has been Rochelle's best friend since high school. I doubt they could go one day without talking, let alone a week. Jake's only exaggerating to prove a point.

"Well, this time I guess she's hiding from all of us, then," I say.

"I guess so," Jake says. "And once everyone has made a big enough fuss over her, she'll come home. And I won't be waiting for her with open arms this time."

I struggle to maintain my composure, the way Dad taught me, the way a Greymont should, but my anger bursts out of me. "You're being such an asshole," I say. "You think she just abandoned her car on the side of the road? She loves that car."

Rochelle's 1972 powder-blue Triumph TR6 is her baby. She wouldn't even leave it in the driveway, let alone on the side of the road next to a nature park. The police have already determined that the car didn't break down, so something else must have made her pull over by the roadside.

"Maybe she met up with someone else," Jake says, a flicker of jealousy in his eyes. "Another guy. He picked her up, and she left the car."

"That's bullshit."

Jake has always been jealous, almost from the very night he and Rochelle met. She thought his possessiveness was charming, at least at first. But I see it for the toxic mess it is. That jealousy is preventing him from helping to look for her. From even admitting something might be wrong.

Jake shakes his head, biting his lip. "Wouldn't have been the first time. Your sister is a—"

I step forward and push him, hard. "I will beat the everloving shit out of you, Jake Carr, if you say one more fucking word."

His jaw clenches again and anger flashes in his baby-blue eyes, but he pushes it down. Instead of lashing out, Jake smirks, his handsome lips twisting into the hipster-cowboy insouciance he projects every time he gets onstage. "Better watch that dirty mouth of yours, Natasha. Don't want people to think you're not a lady."

It takes all my self-possession not to deck him in his smug, beautiful face. "She could be lost and hungry in the woods. She could have been eaten by a fucking bear. She could have been murdered by some psycho. And you're standing here telling me to act like a lady? Why aren't you out looking for her? Why aren't you on the news using what little celebrity status you have to get people to help find her? Why aren't you doing *anything*?" I yell the last part, and Jake takes a half step back.

He looks to one side, a tiny bit of shame creeping into his expression.

"Oh," I laugh, making it as derisive as I can. "I see. You're worried about your image. Bad boy Jake Carr doesn't have a steady girlfriend. Is that why your PR team has kept you out of the news—or is it your family's money? You know, I really tried hard to like you, for Rochelle's sake. But you're a useless piece of shit."

I spin on my heel and bang out of the bar, and am instantly hit in the face with glaring June sunlight and a wave of humid heat. This parking lot feels like the very pit of hell. I yank open the door of my BMW and throw myself against the driver's seat. The leather burns the exposed skin of my shoulders, but I don't care. I'm burning on the inside, so why not the outside too?

"Goddamnit!" I yell, and punch the steering wheel. The horn gives a weak blast, and a homeless man on the other side of the parking lot startles. He scowls at me and continues walking, dragging a black trash bag behind him. Ah, good, another person who thinks I'm a spoiled rich bitch driving my daddy's fancy car. To him, I'm no better than Jake.

Tears sting the corners of my eyes, but I blink them back as I start the car, crank the air conditioner, and turn the music all the way up. I spin out of the parking lot and immediately get stuck at a red light. A herd of college girls with fresh blowouts parade across the walkway. The light changes, but they've paused in the middle of the road to—I swear to God—take a selfie. I consider blaring my horn at them. Instead, I take a deep breath. The voice of my therapist, Dr. Patel, chides me. *You know what this anger is, Natasha. It's fear. It's anxiety.* She says all my rage is a coping mechanism for dealing with trauma. Maybe she's right, or maybe the world is just full of reasons to be mad.

Like my sister going missing and the police having zero leads. Like her shithead boyfriend doing nothing to help us find her. The thought sends a bolt of anger down my arms, and before I know it, I've got my palm pressed hard against the horn. The girls look at me and laugh. They give me the finger but get out of my way in a hurry when I rev my engine.

I drive in stop-and-go traffic for another few infuriating minutes until I'm able to pull onto the interstate. I glance at the dashboard and hit the gas. I told my parents I'd be home by four, but it's going to be at least five. With Rochelle missing, they are more on edge than ever. I didn't tell them I was going to see Jake; in fact, they didn't even know about Jake until a few days ago. Rochelle never told them anything. She has always kept things from them, but after she left for college, she became even more secretive.

As I drive, I start sorting through the facts like I would for a research paper, laying them out in order. The night she went missing, Rochelle was at a party with Jake at some music executive's house. They drove separately because Rochelle was coming from a study group in the library at Highland Rim University. They were both seen at the party until midnight, but after that time, no one remembers seeing her. Jake's friends vouch that he was at the party and spent the night there, and there are photos of him hanging out after midnight. Jake says Rochelle was tired and drove herself home. No one else saw her after that. A park ranger reported her abandoned car after it sat by the side of the road next to the nature park all day. No one knows why she was even driving in that direction. Basically, no one knows anything.

I pull into my family's neighborhood and slow my speed as I drive through streets with massive, imposing houses and enormous, perfectly manicured lawns. I keep thinking that one day this will feel like my neighborhood, the place I belong, but it's been six years and I still feel like that newly adopted ten-year-old gawking at the kind of wealth I'd only seen on TV. Since then I've worked hard to make myself into the sort of person who lives here, from my 4.0 GPA to my shelf of fencing and track medals. Fake it till you make it and all that.

I turn onto my family's tree-lined drive and speed along the curve that borders the Civil War–era wall, slowing only when I see the house. It's a beautiful old Georgian brick with ivy climbing the walls and cream-colored roses growing in the flower beds. Unlike a lot of the houses around here, it manages to be classy without being imposing or overwrought. It reminds me of my parents, with their old money and soft charm. My gentle mother, my steady father. Sure, they can be oblivious sometimes, but they're still the sort of people who adopt two half-grown girls and love them like their own blood.

Mom is waiting in the kitchen, an apron covering her dress, yellow rubber gloves on her hands. She's been scrubbing the sink. Again. "Natasha, I was starting to worry," she says. Her lips tremble, and I hate myself for scaring her.

I give Mom my best good-girl smile. "Fencing club ran a little long, and then some of us went for fries and milk shakes after."

Mom smiles, but the worry lines don't quite disappear from her perfectly made up face. "I'm glad you're spending time with your friends, sweetheart. You've been working far too hard this summer."

She's too distracted to notice the lie—except for Georgia, the people in fencing club aren't my friends. They're a bunch of type-A overachievers who picked fencing because it gives them a chance to release all their pent-up angst. Not that I'm any different. Amid fencing club meets, my summer has been consumed by standardized test prep and internship applications. Well, until Rochelle went missing. None of that stuff matters until Ro comes home.

I plop onto a stool at the kitchen counter. The marble countertop has been scrubbed so clean I can almost see my reflection in it. "Any news?"

Mom turns away quickly, but I still catch the way her face falls. "Nothing at all. The police have finished searching the area along the highway, but there's no sign of her. They . . . they are dredging the river now to see—" She gasps down a sob.

I'm off my stool in a moment. I wrap my arms around her from behind and press my face into her soft hair. "Oh, Mama," I croon. "Oh, she's not in the river. I promise." My mother's small frame shudders.

"You know, you know that boy she was seeing, Jake? He said she's done this before, just taken off when they had a fight." I hate myself for repeating his words, but I have to offer Mom something. "Maybe that's all that's happened. Maybe she'll turn up in a few days or a week. And we'll forget all about this."

"Of course, of course, sweetheart," Mom says, turning to face me. I wipe the tears from her eyes with my thumbs. She tries for a brave smile.

I hold back my own tears and raise my chin. "We Cook girls are tough, you know." Mom startles at my use of my and Rochelle's birth name. "That's what Rochelle used to say to me, when we were little and things were bad. 'We Cook girls are too tough for anyone, Shashi.'" Mom smiles at Rochelle's nickname for me. "And now that we're Greymont girls, well, we're even tougher."

Mom beams at that through her tears, and I almost feel like things are going to be all right. Then her cell phone rings and Mom hurries to answer it. "Hello?" she says. The way her voice shakes makes me want to smash something.

"Yes, this is Cheryl Greymont. Yes. I see. Anything else? No, no, of course." Her face is carefully blank now, but she grips the phone until her knuckles bleed white. "I'll call my husband, and we'll arrange it. Yes. Yes, we'll come. Thank you."

After she ends the call, she stares at the phone in her hand so long I think she's in a trance.

"Mom?" I ask. "What is it? Did they find her? Is she . . . is she—" My voice breaks.

My anguish catches Mom's attention and she meets my eyes, her own steady and sure again. "They found her purse beside the river."

"Oh. Do they know—"

Mom shakes her head. "The police said now that we have a definite starting place, we can bring our own search party out there if we want to. Because we have a place to look now." Purpose enters her voice, and she's the mother I've lived with for six years, the one who organized bake sales and wrangled the PTA. "Now we know for sure she went missing in the nature park. That's more than we had before. We can start at the river."

A horrible image flashes into my mind: Rochelle dead in a dirty river, her corpse gray and bloated, her beautiful blond hair caught in bracken, her eyes eaten by fish. My knees buckle, but I sit back down before Mom can see. I push the hateful images away and give Mom a reassuring smile. Rochelle isn't dead. I'd feel it if she were. I'd know it way down deep inside. Rochelle is alive, and she needs us to find her.

I wave my iPhone in the air. "I'll start rallying the troops."

Less than two hours later, we've got sixty volunteers combing the nature park for signs of Rochelle. The search party has been broken into four sections: one to search along the river where Ro's purse was found, one to check the brush-filled meadows nearby, one to walk the low-lying forest, and one to climb the ridges in hopes of spotting her from above. The Wood Thrush Nature Park is enormous, covering about 2,500 acres, traversing several types of landscape. If Rochelle is here, she could be anywhere.

For the twentieth time, I shout Rochelle's name into the trees that line the road. The echoes of other voices are all that reach me, each one yelling the same word, my sister's name. "Rochelle!" I call again, worrying my voice is too thin and weak to carry. The immensity of the park, the sheer vastness of it, makes me feel small and powerless.

I came here once before, when I was eleven, and I felt exactly the same way then. It was our first summer as Greymonts, and

Dad took us hiking. It was hot and humid, and mosquitoes kept biting me. The woods felt big and mysterious and dangerous and I wanted to go home, back to someplace safe and familiar. Rochelle loved it, though. She asked Dad a hundred questions about the plants and trees, took off her shoes, and splashed in the creek. I didn't let myself whine even once because she was so happy, and I loved seeing Rochelle smile.

The memory of Ro's smile wraps around me like a warm blanket. God, I miss her so much. "Rochelle!" I scream, my voice breaking on the second syllable, ending in a croak.

"We'll find her, Natasha. I promise you, we'll find her," Rochelle's best friend, Margo, says, taking my hand and squeezing. She gives me an encouraging smile, pushing back her curly, carefully styled hair. I wonder if she's trying to convince herself as much as me.

Margo feels almost like family, and she's always treated me like an honorary little sister. But I've never spent time with her without Rochelle, which makes this all feel even weirder.

Georgia takes my other hand, but she doesn't promise anything. Georgia never makes promises she can't keep. It's nearly twilight, and her skin is tinged blue in this light, shadows playing beneath her brown eyes. She looks grim, worried. Somehow that's more comforting to me than Margo's sunny optimism. It's how I feel too.

We continue to follow the line of trees at the road's edge. I wanted to go inside the forest to search, but I could tell Mom and Dad were freaked out by the idea of me going in there, as if I would disappear just like my sister. Instead, I promised that

Georgia, Margo, and I would keep to the roadside near where Ro's car was abandoned. Police and park rangers have already been over this area, but it's possible they missed a clue. Or at least that's what I'm telling myself. Anyway, I need to feel like I'm doing something worthwhile.

We're surrounded by silver tree trunks and healthy green leaves. Yet it's eerily quiet. No birds sing, no squirrels play in the branches. It's still, except for the calls of my sister's name and the occasional whoosh of a car speeding by. The farther we walk, the less frequently the searchers' voices come, until all we can hear are our own shoes crushing the grass, scuffling gravel. Georgia's breathing is steady in my ear, her hand sweaty in mine.

The air seems to hum against my skin, as if it's alive. This whole place feels alive, like a breathing, thinking, watching being. I'm terrified of it, but something inside me pulls toward it too. Every inch of my skin feels sensitive, receptive, expectant. It almost feels as if I could reach out my hand and—

"Kind of creepy, isn't it?" Georgia whispers, jarring me from my strange thoughts. That magnetic pull I was feeling vanishes. She takes her phone from her back pocket and starts filming as we walk. For a few moments I watch our movement along the roadside through her iPhone's screen, and it reminds me of a low-budget horror film.

Georgia can't see anything interesting without wanting to get it on film. Much to the disappointment of her CFO father and engineering-professor mother, Georgia is an artist. But I'd rather she didn't make art out of this particular experience.

"Do you have to do that?" I ask.

"Sorry," Georgia says. "Habit." She stops recording and pockets her phone.

A cool breeze wafts through the humid air, carrying a strange metallic odor. The hairs along my nape prickle, sending small tremors down my back. Even though there's still a half hour of light remaining, the forest is already nearly dark. I'm about to suggest we turn back for the car when there's a crunch of fallen leaves from inside the trees.

The three of us freeze and wait, listening. The woods go silent again. I peer into the gloom, but the trees are merely shadows in the dark. Georgia takes her phone back out and clicks on the flashlight app, shining it into the trees, illuminating the thickly carpeted forest floor.

The flashlight beam reflects off two eyes in the darkness, and an animal explodes into movement.

Margo screams and yanks Georgia and me away from the tree line, back onto the road. "Back to the Jeep!" she yells. Our feet pound the pavement and we don't look back, we don't stop moving, we don't do anything but flee. Georgia and I are good runners from three years of high school track, but after a few minutes Margo starts struggling to keep up. It's no surprise— she's dressed in Converse and tight, high-waisted jeans. I drag her along, trying to take some of her weight. There aren't any sounds of a chase behind us, but my heart is beating in my temples and my breath is coming short and all I can think is that if there are creatures like that roaming the woods, Rochelle might be in more trouble than I thought.

An unexpected sob wrenches itself from my chest and I trip and fall, my knees slamming into the road. The impact turns my vision white with pain, and I roll over onto my side, my arms wrapped around my aching, screaming knees. Georgia and Margo bend over me, talking across each other. They pull me to a sitting position, and all the tears I've been holding back pour out. I sit on the warm blacktop, sobbing and feeling like my insides are being ripped out.

Margo, still trying to catch her breath, kneels in front of me on the road and folds me into a tight hug. Georgia stands over us, watchful, her hand resting against my hair.

The twilight is still and quiet. Lightning bugs begin to light up the tall grass at the roadsides. "Look, fireflies," Margo says, smiling at me through her own tears. Her round face looks beatific under her halo of humidity-frizzed hair.

"Why do you look pretty when you cry?" I ask, wiping away my snot. "I look like a hot mess."

"It's the only thing I got out of my high school acting career," Margo says with a laugh.

"You also got Rochelle," I point out. That's how Margo and Rochelle became friends—acting in a school production of *Much Ado About Nothing*.

"Yeah," Margo says with a sniff, "I got Rochelle."

"Truck's coming," Georgia warns us.

Margo helps me to my feet and we move to the side of the road just as a truck pulls up next to us. Margo pushes me slightly behind her.

"Y'all all right?" a man's voice says.

My vision is still blurry with tears, but I make out a park

ranger in the truck's driver's seat. He is white and about thirty, with a face full of stubble and straight brown hair tucked behind his ears. One slightly muscled arm rests on the open window, revealing a deep tan beneath the sleeve of his beige uniform. He's wearing thick leather work gloves.

"We're fine," I say. "Now." I wipe at my eyes.

"An animal was chasing us," Georgia adds, crossing her arms and eyeing him suspiciously.

The ranger's eyebrows go up. "Are you sure? The animals usually don't bother people, unless you're bothering them. What'd it look like?"

"Had yellowish eyes," I say, not liking the tone he's taking. "Pretty big. That's all I saw before we ran."

"Hmm, might've been a lost dog, I guess," the ranger says with a shrug. "We've had some reports about that. I've run into a few myself. Nothing to get worked up about." He gives us a disarming smile. "Y'all can get in if you want. I'll take you back to your car."

I glance at Margo to see what she thinks. She smiles at the ranger. "Thanks. We're parked just up the highway, on the shoulder," she says. "We'd appreciate the ride."

"I don't know if I want to get into some random white dude's truck," Georgia whispers in my ear.

Getting into a truck with a stranger isn't something I'd normally do either, but night is falling fast and some yellow-eyed beast is roaming the woods. "It'll be fine," I whisper back. "We're all together and he's a park ranger, which is like a nature cop."

Georgia looks even less convinced, and I realize my mistake. Cops don't feel safe to her. "Sorry. We can call my mom if you want. She can probably send someone to get us," I offer. "Or we can keep walking."

Georgia looks around the gloomy, deserted roadside, biting her lip. "Nah, it's way too creepy out here. Let's just risk the ranger dude."

I give Georgia's hand a reassuring squeeze.

Margo is already moving toward the passenger door. "Why don't you sit up front, Natasha? You're probably sore from falling." She pushes the seat forward so she and Georgia can climb into the back of the truck.

She's not wrong. I wince at the pain in my knees as I heave myself up into the cab. At least sitting up front will let me stretch my legs out.

"Y'all part of that Greymont girl's search party?" the ranger asks as he puts the truck into gear.

"She's my sister," I say, and the man's eyes flit to my face again, apparently looking for a likeness. He won't find much of one—my hair is brown where Ro's is blond, my face oval where hers is heart-shaped. Ro is curvy, and I'm all long legs and athletic shoulders.

"Sorry to hear that," he says, his tone soft. "She seems like a sweet girl, from what the news's been saying. I've been assisting the police as much as I can. I live on the park, up by the old ferry access road." I settle into the soft lilt of his voice, suddenly soothed.

"All by yourself? Have you been there long? Don't you get lonely?" Margo asks, leaning around the seat to smile at him.

The man laughs good-naturedly at Margo's rapid-fire idea of a conversation. "Moved here from north Florida a while back. I like the peace and quiet."

"He won't get much of that with Margo in his truck," Georgia stage-whispers from the back seat.

"We can't all be silent and pensive *artistes*," Margo retorts.

"No, the world has a dire need of bubbly fashion designers who never stop talking," Georgia says.

Margo sticks out her tongue at Georgia and goes pointedly silent. Georgia chuckles.

They've been like that ever since the first night Georgia came over for a sleepover in ninth grade and Margo teased and charmed her right out of her broody shell. After three years of being thrown together at family events, constant ribbing is just their thing.

I smile, but their banter can't completely distract me from the empty darkness outside the truck. I didn't realize we had walked so far from the car.

The road arcs sharply around a bend, and my eyes follow the curve of the ridge. I'm surprised to see a house sitting up there. I didn't even notice it when we were walking since I was looking into the trees on the other side. "Is that house part of the nature park?" I ask, pointing toward it. "A historical site or something?"

The ranger looks up. "No, that belongs to the Lloyds. From what the other rangers tell me, they've lived there for decades. The name never changes. Even men who marry into the family go by Lloyd. Strange folks, lots of rumors about them around town. Haven't you heard of them before?"

We all shake our heads. It's not surprising we haven't—we live one town over, in Swylerville, a university town. We shop at different stores and go to different schools and churches than the people around here in Fawney.

"What kind of rumors?" Georgia asks, craning her neck for a last glance of the house. She's always on the lookout for her next documentary subject. Clearly, she thinks there could be a story in that creepy farmhouse.

The ranger laughs. "Nonsense mostly. Folks say they're witches and will sell you spells to get revenge on your enemies. That sort of thing."

"I could use a spell like that," I mutter, thinking of Jake. But then a memory stirs. Rochelle sitting on my bed, holding one of her many crystals in the palm of her hand. She said she wished she could do magic. I told her she should watch this 90s movie about teen witches called *The Craft*, and once she saw the snakes they summoned, she'd change her mind.

But Rochelle shook her head. "I heard about a family of real witches who live in Fawney, in the hills. My friend Sandra went to them when her boyfriend told her she had a fat ass. They gave her a potion to make him ugly. He broke out in terrible acne and all his hair fell out."

I had scoffed at that, and Rochelle laughed. But there was a look of longing on her face. She wanted the magic to be real.

"You ever met them?" Georgia asks the ranger, dispelling the memory.

The ranger shrugs. "Seen 'em around, now and again. They come onto Wood Thrush sometimes. Eerie folk. Especially the daughter, there's something creepy about her."

"You think they really sell spells?" I ask. These could be the same witches Rochelle mentioned. I wonder if Rochelle told

Margo about the witches too.

"They might sell meth, but I doubt they're cooking up anything more magical than that," he says. "Just hillbillies, you know. Not the kind of people a girl like you wants to run into."

I roll my eyes. "A girl like me, huh?"

Georgia puts a hand on my arm and interrupts. "I wonder if the police have questioned them. They live close to where Rochelle's car was abandoned. Speaking of which, there's our car, right there," she adds, pointing at her blue Jeep.

"I hear the police searched their property. Didn't find anything," the ranger says as he pulls up behind Georgia's Jeep. "Y'all be safe now. I hope you find your sister." He gives me a warm smile and a nod.

"Thank you," I say as I climb out of the cab. My legs tremble when I put weight on them.

"Yeah, thanks for the lift," Margo says from the pavement. She blows him a kiss through the window, and the ranger laughs, his gruff mountain man facade giving way to Margo's sweetness. I think Margo got a lot more out of high school theater than pretty crying—she could charm an audience too if she wanted to.

It ought to be annoying that Margo is acting so chipper while on a hunt for her missing best friend, but I know she's just trying to keep up everyone's morale. It's the same thing she did the time we all drove over to Nashville for a concert and our car got towed and everyone was exhausted and arguing. She's a peacemaker at heart, and I have to admit that having her here does make things feel a little less grim.

Georgia sees I'm limping and helps me to the Jeep. As she

tucks me into the passenger seat, the park ranger's truck disappears into the night.

"I don't know what that thing in the woods was, but I'm pretty sure it wasn't a dog," Georgia says. "More like a chupacabra. Let's drive back to the nature center and see if there's any news. I don't want to be alone out here anymore."

I don't bother mentioning that it's Rochelle who is alone, lost in the shadows with, what—otherworldly beasts and creeping witches? Or lost dogs and meth addicts? I need to believe we'll find my sister in these woods, alive and safe, with stories to tell, but spending a single afternoon here is making it hard to hold on to hope. Fear comes easier.

The moment I catch sight of my mother's face in the dim light of the nature center, I know they haven't found anything either. Rochelle is still out there, waiting for us to find her. All we can do is keep searching, keep yelling her name, and keep hoping that she'll finally answer.

But what if being adopted by the Greymonts was the last miracle my sister and I will ever get?

THREE
DELLA

I watch Momma carefully when I visit for the next two days, searching in her eyes, her smile, her songs for any hint that she knows about the missing girls, that she had anything to do with their disappearances. This morning, I asked her point blank if she has ever left the prison. In answer, she sang the first verse of "Folsom Prison Blues" and laughed, making a joke of it. I laughed too, twisted as it was. But then her smile died and she started singing "The Bloody Miller" again.

I couldn't stand to hear that awful song another time and interrupted her. She recoiled, as if she'd been in a trance, and looked at me with enormous, frightened eyes. When I touched her arm to comfort her, she shrieked and started throwing rubble at the wall. I left before she started throwing it at me.

I'm still thinking about her reaction as I lie on the couch after dinner, listening to Da make a racket in the kitchen. Why is she so fixated on that damn song? It was never even one of her favorites. Is she trying to tell me I'm right to think she's guilty? Is she reliving killing Aunt Sage?

Da's voice from the kitchen pulls me from my thoughts. "We're outta nearly everything, Della. I've got nothin' to work with," he complains. When I enter the kitchen, he's frantically shuffling through empty mason jars in the pantry. "If a customer comes by, I'm gonna have to pretend my goddamned spit is magic."

We haven't been able to go gathering on the Bend because of the search parties. They must've combed every inch of the nature park by now, yet still they go on with their flashlights and their yelling, calling for Rochelle Greymont. Some part of me almost envies her. If I went missing, no one would organize a search party; the police wouldn't go banging on doors. In their eyes, I'd be just another trashy girl who took off from a crappy home.

"I'll go," I tell Da. "Less suspicious than your ugly mug. If anyone asks, I'll say I'm helping look for her."

Da nods, ignoring my dig. "Fine. Go on now, in case we get a customer tonight. We sure as hell need one, or I'm gonna have to pick up a shift at the chicken plant again and stink to high heaven."

"The Bend save us," I say, and Da smiles at Granny's old saying. I lean over and give him a quick kiss on the cheek, and he ruffles my already messy hair. I don't look at him again, afraid I'll see something like nostalgia in his eyes. We used to be so close. Momma's transformation should have made us even closer, but all it's done is drive a wedge between us.

In fact, Momma's driven a wedge between me and pretty much every other human being alive. Miles and Da, what few friends I had from school. I can't make new friends either, not with the secrets I've got.

I grab my foraging bag and head across the road and into the woods. We do need a customer. Momma and Da have never been able to hold down a job for more than a few weeks. I can't blame them. It's hard to work a convenience store register or answer telephones when you've touched the magic of the Bend, when you've twisted its power to your purpose, when you've set your will loose on the world. I'm only stocking shelves at the grocery store this summer to make sure our land taxes get paid so we don't lose our house.

I creep through the trees, stealthy as a bobcat, the way Momma taught me when I was little. "We tread lightly on the Bend, Della," she'd say whenever I would break a twig or kick a stone. "We respect what it offers us."

I've always thought of the Bend less as an it and more as a she, since its magic came from a woman—my great-grandmother by five generations. Momma's told me the story so many times it feels as real to me as the ground I walk on. How Erin Lloyd immigrated to Tennessee by way of Scotland in the 1920s and made her living by brewing moonshine during Prohibition. How she sang magic into every brew to make it irresistible. How she was drowned as a witch by a rival moonshine gang. How she sang every drop of her magic into the land for her descendants before she died. How the Bend took her small offering and let it grow wild.

Now each of the Lloyds channels the magic in our own way. Of course, we can all make the brews customers know us for—we learn them with our ABCs. We can all give the people what they come for: healing or cursing. Most people come for the cursing. They trust their health to the doctors and their grudges to us. That's why folks call us vengeance witches, but really, they're just vengeful people. That's something no one in Fawney wants to admit to themselves. Easier to call us evil, hateful, devils.

But the Bend's power is bigger than spells for angry women and brews for cowardly men. Each of us has our own peculiar gift, a way into the Bend's magic that's our own. Aunt Sage could heal, and Miles can track. Momma sings the magic from the water—or she did, before the river siren claimed her voice for its own purposes. And me, I can work with anything that grows beneath the soil.

Aunt Sage used to say that we haven't tapped one-tenth of the Bend's magic yet. That we only understand one-hundredth of what the Bend is, or of what lurks inside this land's heart. She always got frustrated with our piddling trade, and talked constantly about how we could do more, be more. She said we ought to be changing the world instead of slinging petty spells like greasy fast food hash. Momma laughed at her little sister and called her a dreamer.

I can't help but wonder what Aunt Sage would say about how small we're living now. How we hide Momma away behind prison walls. How Miles turned his back on the Bend and the rest of us let him. How the magic is spinning more and more out of control and we're not doing anything to stop it. We're just surviving.

I'm reminded of it with each soft step I take across the loamy forest floor. The smell of magic used to rise up from the earth, fresh and fragrant as honeysuckle. But now it's sour, cloying as dying roses—a rich and dangerous smell.

But as I begin to gather, I forget about Sage and Miles and even about Momma. All my attention goes to the trees, plants, and mushrooms around me. This world is one I understand— grounded and quiet and slow. I stoop beneath a chestnut oak where I often find turkey tail mushrooms growing from an old log, but there aren't any today.

Da will be disappointed if I come home without any, so I'll have to grow some myself. I sit on the ground and press one hand to the soil. I close my eyes and focus on the tiny threads of the fungal network that runs underground, connecting the trees and plants and everything that grows here.

Most of the nature park's guests don't know it, but there's an enormous web of life under their feet. The trees use it to share resources and communicate dangers, sometimes even to spread toxins to rival plants. Of course, it exists in every forest in the world, but here, in the Bend, the fungal network doesn't only convey messages and nourishment between the trees. It also carries my great-grandmother's magic.

My magic.

Breathing slowly, I feel my way beneath the soil until I sense the immense connectedness that binds everything around me together. In my mind's eye, I can see the tiny threads wrapping around the oak tree's roots, pouring life into it. I could delve deep and far, but I don't need to. I easily find the fine white filaments of the turkey tail's underground mycelium and direct nourishment into them. Soon, a cold dampness spreads around my hand, and I feel the soft, familiar nudge of mushrooms.

When I open my eyes, the turkey tails are spreading across the log, their wavy brown-and-white caps each as big as my palm. I break them off and stow them in my bag. Da will laugh at the size of them and call me a show-off.

It takes me a minute to shake off the effects of my magic. Growing things makes me feel slow, as if movement isn't very important. I'd rather lie down on the ground and breathe with the trees, but I force myself up. There's more gathering to do.

Soon, I find a thick patch of poison ivy, spreading across the ground between trees, curling up their trunks. I rip off several handfuls and push them into a gallon-sized plastic bag and seal it closed. Poison ivy is a main ingredient in some of our nastiest spells, and Lloyds have been handling it so long it doesn't harm our skin.

After a half hour of walking through sparse young chestnut oaks, I break from the trees and into the open, weed-choked meadow that used to be farmland. Now it's part of the nature park, its mown paths providing an easy stroll near the river, so long as you don't mind the ticks. It's a favorite haunt of birdwatchers.

I check the area for park rangers and hikers, and then walk to one of the small ponds at the edge of the meadowland. I

stoop at its rim and plunge my hand deep into the water, pushing my fingers into the mucky soil. Soon, a couple of leeches
have gathered. I pluck them from my skin and into a glass jar,
which I fill with fetid water and stow in my bag.

I take a few minutes to collect weeds and wildflowers, as
well as some ticks that try to crawl up my pant legs. I'm about
to take another dip for leeches when voices float toward me
over the water. Instinctively, I crouch low and gaze over a clump
of brambles to where the voices are coming from.

Three girls emerge from a small copse of sickly oaks and
hedge apples on the eastern side of the meadow. They don't
look like anyone who lives in Fawney. They must have come
over from Swylerville.

"I can't get over how creepy this place is," one of them, a
short Black girl with long braids, says. "Even the trees don't
look right." Those trees probably do look eerie to outsiders—
twisted, stunted, and blackened with fungus. They were
damaged in a flood a few years ago and haven't ever recov-
ered. I could probably put them to rights, though it would take
months or years to fix the whole copse. Besides, we sometimes
use their bark for weakening and sickening spells.

"So creepy," her friend agrees. She's a chubby Asian girl
with curly hair and a nose ring. She's way too fashionable for
Fawney—she looks like she walked right out of a vintage clothing catalog.

The last, a preppy white girl, doesn't say anything. Her eyes
are trained on the horizon, her chin tilted up, as if she's watching for a hawk. But these three aren't birdwatchers. I don't

know what they are. I duck farther behind the brambles and still my breath as they come close.

"I really don't think this is safe, Nat," the girl with braids says, only a few feet from where I'm hiding. "What if that dog comes back?"

"We brought pepper spray," she says without even glancing at her friend. She's the least frightened of the three, but she looks out of place here, like she's never spent a day in the woods in her life. Her dark brown hair is pulled into a high, long ponytail, and her eyebrows are perfectly sculpted. Her clothes are new, but they've been snagged and torn. She doesn't know how to walk easy through a wood.

I feel a smile tug the corners of my mouth. If I weren't trying to lie low, I might give them a good scare, send them back to their Swylerville suburbs and off Bend land. But this isn't the moment to scare park visitors. Instead, I decide to keep an eye on them, just in case.

They hurry past my hiding place and across the open field without seeing me. Once, the preppy girl yelps and smacks at her pant leg, probably dislodging a few hungry ticks, which are particularly vicious this year.

"Jesus Christ," one of them mutters. They stop at the edge of the oak forest I just came out of. They peer into the woods for a long time, and then step onto a narrow hiking trail. Once I'm sure they're well into the wood, I follow, keeping off the hiking trail, always twenty yards behind them and to their left.

They walk bunched together, whispering to each other, jumping at every noise. The trails aren't well marked here, and soon they lose their way, blundering onto a deer track that takes them down into a ravine.

"Where the hell are we?" Vintage Girl moans, holding a phone above her head, trying to find a signal.

I sigh. It's only a few hours until dark, and if another person goes missing on Bend land, it's only going to draw more attention to us. I emerge onto the hiking trail above them and call down, trying to make my voice sound like the friendly ones I hear park-goers use with one another. "Are y'all lost?"

"Yes," two of them yell.

"So lost," Vintage Girl adds.

I point the way back to the trail and they climb up. The white girl's face is scratched and bleeding, but she doesn't seem to notice. She's somewhere else, not quite here. The other two girls keep glancing at her nervously.

"You park at the nature center?" I ask. "I can help you find the way back."

"Thanks. I'm Margo, and they are Natasha and Georgia," Vintage Girl says. Before I can introduce myself, she plows on, "I'm so glad you found us. This place is terrifying. I don't know how anyone comes here for fun. I mean, no offense or anything. Do you work here?"

I blink at her for a moment, a little off balance. Da's not chatty, and no one at work really likes to talk to me. I don't think I've had a full conversation since school closed for summer, let alone one with someone like this girl. Finally, I find my voice. "Uh, no, I just spend a lot of time here. I live close by. I'm Della, by the way."

Natasha's head snaps up and she eyes me carefully. "In that old farmhouse that overlooks the road?"

I startle and try to cover it with a cough. "Yeah, actually."

"You hear about the missing girl?" she asks, and Georgia looks at her strangely.

"Yeah, it's sad," I say. "I'd think you three would be afraid to be out here after that."

"Why aren't you?" she demands, a challenge in her voice.

What's she getting at? I shake my head. I don't know and I don't care. I just want her gone. "Some people can take care of themselves," I say, eyeing her clothes meaningfully, "and some can't."

Her eyes go hard and she looks away, clenching her jaw. I can tell she's searching for a retort and not finding one.

But then she sighs. "Yeah, some can't."

Georgia puts her arm around Natasha and pulls her into her side as they walk. I wonder idly if they're a couple, but I don't think so. They both seem solitary.

Natasha's shifts in mood have thrown me off center, so I don't say anything else. The woods are quiet in the last heat of the day, every animal in its burrow or its nest, the predators waiting for night to forage and hunt. Even Margo, who seems like she never stops talking, has fallen quiet, thank the Bend.

Georgia turns back to me. "So, Della, is it true that your family sells, like, spells and magic and stuff?"

"Where'd you hear that?" I say.

"A forest ranger told us."

I can't decide whether to laugh it off or use it as a chance to drum up business. Before I can answer, Natasha throws a question at me, her tone more than curious. "What kinds of people come to you for spells?"

I shrug. "All sorts."

"You ever get students from Highland Rim?" She studies me intently.

I kick a rock out of the path and look out over the hills. "Sometimes. But it's mostly locals. Why? Do you go there?"

"I do," Margo says. "So does—" Before she can finish her sentence, something dives at our heads. Margo yelps and throws her arms over her head, ducking. Natasha trips over a rock and nearly takes Georgia down with her. The creature— hardly more than a gray blur—flaps its wings once more over our heads before disappearing into the trees. At least I think it had wings.

"What was that?" Georgia and Margo yell in unison, but Natasha doesn't speak. She stares off in the direction the thing flew, her face full of conflicting emotions: disbelief, awe, fear. Then she turns to me and her eyes narrow.

"What are you playing at?" she demands, clenching her fists. "How'd you do that?"

I stare at her, puzzled. "It must've been an owl. The barred owls have been really active this year," I say, but something in my gut tells me it wasn't an owl. It might have moved like an owl, maybe even been shaped like an owl, but it wasn't one. The air has gone cool and dry, nothing like the drenching early summer heat we've been walking through. A shiver starts up my spine. I've lived my whole life on the Bend, and I've never felt anything like that.

The way Natasha rubs her arms makes me think she felt it

too. But why is she looking at me with fury and distrust in her eyes?

"Yeah, probably an owl or something, Nat," Georgia says. "Come on, let's go. You know your parents will worry." She gives me an apologetic look and shrugs, as confused by her friend's behavior as I am.

Natasha doesn't say anything, but after a few more angry glances at me, she allows Margo and Georgia to pull her down the trail and toward the nature center. Once the center is in sight, I let them continue on without me, but I watch them until they reach their car and are safely inside. Those are three more people who won't be going missing on the Bend tonight.

As I walk home in the growing dark, I wonder who Natasha is and why she acted so strangely. Did she think I used my witchy powers to charm an owl into dive-bombing her head? The thought makes me snort.

But even so, I search the tree canopy, watching for signs of the creature, or others like it. If they are there, I don't see them. The branches are empty and quiet, only a gentle wind rustling the leaves. The Bend is keeping its secrets tonight.

FOUR
NATASHA

Georgia doesn't say anything on the way home from the nature park. She's got her thinking face on, the one she gets when she's trying to figure out how to sequence video footage or learn a tricky new fencing maneuver. I don't mind—I need a chance to think too. But all the silence in the world isn't going to help what I experienced in the woods make sense to me. What I saw, what I felt. What I *heard*. We're pulling up to my house before I've sorted any of it out.

Georgia puts the car into park and turns to me. "What was the deal with you and that girl Della? Why'd you catch an attitude with her over that owl?"

"What?" I say, coming out of my heavy thoughts. Georgia is eyeing me worriedly. But I don't know how to explain what happened. "Oh. I don't know. I was just . . ."

Part of me still feels like I'm there on the nature park, the muggy air crowding against my skin, the low buzz of insects thrumming around me.

"You were upset about Rochelle?" Georgia asks, her voice gentle.

"I—" In my mind, there's a whoosh of air, the flutter of wings on my face. And something much, much stranger—my sister's voice whispering in my ear, so real it tickled.

I look over at Georgia, her face half in shadow from the porch light. I can tell Georgia anything, can't I? We've been best friends and teammates and practically sisters for three years. I can tell her and she won't say I'm crazy. She would never.

"Find me," I whisper.

"What?" Georgia asks, leaning toward me.

I look up and meet her eyes. "That's what she said. Rochelle. She said, 'Find me, Natasha.'" Or did the bird say it?

Georgia sucks in a breath. "Rochelle?"

"Yeah. When the owl dive-bombed us, that's what I heard."

"And you thought that girl Della was to blame somehow? Like, you thought she was the one who said it, trying to make you think—"

"I don't know what I thought," I say quickly. "It was a knee-jerk reaction. But then I realized it wasn't Della. It was really Rochelle's voice. I'm sure of it."

Georgia is silent for a few beats, thinking. When she finally speaks, her words come slowly, as if she's choosing them with extreme care. "Babe, that's a lot. I can't really imagine. Do you think maybe you want to find your sister so badly that your mind sort of invented hearing her voice?"

"Like a hallucination?" I ask.

Georgia puts her hand on my knee. "Yeah, maybe. Or maybe that girl Della did whisper it, and you were so frightened that you heard your sister's voice. That's just the sort of fucked-up trick someone pretending to be a witch might pull."

Was it a hallucination? I mean, it was a talking bird. So that can't be real, right?

"Yeah," I say. "Yeah, it was probably something like that. It's fine. I'm just . . . it's been a really, really long day. I'm just tired."

But Georgia is still eyeing me. She can tell I'm lying. "Do you remember my cousin Lena, what I told you about her?" she asks.

"The one in Louisiana?" I remember Georgia said they used to choreograph music videos when they were little. Lena taught Georgia how to put on eyeliner. But when Lena was fifteen, she went missing on her walk to school. Georgia brings her up occasionally but hasn't talked about her in a long time.

"Yeah, she—I've been thinking about her a lot, ever since you told me Rochelle was missing. I didn't want to bring her up because . . ."

"Because they never found her?" I guess.

Georgia nods. "Yeah. But her family went through stuff like this too. We all did. I still sometimes get a glimpse of someone from the side and think it's her. Just for a second. Even after four years."

"But Rochelle has only been missing a few days," I say.

"I know." Georgia tries to smile but can't manage it. "I'm just saying that I understand and that you can talk to me. Don't do that thing where you close yourself off. I know you like to manage stuff on your own, but you don't have to. I'm here."

Georgia leans across the seat and wraps her arms around

me. I hug her back, feeling tears sting my eyes. "Take a shower
and get some rest," she says. "Maybe things will look different
in the morning."

I nod against her shoulder and she kisses my cheek and
pulls back, looking at me worriedly. I catch her wide, dark
brown eyes in the porch light. "Do you want me to stay?" she
asks. "I don't mind."

I shake my head and muster up a smile for her. "No, you
have plans with your girlfriend. Go have fun. I'm going to
watch a movie with Mom and Dad and go to bed early. Don't
worry about me."

Georgia hesitates, but then she nods. "We'll be at Crescent
until probably three, and then I'll crash at Odette's place. But I
promise to stay sober, in case you need me. I'm one text away."

"Are you still doing research there, or is this a date?" I ask.

Georgia shrugs. "A little of both? I don't know if the queer
club scene is what I want for my film project or not. I haven't
found the right angle to make it shine. I keep thinking if I spend
enough time there, something will click."

I nod. "At least it's giving you and Odette lots of time
together."

"Yeah, that girl loves to dance," Georgia says, her face
lighting up. "But I need to find something really compelling if
I'm going to win that film school scholarship to help me pay for
NYU. It's so competitive."

"Your parents still say they won't help pay?"

"Not for such an 'impractical' degree," she says with a
scowl. "I don't understand how they can be so supportive about

my being pansexual and dating a girl, but they can't support
what I want to do with my life."

"It's so unfair. But you're brilliant, and you're going to get
that scholarship. I'll help you if I can," I promise. "Just say the
word."

"Okay, but right now let's worry about you."

"I'm fine," I say, even though my throat is tight and tears
are looming behind my eyes. "Get out of here and go dancing
already."

Georgia sighs. "I wish I could tell you everything's going to
be all right. I wish I could. But whatever happens, I'm here for
you, okay? Anytime. Just like always." She squeezes my hand
once and then lets go.

"I know. Thanks, Georgia. Good night." I jump from the
Jeep before the tears I've been suppressing the whole ride home
can make an appearance. I run up the front porch and unlock
the door. The house is quiet, my parents not at home. Once
inside, I lean against the door and let the emotions come.

Suddenly, I'm so weak I can't walk. I slide down the door
onto the cold marble entryway.

My sister's voice beats through me like that owl's wings.
Find me, find me, find me.

And while my brain knows Georgia's right, that it couldn't
have been real, my heart and all the rest of me knows it was.

But Rochelle has always been the superstitious one, not
me. She loves getting tarot readings and hearing ghost stories,
which she believes wholeheartedly. She thinks angels are real
and that bad luck is more than coincidence. She believes in fate.

Our biological grandmother, who died before I was old enough to remember her, used to babysit us. Nana filled Ro's head with stories and her heart with enormous beliefs.

Ro grew up, but she never grew out of her superstition. She continued carrying crystals in her pockets and wishing on falling stars. It isn't that she's stupid or foolish—she scored a thirty-three on the ACT and can solve math problems in her head that I can't even work out on paper. She says she can believe in science and have faith at the same time.

I never laughed at her beliefs, but I never shared them either. I figured they just helped her get through the hard times with our birth parents and the transition to becoming Greymonts. But now . . . what if Ro was right? What if there are things in the world that we don't see or understand, things that sound impossible but are as real as we are?

That bird wasn't just a bird. I felt Rochelle in the brush of its wings. Felt *her*. At a moment when I was feeling hopeless, she swooped down and spoke to me. Gave me faith that I could find her. At first, I thought that girl Della had done it somehow, that she was playing a trick on me. I thought maybe she knew exactly who I was and wanted to mess with me.

But now I don't think so. I would recognize Rochelle's voice anywhere, and it was her. I know it was. Somehow, she spoke to me through that owl, let it carry her voice to me. She wants me to find her. God, why didn't I listen right then? Why didn't I turn to the creepy witch and ask for her help?

I remember that magnetic pull I felt the first time we went out looking for Rochelle, when the whole nature park felt alive and sentient, when it seemed as if I could stretch out my hand and some unseen power would rise up to meet me. Was that Rochelle? Was that my sister I felt there? Or something else?

Now I sit in the dark and the silence, far from my sister, listening to the sound of my own breathing, and wonder what to do next. When my phone dings with a text message, I raise the screen to my eyes without thinking. It's a message from Mom, saying she and Dad are on their way home. There's no news.

I have news, but I couldn't possibly share it with them. They'd look at me with concerned faces and ask if I needed to make an appointment with Dr. Patel. But what I need is to listen to my sister. Ro was telling me to move, to act. I can't sit here all night, waiting for inspiration to strike.

It's time to do what Rochelle asked and find her. I text Mom saying I'm hanging out with Georgia tonight, hurry out to my car, and peel out of our drive. Before I know it, I'm on the highway, gunning the engine, driving faster and faster. I'm going ninety miles an hour before I come to my senses and slow down to sixty, my heart racing. I pull off onto the road that leads to the nature park and take a big, steep twist around a cliff.

I've always believed the only magic we get is the magic we make for ourselves—the lives we choose and build and fight for. But now I'm not so sure. Now I've walked the uncanny paths of Wood Thrush Nature Park. I've felt something there that I've never felt before. If I can be open to the idea of Ro sending me a message in a bird, why not go to a witch for help?

I'm desperate enough to take that clichéd leap of faith. My head says I'm an idiot for even thinking about it, but my gut says there might be more to this world than I've ever imagined, that there *has to be* more.

Most of all, I need for there to be more. For Rochelle and for me too.

The witch's house should be just up ahead. I slow down and watch for a driveway. I almost miss it, but then my head-lights glint off a reflector attached to a mailbox. I slam on my brakes and reverse the car a few feet, then pull up the drive-way, my heart racing. What if they really are a bunch of meth addicts?

It's pitch-black out here, only a small yellow porch light to direct me to the house. I pull beneath a tree and turn off my engine, listening to my pulse pounding in my ears. I close my eyes and try to steady my breathing. "Only for you, Ro," I whis-per. I'm about to open my door when something jumps onto the hood of my car.

I scream and grab the steering wheel, ready to blow right out of here. But it's only a big cat. The damn thing curls up on the hood of the car and goes to sleep. Now I can't chicken out and leave, I guess. I push open my door and walk on shaky legs across the dark yard to the porch, gripping my pepper spray. I'm almost glad it's too dark to see what I'm walking into.

The door opens before I can knock, and Della's eyes widen in surprise when she sees me.

"I need your help finding my sister," I blurt out.

Della stares at me for a long time, moths fluttering around her face, which is haunting in the weak yellow light—all sharp cheekbones and deep green eyes, with a corona of red hair.

The witch closes the door behind her and steps toward me. "Your sister?"

She really doesn't know who I am. It couldn't have been her who spoke with Rochelle's voice. The truth pushes me forward.

"Rochelle Greymont. She's my sister. I don't know if you're the real deal, but if you are, I need you to do a spell to find her."

Della's expression closes off. "I can't help you."

"I heard my sister's voice," I say desperately, "when that owl swooped down. I heard Rochelle, and she asked me to help her."

Della's eyebrows lift in interest, but she shakes her head. "I can do spells, but not like what you're asking for. We do brews. To get back at your cheating girlfriend. Make your best friend admit she stole your boyfriend. Stuff like that." Her tone goes hard. "We're not magical detectives, princess."

My hope deflates in my chest like a punctured basketball, and all the fear rushes back. "Fuck you," I say, and stomp back to my car.

"Anytime," Della calls with a laugh.

When I start the engine, the cat leaps down and dashes onto the porch. I squeal out of the driveway, my blood beating an angry pulse in my ears. I drive without thinking, hurling down dark, twisting roads with trees rising up on either side, my headlights illuminating overhanging branches. After half an hour, my gas tank is close to empty and I don't know where I am. But I know where I want to go.

I text Mom again, saying I'm staying the night at Georgia's. The lie twinges my guilt, but I can't bear to go home. Instead, I drive to Rochelle's. I just want to be near her. And if that witch won't help me, I'll have to find my sister myself. Maybe I'll find a clue at her place.

Rochelle's apartment complex is just a few blocks from the university, so the parking lot is crowded with cars. I finally find a spot and hop out of my car, hurrying across the asphalt lot. Ro's apartment is on the third floor, and there's a light shining outside her door, beckoning me in. I take the stairs two at a time. I knock away the yellow police tape, find the spare key she asked me to keep for emergencies, and let myself inside my sister's apartment.

The smells are the first thing I notice. Lemon and lavender. She always smells like one or the other. The scent brings tears to my eyes. I flip on the lights, illuminating the space. A sense of rightness settles in my chest. It was stupid to go to a witch. I know Rochelle better than anyone, just like she knows me. This is where I should have come to find her.

The apartment is a one-bedroom, with a small combination kitchen and laundry room and a pub-style table for a dining room. It's a disaster zone, partly because Ro is always messy and partly because the police have been searching through her stuff. It's also bright with color—paintings, throw pillows, clothes tossed over furniture. Everywhere I look are bold reds and teal blues and splotches of yellow. There are pictures of our family on the bookshelves, pictures of Ro with her friends, even a photo of the dog Mom adopted for us when we first moved into the Greymont home. He was an elderly, cranky gray schnauzer named Teddy who was utterly indifferent to me but followed Ro around in abject adoration.

The only person there isn't a picture of is Jake. Last time I came over, only a few weeks ago, there was a framed photo of Rochelle and Jake on his family's boat, Jake planting a kiss on Ro's cheek, Ro smiling enormously, her hair wind-whipped, her eyes bright and happy. But that photo is gone now. Maybe the police took it.

I pass over the bare, unused kitchen—Ro used to cook for the two of us when we were kids and our parents were too high or not around, but once we moved in with the Greymonts, Ro gave up cooking. Since starting college, the girl subsists on yogurt and Starbucks. I pass into the bathroom and check the medicine cabinet. I don't know what I expect to see, but there's only a bottle of Tylenol and some allergy nasal spray, a few loose tampons. Her toothbrush is still in its holder, her hairbrush in a drawer. Her makeup is scattered all over the counter—lipsticks and eye shadows and blushes in shades I could never pull off.

Undeterred, I hurry into her bedroom, the last room of the apartment. I flip on the light and want to laugh. If the rest of the apartment is messy, Ro's bedroom is an explosion—her bed is unmade, the quilt on the floor. Clothes are piled on the dresser and hung over a chair and dropped wherever she happened to be standing in the room. There are stacks of books and notebooks, mostly for science courses. Ro is taking summer classes so she can double major in premed and psychology. She says she doesn't just want to treat patients, she wants to understand them.

Sometimes I wonder if what she really wants is to understand our birth parents and the effects they had on us. After all, Ro lived with them for almost fifteen years, and leaving them behind was more complicated for her than for me. They were her parents before they were addicted to drugs; she got to be loved by them at their best, whereas I only got the leftovers. After the adoption, we chose to cut off all contact and move on, but I'm not sure Rochelle ever stopped missing them.

As I sort through her notebooks, I have an idea. Ro kept a journal. Did the police find it? Ro started journaling after we moved in with Mom and Dad because a counselor said it would help her adjust. She never stopped journaling but was always secretive about it. She didn't like for anyone to catch her writing and she always kept the journal hidden where Mom and Dad couldn't find it.

But I knew all her hiding spots because she learned them from our birth parents—places they stashed drugs. Inside wall vents, under floorboards, inside a pillow, taped to the back of dressers. I check all the ones I can think of, but there's nothing. Then I realize Ro would have new hiding places now, in her own apartment, since Mom and Dad aren't living here. I get creative, checking all sorts of unexpected spots. Finally, I open the fuse box in a corner of her bedroom and laugh. There's a little pocket on the inside of the door made from duct tape. A teal-blue Moleskine sticks out of the top.

With trembling fingers, I pull it out and take it over to Ro's bed. I sink onto the soft mattress and hold the journal in my lap, just staring at it. Finally, I pull the elastic string away and open the cover. There's no name written beneath "In case of loss, please return to," only a geometric-style drawing of a crystal. I take a deep breath and then grasp the bookmark string hanging out near the middle of the journal. I use it to flip the pages open to the most recent entry.

Rochelle's looping cursive handwriting springs out at me. May 31. The entry is dated a week ago, only two days before she went missing. It feels wrong, violating my sister's privacy like this. I don't keep a journal, but if I did, I'd be humiliated if anyone ever read it.

But maybe she wrote something here that will help me know what happened to her, where she is. I take a deep breath and start to read.

The entry begins with a discussion of her summer courses, how worried she is about passing chemistry. I skim ahead, looking for something more telling. My eyes snag on Jake's name.

Ro says she is thinking about breaking up with him. Alarm bells sound in my head. Then I read this paragraph: *I'm afraid of how he will take the news, of what he might do. Maybe I can hold off for the rest of the summer, wait until he's about to go on tour. He won't care so much then. And who knows? Maybe I'll feel differently by then. Maybe this has just been a rough patch. Maybe.*

That's the last word of the entry and the last word in the journal. *Maybe.* A word that's half hope and half resignation.

"Maybe" and all the possibilities that word holds make me suddenly tired. I lie back on Ro's bed and breathe in the citrusy smell her hair left on the pillow. I want to pull her quilt off the floor and go to sleep here, cocooned in my sister's scent, in the cheerful disarray of her life. I want to sleep here and forget, for just a little while, that Ro is missing and that it's my job to find her.

But I can't. I need to read every page of this journal and then I need to turn it over to the police.

I drag myself from the bed and sit at her desk, turning on a heavy gold lamp. The journal starts on January first, the morning after she met Jake at a nightclub. And every page that follows weaves together a story I had only guessed at. I knew Jake was a possessive jerk and sensed he might be worse. But I had no idea what he has been putting Rochelle through. How he tried to keep her away from her friends, how he gaslit her, how he made her believe she was lucky that he cared about her at all. With every page I read, my anger grows, blotting out even my fear, until I'm surrounded by a bubble of my own rage.

I don't know what Jake has to do with Rochelle's disappearance, but this journal tells me he knows a lot more than he's letting on. And he has a hell of a lot to answer for.

FIVE
NATASHA

It's three in the morning and I'm struggling to keep my eyes open. I let my head fall onto the cool pages of Ro's journal and allow my eyelids to lower for one sweet moment. I've just started to doze off when the door to Rochelle's apartment slams closed. I shoot up, ramrod straight, horribly awake. I hear someone moving clumsily through the kitchen, opening and closing drawers. A man coughs.

Terror unspools in my body, sending a wave of weakness through me. A man is in Rochelle's apartment, and I'm here alone. Alone and vulnerable, and no one knows where I am. Mom and Dad think I'm sleeping at Georgia's. Georgia thinks I'm at home. I squeeze my eyes closed, trying not to give in to the horrible movie that starts playing in my head—he finds me, he hits me, he rips off my clothes, he—

No.

I ease myself out of the desk chair as quietly as I can,

searching around me for something I can use as a weapon. I grasp a heavy water bottle, then I remember the pepper spray on my key chain. I rifle through my purse until I find it and remove the safety tab. I clench it tightly and grab my cell phone, dialing 911. I'm about to hit enter and call for help when the man in the kitchen starts singing.

The song is "Take Me Home, Country Roads," and he croons it, slurring the words. He elongates his vowels absurdly.

I'd know that voice anywhere. I shove the phone into my pocket, grab Ro's journal off the desk, and barrel out of her bedroom and into the kitchen. I flip on the overhead light.

Jake startles and turns away from the basket of laundry on top of the dryer, his eyes wide and wet with tears. He clutches one of Rochelle's blouses to his chest. "Natasha? What are you doing here?"

I cross my arms. "I missed Rochelle," I say. "What's your excuse?"

Jake blinks at me. "I left one of my shirts here. I need it for a gig."

"You're crying," I point out. "And that's Ro's shirt."

Jake wipes away the tears. "I'm just allergic to all the fucking girly smells in here." He tosses the blouse back into the laundry basket.

"You're full of shit. You act like you don't care Ro is gone and then I find you crying over her laundry. If I didn't know better, I'd say you've got a guilty conscience."

"I don't have anything to be guilty about," Jake says. "Rochelle's the one who left." But then he glances surreptitiously at his feet, and I notice a leather overnight bag filled with Ro's things—clothes, a hairbrush, a bottle of her perfume.

"Why do you have that bag, Jake? Do you know where she is? Are you taking this stuff to her?" Hope and anger swirl together in my chest. Rochelle's okay. She's okay and she's letting us go crazy looking for her, and so is Jake.

But then I see the tears still leaking from Jake's eyes. He's staring at me strangely, his jaw set.

My blood runs cold. "What did you do to her, Jake?" I ask, trying to keep my voice steady. Why else would he be packing up a bag of my sister's things while crying in her kitchen, unless he did something to her? Did he chase her onto the nature park and then kidnap her? Did she try to leave him and so he trapped her someplace? Or are these souvenirs? Maybe she was never at the nature park at all. Maybe leaving her car there and dropping her purse by the river was a ruse.

"I didn't do anything to your fucking sister. She's a selfish bitch who took off. You can't pin this on me." He takes a step toward me. "She left that bag at my apartment. I was just bringing it back."

Is he lying? I can't tell.

"I found her journal," I say, my voice shaking. I hold my ground.

He furrows his brow. "Rochelle didn't keep a journal."

"She did. And your name crops up a lot. Pretty soon everyone will know how you've been treating her. Then we'll see how that alibi of yours holds up."

Jake clenches his jaw and takes another step toward me. I'm

horribly aware of the six inches of height and seventy pounds
he's got on me, of the smell of beer on his breath, the glassiness
in his eyes. He leans forward. "You go to the police with this
and all they're going to find out is what your sister's been up
to."

I will myself not to back away, squeezing my pepper spray
so hard my knuckles hurt. "What's that supposed to mean?" I
force out.

An ugly smile spreads across Jake's face. "I'll show you."
He pushes past me and down the hallway, opening the utility
closet. He pulls out a vacuum cleaner and kneels down, fiddling
with the dust canister. Maybe I'm not the only one who knows
Ro's hiding spots. But what could be in there? God, not drugs.
Please not drugs.

Jake pulls out a quart-sized plastic bag and holds it out to
me. I have to let go of either my pepper spray or Ro's journal
to take it. I shove the spray in my purse and grab the bag from
Jake's hand. I open it with my teeth and look inside. It's filled
with jewelry, some that looks expensive and some that looks
like the cheap kind you'd buy off the rack at Target. The tags
are still on some of the pieces.

Jake snatches the bag back from me. "And that's nothing.
Rochelle steals shit constantly. Makeup, electronics, you name
it. She's a klepto. Ask Margo—she'll tell you."

I shake my head, but his words are ringing true. Ro used
to steal things before, in our old life. Toys for me, snacks from
the convenience store, lipstick from the supermarket. She got
arrested twice, which is how Dad found out about us and

adopted us. But I thought she stopped after we became Greymonts, after she didn't need to steal anymore. Clearly, I was
wrong. That I could be totally in the dark about this—what
else don't I know about my sister?

The thought makes the ground shift beneath me. But I force
myself to meet Jake's eyes. "Why are you showing me this?"

"Because I want to trade. Rochelle's secrets for mine," he
says.

"Why would I do that?" I look past him to the front door.
Even though he's kneeling on the carpet and I'm standing, I
realize he's in between me and the exit.

Jake smiles up at me, flashing his dimples. "Because you
don't want your parents to know. Because you don't want the
police and the media to know. Old Papa Greymont worked so
hard to get her record expunged. You don't want to tarnish
your sister's image now, do you? Get her kicked out of college?
You don't want to ruin her reputation. Just like I don't want
you to ruin mine." His eyes bore into me, cold and calculating.

Fear unspools in my chest, running through my limbs,
wrapping its choking strands around my heart. Jake did something to Rochelle—he kidnapped her maybe or hurt her and
left her somewhere, I don't know. But whatever he did, I know
he's the reason my sister is missing now. And he's staring at me
like he's planning to take care of me too.

I need to get out of here. Right now.

"Give me the journal, Natasha," Jake says, his voice chill-
ingly even.

I clench the journal even tighter, clinging to it. This is the only evidence I have tying Jake to Rochelle's disappearance. It's the only paper trail showing how he's been abusing her. If I give it to him, I'll have nothing to show the police but my own accusations.

But what if Jake tells the police what he's just told me? They'll probably try to paint Rochelle as a mentally ill, traumatized girl with a checkered past. They'll say she ran away, not because of Jake but because she got herself into trouble. What if they even stop looking for her?

I shake my head, thinking through my options. But Jake assumes I'm refusing to hand over the journal. His eyes harden and he slowly starts to rise to his feet.

"I just want to find my sister," I say, tears making my voice go hoarse. "I just want her to be safe."

"I know you do," Jake says. His voice has gone soft, caressing. "But you should worry about yourself. That's what Rochelle would want you to do." He reaches a hand out and grazes my upper arm.

I recoil from him, and that's when he strikes, grabbing the journal and ripping it out of my hands. He flips idly through the pages, like he's thumbing a novel he's thinking about buying. Totally casual.

I could fight him for it, but I know I'd lose. Jake's posture says he knows that too. He's relaxed now, just waiting for me to give up and go home. I wouldn't even be able to get my pepper spray out of my purse quick enough to have a chance to use it.

Instead, I snatch the bag of stolen jewelry out from under

his arm. Jake lets me take it. He's already won the only battle he cares about. He's made me afraid—like he made Rochelle afraid.

I push past him in the hallway and head for the door, my heart beating hard.

"Good choice," Jake says. "You really are the smarter sister."

I don't say a word. I walk calmly out the apartment's front door and close it behind me. And then I run down the stairs and straight to my car, lock the doors, and bite my knuckles to keep from screaming. Terror and rage and hopelessness pour out of me, leaving me weak and shaking.

I hate Jake, but I hate myself even more. I didn't know what Rochelle was going through. I didn't help her. Did anyone else know? Did Margo?

It's the middle of the night, but I dial her number anyway.

Margo meets me outside her dorm and then uses her student ID to buzz us into the building. She moves silently down the hallway in her fuzzy pink robe and bunny slippers. Outside her door, she puts a finger to her lips. "We have to be quiet because Kyle's asleep. They have a class at eight, so I don't want to wake them up."

Shit, I didn't even think about Kyle, Margo's partner, who she met at one of Jake's parties a few months ago. I've been dying to meet them ever since Rochelle showed me a picture of Margo and Kyle dressed up like Frenchy and Danny from *Grease*. But now Kyle is just in my way because I want to yell and throw things around, not whisper in a dark dorm room.

"Can't we go somewhere else?" I ask. "I seriously need to talk to you."

Margo scrubs at her eyes, and I feel guilty for coming here. She's got enough on her plate between her classes and helping look for Rochelle, and now I'm taking her sleep too.

"Of course, yeah, sorry," she says. "Let me get dressed. We'll find somewhere." When she opens the door, the hallway's light falls on her rumpled bed, showing Kyle's tousled black hair sticking out from beneath a blanket.

I lean against the hallway wall to wait as quiet settles around me again. The noise in my head feels unbearable here, in the dim silence. Again, I feel those bird's wings swooping by and my sister's voice whispering *Find me.*

Margo finally comes back out, looking strangely diminished in a pair of leggings and a boxy T-shirt, with her hair pulled into a low ponytail. So much of Margo is her big, stylish hair and her statement dresses. Without them, she doesn't look so sunny and ready to take on the world. She looks like a tired girl whose best friend is missing. Somehow the sight makes me feel less alone.

We go back outside into the half-lit darkness. "We could just walk. No one will hear us," Margo says. "All the partyers have called it a night, and all the early birds are still in their beds."

I nod, and we start down a tree-lined sidewalk toward the heart of campus. "I'm sorry to pull you out of yours," I say. "But I need to talk about Rochelle."

Margo's face softens with pity. "You've got to give it time. The police will find her," she says.

"Do you really believe that?" I ask. "Why are you so sure?"

"Because they have to," Margo says, her voice cracking. "Because I can't bear the thought that she's gone and I didn't even get to say goodbye. That she . . ."

She lets her words trail off and I don't ask what she meant to say. I can't stand to hear it. I've been depending on Margo's optimism more than I knew. As if she realizes it, she forces a smile. "Rochelle and I used to go for so many walks like this freshman year, when she still lived on campus. We would walk half the night, talking and laughing."

"What did you talk about?" I ask. I'm almost jealous—I wish I were the one who got to take all those walks and hear what Rochelle was thinking.

Margo smiles. "Freshman year was when I came out as pansexual, so we talked about that a lot. Whether I should tell my parents, what I'd do if they didn't respond well. Rochelle walked me through every step, helped me figure out what to say and when."

"Were your parents cool about it?"

Margo laughs. "Not really. I mean, they love me and they are trying. They like Kyle a lot, though it helps that Kyle is Korean too."

"Rochelle was the first person I came out to too," I say, smiling at the memory. "She just said, 'Well, duh.'"

Margo throws back her head and laughs. "I remember that. I think she knew you were bi before you did."

Rochelle has always known me better than I knew myself, but do I know her? Does anyone?

"Margo, did you know that Jake was hurting her?" I blurt out.

Margo stops walking and turns to me. "What? What are you talking about?"

"Did you know he was abusing her?" I don't mean to sound accusatory, but the words come out that way.

Confusion knits her brows. "No. No, she never said anything like that was happening."

"You're her best friend. You're with her all the time. Didn't you ever see anything, hear anything? Didn't you guess?"

Margo's face has gone pale. Tears stand in her eyes. "He's—he's been hurting Ro?"

"Yes. She wrote about it in her journal."

Margo's hand goes to her mouth. "Damnit." She shakes her head. "Goddamnit. That asshole." Margo lets out a long sigh and rubs her eyes. "I didn't tell you this, but Rochelle and I haven't really been getting along. We hadn't talked for a few weeks before you called to tell me she—"

"What? Why?" So Jake wasn't lying about Rochelle's fight with Margo.

Margo shrugs. "I don't really want to get into details, but . . . things have been weird between us for a while now, pretty much ever since she started dating Jake. She didn't spend as much time with me. Bailed on me a few times. I guess I was jealous. But also . . . I—I'm sorry, Natasha, but I didn't like how Rochelle was acting. She was always out partying with Jake. She didn't seem like herself. She even—"

"She *wasn't* herself! She was being abused," I say, barely

managing to keep my voice down. "Why didn't you talk to her about it?"

"I did. I tried to. But you know Rochelle had a hard time with confrontation. She clammed up. She started avoiding me."

Her words are an echo of Jake's. He said nearly the same thing. But it's only an excuse. Everyone's just making excuses for letting Rochelle down.

I feel vicious words on my tongue and before I know it, they're in the air. "Well, while you were off having your little feelings hurt, Jake was abusing Rochelle. He was fucking with her head, threatening her, who knows what else. He—he might have done worse than that!"

Margo flinches but stands her ground. I guess this isn't the first time she's seen me lose my temper. Her voice goes infuriatingly calm, the way my therapist's does when I get pissed at her. "What exactly do you think Jake did?" she asks, sniffing and wiping her nose.

I shake my head. "I don't know, but he's behind all of this. He's the reason Rochelle is missing."

"It's possible," she says. "But—"

"Of course it is, which you'd already know if you'd been paying attention at all," I snap. "If you cared about her at all."

"That's not fair, Natasha. You know I love Rochelle. I think you might be taking your own feelings of guilt out on me. Believe me, I've got more than enough of my own. I feel awful that I didn't try harder to make things right with her. And I feel awful that I didn't help her when she needed it. But I want to help you now."

I let out a hard, bitter laugh. "You can't help me. No one can help me. I don't know why I came here."

God, why is everything so futile? Every lead is a dead end. Every door is locked. Every person is a complete and utter waste of my time—of Rochelle's time, which feels like it's dwindling.

Margo reaches toward me. "Natasha, please don't take off. Let me be here for you."

But I'm already walking away.

I leave her standing in the shadow of a magnolia tree and I walk to my car, my insides sparking like it's the Fourth of July. But I don't need fireworks. I need a goddamned flamethrower.

SIX
DELLA

When I stumble into the kitchen just before dawn, I'm surprised to see the lights are already on. My cousin Miles is there, leaning against the counter and drinking straight out of the orange juice container as if he'd never left home. I stop and squint at him, pushing my hair out of my face.

"Miles?" I ask stupidly.

He puts down the OJ and meets my eyes. His own are red-rimmed with dark purple circles underneath. But he still looks happy to see me. "Hey, Deedee," he says, holding out his arms to me.

I laugh and go to him, wrapping my arms around his neck. He squeezes me tight and then stands back to look at me. "Did you get taller?"

"No, but that goatee is atrocious," I say. "Also, you look like shit."

"Pot, kettle," he volleys back, rubbing his beard a little

bashfully. It's brown like his hair, only with a smattering of red patches. He gives me a sad smile. "How are you, really?"

How am I? I have no idea. "Why are you here?" I ask instead of answering. Miles has never been home since his mother died, since my mother killed her. I'm glad to see him, but I know he's not standing in this kitchen for a catch-up.

"I saw the news, Dee. Two missing girls on Bend land. What's going on?"

"I don't know," I say honestly.

"Aunt Ruby—"

"I don't know," I say again. "She's been in the prison every morning when I've gone. I was planning to try to talk to her again today. To ask—"

"If she's been running around killing people?" Miles says with a dark laugh.

"She's gotten worse," I admit. "Harder to talk to. Wilder."

Miles's face is grim.

"Do you—do you want to come with me to the prison?" I ask.

Miles shakes his shaggy head. "No, I . . . I just can't. I'm sorry."

I sigh. I don't blame him for not wanting to see Momma. But I wish someone in this family besides me would step foot in that damn prison. Not only for my sake, but for Momma's too. How can she stay human if the people who love her refuse to look her in the face?

"Don't be mad at me," Miles says quietly.

"Why are you here?" I ask.

"The girls," he says.

"Yeah, but why are you here?"

Miles turns away, running his fingers through his hair. "God, I don't know. I don't know. To see what you and Uncle Lawrence are doing about it." His voice turns bitter. "To see if you're just sitting around letting it happen."

His words are like a slap, and before I can think, my hackles are up. "I'm doing the best I can. All by myself," I say. "I understand why you took off and I don't blame you for it. But you don't have a right to judge me now. Not when you haven't done a damn thing to help."

Miles passes a hand over his eyes. "If it's her, you have to stop her."

"You should leave," I say, horrified to hear the way my voice wobbles. "If you're just here to point fingers. If you're just here to make me feel like a failure. I don't need your help with that," I say, all my happiness at seeing him gone. Then I turn away and stride down the hallway, back to my bedroom, holding back sudden tears. Miles caught me off guard, gave me hope that someone else might help. Of course I was wrong.

"Della," he says. "Look, I'm sorry." But he stands there uselessly, letting me go. When I come back out half an hour later, there's no sign of him.

I drive to the prison a little later than usual, when I'm sure Momma will be as lucid as possible. I spent the morning after Miles left concocting a new brew, which I stirred into her decaf coffee—a potent mix of ground-up ticks and wild-growing passionflower, to draw out anxiety and bring calm. It's a risk—Momma's got keener senses than an old hunting dog and might taste it in the coffee. But I have to try something to keep her level, to reclaim her from the magic that's eating her from inside. And I want to try one more time to find out what she knows about the missing girls. If only to show Miles I'm not just "sitting around letting it happen."

I wish I hadn't gotten angry with him, though. I wish I'd tried harder to get him to help me. What Natasha said about her sister speaking to her through the owl and the determination I saw in her eyes scared me worse than the police at our door. If the cops don't figure things out, something tells me this girl's going to. I need to know what's happening on the Bend and what it has to do with Momma before Natasha does.

Not for the first time, I wish my magic were bigger and grander than it is. What if the forest's fungal network could do more than tell me about the things that grow on the Bend? What if it could allow me to do more than grow some mushrooms or locate a plant we need for brews? What if it could help me understand my mother and the magic that's ripping her apart? Maybe Aunt Sage was right and there's more to our magic. But for now all I've got on my side is a simple brew and a desperate wish.

It's already nine o'clock when I hurry inside the still-cool walls of the prison. Momma steps out from behind a concrete pillar right into my path, and I barely contain a yelp of surprise. She grins, and I'm grateful to see there's no blood on her lips today. She has smoothed back her hair and tucked it behind her ears. Her face looks almost serene, except for the expression in her eyes, which reminds me of the moody churn of a swollen river.

"Momma," I say, trying to gather myself together, trying not to show her how worried I am, how afraid. But my treacherous heart races.

She cocks her head at me like a spaniel, waiting. She's so still I think she must be listening to the beat of blood through my veins.

"How—how are you feeling today?"

Momma lifts one corner of her mouth into a smile and all the tension in my body uncoils like a spool of copper wire. She's more settled today than I've seen her in months. If the spell in her coffee works, I might get two words of sense out of her.

"Miles came to see me this morning," I say.

Her eyes widen.

"He saw the news—" No, that won't do. "He wanted to check on everyone. See how we are. He looks pretty good, except for some stupid new facial hair," I say with a smirk. I don't tell her how he looks like he barely sleeps. She doesn't need any more guilt.

But the mention of Miles turns her attention inward, to bad memories. She starts to rock and hum.

"Here, I brought breakfast," I say, beginning to pull supplies from my pack. I don't want to lose her before I have a chance to ask about the girls.

Momma falls on the food hungrily, wolfing down an entire biscuit before I've finished pulling the lid off the Tupperware container of eggs and bacon.

"Mmm," she says, licking grease off her fingers.

Mmm is almost a word. I feel hope rising in my chest.

"Momma, I wanted to talk to you about something."

She raises her eyebrows at me, the expression so familiar I smile. Even before she was a monster, this was her way of saying *so talk*.

"Two girls have gone missing on the Bend. Samantha Parsons and Rochelle Greymont. The police are getting suspicious of us. They came 'round the house asking questions. Do you—do you know anything about it?"

Her eyes turn to thunderstorms, flashes of lightning piercing their depths. The smell of the river begins to roll off her in waves.

I squeeze the thermos of doctored coffee between my palms, debating whether to offer it to her. "Do you know what's happened to the girls—do you know who . . . who took them?"

A low growl escapes her lips, but she clenches her jaw tight. She closes her eyes and rocks herself, forward and back, forward and back. It's like she's at war, being torn in two—her humanity on one side, the part that is my mother, and on the other the monster who wants to take over for good.

The sight of her tears me in two as well, but I gather up my courage. "Here," I say. It's worth the risk. I hand her the thermos.

She clings to it and stares at it for a long time, running her thumb over the raised brand logo. It's as if the familiar feel of the thermos is bringing her back to herself, reminding her of who she is.

She stares at me, misery etched into every inch of her expression. "D-Della," she says, forcing my name out.

My breath catches in my chest. "Tell me," I say. "Let me help you."

She sets the thermos down and reaches into the pocket of her dress. She holds out her closed fist palm down, waiting for me to catch what's inside.

When I put my hand beneath hers, she opens her fingers and a bloody twist of dark brown hair falls into my palm. The medium-length strands of hair have been braided together and then looped into a ring.

The blood that coats them is clotted and dark, not fresh.

"Momma," I whisper, a chasm opening up inside me. "Where did you get this? Whose is it?"

She gazes into my eyes as if willing me to understand. When I don't get the message, she sighs and picks up the thermos again. I hold my breath as she unscrews it and pours coffee into the lid. She pauses and sniffs at it before taking a small sip.

The moment the coffee touches her lips, I see the monster take over. And it's angry at being tricked into drinking a brew. I begin to scramble backward, but she's too fast. The scalding coffee splatters across my chest, burning my collarbone. I snatch up my empty pack and dart toward the exit.

It's only when I'm safely outside the prison that I realize she was never chasing me. Even so, I run for my truck, holding the wet fabric of my shirt away from my scalded skin. I had hoped Momma would give me some sign that she's innocent, that I was wrong to doubt her.

But all she gave me was a first-degree burn and a bloody braid of hair.

I unclench my fist and realize I'm still holding the braid. The hair isn't only dark brown in the sunshine; strands of copper run through it, reflecting the light back at me. If it weren't for the dark red blood clinging to the braid, it could be one of those old-fashioned lover's tokens.

I stare at it for a long time, trying to understand. Neither of the girls who went missing had brown hair. They were both blondes. But this definitely isn't Momma's hair—hers is much longer and darker. So whose bloody braid am I clutching now, and what does Momma think it means?

A drop of water falls onto the hair, and I realize I'm crying. "Damnit," I whisper, wiping my eyes with the collar of my shirt. Those tears from this morning finally caught up with me.

I head home with only questions and doubts, less sure of my mother than I've ever been.

I ought to go into work. We need the money. But instead I spend all morning on the Bend. I need to fix something. I can't fix Momma, can't fix all the things she's done. So instead I decide to fix the flood-ruined oak and hedge apple trees where I first saw Natasha and her friends. That much I can do. It will be slow and tiring work, but I'll do it one tree at a time.

As I push through the weed-choked wood, I remember Natasha and her friends called this copse of trees creepy. I've heard others call it sinister. But I can see it for what it is—struggling. Struggling against outside forces too strong for it to defeat on its own. But I can defeat them, at least some of them. I pick a particularly pitiful-looking hedge apple tree off the path, where I'm hidden enough that park visitors or search parties won't stumble upon me.

I kneel at the tree's base, between two of its raised, exposed roots. Old, decayed hedge apples still litter the ground around me, their vibrant green gone. I close my eyes, dig my fingers into the moist soil, and begin to search out sources of nourishment. I find a thick clump of invasive stiltgrass, and some privet, neither of which belong here. They push out native species, choke their growth. I can take as much as I want from them. They'll still grow back, but for now they'll do some good.

I stretch all ten of my fingers, imagining them branching out like searching fungal threads beneath the soil, tapping into the root systems of the stiltgrass and privet. I see the life leaving the green plants in tiny shimmering droplets, like the dew on orb weavers' webs in early morning. Those droplets race along beneath the soil, traveling the branching paths to find this hedge apple tree.

I open my eyes to watch the transformation. The blackened bark lightens and firms up, new branches grow, and then the green leaves begin to appear. Huge, heavy hedge apples like bumpy green softballs expand on the branches. I pull my hands slowly from the soil and sit back.

A healthy, widely branching hedge apple tree fills the sky above my head. Green leaves hang low around me. After a while, I reach up and touch a hedge apple, still cool from the soil. I rise up on my knees and cut the fruit from the branch. I can't eat it and we don't have any brews that call for it, but all the same, I put it in my bag to carry home. It feels like a talisman, a promise.

As I walk through the green, green woods, a slow, satisfied feeling spreads through me. I'm tired, much too tired to do any more magic today. But the terrible helplessness that gripped me earlier is gone. I'm a witch, I'm a Lloyd, and there's nothing helpless about me.

When I hear a car door slam in the early afternoon, I figure it's Da coming home from that shift at the chicken plant he had to take after all. I go back to draining leeches into a mason jar at the kitchen table. There's a knock at the door. I pause, and it comes again, impatient and bold.

I slide out of my chair and wipe my hands on my jeans. I take a breath, prepared to find another cop on my doorstep, maybe one with a search warrant.

But when the door swings open, it's Natasha again. Only this time she looks like she's ready to kill someone.

"Back already, princess?" I say, trying for Da's lazy arrogance.

She raises her chin and stands tall, putting her hands on her hips. "Let's be clear. I don't like you. I think you're a rude, unfeeling bitch. But unfortunately, you're the only person I can think of to help me. So can I come in?"

I laugh. "Jesus, what a charmer."

"You don't have to like me either," she says brusquely. "You just have to take my money."

I sigh. "I told you I can't do a locating spell." And I wouldn't if I could—I want to keep myself and my family as far away from whatever's left of Rochelle Greymont as I can.

Natasha crosses her arms. "I'm not here for that."

I pause, debating. Is it more of a risk to let her in or to keep her out? I'm not sure. I guess it doesn't hurt to hear what she came here for. And if I let her inside, I show we've got nothing to hide.

I step back and wave her in the direction of the kitchen. As she walks by me, I get a whiff of her shampoo, something fruity and expensive. She stalks right into the kitchen in her tight designer jeans, her very presence revealing the house for the shambles it is: the cobwebs at the corners of the ceilings, the chipped paint on the walls, the yellowish stains along the door-jamb, where countless nervous fingers have brushed on their way to collect our nastiest spells.

But Natasha isn't nervous. She takes in the dilapidation and the unnerving jars and tools of our craft with her jaw clenched tight. Some anger inside her has carried her here, past fear and past doubt. It lights her up like an overfilled oil lamp, and I'm drawn to her radiance like any common moth. Maybe that's the real reason I let her in.

Once she reaches the kitchen, she spins to face me. "I still don't know what happened to my sister, but I know who's to blame."

When I don't answer, she goes on. "Her shithead boyfriend, Jake Motherfucking Carr."

I squint. "Isn't he a country singer?"

Natasha nods, impatient.

"Why don't you go to the police?" I ask.

"There's no point. The police have cleared him. They say he has an alibi for the night she went missing, and there's no probable cause. But there is. He told me he thought she was cheating on him. He was jealous. And I know she was scared of him, at least sometimes. She said he overreacted to everything, that he just got out of control. Some of the things he said to her—" The expression of rage on Natasha's face slips for a moment, revealing the terror underneath. "I think maybe he kidnapped her, that he's hiding her somewhere. Because she threatened to leave him."

Maybe this girl's got it all wrong, maybe she's blaming an innocent person, but growing up as a Lloyd has taught me there's no such thing. And if it's going to redirect attention away from us, away from the Bend, away from Momma . . .

"I can help, but it'll cost you," I say.

She rolls her eyes and opens her purse. She rifles through her wallet and then slams two hundred dollars on the kitchen table next to my pile of drained leeches. Either she doesn't see the worms, or she's not squeamish.

"All right then," I say.

Maybe it's wrong to take Natasha's money, but it'll give Da a reprieve from the chickens and make sure our lights stay on. Besides, it would look strange if I didn't take it. Anyway, this girl's got plenty of cash to spare.

I slide the money off the counter and into my pocket. "What'd you have in mind?"

SEVEN
NATASHA

"What kind of spells can you do? What are my options?" I ask, pacing the kitchen.

When I first walked in, I had to work hard not to react to the sights and smells around me. Except for the witchiness, Della's house reminds me a little of the one I grew up in before I became a Greymont—the disarray and clutter, the dust inches deep on every surface, the scuffed and unswept floor. A wave of longing and fear came over me, for a home I shouldn't miss but do. A home that shouldn't still have power to make my palms sweat but does. It would be easy to hate that old life, plain and simple. But I don't. It's a part of me, forever.

But now the stranger aspects of Della's house are beginning to distract me: heavy herbal smells, bunches of dried plants hanging from hooks, an enormous brick fireplace that must be original to what is clearly a very old house. Della and I could both fit inside it, with room to spare. A long-ago tale of Hansel and Gretel flits through my mind.

Della leans against the stove, taking me in. Her green eyes are unnerving, a color you expect to see in anime, not on a real person. Her expression is calculating and hungry, and her arms are crossed over her chest, showing off her strong biceps. A red, angry-looking burn runs over her right clavicle, but she doesn't even seem to feel it.

Just when I think she's never going to answer my question about the spells she can offer, Della finally speaks. "Well, tell me what outcome you're hoping for, and I'll tell you your options. Do you want him to confess? Do you want him to hurt? Or do you want him to die?"

I startle. "Die? You can do that?"

Della shrugs, as if life and death is nothing, as if death is only a matter of charging a higher fee, like bundling HBO into a cable package.

The reality of what I'm asking crashes down on me. I'm in the kitchen of a so-called witch asking her for a spell to do what I can't. To get proof of what Jake has done. To show beyond a shadow of a doubt that he's to blame for my sister's disappearance. What I saw in his eyes last night and what I read in my sister's diary tells me he's the reason she's missing. He's got a hell of a lot to hide.

There are so many things I'd like to do to Jake right now. Humiliate him. Make him suffer. Maybe even make him die. But what Rochelle needs most is for me to make him talk. Since I lost Ro's journal, I need to get Jake's secrets out into the world another way.

"I want to make Jake confess to what he's done to my sister."

Della nods. "I can do that." She pulls out a dented old pot from beneath the sink and rinses it out with water. She sets it on the stove. "I can brew the spell, but you have to make him take it."

"Like drink it? Isn't there another way?" The thought of being near Jake again makes me shiver.

"No," Della says. She waits to see if I'll quail.

"Okay, I guess I'll figure it out." Getting a vial of nasty magic down Jake's throat doesn't sound like an easy task, especially after our confrontation last night, but what choice do I have?

Della nods again and then begins moving methodically around the kitchen, gathering ingredients. She pours a small amount of brown water into the pot and brings it to a boil. Then she throws in some green stuff that looks like pesto.

"What is that?"

"Poison ivy."

"Is that—is that safe?" Just looking at it sends an itchy prickle across my skin.

Della doesn't even turn around. "He's a shithead, remember?"

"Yeah. I just mean, won't it make his throat swell closed? Then what good will it do?"

"It's magic, Natasha. It'll do what I want it to." She seems to be warming to the topic and goes on, a malicious glee in her voice. "We call this brew Itchy Tongue because it makes the person who drinks it spill all their secrets. They can't stop talking. They'll confess to everything they've ever done."

She throws a few more ingredients in and then whispers

over the simmering pot. Della turns to me and presses a single leaf into my hand. It looks like mint.

"What's this?" I ask.

"Stinging nettle. State your intention for the spell and then drop it in. And do it quick—before you start itching."

I stare into the bubbling froth of the potion and put all my hope into it. "I want Jake to finally tell the fucking truth," I say, and let the leaf fall into the pot. Della quickly stirs the concoction, and the leaf disappears.

Nothing supernatural happens, but chill bumps erupt on my forearms. I feel it in my bones—my will meeting Della's magic. This is going to work.

Della strains the brew through a sieve and pours it into a small vial. She squeezes the lid on tight. "He needs to drink all of it, all at once."

"And if he doesn't?" I ask.

"Not my problem." She holds out the vial to me.

I know I should take my spell and go, but I can't seem to make myself leave. Della is awful, but at least being with her requires less emotional wrangling than being with my family or with anyone else who actually gives a shit about my missing sister. "How do most of your clients do it?" I ask, just to buy time with her.

Della smiles and studies the vial in her fingers. "It's almost always wives wanting their husbands to confess to having affairs. They put it in their coffee or tell them it's a new juice fast. Once, though, a guy held his brother down and poured it down his throat. Men have no subtlety at all, do they?" She laughs. "But if it were me and there was something I wanted to know . . ." Her eyes cloud over. "Well, sometimes we're better off not knowing." She passes the vial to me.

"Right," I say, drawing out the vowel. "Good night, then." I force myself to make for the door.

"Night, princess," Della says. I flip her off over my shoulder, and she laughs, a true one this time, and I wonder suddenly what it's like inside her head. Making spells like this to ruin people's lives, does any of it matter to her? Does she wonder about the people at the other end of the spells? Does she care about the people she gives her spells to? Who is she, besides a witch?

I shake my head clear of the thoughts. None of that matters now. What matters is getting this still-hot vial of poison down Jake's throat. If I do this, there won't be any turning back. If I do this, I'll know all the horrible truth. Everything Jake has done to Rochelle. But then I might also know how to find her.

"It's always better to know," I whisper to myself as I make my way outside. I pause in Della's yard and gaze out over the nature park across the highway, listening. I watch the skies for wings. I want so badly to hear my sister's voice again, for her to fly that owl over my head again and tell me she's still alive, still waiting for me.

But there's only the electric hum of insects from the tree overhead, the distant whistle of a train. "I haven't given up on you," I whisper, hoping the wind will carry my words to Rochelle. She might need to hear my voice even more than I need to hear hers.

* * *

A quick look at his Instagram tells me Jake is playing another late-night show at Papa's, everyone's favorite seedy dive bar near the university. I text Georgia, asking her to meet me. Then, once Mom and Dad go to sleep, I slip out of the house and climb into my car, more grateful than ever for my BMW's quiet engine. I get into the bar with the fake ID Rochelle bought for me last year so I could help her celebrate her twenty-first birthday. She didn't want her college friends to know she was turning twenty-one because then they'd wonder why she was only a sophomore. Ro didn't like anyone to know she had to repeat two grades, thanks to our birth parents. So it was just me and her and Margo that night, and it felt like old times. One of my final good memories with Rochelle.

I cradle those memories close as I step into the bar, where the air is heavy with cigarette and vape smoke. Papa's must be one of the last places in America where you can still smoke indoors. The bar is hot and crowded, bodies jostling for room. Top 40 music blares through the speakers, so Jake must be between sets. I scan the room for him, but he's not here.

I order a rum and Coke from a bartender who cocks a suspicious eyebrow at me but gives me my drink when I glower. Some asshole in a Tennessee Titans cap keeps trying to chat me up, no matter how hard I ignore him. Ten minutes go by and there's no Jake and no Georgia.

Right when I'm about to text her, Georgia sidles up to me at the bar. She's dressed for Crescent in a pair of slacks and suspenders with a white tank underneath. The guy in the Titans cap eyes us and sneers, sauntering away.

Georgia looks uncomfortable at being here, and I don't blame her. This is really not her scene. I feel bad I asked her to come, but I don't want to do this alone.

"You all right?" I ask.

Georgia shrugs. "This will make some excellent documentary material. A fascinating contrast to Crescent." She smirks.

"I'll buy you a drink," I promise, knocking back the last of my rum and Coke. I almost never drink, and I can already feel the room going fuzzy. I turn toward the bar and catch sight of Jake.

He's standing there with his arm around a girl with long, wavy blond hair that cascades down her back. He leans in toward her, whispering something. She throws back her head and laughs. I'm too far away to hear it, but I know exactly what that laugh sounds like: throaty and loud. The laugh of someone who could never see the point of being ladylike. Then he kisses her cheek, running one hand down her backside. She slaps away his hand coquettishly, and I get a glimpse of my sister's face: her big, heavily made-up eyes, the dimple in her chin. It's Rochelle. My heart drops into my stomach and a whining noise starts in my ears. Jake really was making up that overnight bag for Ro. Then why was he crying? Why did he get so aggressive with me?

I cross the room on shaky legs, pushing people out of my way. Georgia follows me, asking questions I don't hear. Someone spills their beer on my shoulder, but I don't stop.

I grab my sister by the arm and spin her to face me. "Rochelle," I say, my voice laced with painful hope.

She only looks at me blankly. "You need something, sweetie?" she says in a rough Southern accent that's nothing like Rochelle's husky voice.

I stare at her, my head spinning. For a moment, I was so sure it was Ro. I was so sure.

But this girl doesn't have Rochelle's blue eyes, and now I see her hair is dyed blond, brown showing at the roots. She's wearing an apron, so she must be a server here.

"S-sorry," I stutter, my tongue thick. It feels like the ceiling is caving in on me. Then Georgia is there beside me, her hand on my arm. I wonder if she's thinking about how I heard Rochelle's voice at the nature park, and how I've now mistaken another girl for my sister.

"Hey, Shashi," Jake says with a grin, drawing me painfully back to reality. "You and your date want something to drink? Nicole here will get it for you. Won't you, baby?" He nuzzles her cheek with his nose, and I have to put my hands in my pockets to keep from slapping him.

It's like last night never happened.

"Sure, I'll have a Coke," I say. One drink was clearly enough. I glance at Georgia, but Jake starts talking again before she can say anything.

"No, no, no, Shashi," he slurs, "have a beer with me, to make up for our fight. We both said some awful things." He must have started in on the Molly early tonight. "Nicki, bring us a round, you beautiful goddess." He slaps her ass to send her on her way. He used to slap Rochelle's ass like that too. What's he going to do to Nicole when her new car smell wears off?

"I'm so touched you came here to see me play tonight," Jake says, throwing an arm around my shoulder. He smells like sweat and booze and something slightly chemical. I bite down my disgust and fear and squeeze the vial in my pocket, drawing strength from its solidity. "I thought you hated my guts."

Georgia catches my eye, her eyebrows raised, and I shake my head, letting her know I don't need help. Having her close is enough.

"I wanted to say I'm sorry. I think maybe you're right about Rochelle," I say loudly, to be heard over the music and the crowd and to cut through the haze Jake is in. "I think she did take off like you said. Margo seemed to think so too. I'm sorry I blamed you."

Georgia flinches beside me and her hand finds my arm again.

"Oh yeah? See, I knew you'd come around and we'd be friends again," Jake says. Anyone else would be able to tell I'm lying, but Jake seems to buy it. Maybe he's too stoned to remember threatening me. "Your sister's the best, but she's also a real bitch, you know that, right? You wouldn't believe some of the shit she used to say about you."

"Hey now," Georgia says, but I shake my head at her. She glowers at Jake, and maybe at me too.

"Like what?" I ask, playing along, biding my time.

"Oh, you know, how you were such a goody-goody, never did anything wrong. She said it was like you were born a Greymont, born to make your parents proud. She hates you for that, you know. She hates how easy it is for you to walk in our world. She never stopped feeling like a charity case your parents took in."

His words hit me like a punch to the gut, knocking all the wind out of me. Nicole comes back with three Blue Moons, each with a slice of orange perched on the lip of the bottle. I use the distraction to put my mask back on, so Jake doesn't see how his words have gotten through to me, doesn't see how much they sting. I knew Ro had a harder time than me adjusting to life as a Greymont, but I never knew she blamed me. I never knew she resented me for it.

But Jake is probably lying, right? Trying to throw me off balance? From what I read in Rochelle's journal, this is what he does. He's manipulative, an expert at hurting someone while claiming kindness. Last night he used his size to intimidate me and took Ro's journal by force, and now he's got his arm around me like we're friends. There's no way he doesn't remember what happened. I grip the cold beer bottle, which is a shock in this hot room. I hold it to my flaming cheek for a moment.

A guy at a table in the front flags Nicole down, and she hurries off, leaving Jake, Georgia, and me alone together again. "Hold my beer, little sister, I gotta piss," he says before lurching off toward the toilets.

"What a jackass," Georgia says. "Are you all right?"

"I'm fine. Hold this," I say, handing Georgia my beer. Then I dig out the vial Della gave me and pop its cork.

"Shit, Nat, what the hell are you doing?" Georgia asks. "Natasha, are you—"

"I'm getting answers," I say. While the crowd shifts and rumbles around me, I pour the contents of the vial into Jake's beer and swirl it around. He made it so easy. Now I just need to make sure he drinks it. I squeeze the orange slice into the bottle to help cover the taste.

"Oh my God," Georgia breathes, looking around worriedly.

Before she can say more, Jake comes back and I hand him his beer. "To bitches," I say, raising my bottle. He laughs and we clink our drinks together with Georgia, who's eyeing me like she's never seen me before. I ignore her glaring and take a small sip of my beer, but Jake throws back his head and downs half the bottle. If he notices any difference in the taste, he doesn't show it.

A guy dressed in all black comes up and taps his shoulder. "Boss wants you to go back on in two minutes," he says. Jake nods and starts to turn away from me. Between the drugs and the music, he has already forgotten my existence. But I need him to finish his drink.

"Jake," I say, and he turns back around. I lift my beer again. "Here's to a good show."

"To a good show and all the sex I'm gonna have tonight," he says with an enormous grin, clinking the bottle against mine. He takes one more sip of his beer and then tosses the rest into a garbage can. My heart sinks. Della said he had to drink it all. I went to all that trouble and it's not going to work.

I turn to Georgia. "Let's just go," I say. "This was a mistake."

"Damn right it was. What did you put in his beer?" Georgia hisses.

I shrug.

Georgia's mouth falls open. "I know you're upset about Ro, but you can't go around drugging people. You could get arrested for that. Actually, so could I, just by watching you do it. Did you even think about that when you dragged me here?"

"No one's getting arrested," I mutter. "Except maybe Jake."

I glance back at him. He straps on his guitar and leaps onstage, and even in the dimness of the smoky room I can see how high he is, how out of control. "Hey, y'all, I'm back," he drawls. "Did ya miss me?" Sweat beads at his forehead, and his eyes are huge and glassy. He smiles that perfectly white, innocently dimpled smile that belies his leather jacket, his artfully torn jeans. He winks at someone in the middle of the room, and several people in the crowd hoot and whoop. A girl near the front wolf-whistles, and Jake grins appreciatively.

"Look at him," Georgia says. "Jesus, Nat. Seriously, what did you give him?" She sounds scared, and I feel guilty for involving her.

"He was already like that," I assure her. "He's always on uppers."

Georgia shakes her head, clenching her jaw. She's not only scared, she's pissed.

"We can go home, Georgia, it's not going to work anyway," I say.

"No way. Let's finish what you started," Georgia says. She

crosses her arms over her chest. "If you're gonna make bad decisions, you gotta see them through."

I think about telling her she sounds exactly like her mother, which would really piss her off. But instead I huff and push back through the room, sitting at a table of frat boys near the stage. Might as well wait until I sober up enough to drive home. Georgia stays put; she's probably so mad she doesn't want to look at me anymore.

Jake launches right into one of his most popular songs, and the crowd cheers. He is as high on the music as he is on drugs, and some part of me can't help but admire the way he comes to life onstage. If this person performing were his true self, his best self, Jake might actually be all right. The music lights him up so bright I think I can see what Rochelle sees in him, the burning star that is Jake performing.

He finishes the song and the crowd claps and whistles and stomps. He's like a drug for them too. But then Jake's smile falls and he turns serious, his expression troubled. He bites his lip, hard, like he's afraid something is going to come tumbling out of his mouth. "You know, I don't usually talk much onstage 'cause y'all came here to listen to music, not some asshat rambling on."

I lean forward in my chair, a buzzing in my ears, my breath trapped in my chest. Maybe the potion did work. Maybe it had all risen to the top of the beer and he got every drop. Like Jake said, he never talks onstage. Something is happening.

The crowd cheers, and a woman yells, "Yeah, baby!"

Jake shakes his head sorrowfully. "But tonight, I'm gonna

disappoint you. There are some things I need to get off my chest."

A guy at the next table boos, and his girlfriend hisses at him to shut up. "What you gotta say, Jake?" she calls.

"I'm not the man you all think I am," he says. "Not the Jake Carr I show the world." I wrap my arms around myself, preparing to hear the worst.

"Are you a spy?" the frat guy next to me yells with a laugh.

"No, sir, no, I'm not a spy," Jake says, a hint of his stage persona peeking back through the honesty. "But I am a bad man."

"Oooh, Daddy," a girl yells. A guy calls out, "Spank me."

I wish I could scream at them all to shut their mouths. They might distract him before he says what I need to hear.

But Jake is oblivious to their banter, consumed by the need to unburden himself to the crowd. His mouth works and he rubs his lips together like they itch. He scratches his upper lip. "You see, I've done some awful things." Tears stand in his eyes, which somehow makes him even more beautiful.

The crowd goes silent, and I can hardly breathe. He's going to say it. He's going to say what he's done to Rochelle. A few people take out their phones and start recording. I glance back and see Georgia's phone held in the air too. This will be all over social media tonight. A hard, bright satisfaction grows in my gut.

Jake takes a deep breath and then starts talking, fast, irrepressibly. "I stole my best songs from a guy I used to play with. He wrote them all, and then he got in a car accident and died, and I just said they were mine. I said I wrote them and didn't give him any credit. He was a good guy too. I probably would've done it even if he hadn't died, if I'm honest. But I don't think I'll ever write anything as good as those songs, and sometimes it makes me so mad they aren't mine that I'm glad he's dead."

A few people gasp. I clench my jaw, waiting for him to get to what matters.

"And I—I've always had a troubled way with women. I take them for granted, or I get so jealous of them I can't stand it. It makes me wild sometimes. I had a girlfriend who was like the sun shining in the morning, beautiful and perfect and too good for me. I loved her like crazy—I still love her. But I took her for granted, thought she'd always be around. Thought I could treat her any way I wanted. I cheated on her all the time, with just about anybody. Actually, I cheated on her with that girl there, Nicki the waitress, who's just a cheap piece of ass, not even really worth the effort."

"Screw you," Nicole yells, but the crowd stays silent, entranced by Jake's confession.

"Rochelle started seeing somebody else because I wasn't around enough. She said she wasn't, but I know she was. There was evidence of it everywhere, all over her, all over her things." Jake shakes his head for emphasis. He really believes what he's saying, I realize. He can't lie right now. He truly loved Rochelle, in his own twisted way, and he felt like he was losing her. He really has been acting all this time, pretending he didn't care.

Jake plows on. "I swear to God, I could *smell* the bastard on her. It made me so angry I wanted to choke the guy. But I didn't know who he was, so there was only her to take it out on." Tears begin to pour from his eyes.

The satisfaction in my gut melts like ice water and I shiver, wrapping my arms tighter around myself. Anything could come out of his mouth now. Any terrible, awful thing.

"I started following her, watching her apartment. I looked through her phone and hacked into her email. But she was too careful. I couldn't find anything." Jake shakes his head again, but doesn't wipe away his tears. "That's the thing about Rochelle—she's too damn smart for her own good." Without seeming to realize it, he starts picking out a song on his guitar, just a way of fiddling. But he's staring out into the crowd, his eyes wide and wet.

"So finally, one night I slipped something into her wine. Something to make her talk. But even then, she wouldn't admit to it. Wouldn't say anything. I hated myself for doing it, but I grabbed her wrist and squeezed it so hard I could feel her bones grind together. She cried and said she only loved me, that I was crazy, that I was imagining it. I thought I was going to kill her. I thought I was going to explode and turn into a monster and devour her whole." Jake looks terrified, as if he can't believe such violence lives inside him.

The guy from before, the one dressed in black, gets onstage and takes Jake by the arm. Jake struggles against him, clinging to the microphone. "No, I have to tell them all, I have to let everyone know who I am."

"You've said enough," the man says. Another guy, big and muscled, probably a bouncer, takes Jake's other arm. They start to bustle him off the stage. "She's gone now," Jake yells. "She's gone, and it's all my goddamned fault. I'll never forgive myself for—" His voice cuts off as the two men push him through a back door.

Loud music begins to blare over the speakers again.

I stand up, stunned and numb, as snatches of conversation swirl around me.

"Rochelle? Isn't that the girl who's missing?"

"Is he saying he killed her?"

"No, he was saying she ran away."

"God, he's so hot."

"He just ruined his career."

The palm of my hand starts itching, painfully. When I look down at it, red welts cover its lined surface.

One of the guys at my table touches my arm. "You all right, honey?" he says, scratching around his mouth. "I'd like to make you not all right," he says. "I'd like to throw you over this table and—" I lurch back from him, almost knocking my chair over. I get to my feet and back away from the table, but he continues telling me exactly what he'd like to do to my body. His eyes widen, as if he can't believe what he's saying, but he can't stop. His friends egg him on.

I grab my clutch off the table and hurry into the bathroom. I shut myself into a stall and lean against the door, my chest heaving. Jake almost confessed. He was so close. He almost told us what he did to her. I bang my fist against the stall door.

He confessed to stalking and drugging her and physically harming her. Just those are enough to make me feel sick. But is that enough to make the police question him again? To reconsider him as a suspect? To make him tell us where my sister is?

Before tonight I thought Jake had kidnapped her, that he was keeping her somewhere. But now, after what he just said . . . He said she was gone. That either means he truly doesn't know where she is or he thinks he killed her. But she can't be dead—she asked me to help her, to find her, didn't she?

The sound of the bathroom door opening distracts me from my thoughts. Two girls come in and hover at the sinks, probably touching up their makeup. "Is it bad that I think he's even hotter now?" one asks, and the other laughs.

"He can roofie me any day," she says.

I bang out of the stall to confront them, ready to pour out my rage and fear on their heads, but Georgia's already there. "What the hell is wrong with you?" she yells at them. "Idiots!"

They stare at her, shocked, and then start to giggle. One of them is scratching her scalp, and the other her neck, though neither seems to notice.

"Get out!" Georgia yells, pointing at the door. But I barrel out first, pushing everyone out of my way. I need air. I need to breathe. I need to know that this isn't just going to make Jake more popular, that this isn't somehow going to bankroll his career. I hear Georgia swear somewhere behind me.

The bar is chaos. People are in each other's faces, yelling, crying, all while scratching themselves. One woman slaps the man I saw her kissing when I first walked in.

I look down at my own aching, itchy palm. What the hell is happening? Did the spell spread somehow? Is everyone confessing their secret thoughts and desires and misdeeds? I struggle through the maelstrom to the front door.

When I get outside, I start pacing. I know Jake's confession was just livestreamed. How long until Mom and Dad see it too? What will it do to them to hear how he treated Rochelle, to wonder what else he might have done?

I need to tell them first. I start to walk toward my car, but Georgia grabs my arm and spins me around. "That was fucked up, Nat."

I wrench my arm from her grasp, tears clogging my throat. "I have to go." I turn away.

Georgia sighs. "Please let me drive you. The last thing your parents need is for you to die in a car crash."

The thought stills my feet. "Fine," I say. "But let's hurry."

Georgia is still simmering with anger of her own. "When you asked me to come here, did you even think about how it might affect me? That I might not want to participate in something like that? That if it went badly, the consequences might be worse for me than for you?"

"Shit, I'm sorry. I didn't think," I say, still barreling forward.

"I know you didn't," Georgia mutters.

I stop and face her. "You're right. I'm an asshole, and I didn't think. I'm just so focused on Rochelle. I'm sorry. I really, really am." I take her hand and squeeze it. "You know how much I love you."

Georgia's face softens a little. "It must have been terrible, hearing everything Jake said."

I nod, wrapping my arms around myself even though it's eighty degrees out. "Did you get it all?" I ask.

"Yeah, I did. I hope that's okay. It's on my Insta already. I livestreamed it as soon as I realized what was happening."

"Thank you," I say quietly.

We jump into her Jeep and she squeals out of the parking lot. After sitting in traffic a few minutes, we're on the interstate. There's a roar in my head, like a thousand voices yelling at once. All I can think is that I have to get home to my parents, have to be the first to tell them.

But there's an accident ahead and the traffic stops dead. Red taillights for miles. I scream and bang on the dashboard, but it won't do any good. I'm stuck, stuck here with Jake's confession playing over and over in my head, the confession I made happen. I did this. Despite my fear and anger and shame, a sick pleasure runs through me. Is this what Della feels like all the time? Is this what it's like to wield magic? To have all this power? No wonder Della walks through the world like she's bulletproof, untouchable. No wonder she sneers at all of us. We're so weak.

Because of her magic, Jake had to confess his sins. Because of her magic, he might actually be held accountable for what he's done.

Because of her magic, I might get my sister back.

EIGHT
DELLA

I wake up the morning after Natasha's visit with unease still swirling in my gut. I turn on the TV for some background noise while I make Momma's breakfast. The antenna isn't working well, and the news is the only channel coming in. But it's enough to distract me from everything on my mind.

I'm stirring cheese into a pot of grits when a live report comes on. The name Jake Carr catches my ear, and I leave the stove and hurry to the TV in the living room to listen. There's a poorly filmed video showing the musician onstage, pouring out his evil little heart. I recognize the effects of the Itchy Tongue brew right away. Boy's got verbal diarrhea and all his nasty secrets are coming out.

Hell, maybe it really was Jake who abducted or killed or chased off Rochelle. He seems exactly the type. Maybe Da's right and I've been doubting Momma for nothing. I head back to the kitchen with my heart just a little bit lighter. I'm almost cheerful as I drive to the prison. Everything might work out okay. Jake Carr will go to jail and we can get on with our lives.

My good mood doesn't last long. A fog has rolled in off the river and found its way into every crack and crevice of the prison, making it harder to see than usual. Mist hangs in the air outside the windows, heavy as a shroud. The starlings are quiet in their nests, subdued by the weather. The heat will come once the sun is up, but now the air is unseasonably cool and moist. The prison feels weighed down with moisture.

"Momma?" I call into the eerie dawn stillness.

There's no answer, no sound. I walk through the mess hall and down a corridor that leads to the cellblock where Momma likes to sleep. I usually try not to come back here in the mornings because there's less room for me to get away if she's still wild from her nightly transformation. The green paint on the cinder-block wall is badly peeling, sending flakes fluttering down to the floor every time I brush against it. Finally, I reach the cellblock, where grayish light leaks in from the high, barred windows.

"Momma?" I call again.

No answer.

I wander down to her cell, where there's a mattress and a few of her things. Her door is never locked and I've brought in plenty of her belongings from home, but the cell looks as bleak as any prisoner's who lived here before her. The sight of it always makes my stomach ache. I think she's choosing to suffer, choosing to punish herself—because of Aunt Sage.

I peer around the cell, misgiving beginning to tick away inside me. She's not here.

She's not here.

Shit, shit, shit.

"Momma? Where are you?" My voice is gaining that slightly hysterical edge my mother worked so hard to cure me of as a child. She wanted me to be like her—cool, calculating, unruffled. I take a deep breath and push my panic down.

I'll wait. This prison is huge—it used to hold eight hundred prisoners from around the state—and she has full run of the three wings that haven't caved in. She could be anywhere. Eventually, she'll get hungry and want her breakfast and come looking for me.

Unless she's already eaten.

The thought sends me sprinting back down the hall, my boots making dull echoes in the heavy air. I race through the prison, past every open cellblock, every guard room, every bathroom and recreation area. She's nowhere.

Could she have climbed up to a guard tower? Those have been completely blocked off, so I can't imagine how. But I make my way outside and run furtively along the perimeter of the prison, scanning the roof and guard towers. They are as empty as ever.

I circle back to the door I exited, looking for footprints. There are my boot prints, fox and possum tracks, and there— there, in a muddy track of bare soil, a single human footprint, perfectly formed, with the heel and all five toes, the perfect imprint of my mother's long, graceful foot. Momma's escaped the prison. If I don't find her before nightfall, someone could die—if they haven't already.

I bolt to my truck and rip onto the road. I head home first, just in case she decided to go there. I bang through the front door and search the house, but she's nowhere to be seen. Finally, I knock on Da's door and barge in. He's lying with his face smushed into a pillow, hiding from the sunlight that's beginning to break through the fog and sneak through his blinds. I flip on the lights.

"Momma's gone."

Da sits up, still groggy. He worked a night shift at the plant yesterday. He rubs his eyes and blinks at me. "What?"

"I said Momma's gone. I went to the prison and she wasn't there, and I saw her footprint outside. She's gone."

My meaning finally sinks in and Da leaps out of bed, hurrying to pull a pair of jeans over his boxers. "Have you been to the—"

"I came here first, just in case. But you can help me look." I push my sweaty hair out of my eyes.

Da acted on impulse before, simply reacting to my panic, but now his ability to reason kicks in. He stops buttoning his shirt. "Oh, well, I—"

"You have to stop being so afraid of her," I shout, a year's worth of frustration welling up in me. "I've been handling her completely by myself. All alone. All this time. The least you can do is help me find her!" I leave the room, slamming the door behind me.

I don't wait to see if he's going to follow. I am out the front door and across the road, running through the forest. Birds I can't see sing in the branches, their songs off-key, sharp and shrieking like the screams of children on a playground, but more sinister. Like a woman in a horror movie, running from a knife.

I resist the impulse to call out to Momma. If she's somehow still in her creature form, I'll never catch her, and she might do me harm. Once, in the early days, I got too close to her during a transformation. I still have the scar on my forearm where her claws dug in, so deep I probably should have gotten stitches. This late in the morning, she's almost certainly back to her human body, but she's still dangerous, still a risk to herself and anyone she might come across in these woods.

So I run and watch for her, but really I know where she'll be if she's here—at the river. Always at the river.

I burst into the open field and tear down to the river, where fog still curls over the water. She could be anywhere. She could be in the water or along the banks, hiding in the bracken. She could have covered herself in mud and be waiting like a crocodile for prey to pass by. She could be watching me now, from those weeping willows, peering with her green eyes through the leaves.

I walk quickly along the bank, watching for any sign of her. My heart beats hard and fast against my rib cage. I work to control my breathing, to keep my face neutral. She will smell my fear, but I won't let her see it.

"Never show them you're scared, Della," Momma told me once when we came upon a pack of coyotes feasting on a downed deer. "Never show anything like weakness. If you run into the wrong creature with fear in your heart, you're dead."

Now Momma is that creature. Panic threatens to overwhelm

me—she could kill someone, she could kill me. But what I'm most afraid of is losing her—for good.

I bite down every ounce of fear, will my racing heart to quiet, shove my trembling hands in my pockets, and pretend I'm in control. I cut off access to all the emotions that branch rootlike and insidious inside me, including love. My love for Momma might be more dangerous than my fear.

As I act it out, the control comes to me, stealing over me slowly until my heart beats normally and my limbs move with confidence. Then I see a footprint in the mud. Hers.

There's one, and there's another. Her steps lead out of the river and toward the young oak wood. I want to run, but I force myself to walk calmly, at a steady pace.

The birds are still shrieking unnaturally in the canopy, and I could swear they're screaming one word over and over again. *Dead, dead, dead.*

The fog has settled at the forest floor, a knee-high vapor, so I can't see my feet or Momma's tracks anymore. I step softly now, careful not to snap a single twig, not to rustle one fallen leaf. I glance up into the trees, expecting a raucous gathering of crows, but I can only catch glimpses here and there, of gray wings and taloned feet, of sharp beaks. They flit and jump and swoop among the leaves, calling to one another, *Dead, dead, dead.*

The trees open up into the clearing, and there's Momma, stark naked, knee-deep in fog, her long dark hair cascading down her back, all the way to her thighs. She's gazing up into the branches of an enormous honey locust tree, and she's singing. Her high, trembling voice floats eerily above the fog, beautiful and arresting and strange.

I am rooted to the spot, as if mesmerized. The birds—if they are birds . . . I'm not so sure now—they seem to be listening. They flap their wings as if clapping along; they sidle along the branches with their insubstantial gray feathers. They seem to me like a congregation in a church, in a religious ecstasy.

When Momma comes to the end of "Young Hunting," an old murder ballad about a woman who kills her cheating love with a penknife and throws his body in a well, the birds call louder than ever, and begin to fly in a frenzy from branch to branch. Yet I still can't get a proper glimpse of one. They are as shifting and shadowy as the fog, like the play of dull light over river stones. Is one of these the creature that dove at me and Natasha and her friends?

Momma's last note swirls off like the fog, and then she turns. Her eyes are green as moss this morning, bright as jade. "Della," she says, and her voice is almost like her old voice, pure and strong.

"What are you doing out here?" I ask, taking a few tentative steps toward her.

She turns away from me and gazes up into the branches of the honey locust, but the birds are gone. They disappeared in the moment she turned. She seems gentle now, so I close the distance between us. "Why are you here? Were you out all night?"

Momma looks around suddenly, as if only just realizing where she is. She covers her breasts with her forearms, crossing them over her chest. That's when I see the dried blood under her fingernails.

"Did you hurt someone?" I ask, my voice hardly more than a whisper. My relief at finding her is already turning to dismay.

Momma raises her hands to her eyes, staring at her palms, which I now see have traces of blood in the creases.

A train whistle sounds in the distance. Momma drops to her knees and begins to sob.

Once the sound of the train passes away, I take my wrapped flannel from around my waist and cover her bare, skinny shoulders. "Come on, then," I say, my voice firm. I touch her elbow, and she doesn't lash out, so I put a hand under her arm and help her to her feet. "I'll take you home." Her bones feel fragile as winter kindling under my hands, and even though she's a monster, claws and teeth and blood, every ounce of me wants to protect her, to wrap her up soft and warm, to hide her somewhere the Bend's twisted magic can't touch her.

But there isn't a damn place in this world like that. Because the magic is inside her.

She walks with me, humming "Young Hunting." As she hums the last note, I remember it was Aunt Sage's favorite song. After Momma goes quiet, the forest is silent, not a bird, not a breath of wind moving the leaves. The fog is only ankle-deep now, and rays of light break through the trees. We don't see anyone, not a single living thing. Once we reach the road, I wait with her along the tree line until there aren't any cars. When Momma's feet touch the asphalt, she jolts, as if stepping off Bend land shocked her.

We climb the driveway, and I watch for her to resist, to demand to return to the river or to the prison or to anywhere except this old house, where she used to live. I even pause beside my truck, in case she wants to go to the prison, but she only shakes her head and continues toward the house. She stops before the porch steps and gazes up at her home, her brow crinkled, as if she's puzzled.

"Do you want to go in?" I ask, treacherous little wings of hope brushing the inside of my ribs.

She nods, the motion hardly perceptible. She looks tired. But what has made her so very tired? What did she do all night, in her other body? And who did she do it to?

"You can sleep in your own bed," I say.

She nods again, this time more strongly, and I lead her up the steps and through the front door. For a second, I let myself imagine life going back to normal, Momma and Da smiling at each other over the spell work while I make dinner. The three of us together and happy.

Momma pauses in the living room, taking in the clutter and the dust, and then continues down the hall. I think she'll go into her and Da's old room, but she continues on to the kitchen.

She stops abruptly in the doorway, and I have to peer over her shoulder on my tiptoes to see why. Da sits at the table, chopping poison ivy into small, fine pieces that he'll later grind into a paste. The coward couldn't even be bothered to step past our front door. He just left me to handle Momma on my own, as usual.

He has always been a passive man, always pleased to let Momma take the lead. I thought losing her might wake him up, put him into action, but that seems to go against the very grain of who he is.

Da didn't hear us come in, our feet fall so softly. But as if he senses her eyes on him, he glances up and startles, dropping the knife and pushing back his chair.

"Ruby," he says, shock in his voice. He hasn't seen his wife in months. She never wanted to come home, and he refused to visit her. He claimed it was too hard.

Momma doesn't say anything. She watches him, and I can imagine what he sees: her eyes, alert as a cat's, her every muscle tensed to spring.

"Ruby," he says again, a wave of emotions washing over his face: love and shame and fear and others I can't place. I know what's going to happen next, know it as surely as the frozen rabbit watching the fox approach. I reach for Momma's arm, but she's too fast for me—too fast for him too, stunned rabbit that he is.

I've barely blinked before she has Da up against the refrigerator, his knife in her hand, pressed against his throat. Broken glass lies scattered around them, the strong, bitter smells of crushed herbs filling the air.

"Ruby," he gasps, the third time he's said her name.

I shake my head. I knew better than to hope. Now those soft feather touches feel like choking vines squeezing my heart.

"Let him go, Momma," I say, my voice tired. "He hasn't done anything."

That's the trouble, though, isn't it? He hasn't done anything. Not a damn thing. He didn't help her figure out what was going wrong with the Bend before Aunt Sage died. He didn't fix Momma once she turned. And he's not even strong enough to face up to his failures.

Now Momma turns and looks at me, her face twisted up with a rage that doesn't even look like it belongs to her, confusion plain in every line of her face, as though her body isn't hers and she's fighting against another's control.

"Momma, put the knife down. Do you hear me?" I say. I'm not sure if she does, though she watches my lips move. I think maybe she's hearing other noises, so loud they drown out my voice. I step carefully, toeing glass out of my path without taking my eyes off her. "You don't need to hurt him, Momma. He's not doing any harm."

Maybe Momma's as angry at him as I am, I don't know. She's violent with me too, but she seems to have a special hatred of Da. Maybe because he's weak. Maybe because he failed her. Maybe because he, more than anyone, reminds her of everything she's lost.

She turns away from me and presses the tip of the knife deeper into Da's skin. Blood beads and rolls down his neck, and he lets out a whimper. He should know better than to show her his soft underbelly. But he never could learn this craft. He's good at brewing spells and frightening customers, but he's never learned the instinctive Lloyd magic that makes Momma and me what we are. I guess it's because he doesn't have our blood.

"Momma," I say, my voice as firm and steady as if I were shooing away a stray dog. "Give me that knife and go have a rest. You're tired out is all."

She lets me take the knife from her hand, but she continues to hold Da against the refrigerator. He could fight back—he's got sixty pounds on her, after all—but he stays pinioned there, his face pale with fear.

"Let the poor man go," I say, making my voice light and unconcerned now that the true danger is past. "He's got work to do. Someone has to earn a living around here."

Momma releases his shirtfront and gazes at him, studying his face. She cocks her head to one side and contemplates his throat, as though she'd like to rip it out with her teeth.

"Ruby," he whispers. "Baby."

Momma laughs, a high, wild sound. She throws her head back and sings the first verse of "Come All Ye Fair and Tender Ladies," a song about the fleeting and untrustworthy love of men.

She laughs again and turns away from Da. He takes a breath but stays where he is, tensed for another attack. But she has already forgotten him. She wanders off to the living room and collapses onto the couch, still singing.

I let out a sigh that wants to turn into a sob, but I swallow it down and close the kitchen door.

"Where was she?" Da asks. He dabs at the blood on his neck with a kitchen rag.

"The woods by the river. Singing to the birds. At least I think they were birds."

"You think?"

I shrug, numbness stealing over me. "It was a strange morning." More quietly, I add, "There's dried blood on her hands." I do wonder about the birds—what they are, why she was singing to them—but I'm more worried about where that blood came from.

We're silent for a moment, listening to Momma sing behind the closed door. Even across the house and through the heavy wood of the door, her voice is arresting.

When I glance back up at Da, his face is sad and drawn. I have lost my mother, but he has lost his wife, his life's companion. And he has no way to get her back.

"Why do you let her see how afraid you are?" I ask gently, my anger at him gone.

Da sighs. "I never could lie to Ruby. She always saw right through me. That's what I loved about her."

As if she hears him and wants to drown out his voice, Momma sings even louder about how a man's love always fades away.

"My love hasn't faded," Da says, then turns from me, to the kitchen window, where the light comes in hot and bright. "I know you think I'm weak, Della, for being afraid of her, for not helping you."

A good daughter would say he's wrong, that she doesn't think that, but I'm not a good daughter. At least not to him. I've only got room in my heart for Momma right now.

Da's voice is even when he goes on. "To have your wife, the person you love deeper'n anything, turn on you like that, become someone you don't recognize, someone who despises you—it's agony. One day she was my Ruby, and the next . . . I've lost her and I can't stand it."

Almost from the first day of Momma's change, she couldn't bear to be near Da. She could tolerate me well enough, but a single touch from him sent her into a rage, opened up a well of hatred inside her so deep Da would probably drown in it if he got too close. Maybe her decision to stay at the prison isn't only about Aunt Sage; maybe somewhere deep down she still loves Da and doesn't want to destroy him.

The silence between us has taken hold, and the only sound now is the faucet dripping.

"She stopped singing," Da says, a warning note in his voice.

I hurry to open the kitchen door and peer down the hallway. I tiptoe to the end of it. Momma is asleep on the sofa, still wearing nothing but my old flannel, her skinny knees raised to her chest. I take a quilt off the recliner and lay it gently over her. She stirs, murmurs a few words I don't catch, and falls back into dreams. I decide I'll let her sleep awhile before taking her back to the prison, before locking her up tight. I can give her that much at least.

As I gaze down at her peaceful face, I let myself feel for just a moment how much I love her, how much I miss her. Looking at her like this, you'd never know a monster's inside her, eating away at her humanity. You'd never know what all she's done.

NINE
NATASHA

"You let him go? How could you do that? After everything he said onstage. After I told you how he acted at Rochelle's apartment, what I read in her journal." I pace up and down the dining room, while my parents and Detective Long, the detective in charge of my sister's case, sit at the table. He's a middle-aged white man with bags under his eyes. He looks tired and overworked, but I don't give a shit because he's got nothing but excuses on his lips.

The police took Jake in for questioning late last night, and he's already back on the streets again.

Della's magic did its best, but the police couldn't match it. They won't make Jake accountable. They won't make him pay. Worst of all, they won't find my sister.

"Honey, please come sit down," Mom says, wringing her hands. "Let's talk about this." Her voice shakes, and I know I should do what she asks. I know I should sit back down and listen to the detective, but I feel like my heart is going to explode.

"What's there to talk about?" I yell, and Mom rears back from my anger. "Jake did something horrible to Rochelle, and no one cares."

Dad stands, putting his palms flat on the table and leaning forward like he can barely hold up his own weight. "Natasha, I know you're angry, but you cannot speak to your mother that way."

I turn on him too. "My sister is missing. God, she's been missing for *a week*. She could be wandering around on the park, hurt and lost and scared. I know Jake did something to her. Maybe he attacked her and left her there. Maybe he chased her to the river and—" I choke down the rest of the thought, one I still can't let myself consider. I wanted so badly to believe Jake was only hiding Rochelle somewhere. But he said she was *gone*. All the hope I felt last night has vanished.

The landline in the kitchen starts ringing, but we all ignore it. It's been ringing since eight a.m. It's probably yet another reporter wanting a quote about Jake's performance last night. I wanted to tell the first one everything, but Dad made me hang up on her. He said we shouldn't involve the media until we have all the facts. But what more do we need to know?

"How can you sit there twiddling your thumbs while these police tell us that there's nothing else they can do? How can you just sit there?" I yell at Dad.

He hangs his head. Mom looks pleadingly at Detective Long.

The man clears his throat, adjusts his suit jacket. "Miss Greymont, I can appreciate your anger. Jake Carr is obviously not a good man and there's no doubt that he has mistreated your sister."

"And yet you let him go!" I roar.

The detective raises his hands, conciliatory. "But there is no evidence at all linking him to her disappearance, except what you've told us. He denies taking the journal from you, and he willingly allowed us to search his home and vehicle. He has a rock-solid alibi. His whereabouts are consistently accounted for in the period Rochelle went missing. And, unfortunately, that confession he made onstage won't stand up in a court of law. His lawyers have claimed it was artistic expression, and Jake has denied every charge. Our hands are absolutely tied. I'm sorry. I truly am."

"What about the overnight bag? The one I told you he was packing?" I ask, casting wildly about for anything to grab on to.

"The bag and its contents were cataloged back when we searched his apartment the first time. Your sister really did leave it there," Detective Long says. "He wasn't packing a bag for her or anything like that."

"Honey, maybe we should call Dr. Patel, get you in for an appointment," Mom says. "You haven't been in weeks."

I round on her. "I don't need therapy; I need my sister." My voice breaks. Mom tries to say something more, but all she can produce are tears.

I can't stay here. I can't stay in this room for one more single minute and listen to this windbag tell me how useless he is. I can't stay here and watch Mom crumble into nothing, watch Dad melt into himself. I can't. Maybe that makes me less of a

Greymont, but I don't care.

I snatch my purse off the table and head for the front door.

"Natasha, come back here," Dad says, but there's no conviction in his voice.

I'm out the front door and sliding into my car before anyone can follow me. I spin out of the driveway, my mind racing, tears pouring down my cheeks. I put the windows down and let the wind dry my face, whistle through my hair.

There has to be someone in this fucking world who can find my sister. Some person who's not a useless piece of shit. Because clearly the police aren't going to help. And I guess I can't either. Maybe I imagined that bird in the woods whispering to me with Rochelle's voice. Maybe it was stupid to think I could be the one to bring her home.

And yet I know exactly where my car is headed and what I'm about to do. Because what other choice is there? What other choice is there but for me to get on my knees in front of Della Lloyd and beg her to do something, anything, to help me?

I pull up in front of her house and jump out of the car. I bang on the front door. But when it swings open, it's not Della. It's a short, stocky man with a balding head and stained, rumpled clothes. He stares at me, waiting for me to speak. When I don't say anything, he raises his eyebrows.

"Here for a spell, then?" he drawls. "Let me guess . . ." He takes in my tearstained face, the anger in my eyes. "Your boyfriend dumped you, and you want to give him boils."

I see where Della learned all her tricks. She looks a little like him too, except in the eyes. He could posture all day long and never unnerve me as much as Della because he doesn't have her cunning, sharp eyes. I wonder if she got those from her mother, though Della seems too feral to have ever had a woman's touch in her life.

"I wanted to see Della," I say.

He looks surprised by that. She must not have many friends come knocking. "You know her from school?" he asks.

"We're, uh, friends—sort of," I say evasively.

He cocks his head, curious. "She ain't here. Anything I can help with?"

"Will she be back soon?" I don't fancy spending the evening alone with this man. He doesn't have Della's bite, but he smells like a farmyard.

He gives me a surprisingly gentle smile. "I reckon she might turn up before long. You can wait if you wanna."

"I'll wait in my car. I need to make a call anyway," I lie.

"Suit yourself," the man says. Then he locks the door behind him and climbs into a beat-up old brown car and leaves.

I sit on the trunk of my car and peer out over the highway. The trees of the nature park are lit golden at the tops, like a fairy-tale wood. But instead of unicorns and white stags, it holds yellow-eyed beasts and birds who speak with a missing girl's voice. And God only knows what else. As I sit and stare out at the scene, my anger and urgency fade, and a creeping sadness takes their place. I've failed her. I've failed the one person I could always count on.

The afternoon turns to evening and still Della doesn't come. The big, disheveled-looking orange cat from the other night jumps up beside me, startling me. It meows and rubs up against my arm. I slide down off the trunk to get away from it, in case it's diseased. It meows plaintively.

I'm about to get in my car and go home when I hear tires crunching up the driveway. Della's truck rumbles into the yard. She climbs out wearily and sighs when she sees me. "Come on, then," she says, and her voice is tired.

She leads me through the front door and flips on the lights. The cat shoots inside after her and disappears under a beat-up recliner. Della doesn't even seem to notice it, which is exactly how I'd expect her to act toward a pet. That mangy creature is probably a glorified mousetrap.

The house is the same cluttered mess as before, but it looks like someone has been sleeping on the couch. Della picks up a flannel shirt and pulls it on over her tank top, even though the house is warm.

She pushes open the door to the kitchen and throws those lights on too. The smell here is stronger than before, so sharp and bitter it burns my nose. A few pieces of broken glass glitter beneath the refrigerator.

Della opens the fridge and pulls out a can of cheap soda. She pops the top and takes a long draft. She doesn't offer me one, not that I'd accept. Della still hasn't said anything else, so I'm about to tell her why I'm here when she turns back around and meets my eyes.

She looks exhausted. Dark half-moons hang beneath her eyes, and there is a long scratch across one cheek. There's still dried blood at the edges. I didn't think it was possible for her

to be any scarier-looking, but she is. There's something cynical and dead-hearted in the way she holds her head, the way
she curls her lip, as if nothing in this world means a damn
thing.

"Are you all right?" I ask before I can bite the question back.

Della tries to give me that annoyingly smug smile of hers,
but it's barely more than a grimace. "Not your concern."

"I just want to know you're up to doing what I'm paying
you for," I shoot back.

Something sparks behind Della's cold eyes, and I automatically take a step back. She seizes on my fear and leans closer to
me, until we're nearly nose to nose. She's shorter than me and
has to look up to meet my eyes, but I know that doesn't mean
a thing. It would be the nastiest fight of my life if she decided
to take a swing at me. And she looks like she's spoiling for one.

Well, maybe I am too. I clench my fists.

"Let's get something clear," Della says, enunciating every
word. "You don't own me. You're not my boss. If you don't like
how I do my job, you can find yourself another witch."

"There aren't any other witches."

"Exactly," she says, holding my gaze.

She's so close I can see every detail of her face—the tiny
mole at the corner of her left eye, the dusting of freckles on her
nose. My eyes travel down to her mouth, to her slightly parted
lips. They're full and red, with a little white scar carving a line
down the center of the bottom one.

Della sees me looking at her lips, and curls them into a lewd
smile that makes my stomach knot. "I wouldn't have guessed

you swung my way, princess, but I'm down if you are." She flits her eyes up and down the length of me.

I step back quickly, bumping into the kitchen counter. Della laughs. The tension between us breaks.

"Why *aren't* there any other witches?" I ask, trying to recover my dignity. My cheeks burn so hot I know they must be flaming red. I think this embarrassment is the first thing besides sadness and anger I've felt in days. I almost welcome it, not that I want Della to know how much she affects me.

Thankfully, Della's taking another swig of soda and doesn't see my blush. She sips again, as if she's thinking over a response to my question. "People don't know how to pay attention, I guess," she finally says.

That's not a real answer, but I sense I can't push her any further tonight. She's on edge, simmering with some emotion that has nothing to do with me. I can only hope it will work in my favor.

I get down to business. "Listen, I know you said you couldn't do a locating spell, but I'm desperate. Nothing else is working. The police don't have any leads. Jake slithered his way right out of everything. There's got to be something else. Please. I just want to find my sister."

Della meets my gaze, and I can see her thinking, weighing. She's about to speak when someone else steps into the kitchen and Della's eyes go wide.

"Miles," she says. I spin around, expecting her dad. But it's a younger man, only a few years older than Della. He has messy brown hair, thick dark eyebrows, and a goatee. He's tall and

thin, and his cheekbones look just like Della's—sharp. His eyes
are dark brown and gloomy. He's handsome, in a strung-out,
grungy sort of way.

"I can find your sister," he says. "If she's in the nature park,
I can."

"What are you doing here, Miles?" Della asks, moving
around me. I can't tell whether she's happy to see him or not.
She pauses in front of him, searching his face. "Why are you
back? I told you I didn't need you."

"I didn't like how we left things," Miles says to her. "I
wanted to talk. But . . ." His gaze drifts back over to me.

"But what?" Della asks.

Miles ignores her and addresses me. "If she's there, I'll find
her. I can do it right now if you want."

"Who is he?" I ask Della.

"My cousin," she says. "The prodigal witch making his
return." She's trying to act normal, but I can see he's thrown
her off balance. She almost looks afraid.

Miles gives her a grim smile. "You know it's time, Dee."

Della grabs his arm, pulling him from the room. They go
to the living room and begin to argue in low, insistent voices.
I follow them, hovering in the dim hallway. I can't make out
what they're saying until Della hisses, "How could you do this
to me? To all of us?"

"It's not about you," Miles says, breaking away from her.
"It's about what's right."

"Are you coming?" he says to me just as I start to edge
nearer.

I look to Della. I would never have thought of her as a safe person, but compared to this tall, strange boy with ghostly eyes, at least she's familiar. "Will you come too?"

All the fight goes out of her. "Yeah, let's go." She grits her teeth and heads for the door like she's walking to her own execution. Why does she care if he helps me? What's it to her?

Something complicated is happening between Della and Miles, something that might not have anything to do with me or Rochelle. But I can feel the charge between them, the unspoken words. This boy just walked in to give me exactly what I want, but the look on Della's face makes me wonder if I still want it.

TEN

DELLA

Natasha and I follow Miles onto the Bend in silence. My brain is screaming at me to stop this at any cost, but my body keeps moving forward. I knew I couldn't convince Miles not to do the spell, so all I could do was come along. Come along and watch Miles rip what's left of our family apart. Because if Jake Carr's been cleared, if he's not to blame, that means Momma most likely is.

Miles nearly always finds what he's looking for. So if Rochelle Greymont's body is out here, he's probably going to find it. And then police will come and questions will be asked, and before long Momma will be found and the world will know what she is. Miles's tracking spell can only end in blood and death and misery.

We walk through the woods for nearly an hour before the steep slopes give way to gentler terrain, and then we break into open fields, the part of the Bend I feel least at home in. "This way," Miles says, motioning toward an animal track through the shoulder-high brush. He and I push our way in and start toward the river, but Natasha doesn't follow. She stands there staring at me with startled doe eyes, looking for all the world like Bambi.

"Do we have to go this way?" she asks. "Aren't there, like, mown trails nearby?"

I don't love this route either, but I'm not letting Natasha see that. "It's a shortcut. You want to be out here all night? The coyotes will start hunting soon. You look just like their favorite meal too," I add. "Like a tender baby deer."

"Coyotes don't eat people," she says bitingly, but she follows me more closely, so she must not be too sure.

Miles walks a little ahead of us, his shoulders tense. I thought a year away would dispel some of his anger, but it's wound up tight inside him, ready to burst out at any moment. Is that why he's doing this? He said finding Rochelle was the right thing to do, and maybe that's all the reason he needs. But I think this is really about revenge. He's wanted it all along, and now he thinks he has the moral high ground to take it.

Natasha flinches every time a bird rustles the brush, every time a grasshopper jumps out of our path. But she stays behind me and never complains. Until she starts screaming.

"Snake! Oh my God, a snake!" she bellows, leaping backward, grabbing my arm so that I stumble back with her. I glance down to see a timber rattler slithering down the path. It's not even a very big one.

"You trying to save my life? I'm touched," I say with a laugh. Natasha's still got my arm in a vise grip. Her forearm brushes mine when she lets go, and a little shiver runs through me.

"You're welcome," she responds, her voice acid.

I chuckle and squat down to admire the snake. I'd love to get hold of its venom for our store of ingredients, but Natasha is panicking behind me, backing farther and farther away. I hold up a hand to shush her. "Be still, will you."

I lean down and deftly pick up the snake, gripping its head firmly with my right hand, its tail with my left. Natasha moans with fear. I study the snake, taking in its distinctive brown-and-gray pattern. It's pretty and it's poisonous, and I can't think of any creature in this world that's better than that. I sigh as I toss it out over the brush.

The moment the snake disappears, Natasha bolts, pushing me out of the way and pounding down the path ahead of me to walk with Miles.

I trudge behind them, my mind returning to the problem of finding a way out of this. A way to keep Miles from leading this girl straight to our family's demise. Because after the way I found Momma in the woods with bloody hands, I can't fool myself anymore. I can't pretend the monster's been kept at bay.

When I took her back to the jail after her nap, I walked her to her cell and locked her up. When she realized what I was doing, she fought me hard, but I managed to push her inside, earning only a scratch across my face. The original lock doesn't work anymore, but I wrapped a heavy chain and padlock around the bars to hold the door closed. The window's bars are still solid, so I know she won't get out again. Not tonight. But I can't do anything about the nights she'd already been free.

Locking her up like that—it hurt worse than any injury

she's ever given me. The look of betrayal and panic on her face. Having the run of a big prison is one thing; being slammed into a cramped cell is another. But I guess that's going to be her life now, unless Natasha is right and her sister's somehow managed to stay alive in the wild for a week. Or unless we find Rochelle's body and it leads the police straight to Momma. Because that could only end in carnage.

Finally, we emerge from the brush and into the open, grassy meadow, where we can see the river, shimmering gold in the last rays of sun. It looks pretty in this light, safe, like a river from a picture book. But I've lived here too long not to know the river for what it is: hungry. I've watched it swallow earth and trees, birds and rats. It lies quiet for months and then roars up, raging, ready to destroy.

"I saw on TV that they found her purse by the river, so that will be the best starting point," Miles says to Natasha. "Do you know exactly where it was?"

Natasha hesitates, studying the ridges in the distance, trying to get her bearings.

"Downriver," she says, and starts walking. After a few minutes she stops in front of a red flag stuck into the earth. "This was it," Natasha says, motioning to a pile of driftwood and debris at the edge of the water.

I expected to see yellow police tape, but except for the flag, the bank looks untouched. I climb down it carefully and peer into the water, which rushes past, brown and oily.

Natasha stays above and watches me. "The police said that the big storm last week washed away any evidence that might've been here. They didn't see any sign of struggle, and there wasn't any DNA or anything."

"Do they think she went into the water?" Miles asks, gazing down into the depths. This is the river where his mother died, where her body disappeared. I think it was even near this spot, maybe a little farther down. Miles wasn't here. He didn't see it. He didn't see his mother's torn-up body, didn't see the way Momma's claws dripped blood. But all the same, I know that's what he's seeing now, behind his eyes.

"The police don't know anything," Natasha says angrily. "I'm sure they'd like to call Rochelle a runaway and move on. They've cleared Jake with barely a conversation. They'll find a way to spin it so it's Ro's fault. Unless we find her."

I turn away from Miles, the grief etched into his features too much for me. But Natasha's not much better, with the desperate hope in her eyes. All I can see when I look at them is what the Bend has taken. What my mother—I shake my head, refusing to think about it. I harden myself against their pain.

"A pretty rich girl? Not likely," I say. "The media will be clamoring for some big baddie to blame."

"Hmm," Natasha says. I think she's not going to say anything else, but then she bursts out, "There was more to Rochelle than being a pretty rich girl. She was really funny and super smart. She was a sophomore at Highland Rim. She wanted to be a pediatrician."

"Sure," I say, still studying the water.

"And you know what, we haven't always been—" Natasha stops, and I finally look at her.

"Haven't always been what?"

Her eyes flash. "Never mind. Let's just do this spell so I don't ever have to see you again."

I sigh. I've already tried my best to talk Miles out of this. Back at the house I told him that it would end badly for all of us if he finds Rochelle. I told him we should let the Bend keep her since it's hidden her this long.

But I have to try one more time. "Are you sure you want to do this? It's not too late to back out," I whisper to him.

Miles meets my gaze. "It's time to face things, Della. Time to make them right if we can." His eyes are sad and gentle, and I realize I was wrong about his reasons. This isn't about vengeance. He's just a better person than I am. He might not be a healer like Aunt Sage was, but he's got her spirit. And this is probably exactly what Aunt Sage would want him to do.

That means I can't change what's about to happen. If I try to stop him with force, I'll just look guilty to Natasha. "Fine," I spit, and turn back to her.

She's standing over us on the bank with her arms crossed, a look of fear on her face. But when she sees me looking, irritation slides over the expression. "Well?" she demands.

"Are you and Rochelle blood sisters?" Miles asks.

"Yes."

"Then I'll need your blood," Miles says simply.

ELEVEN
NATASHA

All the feeling drains from my face. "How much?" I ask, trying to keep my voice even.

Della zeroes in on my discomfort like the bitch she is. A slow smile spreads across her creepy face. "Oh, I think about a gallon will do."

I know she's messing with me, but the thought of a gallon of blood makes my head swim. It takes all my self-command not to sink to the filthy ground. I square my shoulders. "What do I need to do?"

"Dee, do you have your knife handy?" Miles asks absently. He seems distant, as if he's listening for something, tuned in to another frequency. It's strange to hear someone use a nickname for Della—it's so human, so ordinary. Like she's just a person to him, not a scary and mysterious witch.

For some bizarre reason, Miles scoops a monarch butterfly off some yellow flowers, cupping it gently.

Della climbs up the bank and pulls a pocketknife from the outside pouch of her bag. She opens it and fingers the tip as if she'd like to stab one of us with it. I will myself not to flinch, not to move away. After an eternity, she passes it to Miles with an angry look he doesn't notice.

Miles hands the knife to me. "Make a small cut on your left thumb, or I can do it if you want." His voice is surprisingly gentle. "We only need a drop or two."

I definitely don't want to stick Della's dirty knife that's been cutting God knows what into my skin, but she's eyeing me, waiting for me to give up and go home. I wipe the blade on the hem of my shirt and press the sharp tip against my skin. A wave of nausea runs through me.

"Need some help?" she asks.

"Fuck you," I say, and jam the tip in. Blood wells up immediately, a deep red. My vision goes spotty and I feel like I'm going to pass out. Thankfully, I don't think Della notices, or if she does, she keeps her mouth shut.

Miles grabs my hand before the blood can fall. "Be still now," he says. He holds his cupped palm near his mouth and blows gently. The butterfly alights, fluttering its delicate wings. I flinch when the insect lands on my thumb.

"Salt and water, blood to blood," Miles murmurs. The butterfly dips its proboscis into my blood as if it's drinking. I have to steel myself not to shake it off. I hate the feel of its tiny feet, the brush of its powdery wings. After a few moments, Miles blows on the butterfly again and it takes off, winging away in the erratic way butterflies always do.

I watch until its orange wings disappear into the dimming sky, and then I narrow my eyes. "Is he messing with me? Because I swear to God, Della—"

I don't get a chance to finish my threat because a strange feeling overtakes me, something stronger than my nausea and dizziness, more potent than my anger. Suddenly, my legs feel restless. This spot of earth seems too small. I need to move. It's like there's a rubber band stretched between me and some distant object, stretched so tight it's about to break.

I take a few hesitant steps in the direction the butterfly went and then I sprint along the river, certainty propelling me forward.

As I run, memories of my life with Rochelle beat inside me like waves. The two of us playing in our old backyard, taking turns pushing each other on a rusty swing set. Cowering together in the bathtub while our mother's friend ripped apart the house, looking for the meth he said she stole. The long nights in our first foster home, our arms wrapped around each other, our eyes squeezed closed at the unfamiliar sounds, the other's smell and touch our only comfort. And then the Rochelle my sister grew into: brazen, with that wicked sense of humor, rolling on the floor laughing at some private joke while Mom and Dad looked on, happy but bemused. My sister, the other part of my heart. The only thing that's kept it beating all these years.

Rochelle feels so close to me, so real and present I can't believe she's not running beside me now.

I race along the river, seeing nothing but a blur of earth

and sky. It's my blood and my bones that see for me, that hear. They propel me forward, my feet crashing against the ground. I'm only vaguely aware of Della and Miles on my heels, making almost no sound.

I veer off from the river and launch myself into the trees, a young, bramble-filled wood. The trees are merely obstacles in my path because I'm after something else, something more important.

The feeling of Rochelle's closeness intensifies until I can almost smell her lavender hand lotion. Until I can almost hear her voice in my ears, screaming my name. Wings beat the air above my head, their wind fanning my face. I look up and catch a glimpse of Rochelle's blue eyes just before I crash into a tree and tumble to the ground. I lie stunned, panting and dizzy. The world spins around me. Finally, I open my eyes again and light floods in, dazzling. The smell of the forest surrounds me, a dank, earthy smell. It's silent now, no wings beating near my face. The treetops are still. But I saw her—didn't I? And it wasn't the first time. That night in the woods when I met Della . . . the same thing had happened—a beat of wings, my sister's voice.

My head swims when I sit up and gaze into the huge, reaching limbs of a strangely twisted tree, its deep brown bark covered in wicked spikes. Long leaves droop down, with clusters of some sort of hanging flowers mixed in. A sweet, honeyed smell floats by whenever the wind blows. The tree looks out of place here, among all these skinny saplings. Like a gnarled old woman among children.

Della launches into the clearing, with Miles on her heels. "Is she here?" she pants, looking around frantically.

"No," I say, finally getting to my feet. "But she was." I'm certain of it.

My legs are shaky and I have to grab on to the tree to keep my balance. I wander around the tree and the clearing, searching for my sister. But there's no sign of her, no indication she was ever here except the feeling in my chest.

"It didn't work," Della says, her voice surprised and almost relieved.

The three of us circle the tree and the surrounding area, not speaking. The sun has sunk behind the hills, and the woods are already dim. Della kneels and runs her fingers over the bark.

"What is it?" I ask, wandering back over.

"Probably nothing," she says, but there are huge scratches in the wood, like four long claws sharpened themselves there. That doesn't look like nothing to me.

"What could make those marks?" I ask. The sight of them sends a shiver down my spine.

"A lynx? Could have even been a mowing machine." Della shrugs, but her nonchalance seems studied.

"Over here," Miles calls. He shines his flashlight on a patch of ground. "The leaves were disturbed. Looks like something was dragged through here."

Something like a body? My sister's body? Cold blooms in my stomach and spreads through me.

"Miles, don't," Della says, but he turns his back and follows the trail.

"You should probably stay here," Della says, trying to block me. "Let us check it out. It might be . . . you might not want to see what we find."

"No," I say, pushing her out of the way. "I'm coming." I follow Miles through the twilight-dark woods, my heart beating a staccato rhythm in my ears. Della plods after us.

After what feels like an eternity, Miles's flashlight stops, its beam steady on the forest floor. Bloody leaves. The monarch butterfly flits up from them, fluttering away into the night. Miles turns and looks at me, his eyes hardly more than glints of light in the dark woods. "Are you sure you want to see this?"

"Yes," I whisper. *It's always better to know.*

He moves the light forward a few inches and the world crashes in on me.

Rochelle lies on her side, naked, her hair spread over her face. Her arms seem to reach toward me, the fingers extended. Her nails are still painted pale purple. The twining morning glories tattooed on the inside of her forearm are still impossibly blue. My eyes catch on those flowers and stay there because I can't bear to look at the rest of her. At what's left of her. Because below her shoulders—

Della comes up behind me and stops, and I can feel her eyes on the back of my head. "You don't have to look anymore, Natasha," she says, her voice the kindest I've ever heard it. "You did what she asked. You found her."

But I will never be able to do enough for Rochelle, the sister who made sure I ate and slept and did my homework. The sister who guarded me with her body and her smile. The sister who was home to me, no matter where we lived.

I drop to the ground and grasp Ro's fingers in mine. They are cold and stiff and lifeless. But I rub them with both of my hands as if I can chafe the warmth back in.

The feel of her hands brings a memory back to me. Rochelle, at her birthday dinner with Mom and Dad, sitting at our dining room table. Our parents had gone off to the kitchen, and Ro turned to me. "Look what lover gave me," she'd crooned, holding up her hand to show me a white gold ring with a big sapphire and tiny diamonds. The ring had glimmered in the light from the chandelier, leaving sparkles in her eyes.

But Rochelle didn't tell me what Jake said when he gave it to her. I had to read that in her journal: *Jake made me promise never to take it off, and then he said something weird: "Unless I take it off you." He laughed when he said it, but it made me uneasy. He has such a strange sense of humor sometimes.*

The sapphire ring is gone now, along with the sparkles in Ro's eyes. Jake made good on his threat.

A scream is building in my chest. It's filling me up, claiming every inch of my lungs, my diaphragm, every hollow space inside me. I need to let it out. I need to let it go.

But it lodges inside me, growing so big I think I'll choke.

"Come on," Della says, grasping my elbow. My brain says to fight her off, but the scream inside me is using up all my strength. I let go of Ro's hand and stumble away, back toward the clearing and the tree. It's dark now, only glints of stars through the treetops.

I can't breathe. Can't breathe. Can't breathe.

Rochelle is dead.

I drop to the ground at the base of the tree, dig my fingers into the grass and leaves, and let out a roar so loud and raw and full of rage a flock of birds erupts from the branches overhead, flapping ghostly pale into the night.

As I watch them disappear into the dark, I realize that Rochelle is one of them. That owl I thought she sent to speak with her voice was never a message from my living sister. It was her ghost. She never meant me to find her alive. She only wanted me to find her body and claim justice on her behalf.

And I swear to the broken body that lies in these woods, to the ghost winging its way among the stars, I will get justice for my sister if I have to rip it from Jake Carr's chest with my own two bloody hands.

TWELVE
DELLA

When Natasha stands up from the ground, I know she's not the same girl she was an hour ago. Her scream of rage and pain still seems to echo among the treetops, like the wind caught it and is carrying it as far as it will reach.

But now her tearstained face has gone hard, her still-wet eyes turned flinty. Every breath she takes, every movement of her body—they feel precise, intentional. It's the way an animal moves just before it strikes.

Without meaning to, I take a step back.

Natasha pulls her cell phone out of her back pocket. She clears her throat. I expect her hands to shake as she dials, but they don't. Her voice, too, is steady when she speaks.

"My name is Natasha Greymont, and I just found my sister's dead body," she says, the words lined up like soldiers in a row. "Rochelle Greymont, the one who went missing in Wood Thrush Nature Park. I found her body in the woods." She pauses, listening. "Yes, I'm sure she's dead." She pauses again and then her eyes flick to me and Miles. "No, I'm not alone. Yes, I'm safe."

My stomach drops. We shouldn't be here when the police come. We shouldn't be involved at all, shouldn't draw attention to ourselves. But what choice do we have? We can't leave Natasha alone in the woods with her sister's eviscerated corpse. Besides, our footprints are here, all over the crime scene. It would be much more suspicious to leave now than to stay. But what possible explanation can there be for our presence here?

I turn to Miles, angling my flashlight so I can see his face without blinding either of us. I'm surprised to see there are tears in his eyes. When he looks at me, there's a flash of revulsion.

"What?" I say.

"You're looking more like Aunt Ruby every day," he says.

It's like he punched me. Suddenly, I don't care about whether we look suspicious—I just don't want to be standing feet away from my mother's victim with Miles looking at me like that. "Why don't you go ahead and leave?" I say, my voice hard. "I can tell the police you had to get to work or something."

"Don't be stupid, Dee. I'm not leaving," he says. "How would that look?"

"Then why don't you go meet the police at the park entrance and help them find us? We don't both need to stand out here with her."

I expect Miles to argue, but he only nods. He slips away into the trees without a sound. I turn my attention back to Natasha, who's still on the phone with the 911 dispatcher.

"We're, um—" For the first time, Natasha's voice falters. "I'm not sure where we are. In the woods. I can't hear any traffic from the highway, so we must be pretty far in." She looks at me for help.

Wordlessly, I take the phone, and then tell the dispatcher how to find us. I explain where Miles will be waiting to guide the authorities into the park. She asks if Natasha is okay, if she's in shock. I tell her the truth: I don't know. She promises that help is on the way, that they will be here in fifteen minutes, twenty at most. Right now, fifteen minutes sounds like an eternity.

I hand the phone to Natasha, turn my back to her, and gaze at the honey locust tree in the clearing. This is where I found Momma, naked in the fog, dried blood on her hands, singing to the birds. Those were her claw marks on the tree trunk.

This is where she killed Rochelle Greymont.

That's her work lying bloody and battered in the leaves back there.

The truth hits me so hard it makes me dizzy. The ground turns to ocean beneath my feet. I knew what we were going to find here; all along I knew. But seeing it—seeing Rochelle's body with her sister standing next to me . . .

Nausea washes over me, and I drop into a crouch to keep from puking or passing out. I let my ragged breaths go in and out of my body. I count to ten and then to twenty and then to fifty, my eyes squeezed tight. I let myself feel the hideous, awful truth of it all.

But then I pull myself together. Because I have to. Because I have no choice. I exhale all the air in my lungs like I'm breathing out my fear and misery too. When I inhale again, I'm steady. I open my eyes and rise to my feet. I look away from the tree and into the sky.

There's a crescent moon hanging between two gray-white clouds. Large birds, probably owls, move among the treetops. Otherwise, the forest is still. Several minutes go by, only occasional murmurs from Natasha, answering questions from the 911 operator. I keep thinking about the look of revulsion on Miles's face. After what we've seen tonight, will he think locking Momma in a cell is enough? I'm not sure even I think so. If she could do that to Rochelle . . . I'm not sure a cell is going to hold her. But what else is there?

A twig snaps behind us, back where we left Rochelle's body. I turn sharply toward the sound, listening. Miles went in the opposite direction a while ago, so it's not him. On the phone, Natasha stops speaking. "What is it?" she whispers, the first sign of emotion I've heard in her voice since she screamed. She sounds afraid.

I shake my head and put a finger to my lips. The two of us wait in the darkness, completely still. A long moment passes, and then comes the rustle of leaves. A heavy animal is moving somewhere nearby.

Panic races through my veins. What if it's Momma? What if she broke out of the cell I locked her in earlier today? What if she came to visit her kill?

I signal to Natasha to stay where she is and begin to creep slowly toward the sound. I'd rather face the river siren head-on than be taken unawares. But when I get closer to Rochelle's body, I make out a shaggy, doglike shape circling the area, its nose to the ground. Relief floods me.

"It's just a coyote," I say. Hearing my voice, the coyote looks up at me, its yellow eyes glinting. It watches me, waiting for me to make a move. Goose bumps erupt on my forearms, and the hair at the nape of my neck stands on end.

"A big coyote," I whisper. The thing is the size of a greyhound, or at least that's how it looks in the darkness. And it really should have run away by now. Coyotes are skittish creatures. Something's wrong here.

"What is it?" Natasha hisses from a few yards behind me.

"Just a coyote," I say again, louder. "It was drawn by the smell of blood."

To my surprise, Natasha comes running, crashing through the leaves. She runs right past me and straight for the coyote, already yelling. "Get out of here, get away from her. Get out!" Her voice breaks on the last word.

But the coyote doesn't run. It doesn't even flinch. This isn't normal behavior. It must be sick or rabid. Natasha and the animal stand facing each other, Rochelle's body lying in the leaves between them. The creature hunkers down and lets out a deep, snarling growl.

Every instinct in my body is screaming at me—this thing wants our blood, our meat, our bones. "Natasha, get away from there," I say, forcing my voice to stay even. "I don't think that's a coyote after all. It must be some sort of dog, and I think it's feral, maybe rabid."

But Natasha is undeterred. "No," she says. "I won't let it touch her."

A breeze rustles through the trees, carrying the smell of rot and death. It's more than the smell of a decomposing human body—it's metallic and musky and foul.

The creature begins to edge from side to side, looking for an angle of attack. I shoot forward and grab Natasha, pulling her away. She fights me, trying to stay near her sister. But I wrap my arms around her and hold her back.

Just then, several flashlights light up the woods around us, and voices carry through the trees. "Hello? Natasha Greymont? This is the Fawney Police Department."

"In here," I yell. For the first time in my life, I'm grateful to see the police. "We're over here."

As the footsteps of the police come closer, the coyote or dog or whatever the hell it is backs away. A stray beam of a flashlight catches its eyes again, and they don't look like the eyes of any canine I've ever seen. They are cruel and cold and calculating.

When the cops break into the clearing, the creature finally lopes away into the night. As though adrenaline was all that kept her upright, Natasha's knees give out and she crumples like a marionette whose strings have been cut. I catch her before she hits the ground and ease her down gently. I hate that this is my family's fault, *my* fault. I hate that I'm to blame. I hate myself.

I look for Miles among the uniformed bodies, but he's not there.

The next half hour is a blur of flashlights and voices. First, they tend to Natasha, draping a blanket over her shoulders, putting a bottle of water into her hands. Treating her as if she's the victim. I'm surprised they can't see what I do: that she's more likely to stab somebody than she is to weep.

I try to stay near her, waiting to hear what excuse she'll make for my presence. Finally, she tells them: "I came out here by myself looking for Rochelle. I just had this feeling that I would find her. But I got lost, and these two hikers found me." She nods at me. "Della there and her cousin Miles. They were worried about me being all alone since it was getting dark, and so they offered to stay with me. I think Miles went to try to get help."

I feel a moment of relief, tinged with admiration. Natasha is a good liar. And for whatever reason, she's making us look as innocent as possible. I don't know if it's for our sake or her own, but either way I'm grateful.

"My cousin was supposed to help you find us," I add. "I don't know where he's gotten off to."

As if in answer, Miles comes crashing into the circle of light, a park ranger gripping his elbow. Miles wrenches his arm out of the man's grasp.

"Miles," I say. "What happened?"

"See? I told you. I'm not a poacher," Miles practically yells at the man.

The ranger holds up his gloved hands and laughs. "All right, son. I hear you. I apologize. But you have to admit, it was suspicious." I recognize the ranger—he's new, but he's been around long enough for me to spot him now and again. I don't know his name.

"I didn't even have a gun on me," Miles says through gritted teeth. But then he turns toward me. "Sorry, they went to a different entrance. I waited around for a long time and when I started back, I got held up." He eyes the ranger meaningfully.

The ranger reaches out to shake the closest detective's hand. "Robert Grange. I understand you've found a body. Can I do anything to help?" The detective sends Grange over to another team of people, and he nods at us before he goes.

"Asshole," Miles grumbles under his breath.

Natasha has been watching all of this with empty, unseeing eyes. Whenever no one is speaking to her, when she's not being asked to perform the part of the traumatized little sister, it's like she disappears inside herself. I think the rage that was fueling her up until now has faded into shock and horror and grief. At least for now. At least for tonight.

I close my eyes and wish for all of this to be over. All I want to do is go home and sleep and try to forget the sight of Rochelle Greymont's slashed and bitten and mutilated body. All I want is to forget what my mother has done.

But I stay where I am; I play my part. I guard my family's secrets, and those of the Bend, like the Lloyds have always done, no matter the cost.

It's after midnight when I finally step into the house. It's completely dark. I collapse into a chair and lay my cheek against the cool, smooth wood of the kitchen table. I'm so tired and hollowed out, I don't even have the strength to carry myself to bed.

I close my eyes and breathe in the familiar smells of our kitchen—the earthy herbs and the cloying flowers, the burned smell of bacon grease and the lingering stale coffee. Whatever else this house is, at least it's still home.

I expect my thoughts to turn to Momma, raging in her tiny cell, but it's Natasha whose face flashes across my closed eyes. She's going to find out soon enough that her sister's boyfriend didn't kill her. Then she's going to come looking for more answers. And I'm going to have to find a way to make the magic lie, to keep her from finding out what I've got locked up in a crumbling old prison off the highway. I don't know Natasha well, but I already know she's no fool. Besides, after tonight, I don't think Miles will be on my side. The second the police told us we were free to go, he set off into the trees. He didn't look at me or say goodbye. He just left. His car was gone by the time I got home.

I fall asleep thinking of Natasha's burning, watchful eyes, her fingers clenched into fists. Sometime later, whether minutes or hours I don't know, I wake up to the sound of Da stumbling through the front door. He trips over a pair of his own boots by the doorway and swears. I stay where I am and hope he'll go straight to bed. I hate dealing with Da when he's drunk. He doesn't get mean like some men; he gets weepy. I think I'd prefer the mean.

I curse under my breath when Da flips on the kitchen lights and catches sight of me at the table. I sit up and rub my neck, which is stiff from sleeping in a chair. I push a handful of hair out of my eyes.

Da stands in the doorway blinking at me. "Della," he says with a smile—a real one, not that shifty one he uses on the customers. He's still in happy drunk mode, but weepy probably won't be far behind. Especially once I tell him what we found in the woods tonight.

"Della, Della, kissed a fella, turned him to an armadilla," he says, singsong. He used to make up rhymes like that when I was little, to make me laugh. Now he's the one who giggles.

I smile despite myself, despite everything.

"There's my girl," he says. "Used to be you and me, Della, you know, used to be you and me."

"I don't see anybody else here," I say, rubbing the sleep from my eyes.

Da doesn't hear me and goes on, waxing nostalgic. "No, your momma put an end to that. Never liked to see us get too close. Wanted to turn you into a little Ruby. But remember how we used to play, Della? Remember how we made up funny brews and laughed?"

It's true Da taught me almost all my spell work. How to identify plants. How to combine them. How to speak just the right words at the right time. He made it fun. Momma treated magic differently, like something sacred. That's why it's strange she's the one whose spell went so terribly wrong, why she's the one—

"Della, maybe we ought to leave here," Da says suddenly.

"What? What do you mean?" Did he hear about Rochelle Greymont?

"Leave the Bend. Leave all this." He motions around the kitchen. "We'll take your momma far away, someplace the magic can't touch her. Maybe then she won't change, she'll go back to normal. We could have a different life."

It's like he's speaking pig Latin. "Leave the Bend?"

"Why not? Why the hell not? What have we got to lose?"

"Everything," I say. "Absolutely everything." A Lloyd without the Bend isn't a Lloyd. Isn't a witch. Isn't anything.

"Da, what's going on? Why'd you go get drunk?" I'm suspicious now. Da never drinks unless Ireland wins at rugby or soccer or if something really bad has happened. He can't have heard about Rochelle yet. Maybe Momma attacking him yesterday was bad enough for him to seek out a bar, but I don't think so.

Da lets out a sob. "It's happened again, baby. Another one."

"Another what?" A weight sinks into my stomach.

"Another girl. She went missing two nights ago."

A black hole opens up inside me. Two nights ago, when Momma was running free, right before I found her with blood on her hands. I take a deep breath. Are the police going to find another body in the woods—another beautiful young woman with her insides ripped out?

"How do you know?" I ask. "Was it on the news?"

"No, I heard it at the plant. From the girl's uncle."

"Who is she?"

Da sighs. "Local girl. Went out with a few of her friends to get high in the woods. They got separated and couldn't find her. Her friends waited to tell the girl's parents what happened— they were afraid of getting in trouble. So the search was delayed,

and then the police found her jacket with, uh, claw marks in it."
Another sob escapes him and he stops talking, slumping down
into a chair. I guess even Da can't deny it anymore—there's
more than a little chance that his wife is the monster behind all
these missing girls. And he doesn't even know what I've seen.

How long before the police find her trail? And what will
they do when they find her?

I consider telling him about Rochelle, but he already looks
so miserable. It will only hurt us both. "I'm going to bed," I say,
standing up abruptly from the table. "For God's sake, drink a
glass of water before you go to bed. I've got enough to deal with
without adding a drunk into the bargain."

Da's got his head on the table and he's weeping loudly when
I leave the kitchen. I'd like to sit beside him and weep too, but
that's a luxury this family can't afford. Instead, I harden every
soft place inside my heart and slam the door to my room.

All my doubts, all my hopes are gone now. There's only
cold reality before me. My mother is not only a witch, a river
siren, a monster. She's also a killer.

Now I have to decide what to do about it.

THIRTEEN
DELLA

I climb out of bed, groggy and sleepless, when it's still dark. I go out to the front porch and slump onto the steps. Hopelessness is spreading through me like seeping water. Absolutely everything is shit. And I'm shit too. I press my forehead to my knees and wish I could cry. But there aren't any tears in me. Only an echoing, empty feeling.

I wonder if this is how Natasha feels too. Does she feel like she failed? Can she feel anything at all? Or is she lying awake in bed now, staring at the ceiling, while a lonely wind howls through her?

"Hey," someone says from behind me, and it's a testament to my exhaustion that I don't jump out of my skin.

Miles is sitting in a cobweb-covered rocking chair at the corner of the porch. I can barely make out his disheveled hair, his long, lanky build.

"What are you doing here?" I ask.

"Wanted to catch you before you left. I know you go out to the prison early."

"So?"

"So we need to talk."

A broken laugh leaves my mouth. "What's there to talk about, Miles? Haven't you done enough?"

"She's killed at least two people, Dee. Probably more." His voice would sound calm to anyone else, but I hear the slight tremble in it. "And I think I know why."

I look up quickly, trying to make out his eyes in the darkness.

Miles stops rocking and crosses his arms over his chest. "She's reenacting my mother's murder. She's acting out what she did to her, over and over again. All the people who have gone missing on the Bend are white women, all of them are blondes. Like Mom was."

"Why would she do that? What kind of sense does that make?"

Miles shakes his head. "Maybe that's part of the spell that turned her. Maybe she can't help herself."

I pause, considering. "I locked her up. She's in a cell now," I say. "She can't do it anymore."

"And you really think that's good enough? You think that's a permanent solution?" Miles's voice sounds strained now.

"What else can I do?" I'm not making excuses. I genuinely want to know what he thinks I should do. Because there are no options, not really.

"You know what you need to do," Miles says. "And if you

won't do it, then—then I will." He stands up from the chair and walks past me down the steps.

"I don't know what you mean," I say, even though I do. But it's unthinkable.

Miles sighs. "Do you remember when Foxy got bitten by that rabid raccoon? What did Aunt Ruby tell me?"

My blood runs cold. Foxy was Miles's rat terrier, a sweet little wiry-haired dog. She's been buried in our backyard for a decade. Momma shot the raccoon that bit Foxy, and then she turned the gun on the dog. Miles dove in front of his pet, begged and pleaded, but Momma shook her head. "Foxy's already dead, you just don't know it yet," she said. And then she pulled Foxy from Miles's arms, carried her behind the house, and put a bullet in her brain.

"You're asking me to kill my own mother," I say, disbelieving. "If Da heard you . . . if he knew you were even thinking about it . . ."

Miles turns and I can just make out the sadness in his eyes. "He'll be devastated at first, Dee. But later, later I think he'll be relieved. Later, I think he'll thank you."

Before I can respond, Miles walks to his car, cranks the engine, and drives away.

I slump back down onto the steps, suddenly dizzy. I tuck my head between my knees and take a long, deep breath. Miles wants me to kill her. He wants me to put a bullet in her brain and an end to all this.

But he's only thinking of the monster, not the woman. The river siren, not Momma. They aren't the same . . . are they? The carnage of Rochelle Greymont's ruined body flashes across my mind, the long-dried blood, the glistening entrails, the—

I bolt to my feet. Miles said if I won't do it, he will.

I can't sit here all day, giving in to despair. I have to come up with a plan. I have to find a way to fix this. Most of all, I need to see her. I need to look her in the eyes and see how much of Ruby Lloyd looks back at me.

I'm on the road just as the sun begins to rise, nerves making my guts churn. Momma's breakfast sits beside me on the seat. I'm not sure why, but I cooked all her favorite foods: fried sausage and mushrooms, with cheese grits and scrambled eggs. I poured her black coffee—no spells this time—into the thermos. It felt like I was preparing her last meal. On a whim, I grabbed her old harmonica and slid it into my pocket on my way out the door.

My hands shake as I near the prison. I can't quite dispel the feeling that I'm driving here for the last time. That an end is coming, one that's out of my control.

I'm about to pull into my usual place when I spot a police cruiser in the prison's old visitor parking lot. The car isn't the sheriff's, which is about all we see out here. It's the police who come from the city. I stay straight and keep driving, but my pulse has exploded in my head. Goddamnit. God. This is it—the end to all my efforts to keep Momma safe.

I was right not to want to help Natasha find her sister's body. Because it's led the police to Momma, just like I knew it would. And now what can I possibly do to stop what comes next?

I turn into a lot that belongs to a defunct glass factory. I park behind a forgotten dumpster and wait, though I don't know what I'm waiting for. My breath is coming so fast I can hardly think. It's not the first time I've seen police at the prison. The sheriff does drive-bys most days to make sure kids haven't broken in or destroyed anything, to make sure homeless people haven't pitched their tents. But those cars come later in the day and the officers never park or go inside. They simply drive by, giving the barest nod to security.

Now they're going to find her. They're going to go into that decaying old prison, maybe with dogs, and find my momma locked up inside. And then what? They'll probably think Da has done it—a madman locking up his poor wife. They'll let her out of the cell and then, and then—

I throw open my door and retch onto the gravel. Every bite of my breakfast comes up, burning my throat and nose.

Vomiting seems to clear my head. I swig a bottle of water I had brought for Momma. Then I get out and skirt through an empty, overgrown lot, heading for the prison. I have to see what's happening. I have to help Momma if I can. I have to help us all. I go around the back, where the police won't see me, and slip through my usual entrance. It doesn't look like they've made it this far inside.

I creep through the dark prison by memory, making my way toward her cell. There are men's voices far across the prison, toward the front entrance. I move faster, willing my feet to be as silent as Momma taught me. The voices come closer, grow louder. I still can't make out their words. Luckily, I don't hear the soft gait or panting breath of police dogs. There are only the heavy footsteps of men, the occasional glint of a flashlight.

I don't understand how they tracked her footsteps in the dark. But maybe they found the trail yesterday and waited until today to investigate? I don't know. Surely Miles didn't send them here.

I finally find her cell without tripping over anything in the dark. I can hear the steady rise and fall of her breath. "Momma," I whisper, trying to keep my voice calm. It won't do to let her know how rattled I am. "Momma, are you awake?" I grip the bars of her cell.

Soft, nearly silent footsteps, and then a face looms up before mine, shadowy and indistinct. "Shhhh, shhhhh," she says. "Shhhh," her voice a croon.

A shiver runs down my spine. She hasn't turned back yet. It's not my mother here; it's the river siren.

"Momma, I need you to come back," I say desperately. "I need you to change." The police are at the far end of the cell-block, only thirty yards or so away.

She sings wordlessly, her voice a low, seductive pull like the current of a river that wants to drown you. Is that how she lured Rochelle and the others? Did she draw them in with her voice and then rip them open with her claws?

The footsteps are so loud now, so close. They're going to find her.

An idea comes to me. It's mad and foolish, but it's all I have.

I pull my hair out of its bun, tear a hole in my shirt, and wipe dirt from the floor onto my face and clothes. I rip off my boots and toss them behind me, along with my socks. Then I run toward the men, loudly, like any other person would, letting the rubbish of the prison cut and scrape my feet.

"Hello?" I yell, making my voice as helpless-sounding as I can. "Is someone here?"

"Who's in there?" a deep voice yells, pointing a flashlight at me.

"Help," I say, practically falling into his arms.

"Let's get her outside," says another voice. "I can't believe we found her."

"Thank you, thank you," I gasp, letting them guide me. I catch my toe on a brick and cry out.

"My God, she's barefoot," one of them says, touched by my apparent suffering.

"I'll carry her," says a man. And then I'm lifted into strong, muscular arms, cradled against a man's hard chest. He smells like deodorant and aftershave. I make myself go limp and let him carry me.

One of the men speaks into a radio, using code words I don't recognize. But then his voice breaks with emotion and he adds, "I really think we found her."

Self-loathing floods me. This is despicable. This is the worst thing I've ever done.

We emerge into early dawn light, just bright enough for me to see the faces of the men who think they've rescued me. They set me down gently on the front steps of the prison.

"What happened to you, darlin'?" the man who carried me asks, his voice gentle. His accent's different from the others'.

And he's not a policeman. He's wearing the tan forestry uniform. It's the same ranger who nabbed Miles in the woods last
night. Any minute now, he'll recognize me.

I hide under a fall of hair, wishing it wasn't such a recognizable red. I never cry in front of people, but for once my tears
will be an advantage. I let them fall, let all my terror and despair
leave my body in shuddering gasps.

"You're safe now," one of the men says, but his voice isn't
gentle like the ranger's. It's annoyed. He wants me to talk. I
risk a glance at him and see he's not in uniform. He must be a
detective.

"Maybe we should send a few men back in, to see if there's
anything," one of the officers says.

Shit. I can't let them go in there. I can't let them find her.

"There's nothing in there. Only me. I was hiding," I say, my
words disgustingly blubbery-sounding. "It was the only place I
could think to go." I hide my face in my hands.

I need to get out of this fast. I need to find a way to keep
them out of the prison, at least until I can get Momma out too.
"It's just—it's just rats in there. And roaches." I shudder. The
men step back, as if vermin are going to run out of my clothes.

"What were you hiding from?" the park ranger asks. "Was
someone trying to hurt you?" I glance down when he touches
my knee. He's missing the last two fingers on his right hand.

"How did you find me?" I gasp, as if I didn't hear him. I
need to think, fast. My mind flits to the strange dog I saw last
night. Maybe I can use that.

A police officer crouches down next to me. "There were

footprints all around the river, near where we found—well, we thought it was odd. A woman's bare footprints."

I bet he means near where they found Rochelle. "Yeah, that was me," I say miserably.

"You didn't swim across the river, did you?" he says, shocked. "There were more prints on the other bank just like them, leading up here."

"No," I say. That lie won't work. I don't look like someone who swam across a river—my clothes and hair are dry. "I ran across the bridge and then back down to the river. I was panicking, but then I thought to come here."

"Are you—are you Kaylee Robins?" the officer asks hopefully, that catch I heard earlier in his voice again.

I finally look up to meet his eyes. "No, my name is Della." Kaylee Robins must be the girl Da told me about last night.

A sigh of disappointment escapes him. The other men's shoulders slump. They begin to murmur to one another.

"Another one? Already?" one of them whispers.

The gruff detective takes my hand, trying to make me pay attention to him. "Listen, sweetheart, my name is Detective Long. I'm here to help you. But to do that I need you to talk. I need you to tell me what happened to you."

"Maybe she'd feel better if her parents were here," says the gentle cop. "Della, can we call them for you?"

"We don't have a phone," I say. Momma and Da never wanted anyone to be able to get in touch with them. Since they didn't have a phone, I never needed one either. Nothing really mattered to us outside of the Bend.

"I just want to go home. Can you take me home?" I ask. "I don't need to go to the hospital. And we can't afford an ambulance ride. We don't have health insurance," I add. "My da can take me there." I'm babbling, like any traumatized teenage girl would.

Detective Long sits on the steps next to me. "Della, I know you're tired and scared. And you'll be able to rest soon. But right now I need you to be brave and tell me what happened. Why were you at the nature park? And what made you so afraid that you ran over here to this prison?"

Now is my chance to turn their attention away from Momma for good. I can say it was a man with a knife. I can say it was Jake Carr with a cowboy hat and a machete. I can say almost anything I want and they will believe me. I don't even need a spell.

"Wait," Grange says. "You're Della Lloyd." My heart sinks. "Weren't you there last night when we found the body? You and your cousin?"

"Yes," I whisper. The men around me shift uneasily, the compassion on their faces changing to suspicion.

"Her family lives by the nature park," Grange says. "She helped find that Greymont girl's body."

The detective's eyes sharpen. "Why did you go back there, Della?"

"I—I couldn't sleep. I couldn't stop thinking about Rochelle. The way her body looked. And I remembered that another girl had gone missing before her. I thought maybe I could find her too. So I went back out into the park."

"By yourself?" the detective asks. He doesn't believe me. It was inevitable that they'd connect me to last night. But maybe I can make it work in my favor.

I nod. "I know it was stupid, but I just—I couldn't get the thought out of my head—of another girl lying out in the woods like that, exposed and alone. No one knowing what had happened to her. It didn't seem right."

"What happened? Did you meet someone?" the detective asks.

"No," I say. "No one."

He changes tack, as if hoping to trip me up. "How did you lose your shoes, Della?" He motions to my bare and bleeding feet, which are nicked with cuts and smeared with dirt.

"I . . . I'm not sure. I don't remember."

"Della, you know a few girls have gone missing on the nature park, besides Rochelle Greymont. Maybe you can help us find them."

"That's what I wanted to do," I say, "but I didn't see any other girls. Just—just Rochelle." I burst into a fresh round of tears.

"What made you come here to the prison?" he asks.

"Dogs," I say, taking a rattling breath. "A pack of them." Maybe that will keep them from exploring the prison more. If I'd said it was a man with a knife, they would have to look. But now, now they have no reason to go in there. And they clearly don't want to go back in anyway. I can see the fear of the place etched into their features. Fear of angry ghosts, of falling debris, of rats and roaches and everything else that lurks in the dark.

"Dogs?" Detective Long asks. "Are you sure?"

"Yes," I say, my voice a whimper. "There were six or seven of them, and they all looked different. Brown and black, one was some kind of pit bull. They chased me, but I got away. They didn't bite me."

"You're a very lucky girl."

"I think . . . I think I threw my shoes at them. I had climbed a tree and threw my shoes at them to make them go away. That was stupid."

"But they did go away?"

"Yes, they finally wandered off and I climbed down and ran. But then I thought they were after me again and I was so scared and so I just ran and ran and ran."

"Jesus," the gentle officer says, the word barely more than a breath.

"I—I'm really scared of dogs," I say, to offer an explanation. "One bit me when I was little."

"Well, I'd be scared of six feral dogs too," Long says, satisfaction in his voice. Feral dogs aren't his problem. That's a problem for the parks department and animal control.

But Grange, the park ranger, eyes me suspiciously. "Her family lives right by the park, literally right across the highway," he tells the others. "Why didn't you run home?" he asks me.

I put my face into my hands again. "I was confused," I say. "I got lost. I didn't even think about it, I guess. I just ran and then suddenly I was here. I went through a slit in the fence and climbed in a broken window," I lie.

"Is that how you got the cut on your cheek?" the officer asks.

I touch my face. The wound still stings, but it's already scabbing over. "No," I say. "That was . . . something else. A branch in the woods." It was actually Momma, from yesterday afternoon when I locked her in her cell. Just human fingernails.

Grange shrugs. "I know where her family lives. I'll have one of my guys go knock on her door," he says. He steps away and makes a phone call.

This was a mistake. I kept them from finding Momma in her river siren form, but I've made myself look suspicious. What sort of girl goes back alone into the woods where she found a dead body? And if they really try to look closely at those prints they found . . .

Before long, an ambulance comes, and an EMT examines me. She wants to take me to the hospital, but I refuse, so she has to content herself with cleaning and bandaging the wounds on my feet. Da pulls up ten minutes later in his ugly, rusted Toyota Corolla. The officers watch as he gets out of the car. His skin is pasty and unhealthy, dark circles blooming under his eyes. He looks hungover and his shirt is buttoned wrong. Not a good impression to make on these policemen.

"Della," he says, a question in his voice.

"I'm fine, Da. Got chased by a pack of dogs in the woods."

Understanding fills his eyes, but his concern for me still looks genuine. He sits down and touches my face. "I'm so sorry, baby."

"Sir, I'm Detective Long," the gruff cop says, reaching out to shake Da's hand.

Da stands and takes the detective's hand hesitantly. "Thank you for helping my daughter."

"Are you aware of what your daughter went through last night?"

Da meets my eyes, asking whether to play along or reveal his ignorance. I give him a barely perceptible shake of the head.

"Ah, no, I'm afraid I don't. I was working last night. Della's seventeen and very responsible, so she mostly keeps an eye on herself."

"I see," the detective says. Then he begins to tell Da about my finding Rochelle's body with Natasha Greymont. It's not how I wanted Da to find out, but at the same time, I'm glad I don't have to tell him myself.

He grows paler and paler as the officer speaks, darting unbelieving looks at me. He can't bring himself to speak at all, just keeps shaking his head in horrified amazement. Right when I think his knees are about to give out, the detective finishes filling him in on my fictional canine adventures.

"You should take her to the hospital and have her checked out," he says to Da, and then turns to me. "Now, Della, don't go into the woods by yourself anymore. It's dangerous out there for a girl on her own." His expression is one of fatherly concern, but I sense the suspicion in his tone. He's acting as though I'm in the clear, but they'll be watching us now. All of us—Da, Miles, and me. They might even start asking about Momma.

I give him a weak smile. "I won't. Thank you for your help."

The police begin to head back to their cars, and one of the officers draws Da to one side to file a report. Then Grange, the forest ranger, sits down beside me. "You know, I live in the park as a caretaker, and I haven't seen any feral dogs, let alone a whole pack. You'd think they'd come sniffing around my place if they're hungry enough to chase down a girl."

"It's a big piece of land," I say. "Lotta room for dogs to roam."

Grange is quiet for a moment. "And even if there were feral dogs out there, I wouldn't expect a Lloyd to be afraid of 'em. Not from everything I've heard about your family."

I meet his eyes and realize he knows I'm lying. Some of those cops might have bought my tale, but not him. He knows what the Lloyds are. What I am.

"We've all got our weaknesses," I say, my voice acid. Then I climb off the steps and limp to Da's car. I lie back in the passenger seat with my eyes closed until he returns. He slides into the driver's seat and I can feel him looking at me.

"Is your momma—" He can't finish the question.

"She's fine. Still in her cell. I did what I had to do to keep them from finding her. She hadn't—she hadn't even changed back yet."

"Jesus," he says. "If you hadn't locked her in that cell instead of letting her have the run of the prison . . ."

The thought makes me shudder. Every one of those men who "rescued" me would be dead, and she might be too.

"Did you understand what the cop was saying about Rochelle Greymont? About her body? Are you good and convinced now?" I ask.

Da nods and then bursts into tears. He puts his head in his hands and weeps. Finally, he looks at me. "I'm sorry, Della. You shouldn't have had to handle this yourself. You shouldn't have had to see . . . I'm sorry for all of it. I just wish . . ."

"If wishes were fishes, I'd have a full belly," I say, too exhausted to comfort him, to make up for everything he lacks. "Let's go home. Momma's going to have to sit tight awhile. We'll have to hope those cops are all too big of cowards to go in the prison. I said everything I could think of to keep them out. There's nothing else we can do."

My truck will have to sit tight too. If the police see me drive it out of the factory lot, they'll know I made up my entire story. And then we'll be right back where we started. If all of this actually works out, I'll be amazed. Because right now the Lloyds look more suspicious than we ever have before.

We drive home in silence, but as Da pulls the car up the driveway, I turn to him, pushing down my pride. Miles wants me to kill Momma and has promised to do it himself if I won't. But this morning has only proved to me how impossible it is for me to let anything happen to her, no matter what she's done. I couldn't bear it.

"You're going to have to help me this time, Da. If we're going to move her, I can't do it alone. Not with my feet all tore up like this. I know you're scared of her, but I'm scared too." My cheeks burn with the admission, but Da's face softens and I know it was exactly what he needed to hear. That I need him.

Da cradles my cheek in his hand. "We'll handle it, baby. Lloyds stick together."

That's always been true. Lloyds stick together. We close ranks against the world, putting family and the Bend first, above everything. No matter what it costs us. I just hope it doesn't cost us all our lives. There aren't any Lloyds left to spare.

FOURTEEN
NATASHA

A day and a half passes, with hardly more than the shift of light on the walls of our home. Like a boat without an anchor, I drift through the house, aimless and unfeeling. I open and close the fridge without ever eating anything, look out the windows, stare at the powered-off TV. I don't know what to do, where to go, what to say. Mom has barely left her bed since she and Dad claimed Ro's body at the morgue, and I can hear her weeping no matter which room of the house I'm in. I can't sleep at all, but I'm so tired I lose track of time for long stretches.

That rage I felt in the woods, the purposeful, deadly anger that allowed me to call 911, speak to police, and deal with everything that came after finding my sister's body—it fizzled out the moment I saw my parents' faces, the grief etched into the skin around their eyes and their mouths. Rage couldn't stand up against my mother's keening wail, my father's silent, streaming tears. I fell into their arms like a little girl, and I don't know how I'll ever find that sure purpose again. All I feel is bereft, empty. Like one of those moons that somehow break free of their orbit and float out in outer space, alone and lost.

My friends keep texting and calling, sending me messages online. I tell them I'm okay but don't want to talk. I don't think I could stand to be around a single one of them, not even Georgia. She knows I'm not okay, but she also knows she can't help me now. She checks in every few hours, and I can only imagine how useless she feels. Margo texted a bunch and left me a voicemail saying not to worry about our fight and that she was here for me if I need her. I couldn't summon the energy to respond.

Reporters are still calling, and some have tried to camp outside our house. Dad threatened them all with trespassing, so they backed off to the street. Right now, they only care that Rochelle was young and beautiful, but it's just a matter of time before they dig up her past. Before they turn on her.

The thought makes me pad down the hall to Mom's room and climb into bed with her. Dad is outside on the back porch, on the phone with someone. Mom lies in the fetal position, exhausted and finally out of tears. I lie against her and tuck my knees into the space behind hers, put an arm over her side, nestle my face into her neck. She grips my hand and presses it against her stomach.

"Can I get you anything?" I ask, just for something to say.

"No, sweetheart, thank you," she says, polite even in her grief.

"I'm so sorry, Mom," I say. "So sorry."

"Me too," she whispers. Her voice is as soft as leaves shushing together in the wind.

For the first time in two days, I fall asleep.

Dad's voice wakes me. "Cynthia, the police are here," he says, hovering at the side of the bed. It's dark in the room and he's hardly more than an outline. "They have news. Do you want to come down?"

"I do," I say. "Come on, Mom." I pull her arm gently. "Let's go hear what they have to say."

Painstakingly, as if her body has aged in a few days to that of an old woman, she drags herself from bed and begins to dress. Anyone else would go down in their pajamas, their robe, but Mom is a Greymont, which is to say a lady. She manages to slip on a dress and cardigan. She washes her face and I brush her hair, and then Dad helps her down the stairs. She still doesn't look like herself—red eyes, no makeup or jewelry, her gracious smile worn to tatters.

I hear the voices of Detective Long and another I don't recognize drifting across the house. They both stand when we enter the living room. The other detective looks Filipino, maybe early thirties, with light brown skin and close-cropped black hair. I nod at her and take a seat on the couch next to Mom, who grips my hand.

"This is Detective Ocampo," Detective Long says as he perches on the edge of Dad's favorite Morris chair. "She's the one who interrogated Jake Carr."

"What happened?" I say. "Is he going to prison? Did he tell you what he did?"

Ocampo starts to speak, but Long raises his hand to stop the conversation. "We'll talk about Mr. Carr, but first let's go over the results of the forensic analysis."

Dad takes in a shuddering breath and I know he's forcing down a sob. I can't cry. There are no tears in my body. I'm as dried up and empty as a tumbleweed.

Long's face assumes a nearly plastic quality, he's controlling it so carefully. "This is going to be extremely difficult for you to hear. You may want your daughter to leave the room."

"No," I say, my voice louder than I meant it to be. "I'm staying. I already saw her—her body. Nothing you say can possibly be worse than that."

"She's right," Dad says, his voice hoarse. "She can stay."

Mom squeezes my hand even more tightly.

Detective Long nods. He leans forward in his chair. "The injuries that Rochelle sustained are many, but they don't give us a clear picture of what happened. I won't go into the details, but suffice it to say that there is no evidence that Rochelle was injured by a human."

"What? What are you saying?" Dad asks.

Long takes a deep breath. "There were no drugs found in a toxin screen, no knife wounds, no bullet wounds, no blunt force trauma. There is also no evidence that Rochelle was sexually assaulted."

Mom begins to sob uncontrollably.

"Then what the hell happened to my daughter?" Dad asks, his voice rough and angry.

"Right now our theory is that Rochelle was attacked by a feral dog, possibly more than one."

Dad shoots to his feet. "Dogs? Dogs? You want me to believe that? This is bullshit."

"Please sit down, Mr. Greymont. It is possible that animal scavenging has obscured additional injuries."

"Animal scavenging?" Mom whispers. She puts her hand over her mouth and squeezes her eyes closed. I remember the coyote standing over Rochelle's body, its glinting yellow eyes.

Long grimaces. "I know it seems strange, but there was a report just the other night of a young woman who says a pack of feral dogs chased her in the nature park. It's likely that—"

"No, you lot have missed something," Dad says, beginning to pace. "Something important. Why was Rochelle on that road at all? Why did she go into the park? You said she wasn't drunk or drugged, so it surely wasn't accidental."

"At this time, we don't have answers to those questions," Long says.

"Jake," I say. "What do you have to tell us about Jake?"

Detective Ocampo finally speaks. "I have to tell you, Miss Greymont, that Jake Carr has been cleared as a murder suspect. He has an alibi for the night of your sister's disappearance. His whereabouts are accounted for, for the day of her disappearance, as well as the days surrounding it."

"He practically confessed to killing her onstage," I say. "Who cares if he has an alibi?"

"We've already been over this," Long says.

"Did you question him again? Now that we have Ro's body?"

"Yes, we did." Long looks to Detective Ocampo.

Ocampo speaks gently but firmly. "We will continue to

investigate his earlier actions toward Rochelle, but we have no ground to stand on here. There is no forensic evidence tying him to her death, nor any circumstantial evidence. It's very clear that Jake Carr did not kill your sister."

"Clear to you maybe, but I know what he is," I say. I'm shedding my days of numbness like snake skin as anger takes over.

Jake won't be blamed for my sister's murder. He probably won't be held accountable for anything he's done. I want to yell and smash things, but I narrow all my attention to the grip of my mother's fingers on mine. I have to stay calm for her. After all, I'm a Greymont too.

"So at least three girls have gone missing on the nature park?" I ask, my voice calm, rational. I saw an article about Kaylee Robins, the latest girl to go missing, online.

"That is correct," Long says, his face sober.

"All of them young women? All of them attractive?" I ask, a horrible thought taking root in me.

"Yes," he says, "but—"

"So Jake's a serial killer," I say. "He's been picking off girls for weeks."

"All the evidence suggests your sister was killed by a dog, Miss Greymont," Long says, the barest trace of impatience in his voice.

"That's ridiculous," Dad thunders. "Three girls missing, all with similar identifiers, and you're saying feral dogs killed them all?"

"We don't yet believe the cases are linked," the detective

says. "The first girl who went missing was out hiking with a boyfriend. He has since admitted that they argued and he left her in the nature park. She could easily have gotten lost, fallen into the river, anything. She may even have left the park. Her disappearance is not a murder investigation."

"And Rochelle was second," Mom says, her voice like an eggshell so fragile you could crack it with a single tap of your fingernail.

The detective nods. "The third, as I'm sure you've seen on the news, was a high school girl who was smoking marijuana in the woods with her friends at night."

"So she deserved to die?" I spit.

"Of course not, Miss Greymont," Detective Ocampo interjects. "We grieve for all these girls and their families. We're going to figure out what happened to each of them." She looks like she means it, but the police haven't given me any reason to trust them.

I start adding up the information, trying to make sense of it. Three girls reported missing on the nature park, all within a few weeks of one another. Only one body, with no evidence tying it to a killer. The other two girls are probably rotting in the woods or at the bottom of the river or in some hole under the ground. And there could be more. There could be dozens, for all we know. Girls no one cared about enough to report as missing, undocumented girls, girls with no connection to the park at all.

"Wait, did you say there was a girl who escaped from a pack of feral dogs the other night?" I ask, seizing on the only thing I can think of. "Why don't you talk to her again?"

"There's no need for that," Long says, shaking his head. "She already told us everything she knows."

"Well, I'd like to talk to her! What's her name?" I ask.

"I'm not at liberty to disclose that information," Long says, exchanging a wary look with Detective Ocampo. "I'm very sorry. But we've certainly taken her testimony into account. Park rangers have been searching the park for evidence of the dogs. If they find the dogs, they may be able to locate any additional victims. There may be a den."

I lean back against the couch and close my eyes. Either the police are very, very stupid or they are lying. There's no way three young women go missing and a pack of lost dogs gets blamed.

We're right back where we started. Rochelle's killer is still free and girls are still going missing. The police aren't going to stop this.

But I will. The meeting with the detectives has dispelled the fog I've been living in for days. The world looks clear again, horribly clear. I'm ready to move, to act, to fight. I text Margo and Georgia, asking if we can meet somewhere. Georgia volunteers her house since her parents are at work. When I pull into the driveway, a newly built monolith of gray stone, Margo's Nissan is already there next to Georgia's Jeep.

I shove out of the car and walk to the front door. I lift my chin, square my shoulders. I'm afraid to go soft again, to let this powerful anger slip through my fingers. If I do, I'll wind up in bed, wishing I were dead, instead of Rochelle.

The door swings open before I can press the doorbell.

Margo's eyes widen when she sees me. Her mouth trembles as she struggles not to cry. She has every right to grieve—she lost her best friend. Yet somehow, the sight of her pain irritates me. I let her give me a hug but pull away as soon as I can. I kick off my shoes and leave them by the door.

Georgia is lying on the white couch, one arm behind her head. She meets my eyes, and I can tell she's gauging how she should act, trying to make out what it is I need. Whatever she sees makes her stay where she is. She doesn't try to hug me or offer me any consoling words. She just holds eye contact with me and waits for me to speak.

I sit in a chair by the window and look out at the perfectly manicured lawn, seeing only dark woods and bloody leaves, my sister's white, reaching hand. The silence stretches out and out and out. I remember the way Della's voice dipped when she said I didn't have to look at my sister's body anymore. But will I ever be able to stop looking?

"Natasha," Margo whispers. "Please, say something. Tell us how we can help."

I think of all her texts saying she's here for me, the ones she kept sending even when I didn't respond to them. I wish she had been there for Rochelle like that. I wish she'd pushed as hard for her as she's pushing for me now.

I shake my head. "I don't know. I honestly don't. The police are convinced Rochelle was killed by feral dogs, which is the stupidest thing I've ever heard."

"Feral dogs?" Georgia echoes.

I nod. Margo makes a choking sound.

I let them sit with it for a moment before I launch into the real reason I'm here. "But I know that's not what happened. It's so clear Jake is to blame."

"Why are you so sure it's Jake?" Georgia asks carefully.

"You saw him at Papa's, you heard everything he confessed," I say.

"I did," Georgia agrees. "But besides Papa's, what makes you sure?" She sounds the way she does when she's quizzing me for an exam—calm, analytical, dispassionate.

"It's the only thing that makes sense. He was abusing her. She wanted to break up with him. And he's acted so strange ever since she went missing. So suspicious."

Georgia sits up and leans forward. "People are complex, Nat. Maybe he's acting guilty because he feels guilty about everything he did to her before she went missing, not because he killed her."

"I think he's a serial killer," I say.

"What?" Margo asks, so shocked she stops crying.

"Three girls. All blondes. All white and young and beautiful. That's his type."

"That's a lot of men's type," Georgia says.

"What are you saying?" I ask.

"You've lost your sister. You're grieving. You're angry. But I have to tell you, Nat, that I think you're wrong. If Jake were the killer, there would be more evidence. There would be something more to tie him to this. You're fixating on him. You're not seeing the bigger picture." Georgia climbs to her feet and crosses the distance between us.

I meet her eyes. "The police aren't looking hard enough. Because of his family, his money. They're afraid of the Carrs, like everyone else."

She shakes her head. "Your family aren't exactly paupers, Nat. Your dad's an attorney. Your mom's old money. Rochelle was a beautiful, wealthy white girl with family and connections and prospects. If the police try hard for anyone, it's girls like that."

"You don't know what you're talking about," I say. "Our past—"

But Georgia shakes her head again. "I know when you look in the mirror you still see a poor foster kid, but that's not how the world sees you. They see a Greymont, and that's how they see Rochelle too."

Georgia grasps my shoulders and holds my gaze. "I'm not saying you can't be upset about the police and where their investigation is going. I'm not saying their feral dog theory is right. I'm saying maybe there's some other stuff besides Jake you should consider." She looks at the ground. "Before you go off about him to the media and get sued for slander."

"What kind of stuff?" I ask. "What do you know?" Since when does Georgia hold back the truth for anybody? She's been free enough with it already tonight.

Georgia looks at Margo, and some agreement passes between them.

"What the fuck, you guys?" I ask, anger already creeping back up my throat.

Georgia sighs. "We know why Rochelle left the party that night. It wasn't because of Jake."

"And how do you know that?" I ask, my voice icy.

"After Jake's thing onstage, after he—well, I started looking through people's photos and videos from the party, just stuff they posted online. Margo helped me with finding the accounts and everything."

"Why?" I ask.

"I thought maybe someone might have caught something—maybe an argument between Jake and Rochelle or something, anything suspicious. Jake's just famous enough for that to happen."

"Oh . . . and you found something?"

"Actually, I did," Margo says quietly. "It was a video on Kyle's phone. Kyle was at the party with some of their musician friends. The video wasn't posted online, and I deleted it off Kyle's phone. Georgia has the only copy."

"Let me see it," I say, holding out my hand, adrenaline suddenly surging through me. What could this video show that could possibly make me think Jake isn't to blame for Rochelle's disappearance?

Georgia queues up a video and holds the phone out, her expression apprehensive.

I take the phone and hit play. The video is of some very drunk musicians singing "American Pie" together. But my eyes immediately go to the girl in the far background. It's Rochelle, standing apart from everyone, surveying the room. She absentmindedly runs her hand over an antique table laden with very expensive-looking knickknacks. With her spangly vintage dress and her hair pinned back with a ruby clip, she looks at home there, among the valuable old artifacts, like she belongs. This is what Georgia means, about how Rochelle looks to the world. You'd never guess life had ever been cruel to her.

Smoothly, slowly, her pace completely unhurried, Rochelle picks up one of the objects from the table and slips it down the front of her dress. She smiles to herself, as though pleased no one noticed.

But someone did. I see Rochelle's face fall just before a man comes into the frame. He's older-looking, maybe in his early forties, broad-shouldered, wearing a cardigan and glasses. I don't recognize him, but Rochelle seems to know him. He motions at her chest, shakes his head. At first, Rochelle seems to be laughing it off, as if he has caught her in a prank. But he says something to her that changes things. Rochelle's face twists into anger. She reaches into her dress and slams the stolen item back onto the table. A few heads turn toward her and the man. I can't make out what Rochelle is saying, but it's clear she's angry. He reaches out to grab her wrist, but she snatches it out of his grasp. She pushes him hard enough that he knocks into the table.

Rochelle turns on her heel and leaves, but the man doesn't go with her. He crosses his arms and leans back against the table casually, as though nothing happened. He looks right at the camera, and I recognize him. He's a music executive from Jake's new label. It must be his house where the party took place. But what did he say to Rochelle to make her act that way?

"*That's* why she left the party," Georgia says, breaking me from my thoughts. "It was nothing to do with Jake. She got caught stealing."

I close my eyes and breathe carefully through my nose. "Who else has seen this?"

"No one," Margo says hurriedly. "I don't think Kyle even watched it after they recorded it. Only you and me and Georgia."

"Let's keep it that way," I say, meeting her eyes and then Georgia's. "All this video would do is give the media more to speculate about. 'Oh, Rochelle Greymont, that dead girl, did you hear she's a kleptomaniac? Do you think she was fucking her boyfriend's boss? Maybe she got what she deserved.'" I shake my head. "That's all that video would do."

"I wasn't going to show you this at all, but with how you're talking about going after Jake all the time . . . how you drugged him at Papa's . . . I just thought you should have a little more information."

"You dug up stuff on my sister and you weren't even going to tell me? God, do you have to treat everything like a fucking documentary subject?"

A horrible idea takes shape in my mind. It can't be true, but it's too powerful to ignore. I close my eyes and count to ten, trying to calm myself down. But it doesn't work. "You're making a documentary about Rochelle's disappearance, aren't you?" I spit. "That's why you were looking for video of the night she went missing. That's why you filmed out at the nature park and at Jake's show. You think Rochelle's your ticket to NYU."

Georgia's mouth falls open. "Excuse me?"

"Dead, rich white women get attention. Isn't that what you've been trying to say?"

Georgia flinches. She breathes in so deeply her nostrils flare. "Nat, you know that's not what I meant. I'm not making a doc about your sister. I swear to God. I'd never do that, and I can't believe you think I would. I'm just trying to help you see the truth."

"Yeah, all you care about is the truth," I say, with a brutal laugh. "You want to confront the truth in all its raw glory? You think you're some artist, some truth teller with a camera, but you're a voyeur."

"A voyeur?" Georgia takes a step back like I slapped her.

"Natasha, you need to calm down and take a breath," Margo says decisively, stepping between us. "Before you two ruin your friendship. Georgia was trying to help."

I turn to Margo. "Why did you even give that video to her? What good could it possibly do?"

"We thought it could help you not go after the wrong person. Georgia told me about you drugging Jake at his show," Margo says. "Your behavior is scaring us. We're trying to be good friends. Please let us."

"Oh, you want to talk about friendship," I say, carried so far past the Greymont restraint I might as well change my name. I'm falling off a cliff, and I'm going to take them both down with me. "Let's talk about how good of a friend you were to Rochelle. You should have noticed your best friend was drowning. You should have helped her!"

"Natasha," Margo says, a sob working its way out of her throat. "That's not fair. I didn't want to say this before, but the reason Rochelle and I fought wasn't over her spending too much time with Jake, it was over her stealing stuff. She stole something from an estate sale when we were out together. I saw her and confronted her. And she just shut down. She wouldn't talk to me. I thought if I gave her some space, she'd let me back in."

"And look how that turned out," I say.

"I didn't do anything wrong!" Margo yells. "Feeling guilty about something and being responsible for something aren't the same. And I suggest you learn the difference. Because the only reason you're mad at me is because you're mad at yourself. Do you really think I'm the one who let Rochelle down, or are you afraid that you are?"

"Fuck off, Margo," I say, brushing past her. "I don't know why I thought you two could help me." I snatch up my shoes and push them onto my feet. Then I slam the front door behind me and throw myself into my car.

I wanted Georgia and Margo to take up the cause with me, to go after Jake and make him pay. I wanted them to be on my side. But they've only proved to me what I already knew. No one is going to give me justice for Rochelle. If I want it, I have to go out and get it for myself. Not through some bullshit social media campaign, not through politics or police.

No, there's only one way I can get what I need. Magic. Magic, and Della Lloyd, the only person who has actually helped me with any of this.

Her magic might be nasty, but so is the world. It's bloody and brutal. It takes and it takes and it never gives anything back.

Well, I can take too. And I'm going to.

FIFTEEN
DELLA

Da and I drove back to the prison as soon as the police were gone. We decided it was too dangerous to leave Momma there, that they might decide to do a thorough search of the place after all, or at least increase security. So now Momma is locked in our basement. This is where we tried to keep her when she was first changed, but the noise was so bad we couldn't sleep, and she kept trying to lure Da down there. Once, I found him trying to get through the barricades in front of the door at three in the morning, desperate to reach her. After that, I moved her to the prison. So I guess I'll be locking Da in his room tonight too.

Isn't this every daughter's dream—to be her parents' jailer? Our farmhouse will sound like a horror movie tonight, and I'll be lucky to snatch even an hour's sleep. I can only hope to move her back to the prison once the police lose interest. I know now that, whatever Miles might want, ending her life isn't something

I can do. And despite how angry he is at her, I don't think Miles would be able to do it either.

It's only eight o'clock, but I already feel tired, deep down in my soul. Momma was angry at being left so long and even angrier to see Da. Somehow, between the two of us, Da and I got her into the back of his car. Once, she pulled my hair from the back seat, and then she tried to make Da run off the road. But we made it home in one piece and shuffled her straight off to the basement, with stores of food and water. She'll probably shred her cot and punch holes in the walls, maybe yank the electrical wires from the washing machine. But there's nothing else we can do, nowhere else she can go.

"Let her roar," I whisper to myself. The roaring isn't what's dangerous. It's when she goes quiet we have to worry. Or worse, when she starts singing.

I'm feeling sorry for myself, I realize—as if I have any right. How can I complain when Rochelle Greymont's body lies in a morgue somewhere and her family weeps for her? When Natasha has had her sister ripped from her, has had to see the carnage with her own eyes? I've been trying not to think about Natasha, but she's haunting me, in a way I didn't think a customer ever could. She's more than that now—only there's not a name for it. But her scream is lodged in my brain, and her burning eyes are always on me now. Is she my victim, like her sister is Momma's?

As if she knows I'm thinking about her, the river siren starts to make a terrible noise downstairs. It sounds like she's banging a frying pan against sheet metal. Da is silent on the couch, his expression one of misery. Da might try to escape it, but he's as bound to the monster as I am, especially now.

She's not only a monster, I remind myself. She's my momma, even if she's locked away in there, her mind gnawed to bits, her nerves strained to breaking. Even if the truest part of her is fading, she's still the woman who gave birth to me, who fed and clothed me and taught me my magic, who made me what I am. I just wish I could get through to that part of her again.

Momma has always been mysterious, but now I don't understand the urges that drive her, the blood that pumps in her veins. I don't understand where she goes when the monster takes over—how much of it is her, and how much of it is the Bend's twisted power? When the monster takes these girls' lives, when it rips them to shreds, does Momma know what's happening? Does she try to fight it?

Because of her, the Bend feels strange now too, almost alien. I always felt I belonged to the Bend, that I understood it more than I understood my own family. But now . . . now I'm not sure I understand its magic at all. I don't understand our relationship to it, or what it wants from us—if it wants anything. Maybe it's all accidental, happenstance. Maybe we'll never know what went wrong. But some part of me feels that there must be an answer. The Bend was steady and faithful for a hundred years, and then one day it started going wrong and changed Momma into a monster. Why?

With all these girls missing and most likely dead, I can't help but wonder if the land is exacting its own vengeance— against us. Or if it's taking its due. Maybe this is a tax we owe for ten decades of free magic. Maybe somehow it's all our fault. And if it is, I don't know how to make it right.

Because as much as I want to blame those girls, say they were stupid for coming on Bend land, for not keeping themselves safe, I know that isn't true. We're responsible for anything that happens on the Bend. It's not just Momma who's a monster. We all are. We're the ones sending its magic out into the world, to poison and punish. Maybe Momma's monstrous form is just one more vengeance spell gone wrong. Only this time the curse was meant for us.

The thoughts are terrible, but they are no match for my exhaustion. Without meaning to, I fall asleep in the recliner, with the muted TV casting shadows over the room and distant thumps coming from the basement.

I don't know what wakes me. The room is filled with moonlight and the basement has gone silent. Someone has turned off the TV and laid a blanket over me.

I must have been asleep for hours because my eyes are crusty and my mouth is dry. I push out of the chair and grope in the darkness for a light switch. The room is heavy with silence, the only sound the electric hum of our old refrigerator. I finally find the switch and flip it on, casting a weak yellow light over the room. Everything looks the same.

But something is wrong.

Goose bumps are rising on my forearms, and my nose itches like it does during a thunderstorm.

I tiptoe down the hallway to check on Da first. His door is ajar and when I push it, it creaks open, revealing an empty bed, the sheets and covers thrown back. I forgot to lock him in, I realize. I fell asleep and I forgot. I close my eyes for one moment, two, three.

Then I walk as quickly as I can toward the basement door, careful not to make a sound. Through the kitchen and into the boot room. To the door that should be blocked up with heavy bricks. The bricks have been pushed aside, and the door is wide open to the darkness below. I don't know how she lured him here without my hearing, without waking me.

I pull the string bulb at the top of the stairs, casting brilliant light over the steps and across the basement floor. When Momma first changed, Da put the brightest light bulbs he could find down here, thinking the light might keep her from changing. It didn't, but I'm grateful for the glare now.

I want to race down the stairs, but I force myself to take them slowly, one step at a time. I keep my pace even and sure. She's probably not here anymore, but if she is, I don't want her to know I'm rattled. No sound comes from below.

At the bottom of the stairs, the washing machine and dryer come into view, and I was right about Momma ripping out their electrical cords. They're a tangled mess, and there are huge dents in both machines, as well as rents in the metal she must have made with her claws. I don't understand how I slept through any of this.

Then I recognize it. That heaviness that lies in all my limbs. It's from a sleeping brew. Da must have done it, but why?

I turn the corner and steel myself to face Da's bloody, mangled body. Instead, I find him and the river siren in a face-off, him with a rifle pointed at her face, her on all fours, ready to take his legs out from under him. In the glare of the lights, her monstrosity hits me like a punch to the teeth. Dark, seaweed-like hair snakes down her back and over her face, which is almost human except for the mouth filled with teeth like a shark's, waiting to gobble up her prey. Her skin is green-gray, and her powerful arms end in hands with two-inch claws that glisten with Da's blood. Her legs are more powerful still, muscled and roped and poised to strike. Her feet are the most human thing about her—long and slender as they ever were. She gives off a smell like river murk, pond algae, plants decaying in mud. Underneath all that is the sharp, metallic tang of blood.

Then she turns her head with a movement more lizard-like than human, and her eyes meet mine. Except for her feet, they are the only unchanged part of her: green, so green, so green you can't look away.

"Get outta here, Della," Da says in a low voice.

"How did she lure you this time? I didn't hear anything," I say, keeping my voice calm.

But Da's voice sounds desperate when he answers. "She sang in my head, in my dreams." He shakes his head now, as if to get rid of her voice. "Told me to spell you. I couldn't help myself coming down here, but I had enough will to bring my gun."

Jesus. If she can sing inside our minds now, what else can she do? What new powers will she develop? And how will we ever contain her?

"Momma," I say, still staring into those unnerving green

eyes. "Momma, don't you want to go to sleep? Aren't you tired? Can't you lie down and let Da go back to bed?"

She skitters a few steps toward me, like a crab, hunger in her every movement.

"You stay there, Ruby," Da says, pointing at her with his gun. She turns her head and hisses at him. He takes a step back, right into the wall, and almost loses his grip on the rifle. Momma bolts straight at him, ripping the gun from his hands and throwing it across the room, over my head. She swipes him across the face, leaving three deep gashes in his cheek, then retreats.

She's playing with him. If she'd wanted him dead, he'd be dead. Those claws could have taken off his head with one swipe. All she really wants is her freedom, and I'm going to have to give it to her, whatever may come of it.

"Just go," I say to her, standing out of her way. "We won't stop you. Go."

She cocks her head, assessing me. I'm not sure if she even understands human language. But she seems to understand surrender.

"No," Da says, taking a bold step toward her. "We won't lose you, Ruby."

The monster moves so fast, like a snake striking, that I don't see her wound him. But he's on the ground, with three huge punctures in his leg, groaning and bleeding. And she's gone, only her scent remaining to show she was here.

"I'm so sorry, Della," Da sobs, clinging to his injured leg. Blood gushes from it, pooling around him. Thoughts spin so fast through my head, and I can't seem to concentrate on what matters. He needs a hospital, but I don't know how to explain what's happened to him. He won't be able to work for a few weeks on that leg, which means we're not going to be able to pay any of our bills this month, unless I can bring in some customers. I shake away the wayward thoughts and focus on what's in front of me, what must be done. I grab a clean T-shirt from the floor and wrap it around his leg. I grab another and tell him to hold it to his face.

"Let's get you to the hospital," I say, helping him up. He cries out and nearly tumbles back to the floor, but I hold him up. "These stairs are gonna be a bitch," I say, "but you gotta do it now before you get any weaker."

Da grits his teeth through the pain and lets me guide him across the room. I take as much of his weight as I can, but it's ages before we get to the top of the staircase. By the time we make it into the kitchen, I'm weak and covered in his blood.

"No hospital," Da grunts out. "Just put me in my bed."

"You're going to bleed out," I argue.

"Won't," he pants. "Bed."

"Fine," I yell, propelling him down the hallway. I push him into bed a little more roughly than I need to. "But if you die, I'm going to be really pissed off at you."

Da grimaces. I think he's trying to smile. "Baby, if I die, you just get the hell on out of here. You get in your truck and drive as far as you can get and make a new life for yourself."

I roll my eyes, but he doesn't notice because his whole face is scrunched up with pain, his skin ghostly white with blood loss. The T-shirts are already soaked through. I have to do something or he really may die.

I change out his T-shirts for two thick bathroom towels and then race to the kitchen. I scan the bottles and bags of brew ingredients. No one in this house has made a healing brew since Aunt Sage died. We're more about poisoning than healing around here. An actually good human being in the family would really come in handy right now.

Miles could help. He learned a little of his mother's ways. But I can't call Miles. I can't tell him we let Momma slip through our fingers again.

But I do know how to knock someone out so well they won't feel pain. An old family brew called Lights Out. If Da had used it on me instead of whatever he spelled me with earlier, I'd still be asleep and he'd probably be dead.

Lights Out was one of the only brews Momma was picky about selling. She wouldn't sell it to men, only women. People hardly ever asked for it, but every now and then a desperate mother would come in, so out of her mind with sleep loss that Momma would brew it up for her. It's about the only softness I ever saw in her. I rack my brain now for the ingredients.

It's our gentlest brew: dandelion puffs, honeysuckle flowers, and hazel bark simmered with a teaspoon of honey. Even the words that go with it are soft as a lullaby: "Sleep and forget, forget and dream, dream and be." I whisper them over the boiling brew, praying Da won't bleed to death before I'm done.

Once it's cool, I take a bowl of it to his room and smear it over his forehead. His expression softens and his eyes close, so

I rub it over his eyelids too. His face goes slack and his body limp. I breathe a sigh of relief. I wish all our problems could be solved this easy. We did try this spell on Momma once, but it wore off the moment she turned.

Da sleeps deeply now, his chest rising and falling evenly. But he still looks like he's dying. His skin is pale and clammy, and sweat glistens at his forehead. I go back to the kitchen and grab a bottle of Jack Daniel's and a sewing kit and get to work.

An hour later, Da's leg is crudely stitched and his face is carefully bandaged. I didn't think he'd thank me for trying out my ninth-grade home economics knowledge on his face. That will have to heal on its own. But he's stopped bleeding and he's still sleeping deeply, so I've done all I can. I throw the bloody towels and clothes in the trash can in the kitchen and go to my room, stumbling as if I'm the one Momma ripped open.

The monster's out in the world now, probably rampaging through the Bend. Maybe she's killing someone, or maybe she's running from the police. There's nothing I can do about it until the morning. I strip off my bloodied clothes and fall into bed. Exhaustion hits me and I sleep, dreaming of gnawed bones and dripping blood, shadowy birds and a gray-green monster flitting through the darkness, singing a high, wild song.

I jerk awake just before seven. The sky is foggy, orange-yellow light bursting through as the sun rises. The events of last night come rushing back to me and I scramble out of bed. I need Miles. I hate to admit it, but I do. He's the only one who might be able to track Momma. What he'll want to do with her once he finds her is a bridge I'll cross when I come to it. For now, we just need to locate her.

I go to Da's room to make sure he's still alive. He's gray and wasted-looking, but still breathing, so I'll worry about him later. I want to run straight out the door, but instead I shower quickly and get dressed, run a brush through my hair—I need to act like everything is normal. No matter how panicked I feel, showing that panic to the world won't help anyone.

For the first time ever, I wish we had a phone in the house. I wish we weren't so isolated. But I'll have to drive to the grocery store and use the one in the workroom. I only hope no one will spot me before I can get to the phone, especially since I've missed so many shifts lately. The last thing I need is to get yelled at and fired.

The parking lot is nearly empty when I arrive. I manage to sneak through the front entrance, past the registers, and all the way to the back of the store without detection. But right as I close the workroom door, a voice says, "Well, good morning, Della."

I flinch and let out a sigh. It's my manager, Keandra, sitting at the break table eating yogurt. She's a middle-aged Black woman who's worked here forever and does not abide fools. "You're not on the schedule today," she says. I suspect she's about to tell me I won't ever be on the schedule again after all the work I've missed.

"No, ma'am," I agree. "I just needed to use the phone."

Keandra raises her eyebrows. "I see. Everything all right at home? It's not like you to miss so much work." If I didn't know better, I'd say she's concerned about me.

I fidget, suddenly uncomfortable. "My dad isn't well," I say, the first thing that comes to mind. It's sure as hell true now.

"And your momma gone too," she says, shaking her head. "That's a lot on your plate."

What does she know about Momma? I've never mentioned her. I don't know how to respond. I just nod and glance toward the phone in the corner.

"I've met your parents before," Keandra says. "Like most of us in Fawney have at one time or another." She chuckles lightly.

I meet her eyes. "They made you a brew?" I ask.

Keandra nods. "I'm sorry to hear things aren't going well. I know how difficult family can be."

"Thank you," I say. I study her, as if I'll see my parents' handiwork written somewhere on her face. But all I see is sympathy, which isn't a way people in Fawney tend to look at me. I don't know how to feel about it.

"You know, sometimes you find yourself caught in between a rock and a hard place, and you need somebody else to get you out of there. You got anybody like that?" Keandra asks.

I glance at the phone again. "I hope so."

Keandra nods and tosses her empty yogurt into the trash. "I'll leave you to it, then." She pushes herself to her feet and heads for the door. Before she closes it behind her, she turns and points her finger at me. "And don't miss any more shifts unless you want to start cleaning bathrooms."

"Yes, ma'am," I say. As soon as she's gone, I snatch up the ancient, yellowing phone book. I find the number for Highland

Rim and then wade through a long series of automated record-ings until I hear something that sounds like it might get me to Miles's department.

I speak to two people and get transferred both times until finally a gravelly voice tells me Miles isn't at work yet. I don't have a number to leave for him to call me back. "Will you tell him his cousin Della called? It's an emergency. He'll know how to find me," I say. "Tell him—tell him I said please."

"Sure thing, honey," the man says. I hang up.

I sneak out of the store and back to my truck. I swear I can feel the weight of my whole family on my chest, pressing down so hard I might just stop breathing. Da and Momma, Momma and Miles, our magic, our murders, our infinite crimes. I might be the youngest Lloyd, but what happens to us now, it's all on me. I want Miles to be the one who can get me out from between this rock and hard place, like Keandra said, but that's only wishful thinking. This family is mine to save or destroy.

I just wish I knew how.

SIXTEEN
NATASHA

My eyes are on the road, but all I can see is Rochelle's body lying in a morgue. Inert, cold, hardly her at all. Today that body is going to be fed into an incinerator and its ashes poured into an urn. Tomorrow, we will sit in a church and gather all our grief together in farewell. Her old high school friends will come, all the relatives we hardly talk to, some students from the university. Margo, who might not even look at me after what I said to her. We'll sit in that church and pretend to find some measure of peace.

But what peace can there be? Rochelle was ripped apart, her life extinguished, and the person who did it is just walking around town, performing shows. The media has stopped even mentioning him. Now it's all feral dogs and cries for reforming the animal control department. How can we all move on like this? How can we lay my sister's body to rest when her soul is trapped on a lonely nature park, crying out for vengeance?

And no one wants to give it to her. Except for me. Yet I've never felt more powerless.

Women spend so much time trying to make ourselves small so we won't get hurt, or we make ourselves so visible our visibility becomes a shield. We've got a hundred weapons to use against men like Jake, and none of them work. Not a damn one of them could save Rochelle, could protect Georgia's cousin Lena from whatever happened to her. But magic like Della's— now that's something else, isn't it? That's a weapon with sting, with bite.

With power like that, imagine what women could do to the men who want to break them. We'd never have to be weak again. We'd never have to be afraid.

I'm going to find a way to get that power. For Rochelle and for myself.

I once asked Della why there weren't any other witches besides her and her family. She didn't say it was because her blood was special or because she had secret knowledge the rest of us didn't. She said it was because people didn't know how to pay attention.

If magic isn't about bloodlines, if it isn't something you either have or you don't, that means it can be learned. Maybe you won't be as good at it as someone raised to it, but that doesn't mean you can't try.

What if magic is like anything else in life—what if it's there for the taking, so long as you're willing to fight for it?

I'm good at paying attention. I always have been. I learned to read my birth parents' moods by the time I was five so I knew exactly how to behave. When it was safe to ask for something, when it was better to go and hide.

I learned to read the social cues in my adoptive family just as quickly. Theirs were more subtle than anything I'd encountered before, but I was a quick study. I learned to read their manners like others read books, to learn my place in their world. Learned the meaning of every silence, every raised brow, every sigh. And those gestures became mine too.

I can pay attention.

That's what I tell myself as I climb out of my car in the parking lot of Wood Thrush Nature Park. I grip my pepper spray in one fist and check to see that the little knife I borrowed from Dad's dresser drawer is still in the pocket of my jeans.

From what I can tell, Della's magic is tied to this place. She knows this park better than any ranger, and her ingredients all seem to come from here. The locating spell that Miles did—it seemed to draw from this place too. I think the nature park is the source of their magic, and I hope it will be the source of mine.

I start toward the first hiking trail I see, but then I notice yellow police tape over the entrance. A sign is posted there: "Closed for maintenance."

I snort. "Closed due to mysterious disappearances, murders, and maybe feral dogs" must have been too much to fit on the sign.

I check around to see if anyone is watching before I duck beneath the tape and start down the trail.

Before long, I'm swallowed by the trees, encased in shadowy

green light. I try to step quietly so that I can listen to what's happening around me, but my footsteps still seem loud in the empty park, my breathing louder still. My tennis shoes scuff against the gravel that's been scattered over the dirt path, I trip on a root, I swear when a squirrel rustles the dead leaves beneath the trees. Here, I'm everything that Della isn't—an outsider.

I walk like this for half a mile until a smaller path branches off toward the creek. I take it, feeling the soil beneath my sneakers grow wetter, the air a little cooler. The water isn't very deep here. If I went in, it might reach my knees. I dip a hand in and am surprised to find it cold. I quickly wipe the water off on my jeans, wondering if I've exposed myself to harmful bacteria.

No. I can't think like that. I have to think like Della.

I take off my shoes and socks and roll up my pant legs. Slowly, I step into the creek. The bottom is slicker than I expected, and my feet almost go out from under me. I automatically dip into a crouch I learned while fencing, just in time to keep from toppling backward. I totter out farther over the algae-covered rocks until I find a large, smooth stone raised high enough out of the water that I can sit on it.

My feet stay in the water, but the drops of water on my calves bead and roll, making me shiver. I sit on the rock and I try to pay attention.

First, the creek. The water flows smoothly, except where it meets rocks that stick up, and then it froths a little, flowing around them. There are minnows in the creek, tiny little ones and slightly larger ones that make me want to pull my feet from the water. But I leave my toes where they are.

Next, I turn my attention to the trees. They are smaller here, as though newly planted. The leaves look like the ones on the Canadian flag, which I guess means they are maples. The light shines prettily through them.

God, this is boring.

At least learning to read people is interesting—people do more than exist, after all. But nature is just . . . inert. It's there. The wind blows and the water flows and the minnows swim. Simple.

But Della said to pay attention, so there must be more I'm missing.

I'm silent for another few minutes, waiting. I stare at the water and let my mind drift, my senses unspool. And there it is—that thing I felt on the night of the first search party, that quivering, goose-bumps-inducing feeling. The certainty that something is here besides dumb matter, that there is a—

A twig snaps behind me, making me flinch. My eyes come into focus on the creek beneath me and before I even know why, I'm screaming. I yank out my feet and hop quickly onto my toes, balancing precariously on my rock. A small brown S wiggles away with the current.

"It's only a water snake," someone says from behind me. I swivel so fast to locate the source of the voice that I nearly pitch into the water.

"Sorry," Della says. She gives me a weak smile. She moves forward so I don't have to look behind me to see her. Awfully considerate.

I narrow my eyes. She ought to be laughing at me. Snorting.

Calling me princess. Surely seeing my dead sister in the woods wasn't enough to turn her human.

"What are you doing here?" I ask, trying to regain my balance in more ways than one.

Della shrugs. "Out for a walk."

I study her. Now here's something worth paying attention to. Her hair is washed; her clothes are clean. And yet she looks . . . shaky, like she's coming apart. It's more than the dark circles under her eyes. She seems to be constantly surveying our surroundings while trying to pretend she isn't. She's acting like someone who just returned from war—wary and jumpy and jaded.

"You look like shit," I say.

Della smirks. "People keep telling me that. I'm going to get self-esteem issues."

I watch her, waiting to see if she'll treat me like a fragile creature the way everyone else has been doing or if she'll just be her usual asshole of a self. She can't seem to decide.

"What are you doing here?" she finally asks, shoving her hands into her pockets. "The park is closed to visitors."

"I don't see a ranger hat on your head," I say.

Della bites her lip. "It's not safe out here for you, Natasha. You ought to know that. You should go home."

"Nowhere is safe," I mutter.

"Maybe so, but there are a lot of places safer than here right now."

I raise my eyebrows. "What's that supposed to mean? What do you think is going to happen to me?"

Della looks away, off into the trees. "Well, there's that dog we saw."

"Not you too," I say. "I can't take one more person who thinks my sister was killed by some stray dogs."

"Why are you here? Really?" Della asks. She crosses her arms over her chest. The sun highlights the fine blond hairs on her arms, the contours of her muscles. She looks so strong, so competent, I can't help but hate her for it.

That's what I want to be. More than anything.

I study her, wondering how to admit how powerless I feel, how impotent.

Suddenly, a bird's song catches my ear. It's flutelike. *Ee-o-lay. Ee-o-lay.*

Della's face breaks into a genuine smile.

"What is that?" I ask.

"It's a wood thrush."

"Oh, like the name of the park," I say.

Another bird answers, its voice almost the same, but the song is slightly different.

"They do that," Della says. "Sound off to each other. One bird can harmonize with itself too." She tips her face toward the trees and her expression is one I never expected to see her wear, something like adoration mixed with joy. She opens her mouth like she means to sing, but then her smile disappears.

"How do you know all that?" I ask.

Della looks off into the trees again, a frown creasing her brow. "My mother taught me. She could sing to the birds, communicate with them."

"*Could?*" I ask, holding my breath.

Della turns, and her unnerving green eyes settle on me. "You're here for more magic, aren't you? Things aren't working out so well with your serial killer theory?" Her voice is the one from before, hard and cynical.

I feel my spine tauten. Now we're back on footing I know. I raise my chin. "Yes, but not your magic. I want my own. I want to deal with Jake myself."

Della laughs. "Rich people, think they're entitled to everything."

I bite back a snarl and speak calmly. "You said before the only reason there weren't more witches is that people don't pay attention. Well, *I* can."

"And you think you can just sit out here in the woods and absorb magic through osmosis? That's not how it works."

"Then tell me how," I say, gritting my teeth. "And I'll be out of your hair."

"You won't be able to learn," Della says with a cruel little laugh.

It's a lash on my already screaming skin. I want to fight back—with my fists and my nails, my elbows and my teeth. I want to let myself loose like a wild thing and wrench the lash from Della's hands.

I'm tired of playing the part of a good Greymont girl. I want to explode. I want to let the pressure inside expand and expand until it hurtles out of me with the force of a bomb.

Instead, my anger scalds me from within. How do I let it out so it can hurt someone else?

Suddenly, Della takes a quick step back and her laughing eyes leave my face. She studies the creek water that's now inches from her boots. Her brow furrows.

"What?" I say.

Della's eyes widen, and I finally look down. The creek has risen up, up, up and covered my ankles. The water swirls beneath me, agitated. I leap to my feet, standing at the very tip of the boulder, where the water can't reach.

"What the hell?" I say, startled out of my angry thoughts. Creek water doesn't move with a tide like the ocean. It shouldn't have been able to creep up on me like that. And my skin, it's covered in chill bumps, humming with that strange energy I felt before, not my own—the energy of the woods.

Then the water starts to recede, slowly, like someone pulled a plug in a clogged-up drain. I can feel my anger draining with it, leaving me empty.

"You did that," Della says, disbelieving.

"I didn't do anything."

"You did, though," she says, her voice filled with wonder.

And even though it seems impossible, I know she's right. Somehow this creek responded to what I was feeling, matched up with my emotions. Its waters rose with my anger, ready to do my bidding. Why does this all feel so familiar, like a promise fulfilled?

Because, I realize, this is what I felt the first night I came here, when something in me seemed to respond to something here—something powerful and alive. Later, after the owl incident, I had thought it was Rochelle I was feeling, but now I think it was . . . magic? Like the power was there for me all along and my anger just let me use it.

Maybe my anger isn't the problem everyone thinks it is. Maybe it's the solution. The thought fills me with the same satisfied pleasure I felt after using Della's potion on Jake. Like maybe I don't have to be helpless anymore.

"What was that you were saying about how I couldn't learn magic?" I laugh, the sound strained and strange in the empty woods.

Della's face turns troubled. She shakes her head. "You shouldn't have been able to do that."

I hop down from my perch, splashing into the creek. I wade toward Della. "What are you so afraid of?" I ask. "Why is my learning magic such a threat to you?"

"What if someone saw you do that? Can you imagine what would happen to this land?" Della asks. "Can you imagine the people who would come stomping through here? What would be lost?"

Now that I recognize the magic for what it is, I can't believe I didn't see it sooner. It surrounds me, heady and powerful and *present* in a way that's almost human. How hasn't the whole world come running to this place?

"Then you couldn't hoard this magic for yourself anymore," I say.

"It's not about that," Della says.

"What's it about, then?" I ask, finally stepping out of the water. I shiver, as if the world outside this creek is winter. But then I feel almost normal again, myself, distant from the magic

I had tapped into. The heat and noise of the woods rushes back to me. Della is startlingly close.

She studies me. Her expression shifts. "All right, I'll teach you magic."

"Are you serious?" I can't imagine what would make Della agree to do that.

"On one condition."

"What's that?"

"You keep it to yourself. Don't tell anyone else about it. Don't bring anyone here. It's only for you."

"And Jake," I say, "when I use it on him."

"Fine, but not yet. Not until you know how," Della says. "You have no idea what you could do, what could happen."

"I'll wait . . . a little while," I say. "But not too long. So you'd better teach me fast."

Della looks like she already regrets it, but she nods.

Excitement courses through me. I'm going to learn magic. I'm going to become a witch. I'm going to make Jake Carr wish he'd never been born.

SEVENTEEN
DELLA

I came out here to look for Momma and instead found Natasha. The wood thrush is still trilling away in the distance, singing songs I can't translate. I wonder how close Momma is, whether she can hear it, whether she knows what it's singing about.

But now I have something else to worry over besides Momma's whereabouts, because here's Natasha, barefoot in the creek, screaming at little snakes. Natasha making the water rise like she's the goddamned moon.

I've never seen anyone outside our family interact with the Bend like this. And Natasha is untrained, ignorant, and angry. She's dangerous—to herself, to me, to the Bend itself. I can either teach her or I can let her loose, and we've already got one wild card running around out here.

Whether I help her or not, an outsider using the Bend's magic . . . it could be catastrophic. I might be making a terrible mistake. But still, there's a part of me that wants to see what happens. That wants to see what this girl who burns like a wildfire is capable of, what she can do with the anger inside her. I only hope she doesn't burn the Bend to the ground.

"Well?" Natasha asks, impatience in her voice. "Where do we start?"

I glare back at her, but there's a feeling like a splashing fish in my stomach. I think it might be excitement. But Natasha doesn't need to know about that.

"What do you want to know?" I ask in my most resigned tone.

Natasha thinks for a moment. "Where does the magic come from? Has it always been here?"

I shake my head. "Not always. This land used to be ordinary, like any other place."

"What happened to change that?" Natasha asks, leaning toward me.

I hesitate. I've never shared the history of our magic with anyone. I wonder what Natasha will make of it. I decide to use Momma's words, instead of my own.

"I'll tell you the story the way I learned it. Whether you believe it or not . . . that's up to you," I say.

Natasha nods.

I close my eyes and settle into the story. It was a bedtime story Momma told me, not to comfort me, not to send me to sleep. She said it was my birthright. When Momma told this story, she slipped into storyteller mode, her voice trailing like honey, thick and viscous. Her accent deepened; her eyes seemed to grow dark. I never interrupted.

I haven't told the story before, but I think I can tell it the way Momma did. I clear my throat. "It's about my ancestor,

Erin Ruby Lloyd. She and her family were moonshiners here during Prohibition."

"Seriously?" Natasha asks. A smile hovers around her lips.

I stare stonily back at her.

"All right," she relents. "I'm listening."

I launch right into the story. "Two big, burly men had Erin Lloyd in their grip, their fingers digging into the tender space above her elbows. Her daughter, Rosie, followed behind, begging them to stop. Erin couldn't see where they were taking her through the itchy burlap sack over her face, but she knew the land well enough to know they were headed for the river, somewhere near the hidden limestone cave where she brewed the best illegal moonshine in Tennessee."

I glance at Natasha's face to see if she's laughing. But she already seems engrossed. So I go on.

"She should have known it would come to this. First the little girl dying, then the herd of goats. She'd heard of witch hunts in America, but she thought they'd long since died away. It was greed that did her in—not her own, but these men's. Seemed like it was always the greed of men that undid a successful woman.

"The sound of the river reached her ears. There had been a lot of rain and the river was high, barely staying within its boundaries. Its rushing should have filled her with panic, but instead a calm washed over her. She stopped struggling against the men and went still."

I can hear my voice changing, slowing and deepening the way Momma's used to when she got to this part.

"But her daughter wasn't finished fighting. Rosie's sobs

were louder than the river. 'Please, please. Please don't drown my mam. She isn't a witch. I swear, I swear. We'll leave this town, we'll go far away and never come back. Please.'

"The men ignored her.

"One of them yanked the sack off Erin's head, allowing the dim, green-tinted light to fill her dazed eyes. They were at a bend in the river where a young honey locust tree grew, only a few yards off from the water, its branches heavy with seed-pods."

I pause, thinking. A honey locust tree. A honey locust tree like the one in the oak forest, the one that's too big and too strange and very much out of place? Could it be the same one, and the oaks grew up around it in the years after Erin died? Maybe. Is that why Momma was drawn to it?

"Della?" Natasha asks, recalling me. Her brown eyes are wide, her face full of suspense. She's thirsty for the rest of the story.

I nod, pushing thoughts of the tree from my mind.

"Erin expected the men to march her to the bank and shove her right into the river, but now that they were here, at the crisis of the thing, they seemed to have lost their nerve. They looked at one another, waiting for the other to go.

"Rosie was on her knees, begging and pleading, her tears watering the earth.

"The men seemed moved by her pain. But this had all gone too far now. It wasn't even just about the moonshine anymore—not just about Erin putting them nearly out of business with her bewitched brews that no one could resist. Now their pride was involved. If they came home and the witch wasn't dead . . . well, then they couldn't go home at all.

"Erin knew she was going to die today. All that was left to her was to choose the manner of her going."

I glance at Natasha and see her eyes wider still, her hand over her mouth. She's a good audience, I'll give her that.

"'I'll go into the water myself now. I won't even make you do the deed,' Erin said to the men. 'On one condition only: you leave my daughter be. She'll give up moonshining and go quietly home. And if you agree to that, I'll go into the water myself.'

"The men exchanged puzzled looks, but neither truly wanted a murder to his credit.

"'Aye,' said one.

"'Aye,' said the other.

"The witch drew herself up to her full stature, which wasn't much, but her bright green eyes made up for what she lacked in height. 'And I promise you this, lads. You go back on your word, you harm one hair on my girl's head, then the devil himself will come up from hell to snatch your sorry bodies.' As if to accentuate her point, Erin snatched a handful of hanging pods from the honey locust tree.

"The men grew pale and nodded. 'First, we'll tie your feet together so you can't swim,' said one. Erin didn't resist. After all, the men had already made their most fatal mistake: they didn't gag her.

"Erin stood patiently, allowing them to twine some rope around her ankles. Rosie came to her and gazed into her mother's calm face, her own cheeks streaked with tears.

"Erin leaned forward and whispered in her daughter's ear. 'The land will always take care of you, child. You know how to forage here for what you need. You'll survive. But there will be more here for you than food.'

"Confusion wrote itself in her daughter's big brown eyes, but Erin could only hope the girl would understand eventually.

"'Go on now,' said one of the men, giving Erin a push. Anger threatened to undo her deadly calm, but she couldn't afford a mistake now. So she only lifted her head a little higher and began to take tiny steps toward the water. The men, impatient, carried her the rest of the way and down the bank. But then they let her go.

"When the river touched her toes, Erin began to sing. The words didn't matter—it was only the power of her voice that made the difference. That had always been the beauty of her magic—a middle-aged woman singing mountain ballads over her moonshine, what harm could it do?

"A middle-aged woman, bound at the ankles, with only a fistful of seedpods to cling to, shuffling herself into the river— so what if she sang, if it comforted her?

"But as she sang, she wove. She sang her magic into the water, just as she had sung it into the moonshine. Only this time she sang it all, every last drop. The river carried her magic throughout the surrounding land, letting it leach into the soil, wrap around the roots of plants, aspirate into the air. The men didn't notice; they only heard a woman singing an old ballad, singing until she was knee-deep, chest-deep, throat-deep. She sang until her words were only bubbles surfacing at the top of the water, until her body was dashed away in the current of the river.

"But Rosie felt the land under her feet change, felt her

mother's magic roll across it. She dropped to her knees and pressed her palms against the ground. That's where the men left her, bowed down over what was left of her mother's life.

"And so the magic took to the river and the soil, twisted into its fabric and grew strong. It twined itself like roots through the earth. It offered up its magic to Rosie and Rosie's children and grandchildren.

"And to me," I say, since Momma always finished the story by saying the magic was mine now too. "And I guess to you too," I add grudgingly.

Natasha comes out of the spell of the story with a laugh. "Well, that's quite a tale," she says.

"You don't believe me?"

"I believe that you believe it," she says.

I shrug.

"I have questions," Natasha says. "First of all, where did Erin's magic come from in the first place?"

"No idea," I say.

Natasha rolls her eyes. "Second, if Erin was so powerful, why didn't she use her magic to kill the men?" Now she raises her eyebrows as if she's caught me in a trap.

I smile. I asked Momma the same question when I was eight.

"She didn't have that kind of power. She could sing her magic into a substance like whiskey or water, but that's all. She was limited."

"Then how was she powerful enough to create all this?" Natasha gestures around at the trees, the creek, the wildflowers.

"That's the mystery, isn't it?" I say. "Maybe it was the idea of sacrifice or surrender. Maybe her death bound her magic to the land."

"It doesn't bother you—not knowing everything, not understanding how your magic works?"

"It's not science," I say. "Shouldn't magic have a little mystery in it? Shouldn't it require some faith?"

"So you have to have faith for the magic to work?" Natasha asks. "Like, you have to believe that when you boil a handful of poison ivy leaves in some dirty water, it's going to make a potion to make an asshole confess his crimes?"

"Well, not exactly. But you have to mean it. You have to intend for the asshole to confess his crimes. Intention is everything. You have to know what you're trying to accomplish."

Natasha nods. She starts to ask another question when a hackberry emperor floats down and lands in my hair. Instead, her face turns pale at the sight of the butterfly. I can feel its wings fold and unfold against my forehead. It must remind her of Miles's spell to find Rochelle's body.

A twig snaps and our heads both turn toward the noise. The butterfly takes off again.

"Miles," I groan as my cousin emerges from the trees. My heart is already racing—what if it had been Momma lurking there? If I hadn't been so distracted by Natasha, the butterfly would have tipped me off. It's Miles's favorite way to track.

His eyes flick between us, clearly trying to understand what on earth is happening here. "Uncle Lawrence said you'd be here," Miles lies. The butterfly lands on his cheek.

"Natasha asked me to teach her some magic," I say.

Miles's mouth spasms. "And you agreed?"

Before I can answer, Natasha is speaking. "You used the butterfly to find her," she says. "Just like with Rochelle. How?"

"I think Miles's magic is a little too advanced for you," I tell Natasha.

"Try me," Natasha says, her eyes narrowed.

Miles looks deeply uncomfortable. The butterfly crawls up his cheek and then onto his ear. "Maybe later, okay? I need to have a word with Della." He motions me toward the direction he came from.

"Why did you call me at work?" Miles asks once we're out of hearing range.

"Momma escaped last night," I say fast, wanting to get it over with.

"Della," he says, his voice a broken, pitying sound. He rubs his face hard, leaving one side of it red. "After we saw what she could do . . ."

"I know," I say quietly, my mind too full of images of Rochelle Greymont's broken body to be angry at him anymore.

"Any sign of her?"

I shake my head. "Nothing."

Miles bites his lip. "You should have—"

"What? Killed her while I had the chance?" I say drearily.

Miles ignores that. "What if we can't find her?"

"At least they've closed the park."

"Yeah, and look how well that's working out," Miles says, nodding toward the creek.

"I'll keep an eye on Natasha," I promise. "You focus on finding Momma."

"Fine," Miles says.

"And if you find her, Miles . . ." I trail off. "I know you're still angry about Aunt Sage, but please . . . for me. Just remember she's *my* mom, okay?"

Miles looks like he wants to argue, but he only sighs.

"If I find her, I'll bring her to you. I promise. Don't worry. We'll figure it out together," Miles says. He puts a hand on my shoulder and holds my gaze. "I'm sorry I left," he says.

I reach up and tug his goatee. "You did what you had to do. I understand."

He smiles. "Okay, I'll come by when I can. In the meantime . . ." He pulls a cell phone from his pocket. "I loaded it with minutes and put my number in there. Call me if you need to, okay?"

I wrinkle my nose at the phone.

"We don't have to be our parents," Miles says. "That cell phone doesn't make you any less a Lloyd. Besides, wouldn't you rather Natasha call you instead of showing up whenever she wants?"

He's right. The more control I have over Natasha's comings and goings on the Bend, the better. I take the phone and its charger and shove them into my pockets. "Thanks."

Miles studies me. "And Della, watch yourself. With her." He motions toward the creek again.

"What do you mean?"

Miles raises his eyebrows. "You know what I mean."

I feel the blood rush to my cheeks. "Don't be ridiculous. I've got bigger things on my mind, in case you haven't noticed."

"Oh, I've noticed a lot of things," Miles says. "Don't try to tell me you wouldn't go there."

I laugh, surprised by how bitter the sound is. "Well, she sure as hell wouldn't—"

"She might," Miles says. "The way she was watching you back there. She just might."

There's an unexpected swoop in my stomach. "Oh, fuck off, Miles," I say. "Mind your own business."

I can tell he wants to tease me about Natasha, like he would have done in the old days. But this new Miles is too solemn for that. He gives me half a smile. "Just don't make things more complicated than they already are, okay?" Before I can retort, he turns away and walks into the trees.

After he's gone, I look back toward the creek. My traitorous feet want to hurry back to Natasha, but I make myself walk slowly. Maybe Miles is right and I do need to watch myself.

Falling for Natasha is the last thing I need. It won't help me, Momma, or anyone else. Least of all Natasha.

But if I didn't have so much to worry about already? If I weren't Della Lloyd, with all that name demands? Maybe, just maybe I'd like to. And that's almost as scary as everything else that's happening.

EIGHTEEN
NATASHA

Rochelle's funeral. I stand wedged between Mom and Dad in the Episcopal church where we come for Christmas, Easter, and the occasional wedding. I stare at the blown-up photo of Rochelle at the front of the room, draped in white roses. I feel so much grief I'm afraid it might swallow me.

Mom is shaking on my right, and Dad keeps clenching and unclenching his left hand, the one that's not holding mine. They are trying with all their might to hold their bodies in one piece, not to fly apart.

I saw Georgia here with her parents and Odette when we walked into the chapel after everyone else. Mr. Greer had his arm around Georgia and tears running down his cheeks, as if imagining his own daughter being taken from him the way Rochelle was taken from us. Or maybe he was thinking about Georgia's cousin Lena and how they never even had a chance to bury her.

Georgia met my eyes for just a moment before I had to turn into our pew. I feel like shit about our fight. Yeah, it was fucked up for her and Margo to be digging up stuff on Rochelle like that. Especially to then use it to try to clear Jake's name. To try to convince me he's not to blame when I know that he is.

But I have to believe they really were trying to help. I shouldn't have called Georgia a voyeur. I shouldn't have accused her of making a documentary behind my back. But I can't stop thinking of the harm that video of Rochelle stealing could do. I couldn't stand to see my sister's name dragged through the mud. What if all these people here to honor her memory knew about her stealing? It would change how they saw her. It would change how they felt about her death. Her murder.

I push away these thoughts and try to focus on the reason we're here: to say goodbye.

Up front, Reverend Jordan makes her slow and quiet way through the funeral liturgy. It's one I've heard a few times, for the deaths of my grandparents and for a friend of Dad's who had a heart attack. I wish the words could comfort me the way they do Mom—I feel her body relax a little beside mine.

But I can barely take in the words. I stand when I am told to and sit when I am told to. I open the Book of Common Prayer to the correct pages. I listen to the words, but I don't hear them, not really. They are like the babbling of a brook in the woods, and just as mysterious.

Finally, finally it is over. The prayers have been recited, the hymns sung, the benediction given. We flow out of the nave in a tide of tears and whispers. But I can already hear stomachs growling, people no doubt looking forward to the hors d'oeuvres at the reception. Life moves on for them.

But for us? Life has stopped. Mom and Dad will forever be sitting in this church weeping for their daughter. And I'll forever be standing in the woods, staring down at the broken body of my sister, feeling a howl rise up through my chest.

Margo gives me a small wave from a corner, where she stands with Kyle, who has their arm around her. Her eyes are red from crying. I should go over. I should apologize. I've done nothing but dump my feelings on Margo from the start. And she was right—I was angrier at myself than her. Somehow it's so much easier to forgive her than it is to forgive Georgia.

I take a deep breath and walk over. Margo's eyes well up and overflow at the sight of me. She moves away from Kyle and opens her arms to me. I go into them without thinking. "I'm sorry," I whisper into her hair. "I'm so sorry." Sorry for how I've treated her, for being too caught up in my own pain to acknowledge hers, sorry she lost her best friend.

"Me too," she says. "This is surreal."

"Can I meet Kyle?" I hope they don't already hate me with how I've treated Margo.

Margo smiles. "Of course." She leads me over. Slim and fashionable, with dark eyes and sharp cheekbones, Kyle looks like a model. They bashfully push a handful of fluffy black hair from their eyes and reach out for a handshake. But their lavender-colored nails immediately remind me of Rochelle's, and the image of her hands reaching out in the beam of the flashlight sends a wave of horror through me.

"Nice to meet you," I manage to say.

"Your sister was an angel," Kyle says in a soft voice, putting their arm around Margo again. "She introduced us."

Margo kisses Kyle's cheek, smiling through her tears. She's not alone in her grief. I wish I was the same. The sight of them together makes me happy, but it makes me lonely too.

"I'm going to go find my parents," I say. "Margo, I'll call you in a few days. Take good care of her, Kyle."

"Okay, babe," Margo says, giving me another hug. "We'll go out for coffee or something."

"I'd like that," I say. "See you both later."

With at least one weight off my chest, I start toward my parents, where they stand with Reverend Jordan.

But then I catch sight of a familiar-looking man hovering near the door, as if unsure if he should be here. He has shaggy salt-and-pepper hair, boxy glasses, a gray beard. It's the music executive from Kyle's video. Without thinking, I move in his direction. His eyes widen slightly when he sees me coming, and he takes a step back.

I reach out my hand to shake. "I'm Natasha Greymont," I say, calling on my mother's charm to put him at ease.

"Greg Paulson," he says. "I'm sorry for your loss."

"Thank you for coming. You're from Jake Carr's label, aren't you?"

He looks surprised. "Yes. I hope—I hope you don't feel I'm intruding, but I . . . your sister was a lovely human being. I am—we all are . . ." He lets his words trail off, and his cheeks flame red.

"Has your label dropped Jake yet?" I ask baldly. I'm too tired to keep up the game.

"Well, n-no, not yet. B-but that's not quite up to me. I've made my recom—"

"She tried to steal from you the night she died," I say, cocking my head.

"How did you . . . I mean . . . what are you saying?"

"Rochelle tried to slip some trinket from your house down her dress. You saw her. The two of you had words. You grabbed her wrist, she snatched it away. She left the party."

Tears fill Greg's eyes. "I might have been the last to see her."

"No, Jake Carr was the last to see her. When he killed her."

Greg's mouth opens, trembles. "Jake has an alibi."

"All I really want to know is what you said to her. To make her so angry. Did you call her names, hit on her?"

Greg shakes his head. "I asked her when she was going to learn to stop hating herself. That her stealing, her relationship with Jake—it was all self-sabotage. I told her she was better than that, and she deserved better. And that the world deserved better from her." His voice trembles on the last word. "I cared about her."

"You were seeing each other?" Was Jake right about her cheating?

"No, nothing like that. We had coffee a few times, purely platonic. We mostly talked about Jake. I tried to warn her to leave him."

"You did?"

He nods. "I know what Jake Carr is. A womanizer, a drug addict. He's a black hole." Greg smiles wryly. "The label knows it too, but—"

"But they think he'll make them money," I finish.

"Yes, I suppose so," Greg says. He sniffs, stands a little straighter, as if remembering his duty to his employer. "But for all Jake's vices, I know he wasn't responsible for your sister's death. If I thought he were, I'd have told the police that."

"The police don't want to know what really happened to my sister. They like their little dog theory. But I know what happened to her, and I'll make sure Jake pays for what he did."

Greg's face twists with pity. "Your sister wouldn't want you to grieve her this way. She'd want you to let her go, to move on and be happy. Not to spend all your time on trying to take down Jake. Rochelle wouldn't want that."

"You know, Mr. Paulson," I say, "I bet you think you're one of the good guys, don't you?" And with that I walk away. He has nothing else to tell me, nothing to offer but empty words. But at least now I have one more tiny puzzle piece of the night Rochelle died. I snap it into place and move on.

Maybe in a small way, Georgia was right to say I was fixating on Jake and not seeing the bigger picture. Because it's not only Jake. It's *all* men. Men like Detective Long, men like Greg Paulson. Men who are content to sweep a girl's murder under the rug while her killer walks free. Because that's just what happens to women, isn't it? We get beaten and brutalized and buried, and it's just another day on this fucking planet. It's expected. It's tolerated.

Everyone in this church might think we laid my sister to rest, but I know the truth. She's winging her way around Wood Thrush Nature Park, and that's where I should be too. Learning to wield its magic, learning to speak its language, learning what I need to fight back.

Because I'm not playing by their rules anymore.

When I pull into Della's driveway, her orange tomcat comes bounding off the front porch like a dog and stands with its feet planted firmly in my path, meowing in a demanding sort of way.

"Shoo," I say, trying to walk around it. The cat neatly swerves into my path, still meowing. I try the other way and the cat makes for my legs, rubbing itself against my jeans.

"What? Are you that starved for attention?" I ask. The cat gives a pitiful meow.

"Oh my God, just pet him," Della says, watching from the porch.

"I don't like cats," I say.

"Ugh, you're a dog person, aren't you?" Della sneers. "Should have known."

"I'm not an animal person at all," I argue. "They stink and they shed and they're all way too needy. And this one looks like the worst of the bunch," I add, eyeing the cat's thick, dusty fur.

"Don't let my da hear you say that," Della laughs. "He loves that damn cat."

I struggle toward the porch, but the cat twines between my feet, trying to trip me.

"Just pet him and he'll leave you be. He's stubborn."

"Fine." I squat down and run my fingers over the cat's head. He purrs. I run my hand down his back once, rub behind his ears, and then start to stand. He reaches his head up and nips at my fingers, and I snatch my hand away. "Hey!" I yell. The cat bolts away around the side of the house.

I survey my hand to see if he got me.

Della laughs again.

"You knew he would do that, didn't you?" I ask, striding toward her.

She shrugs and gives me a playful smile.

"Bitch," I mutter, and her smile widens.

Almost against my will, I start smiling too. "You ready to go?" I ask.

"I thought we'd start our lessons here today," Della says, almost shyly. "If that's all right."

"Well, I guess you're in charge," I say. "Lead the way."

I follow Della into the house, straight through the living room, down the hallway, and into the kitchen. To my surprise, she opens another door and leads me into a small, windowless room like a large pantry. She pulls a string and a single light bulb flares to life, illuminating large barrels and old tubing.

"What is all this?" I ask. It looks like a bunch of junk.

"This is where it all started," Della says. "This is what's left of Erin Lloyd's whiskey still."

"She made moonshine with all this?" I ask.

"Yep, until she died. And then her daughter made something else."

Her tone makes me look up sharply, and I realize we're standing much closer to one another than I had thought. Della's eyes faintly glitter in the light from the bare bulb. I force myself to rally my thoughts. "What did she make?" I ask, though I think I already know the answer.

"Well, first she made a brew to poison the two men who drowned her mother. It made them go wild with anger and murder one another."

My mouth drops. "Was she caught?"

"No, because it looked like a drunken brawl to the police, and even the men's family was fooled. She got her revenge and no one was the wiser."

I'm surprised to feel a rush of pleasure at hearing Rosie's story. "They deserved it," I say.

Della cocks her head at me. "Taking someone's life in revenge might not be what you think, you know. It took its toll on Rosie."

"What do you mean?"

"She was a sweet girl in the beginning, innocent really," Della says musingly, running her fingers over a length of tubing. "She didn't have her mother's magic, so she'd only planned on marrying a nice boy and settling down to have kids. Now she was a witch and a murderer to boot."

"So?" I say.

"So she wasn't the same after that. She took pleasure in other people's pain. She made up the worst of the spells we use now. She lived to punish people."

"Did she ever marry?"

Della shakes her head. "No, she had a one-night stand with a boy in town to get herself a baby to carry on the Lloyd line. She did it again a few years later, and then again. She wanted to make sure one of her babies would live so her mother's magic wouldn't be wasted."

"So what generation are you?" I ask, trying to do the math in my head.

"Sixth," Della says. "Erin to Rosie to Charles to Bula to Ruby to Della," she recites, as though rattling off a child's rhyme. "Momma made me learn our family's history right alongside our magic."

"Wow. So you've got six generations' worth of knowledge," I say, a sense of futility hitting me so hard I want to walk right out of the house.

"And you've got about five minutes' worth," Della adds with a meaningful look.

Then a more hopeful idea occurs to me. "Your mom is Ruby, right? But your dad—he's not Erin's descendent. And he does magic, doesn't he?"

Della nods. "But he's rare. Not everyone has the knack for it. You might or you might not. Probably not," she adds with a smirk.

I want to argue with her, but I bite my tongue. "Do you still use moonshine methods to make—what did you call them? Brews?"

"Well, not the equipment. It's hard to arrest someone for witchcraft, but moonshining is still illegal, and that would be an easy charge to get us on. But the principles of it have sort of stayed, I guess." She pushes open the storage room door and waves me out.

"What principles?" I ask, trailing after her.

"Distillation. That's how making whiskey works, right? You ferment the corn or whatever and then you distill it down to its purest form. The liquor comes from the steam that rises. So basically, you start with a raw material, add fermentation, and then draw out the liquor. That's sort of how magic works, at least for us."

I lean forward, my mind working hard. "The nature park— Erin's magic bound itself to the park, so anything that comes from there is the raw materials."

"Right," Della says.

"What's the fermentation?"

"Intention, I guess," Della says. "You add human desire to that magic to activate it. And then you draw out the liquor of the magic, so to speak, through whatever means you can. Whatever you're good at. For Rosie, it was brewing. For Miles, it's tracking."

"So what's the deal with me and water?" I ask, thinking of the way the creek rose up around me.

"Let's find out," Della says with a quick grin. "Let's go to the river."

NINETEEN
DELLA

We trudge through the meadow, through snakeroot, milk-weed, and thistle. The sun is hot and bright, the sky a perfect blue. There aren't any clouds, not a hint of rain or darkness. Yet there's something unsettling at ground level, in the way the brush around me rattles, as if it's October and not mid-June. There's an eerie, expectant feeling in the stifling air like a nail grazing the skin. Everything feels wrong.

"This way," I say. We cut briefly into a scattering of trees that line the meadow, but the heat doesn't drop away. If anything, it intensifies. The air is heavy like before a thunderstorm. The birds are silent, and there aren't any squirrels or other creatures about. It feels like the entire Bend is holding its breath, waiting for something to happen. Goose bumps trail up my arms, and Natasha shivers beside me. It's strange how she can sense the magic too, when otherwise she couldn't be less at home here.

I wouldn't take Natasha to the river at night, but it should be fine during daylight. I wonder where Momma is right now. Is she asleep in a cave? Perched up in a tree? I am desperate to find her, but not while I'm out here with Natasha.

When we break out of the trees and into the open, Natasha breathes a sigh of relief. But the sound of the river worries me. We've barely had any rain lately, yet I can already hear that the water is high, rushing unusually fast. When we reach the bank, my heart starts to race.

I nod at the water. "Is that anything to do with you?"

The water is a deep, dark brown, but it's moving so quickly that the surface is frothy white in places. It looks angry, agitated.

"What? No," Natasha says. "Jesus."

I figured that wasn't the case, but I sure wish it was. There's something strange going on here. The river's powerful enough on its own without adding supernatural shit to the mix.

I've never cared much for my English classes, but we read a poem by a British guy once where he said the river was a sullen god waiting for its chance to strike. He said people would go about their business and forget it, but it was always watching and waiting.

That's how I feel about our river—since even before Momma became its siren. I've seen this river leap its banks and drown animals, flood whole sections of forest. It's peaceful until it's not, quiet until it's not. Then it rises up to eat you. That's the thing people don't realize about the river—it has teeth. It's the hungriest thing around here for a hundred miles.

"Why's the water like that?" Natasha asks.

"Dunno," I say. I pull off my boots and scramble down the bank. I step into the water so I can feel the river's hungry pull. There's something here I need to know. The water seems to nip and lick at my feet, as if tasting my blood. I wade deeper.

"Is that saf—" Natasha stops her question before I can roll my eyes at her. She comes down the bank too and stands at the edge of the river. She's very careful not to touch the water. Maybe she thinks it's dirty. Or maybe she's one of the rare outsiders able to use the sense God gave her.

We stand in silence a long time, me with my eyes closed listening to the river, feeling its tug. I let my heartbeat slow to the splashing rhythms of the water until it feels like the water is moving through me, splashing through my veins. It's a little like it feels when I connect with the forest's fungal network, but wilder, more unpredictable, more . . . emotional.

"It feels angry," I say, realizing it as the words leave my mouth. I open my eyes.

"What does?" Natasha asks.

I nod at the water.

"How can a river be angry?" she asks, wrinkling her nose.

I shake my head. "How can I make brews that compel shit-heads to spill their secrets?"

"Fair enough," Natasha says. It surprises me how simply she accepts the magic. Momma once told me Da was like that, the first time she brought him to the Bend. He seemed to understand the land right away, like it spoke in his ear, she said. He was making spells almost as well as her before he'd lived in the

Lloyd house a year. By the time I came along, there was little to show that Da hadn't always been a Lloyd.

Da chose our life, even chose our name. I need to remember that the next time I think he's being cowardly.

"I wish I could feel it," Natasha says. "Feel something as angry as I am."

I regard her for a long moment. "Come on in," I say. It's a dare and she knows it.

She reaches down to unlace her sneakers, pulls off her socks. I smirk at her pedicured toes, which shine metallic purple against her olive skin. But she sticks those pristine toes into the rushing water of the river and then her legs, all the way up to her mid-calf. She turns and quirks an eyebrow at me, proud to have met my challenge.

"Be careful, there's a drop-off right behind you. Goes down fast, like ten feet deep."

Natasha glances nervously at the dark water.

"Close your eyes," I say. "Put all your focus on the river."

Natasha goes quiet and still. Long minutes pass. When she finally looks up at me again, there are big, welling tears in her eyes. "That's what it's like. That's what I feel like all the time now," she says. "Like something in me is going to rise up and swallow the whole goddamned world."

I wonder what we're feeling here. Is it Erin Lloyd's magic or something else? Is it Momma's emotions, some vestige of binding herself to the river and becoming its monster? I don't know. But I can see from Natasha's expression that the river's anger is every bit as real to her as it is to me.

When I was little and first went to school, I started making friends with some of the other kids. When I came home talking about a new little girl I liked, who wore pink bows in her hair and brought sandwiches for lunch shaped like hearts, Momma lifted my chin and looked me in the eyes. "Della, you'll never be like that girl or any of the rest of them, you hear? Magic comes from need, and kids like that don't need nothing."

For the first time in my life I think she might be wrong. Because the wealthy, pampered girl standing next to me in this river with angry tears in her eyes is every bit as capable of magic as I am. One single spell and she could undo us all.

I ought to push her in the river now and let her drown. Instead, I step toward her, as though drawn into her current.

Her blazing eyes meet mine and then go to my lips. She flicks her eyes back up at me, a dare in them. I step toward her again. She doesn't move, rooted into the silt of the river as though standing on dry land.

The water pushes me from behind, and I tumble against her, steadying myself by grabbing hold of her hips. Natasha grins, and I realize it was her doing. So it's not only anger that makes her magic work.

I don't let go of her once I've regained my balance. Instead, I slip my thumb under the hem of her shirt and trace it across her skin.

That single touch sends Natasha hurtling toward me. She grasps my face in her hands, knots her fingers in my hair hard enough to hurt. She tips back my head and presses her lips against mine. Her mouth is hot and urgent and greedy as the river that laps at my legs.

I pull her hard against me until her chest is pressed against mine, her thigh sliding between my legs, making me ache. Her hand goes under my shirt and up my back, her fingernails digging into my skin.

Her lips find my throat and I throw my head back, gazing up at the sky. A single pale moth floats over my head, and suddenly I remember where I am, who I am. And who she is. This is exactly what Miles warned me about.

"I can't do this," I say, yanking myself out of her grip.

"Do what?" Natasha asks. "Kiss me?"

"I said I'd teach you. I didn't say I'd . . ."

"Like me?" she asks. "Want me?"

I'm shaking. With desire, with fear. I hate how much I want her. How much I want her to want me back. But look at us—she's a grieving girl, set on vengeance, and my family is the reason she needs it. And once she gets her revenge on Jake, she'll go back to her life, like every customer who's ever stepped through our kitchen door. After that, she'll forget me. I'll be alone again.

I turn away from her. "Go home, Natasha," I say.

"Della, please," she says, grabbing for my arm again. I push her away, and she stumbles back a step. Her feet go out from under her, and she plunges into the water, straight into the drop-off. She cries out once and scrabbles for something to cling to. But the current sucks her up fast and she goes under and then away, quicker than I can blink.

I start to follow her and almost lose my footing. Instead, I push my way back to the bank and run along it, watching for her head to pop back up. She surfaces a few yards down and gasps in a breath of air. I fly along the bank, dodging rocks and debris. She's trying to swim, but the current is too strong and keeps sucking her back under. The next time she surfaces she screams.

There's more than fear in that scream—it's agony and anger and a thousand other things I can't place. It's like she absorbed the spirit of the river into her body and gave it a voice. I'm stopped in my tracks by it.

But then she goes under again and I'm running after her. I have to get her out before she drowns or crashes into a boulder.

Next time she surfaces, I yell, "Grab that tree!" I don't know if she hears me or not, but she clutches on to a slender branch from an elm that fell over and now lies partway across the river. She manages to keep hold of it, but her body is buffeted hard by the current. She's going to get tired soon.

I clamber out over the tree, walking for as long as I can, then crawling. Finally, I have to scoot along the thin top, up to my thighs in the rushing water. If I fall in too, we might both drown.

"Natasha," I yell, "try to move this way. Use the branches to pull yourself over here."

Her arms tremble with the effort, but she finally gets close enough for me to grab the back of her soaked shirt and haul her through the water. It's slow-going, and she's coughing and sputtering the whole way, but finally, I pull her onto the bank of the river and she crawls frantically onto the muddy, overgrown shore.

Once she knows she's safe, she rolls onto her side and

coughs up river water. I crouch beside her, waiting for her to stop. Finally, she falls back onto the bank with her eyes closed.

"Are you all right?" I ask, touching her shoulder. Her skin is ice cold, so different from the heat I felt only minutes ago.

Natasha opens her eyes and gazes up at me. "You bitch," she says, her voice hoarse.

"Sorry, princess. I swear I didn't mean to."

She reaches up and tries to punch me in the face, but she's too weak and manages barely more than a tap on my cheek.

"Good form, though. On another day, that would have really hurt," I say.

To my surprise, she laughs.

"Come on, let's get you up," I say, pulling her to her feet. "You can borrow some of my clothes . . . if you can stand to wear something off the rack."

Natasha snorts and then has a coughing fit. "I'm not *that* rich."

I help her up the bank, and she has to stop to rest. We sink down onto the grass.

"Where'd you learn to punch like that?" I ask, rubbing my jaw in mock pain.

Natasha smiles weakly. "My dad taught me."

"Mob, huh?"

Natasha rolls her eyes and then closes them as if it made her dizzy. "My biological dad."

I whistle. "You're adopted? Did your parents get you from, like, Russia or something?" I regret the words the moment they're out of my mouth.

"You're a real piece of shit, Della," Natasha says, but there's no bite in her voice. "My birth parents were addicts and in and out of jail. I was ten when I got adopted. Rochelle was fifteen."

"Wow," I say, genuinely shocked. "That is . . . unexpected." I study her, trying to make sense of this new piece of information.

"I really thought you'd make a Cinderella joke," Natasha says. She laughs and then grimaces at the pain in her chest.

"Thought about it," I admit. "You don't tell a lot of people about your past, do you?"

"No, I don't," Natasha says, and she almost sounds surprised. Maybe she didn't mean to tell me about it either. Maybe she has trouble holding back around me just like I do around her.

"We'd better get you home," I say, helping her back to her feet. I'm careful not to touch her too much; I can't let her pull me in again like she did earlier.

We make it to the edge of the trees before she has to rest. It's midafternoon and the woods are still quiet and eerie-feeling. We sit in silence for a full five minutes, and I don't hear a single bird.

"I really felt it when I fell into the river," Natasha says.

I look up quickly from the leaf I'm spinning between my fingers and meet her eyes.

"It's more than the river," she says. "It's everything. Everything here is filled with rage. The earth, the trees, the water, everything."

I don't answer. I feel spellbound by Natasha's voice. Usually her words come out sharp, pointed. But now they're softened with a kind of reverence.

"And there's something else. A feeling I had. Why they're all so angry. It's because . . . because something is wrong. There's an intruder." Natasha's words are slow and halting, filled with uncertainty, like she can't quite believe what she's saying. "A monster." Her enormous eyes lock onto mine, and a tear runs down one cheek.

I will myself to be still, to betray nothing. "Maybe—maybe that's just what you're feeling because of your sister, because of Jake."

Natasha shakes her head uncertainly. "No, this rage was so much bigger than mine. I know what anger feels like. I'm so angry all the time. This is different—this is massive. Like it could crack the world in two.

"I think—I think that if I'd died in that river, I would have become part of it. That I would have been swallowed up by it. And that it would have made use of me. Is that what it feels like for you, when you do magic?"

We're sitting so close, our knees almost touching, and I can smell the river on her, and the fragrance of her hair underneath it. Her lips tremble, and I realize how perfect they are. She is my enemy and could undo me, and yet—and yet, all I want is to put my arms around her and tell her that yes, yes, that's what it's like.

"No, not really," I say instead. "The only will I'm doing is the person who hires me. I'm just the hands that make the magic. Come on—we need to get back." I turn away, not helping her up this time, though I can hear her struggling to find her feet. I can't let her make me weak.

We walk in silence back through the woods, and I can almost hear the cry of the wood, the cry of the earth, the cry of the water that runs underneath it all. And Natasha's right—the Bend is filled with a great, terrible anger. A monster walks here.

Maybe it's me.

TWENTY
NATASHA

Della lends me a pair of sweatpants and a tank top and gives me a towel to dry my hair. She's strangely delicate with me, quiet and gentle, yet distant. Brittle as one of my mother's china teacups.

My skin feels cool under the rough fabric, and something about being in Della's clothes makes me aware of every point of my skin that touches the cloth. All I want is to go home and change into my own clothing, lie down in my bed and try to understand everything that happened today.

What did the river do to me?

Why did I kiss Della like that? And why do I want to kiss her some more?

Afraid to be near her any longer, I let myself out of the house while Della's in the bathroom and walk shakily to my car. I lean against the open door for a moment, trying to regain myself.

Before I can climb in, a pickup truck comes up over the hilly driveway and parks next to me. It's a park ranger, the one who gave Margo and Georgia and me a ride, the one who was there when we found Rochelle's body. I can't recall his name.

"Miss Greymont," the man says, coming around the side of his truck.

"Hello, sir," I say, automatically offering him a handshake.

"Sorry," he says as our hands meet. "Chain saw injury." He's missing two fingers and is apparently self-conscious about it. He must have been wearing gloves last time we met.

"Are you all right?" he asks, surveying me. I realize I probably look like a mess.

I give him a sheepish smile. "Fell in the river."

"Huh," he says. "Glad you made it back out. I'm surprised to see you spending more time with the Lloyds. Not exactly in your circle, are they?"

"Oh, well, Della's been helping me learn my way around the nature park." I pause, realizing my mistake. "I know it's closed and we're not supposed to be there, but—"

"I can't see how you'd want to go anywhere near that place after what happened."

I shrug. "It helps, somehow. I don't know why."

He nods but his brow furrows. "Matter of fact, I'm surprised the Lloyd girl's going anywhere near it either," he says, "on account of the dogs." His voice is nonchalant, but there's some meaning behind his words.

I'm not sure how to respond, so I make a joke of it. "I think a dog would run from Della if it knew what was good for it."

He squints at me. "I meant because of how she only barely got away from that pack of feral dogs the other night."

My blood runs cold. The girl detective Long mentioned being chased . . . "That was Della?"

"Well, you know, off the record, yeah. She didn't mention it?"

"No," I say. No, she didn't mention that she's the person who has pushed an entire police investigation away from Jake Carr and toward a pack of feral dogs no one else has seen. "What happened exactly?"

"Well, you know, the police had tracked some footprints out of the park to that old prison by the highway. I was with 'em. We went inside the prison, and the girl came running out at us screaming for help. Said the dogs had chased her and she just ran to the prison. She was barefoot, and her feet were all cut up. She had a big scratch on her face. Nothing else the matter, though. She's a strange one for sure."

"She is," I agree. A strange girl whose tongue was in my mouth less than an hour ago, whose fingers were twined in my hair, whose body was—

"I think you'd be better to avoid this family, Miss Greymont. The mother was always a wild one, though no one's seen her in months. And the father is a nasty sort of fellow, not at all the kind of people your family would want you keeping company with. Maybe they don't know any better—you know how it can be with poor folk—but I think they like being that way."

I bite back a retort. "Thanks for the warning," I say blandly as I slide into my car. "I'd better get on home."

He nods at me. "And please stay out of the nature park until it reopens," he adds as he continues toward the house.

"I will," I lie. I turn my car around and head down the driveway. The air inside is hot and stuffy and the smell of the river wafts off me powerfully, along with the acrid, herbal scents from inside Della's house.

I need to get this girl out of my nose, so I roll down all the windows and let the air blast me, blowing back my hair as I fly down the highway. I'm shaking, but I keep letting the air buffet me, let its sharp pressure clean my skin.

This ranger wants me to believe Della was the girl who ran from the dogs. Who started this whole feral dog story. She acted like she'd never heard anything about feral dogs when I mentioned it, didn't she? I brought it up, so she could have said something about being chased by dogs. There's no reason for the ranger to lie about it.

I can't really picture Della being chased away from the nature park by feral dogs. And if it did happen, wouldn't she have said so? Everyone else has been so eager to make me believe the police's paltry explanation for Rochelle's death.

But there was a little truth in the ranger's story. Della's feet really were injured—I saw that for myself at the river. And she did have the scratch on her face. And how many other injuries have I seen on her? She always looks like she's just come from a fight. So who's doing it to her? She's definitely hiding things from me. She never gives me a straight answer. And look how she pulled away from me when we kissed.

What if she was running, only not from dogs? Maybe her

father is abusive. Maybe he's the one who chased her, and she fled to the prison to get away from him. Maybe he's the source of all her injuries, her need for money. Maybe she's trying to save up enough to get away from him.

But why wouldn't she use the opportunity when the police found her to tell them who he was, what he'd done? Maybe she didn't want him to get in trouble. I know how complicated domestic violence can be, how ashamed it can make you feel. How twisted your thinking can get when you love the person who is hurting you. I was so young, but I still remember it clearly.

But Della seems less like a victim than anyone I've ever known.

I grip the wheel and accelerate. If I drive fast enough, let the wind hit me hard enough . . .

Just when I thought I was getting to the bottom of Della Lloyd and her magic, there's another twist to the story. Another mystery to unravel.

The ranger told me to stay away, but hearing his tale only makes me want to be around Della more. There's something going on here. Maybe it's something to do with Rochelle and maybe it isn't. But it's clear to me that Della's not trouble so much as she's *in* trouble.

She agreed to help me with my magic. Maybe I can help her too.

When I pull into my driveway, Georgia's Jeep is there, and she's sitting on the front porch steps, staring off into space. A mix of feelings swirls in my stomach, making my face burn red. Anger, guilt, relief, longing, embarrassment, annoyance. Mostly, this is not what I want to deal with after everything that just went down with Della.

"What are you doing here?" I ask stiffly.

Georgia looks me up and down. "What are you wearing?" she counters, noticing my clothes. And then she sees my wet hair, the cuts and bruises along my arms where I ran up against debris from the river. "What the hell happened to you?"

"Nothing for you to worry about," I say with as much dignity as I can muster, walking past her and to the front door. I consider slamming it behind me, but she's already there, with a foot in the jamb.

"Please talk to me, Nat. This really isn't fair. I didn't do anything wrong."

I spin around. "Not fair? You know what isn't fair? My sister's dead."

"I know," she says. "But being angry at me doesn't change that. And I really am trying to help. I want to find out what happened to Rochelle too. In fact, that's what I've been trying to do."

"What do you mean?"

Georgia fidgets. "You were right when you said I wasn't doing enough to help. I thought the truth was what mattered, but maybe that wasn't the time for it. I should have listened to you. I should have backed you up. That's why I—"

"Please tell me you don't have more videos of my sister."

Georgia shakes her head. "I set up some wildlife cameras

out on the nature park, near the area where Rochelle was found," she says, biting her lip. "It wasn't hard to find between the news reports and the police tape."

A rush of images assaults me so fast I have to hold on to the door frame. Smears of blood on dead leaves. Rochelle's hair thrown over her face. Rochelle's body—

"Why?" I gasp.

Georgia takes a deep breath. "Sometimes killers like to revisit their kill sites."

I snap my head up to look at her. "You believe me? That there's a serial killer?"

"Yeah, or at least I can see that it might be a possibility. I shouldn't have shut you down so fast. I'm sorry about that. I'm sorry about everything."

"I'm sorry too," I say. "For the shitty things I said. For accusing you like that."

"Yeah, you were kind of an asshole. You got me to thinking, though, when you said I was a voyeur."

"God, Georgia, you're not a voyeur," I say. "I was just pissed. I knew the words were awful as soon as they came out of my mouth, but I couldn't seem to stop."

Georgia smiles wryly. "We've been friends long enough for me to know what it looks like when you lash out. I know you didn't really mean it. But it made me think more about my night-club project. There's no story there, at least not the one I want to tell. It's not a story that comes from a personal place. I mean, that's not even really my scene." Georgia drops onto the steps. "It was Odette's idea, and I thought it was a good one, but . . ."

I sit down next to her. "But?"

"I can do better. 'Excellence in all things,'" she says in a perfect imitation of her father's voice. She laughs. "I'll find a project that really matters to me, that has my ethos."

There's no reason for me to keep being mad at her. No reason for me to shut her out. She's here and she's listening and she's helping. It's probably more than I deserve.

I put my arm around her. "You'll figure it out. You're already excellent."

Georgia laughs.

"I've been thinking about Lena," I say.

"What about her?"

"She was on your mind when you told me the police try harder for girls like Rochelle. Wasn't she?"

"Yeah, she was," Georgia says. "When Lena went missing, the police didn't even look for her. They did nothing. Absolutely nothing. And she was only fifteen. It's been four years and we still don't know where Lena is." Pain rips through Georgia's voice. "Because she was Black and poor. She didn't get police-organized search parties. She didn't make the news. The only people who looked for her, who cared, were her family and her church."

"It's so unfair that happened to her," I say.

"Her and seventy-five thousand other Black girls," Georgia says, rubbing her face.

"What do you mean?"

Georgia shakes her head. "That's how many are missing in the United States. Victims of sex trafficking mostly. Can you imagine what would happen if seventy-five thousand white girls disappeared?"

"The world would shake," I say. Despite my feelings about the detectives on Rochelle's case, I know that's true.

"Exactly."

We're both quiet for a long moment. "We should make it shake," Georgia says quietly. "Whether it wants to or not."

I meet her eyes. "What do you have in mind?"

"I don't know yet," Georgia says. "But we don't have to take this shit lying down anymore. Other people are already fighting. We can fight too. For all the girls who are missing. For Black trans women. For Native and Indigenous women."

Her words catch fire inside me. That's what I want—to fight. Not just for Ro. For Georgia and Lena. For all of us. "Let's give 'em hell," I say.

Georgia's face breaks into a true smile. "Let's give 'em hell."

I wrap my arms around her and squeeze her tight. Georgia hugs me back but then pushes me away so she can study my bedraggled appearance. "But before any of that, you're gonna have to tell me why you look like a drowned rat."

I laugh, wiping my tears away. "Do you remember that girl Della we met on the nature park, who helped us when we got lost?"

Georgia's eyes widen. "Oh my God, Natasha. You—you aren't . . . ?"

"I mean, we kissed, but that's not really important."

"Not important?" she demands, outraged. "You kissed that—that—that witch?"

"She really is a witch," I say. "She's the one—her and her cousin Miles—they are the ones who helped me find Rochelle."

"What are you talking about?" Georgia asks, scrunching up her brows.

I dive into the story, telling her everything from the spell for Jake to finding Rochelle's body. I don't mention what happened at the river today, how Della pushed me in or what I felt. But what I've told her is enough. Georgia's face has hardened.

"Those people are fucking with you, Nat. They're preying on your vulnerability. There's no such thing as magic or witchcraft. You're being swindled."

I shake my head. "No, it's real. You know me, Georgia. Do I seem like someone who would fall for something like that?"

Georgia shrugs. "When Lena went missing, this psychic contacted the family. Promised to find Lena for this huge sum of money. My parents lent my aunt the money, not knowing what it was for. The psychic disappeared once she had it. What I'm saying is that grief makes people believe stuff they wouldn't normally believe. Because they're vulnerable and want to hold on to hope."

"This isn't the same," I say.

"Isn't it?"

Suddenly, I see myself through Georgia's eyes. A heartbroken little sister, hell-bent on punishing a man the police have exonerated, raving about serial killers and witchcraft. I sound like I've gone off the deep end.

I mean, I literally did go off the deep end. But I know what I felt in that river. I've seen Miles's and Della's magic at work. I've felt my own, too, simmering beneath my skin.

There are some things you just can't understand until you experience them.

Like grief. And magic.

Like Della Lloyd.

TWENTY-ONE
DELLA

When I come out of the bathroom, Natasha is gone, and I'm alone in the house. I sink onto the sofa and groan into my hands. This has all gotten so out of control. All I wanted was to protect Momma, to keep the outsiders out, but they just keep pouring in. And I'm not sure I'm right to protect her anymore. Not with this many lives lost and more at risk.

There's a knock on the door, a man's hard fist. I ignore it. Whoever it is knows I'm here, but I don't care. He can knock all damn day. He waits a few moments and tries again, but finally he goes away, and a truck starts up and drives off.

But I don't enjoy the silence for long before the phone Miles gave me rings. "Did you find her?" I ask.

"In the real world, people say 'hello' when they answer a phone, Dee," Miles drawls. "But no, I didn't find her. It's like she's vanished."

"Do you think—do you think something happened to her?" I ask, stupidly conjuring up Natasha's serial killer.

Miles snorts. "What could possibly hurt Aunt Ruby? Even before she changed, she was the most feral thing I've ever met."

I smile a little. That's the sort of thing the old Miles used to say, before Momma's transformation, before Aunt Sage, before everything. Back when we were friends and used to make fun of each other's parents. Before it hurt too much.

"How are things with Natasha?" Miles asks.

I must pause for too long because he says, "I told you."

I could argue, but what's the point? "You told me," I agree.

"What are you going to do?"

"I don't know. Sometimes I think—I think that you're right about Momma. That I should stop protecting her. That it's all gone too far." I shake my head, the traitorous words burning my tongue.

"We'll worry about it when we find her," Miles says with a sigh.

"Okay," I say. Miles hangs up.

The next morning, I have an idea. Maybe it's silly, but at this point anything is worth a try. And I need to think about something besides Natasha, need to do anything except wonder about what will happen when I see her again.

I cook Momma's favorite breakfast and hike to the river just as the sun is coming up. Maybe if I catch her right after a transformation, when she's hungry, she'll show herself. I lay the meal out on a log and sneak into the trees to wait. But fifteen minutes go by and Momma doesn't appear. The longer I sit, the more uncomfortable I become.

The Bend still feels strange, wrong. The birds are deathly

silent in the trees, and the fitful breeze rustling the leaves of the oaks feels restless. The river is still high and surging, its unrest so obvious even an outsider would notice. Natasha was right—that anger we felt isn't only the river's. I can feel it coursing underground too, spread from tree to tree like gossip. It feels like a part of the Bend but also not, like a tumor growing on a blood vessel. Is it Momma's anger, or something else? Is it the same trouble that started our family's unraveling, or something new? Whatever it is, it makes my skin crawl, sets my teeth on edge.

I'm about to leave my hiding place when a twig snaps, the sound echoing like a gunshot in the stillness. My heart leaps into my throat. I hold my breath, waiting.

That was far too big to be a squirrel. A human made that sound, or else another very large mammal. I wait another five minutes, but there's not so much as a sigh of wind to break the stillness now. I climb out of my hiding place and move on soft feet toward where I heard the sound.

No one is there. I search the ground and spy animal tracks. Paw prints. Enormous ones, large enough to put my entire hand into. Huge pads left deep impressions in the soft ground, and long talons have pierced into the soil. I squat down and study it, trying to figure it out. It's like a bear's, but we don't really have bears in this area. And this looks more like a dog or a coyote anyway. But what dog is this big?

A smell wafts toward me from inside the trees—it's rank and musty, like fetid water, with an undertone of blood. Every hair on my body stands on end at the smell of it.

I search for more tracks and find them, leading away from

the river and into the oaks. I think about following, but a strange, unfamiliar fear is wrapping itself around my insides. I've never felt fear like this here, where every inch of the land is known to me. But my body won't take another step into those woods, every muscle in my limbs refusing to work.

I grit my teeth. This is absurd—I won't be run off the Bend by a paw print or two. The worst thing in these woods is Momma, and she's got to be out of her river siren form by this time of day. I take a deep breath and step into the gloom of the oaks.

The moment my foot connects with the earth, a bunch of birds fly at me from the trees, screaming and slashing with their talons. As I stagger back from them, I realize they are all like that owl I saw with Natasha, the one she thought she heard speak. I take another step back, but the birds pursue me, beating their weightless wings. They scream so loud I cover my head. Finally, I turn and run, still ducking, my heart beating hard and my blood rushing in my ears. The birds' cries turn victorious, satisfied with their efforts. Even once they stop pursuing me, I don't stop running. I run all the way home, dash through the front door, and collapse onto the living room rug, panting and shivering.

"Della," Da says in surprise, half sitting up from where he lies on the couch. He's still practically gray from his injuries, but he's healing. "What's happened? Is it Ruby?"

I shake my head, but that's all I can do. I can't catch a breath to answer him. And even if I could, what would I say? Owls are solitary creatures. They don't flock. And they certainly don't fly at people's heads for no reason.

But I already know those weren't owls. They were Momma's ghostly birds from the honey locust tree. And those tracks didn't belong to any dog I've ever seen.

The Bend has finally twisted completely out of our control. It isn't only Momma I've got to worry about—the Bend is making its own monsters now.

I've calmed down a little by the time I get to work, the trembling in my hands gone. My mind is still racing with questions, but I don't have any answers. It feels outrageous to be standing in this little country grocery store, aisle four, shelving canned green beans, when the Bend is coming apart at its seams. But I need time to think and regroup. This monotonous, steady work is good for that, if nothing else. Besides, we really need the money. Da's not making it to the chicken plant anytime soon. And I'm not about to be on bathroom duty for missing more shifts.

Someone taps me on the shoulder, and I startle so badly I nearly hit my head on the shelf. Customers usually leave me alone, so I expect it to be my manager, Keandra. Instead, it's a girl who looks familiar—she's Black, kind of petite, with long braids. It takes me a moment to place her. Georgia—Natasha's friend.

"Della, isn't it?" she asks, cocking her head at me. She studies me with curious eyes, taking in my appearance with a slightly puzzled expression.

I nod. "I'm sorry, I don't remember your name," I lie.

"Georgia Greer. Natasha's best friend."

"Can I help you with something?" I ask, even though I know she's not here for groceries. She knows where I work, which means Natasha has probably told her about me. But how much has she shared?

Georgia leans against the shelf. "Actually, yeah. I'm trying to help Natasha get some answers, which means I need to fill in some gaps in what we know."

"Okay," I say.

"I was hoping you could clear a few things up for me. About how you helped Natasha find her sister's body."

My fingertips tingle a warning. "Look, I'm kind of busy here," I say.

Georgia crosses her arms over her chest. "Yeah, those green beans really need to get onto those shelves in a hurry. All these customers." She nods at the empty store.

I grit my teeth. "What exactly do you want to know?"

"How did you and your cousin—sorry, what's his name?"

"Miles."

"Right, Miles. How did you and Miles know where to find Rochelle?"

"What did Natasha tell you?" I ask.

Georgia smiles. "She said you used magic."

I smile back. "Well, there you go."

"Uh-huh," Georgia says. Her eyes range over my face, as if looking for some hint of weakness. "Was there anything special about the place you found her? Anything unusual the cops might not have noticed?"

I shrug. Why does she need to know this stuff?

Georgia seems to read my thoughts. "I'm asking because I know you're familiar with the land. I thought you might see things a little differently."

I pause, deciding how much to share. "It was close to the river but under cover. A little ways from a huge honey locust tree." And it's the place I found my mother singing to some strange, ghostly birds in a fog, with blood on her hands. I breathe deep through my nose.

But Georgia has already moved on. "Did you ever meet Rochelle before? Seemed like she could have been heading out to your place the night she died."

I shake my head. "Never heard of her until I saw her on the news." I'm getting a sense of where this is going, so I continue, "And let me remind you that Natasha came to me. I didn't seek her out. She came to me because no one else would help her."

"Well, you helped her, so why is she still hanging around you? You and Nat have been spending a lot of time together," Georgia says.

There it is, the real reason she's here. She wants to warn me off Natasha. "So? Are you jealous?"

Georgia laughs. "You two don't have much in common."

I don't say anything and go back to putting cans on the shelf.

"I want to know what you're playing at. What you want from her," Georgia says. "She's my best friend, and she's been through enough."

"I don't want anything," I say, though really I want everything, everything I can't have.

"See, 'cause I think you're putting weird ideas into her

head, giving her unreasonable hopes. I think you've got her under some sort of—"

"Spell?" I interrupt, finally meeting her eyes with a glare.

Georgia takes a step back but tries to cover by laughing. "Not a real spell, of course. But every charlatan has some kind of power, some sort of charisma or something that lets them rob people blind while staying their personal hero." Bitterness laces her words.

I snort. "If you think I'm Natasha's personal hero, you're an idiot. The girl barely tolerates me."

"And yet she's been with you all the time, even kissed you," Georgia says. "Ignoring her real friends, far away from everybody who cares about her."

"I care about her," I snarl, and then quickly look away, stung by the truth in my own words. I care about her, more than I've cared about anything except Momma in a long, long time.

"If that's true," Georgia says, seriously now, "then send her home. Tell her not to come back. Because whatever you are, you're not good for her. I don't trust you. I don't think Natasha is safe with you."

She's right. She's a rich, snotty asshole, but she's right. I slam the next can of beans onto the shelf a little harder than I need to.

"Look," Georgia says. "I'm not about telling people who they should be with. If her sister hadn't just died, I wouldn't say a word. But I'm going to do everything in my power to help her, and I think that means keeping her away from you. That's all I wanted to say. See you around, Della." Then she sighs and walks away.

I squeeze a can until my fingers ache as I watch her leave.

I was right to tell Natasha I couldn't do this. I was right to send her away. And if she knew who I am and what I've already done, what my family has already cost her, she would listen. She would run as far and fast from the Bend as she could.

But, no, that isn't true.

If she knew, Natasha wouldn't run. She'd burn us to the ground. And that might be exactly what we deserve.

TWENTY-TWO
NATASHA

I pull into Della's driveway and cut my engine.

Georgia said I was stupid to come back here. She said Della was a mistake I didn't want to make. She might be right.

But there's something going on here. I don't know what the feral dog story is about. Whether it means anything at all. But the way Della pulled away from me when we kissed, even though I know she wanted me, I know she did. . .

There's something holding her back from me. She's afraid.

Whether Della really did run from the dogs and chose to hide it from me or made up that lie for the police—either way, there's something strange about it.

I thought I needed Della's help, but I can't shake the feeling that she needs mine.

She gave me her phone number, but she hasn't responded to my texts or calls. All I can do is confront her face-to-face.

I push open my car door and start toward the house. The

place looks even more neglected than usual. The grass is knee-high, clotted with thorny pink thistles.

Della's father opens the door before I make it up the steps. He starts to limp onto the porch with the help of a cane until he catches sight of me. He stops, and we sort of take each other in for a moment. A bandage covers part of the left side of his face.

"Hello," I say.

He blinks at me for a moment and then leans against the doorframe and surveys me. "Della's friend, right?"

"Yeah," I say. Friend. Something like that.

"My daughter said she gave you a spell for your cheating boyfriend. Didn't it work?" He raises his eyebrows at me.

So I'm not the only one Della has been deceiving. Another secret, another lie.

"I just wanted to see Della," I say, hedging. I won't be the one to give her away.

"S'not here."

"Her truck is here," I counter.

He smiles and then winces at the pain in his cheek. "Off with her cousin."

"Will she be back soon?"

He shrugs. "Might be. I don't keep tabs on her. We both know she's the one in charge around here," he mutters.

"Sounds about right," I say with a laugh. He looks up, surprised. He must not be used to anyone knowing Della the way he does.

But looking at him now, I realize what he says is true. He's definitely not the one Della is afraid of. She's no abused daughter.

"I'll wait, I guess," I say.

The man nods absently. Then he locks the door behind him, limps painfully down the steps, and climbs into his beat-up old brown car without another word. He has to try twice to get it started before he drives away.

I stand still in the yard for a moment, my mind racing through what I've just learned. Della isn't the only one covered in injuries. He looks like he fought with someone recently. And Della lied to him about my coming here.

This family is definitely suspicious. But I still can't decide whether they have anything to do with Rochelle or if I've simply walked into some weird domestic drama.

I'm suddenly filled with misgivings. Should I have listened to Georgia and stayed away? Am I putting myself in danger? My parents have already lost one daughter.

My eyes are drawn instinctually toward the nature park. The trees look innocently green from here. Idyllic even. There's no hint that magic grows up from soil right alongside them, no hint of spell-casting witches. No hint of murdered girls. You'd never guess that my sister's body was brutalized and left there, that her spirit still lurks in the woods, waiting for justice.

"Rochelle," I whisper, and suddenly I miss her so much it feels like someone has punched me in the stomach, knocking all the air from my body. I make it to the car and then sag onto the trunk, squeezing my eyes shut. "Rochelle," I say again.

Before I know it, I'm weeping, the tears gushing out, my breath coming short.

"Please don't be dead anymore," I say to the air. "Just please don't." I know my words make no sense, but I've never wanted anything so badly as I want my sister to not be dead. But there's no end to this hurt, no way to make it better. Rochelle is dead, and her last hours were terrifying and painful and so horrible that some part of her got left behind.

I can't bring her back to life. All I can do is try to lay her to rest.

A car struggles its way up the drive, and Della and Miles both get out. I hurry to wipe my eyes and nose, but there's no disguising what I'm feeling. Miles takes one look at me and goes straight to the house, but Della walks slowly over.

Her hair shines red in the sunlight, but her eyes seem cast in shadow. I can't tell what her expression is until she's right in front of me—and even then I don't know what she's feeling. She steps up close, not speaking, her eyes flitting over me.

She looks at me for a long time and then she sighs.

"What?" I say, hating how shaky my voice is.

Della holds out her hand, and to my surprise I take it without hesitation. "Come on," she says.

"Where are we going?" I ask.

Della gives me a sad, lost sort of smile. "To burn it all down."

"I don't—what do you mean?" I ask, letting her lead me down the driveway.

"Let's make you a proper witch," she says, her voice certain now. But somehow I'm not at all sure that's what she meant.

"Della," I say, when we get to the bottom of the hill. "Stop." I pull my hand from hers and make her face me.

Her eyes are the color of light shining through emeralds,

and they're gazing at me like I'm her salvation and damnation in one. She slides her hand behind my neck and knots her fingers in my hair. I think she's going to kiss me, but she doesn't.

"The Lloyds have done a lot of damage with the Bend's magic," Della says. "We've cursed people, broken up marriages, ruined people's lives, even—even killed people with our magic. I've never felt bad about any of it, until . . ." She trails off, gazing at me.

"Until what?" I whisper.

She shakes her head. "I just think . . . I think maybe someone else deserves a go now. You. You deserve it. And if I can, I'm going to give it to you."

"I thought you already were," I say. "You agreed to teach me."

"There's a lot you don't know. A lot I haven't told you," she says. When we cross the road, Della grabs my hand again and pulls me forward. We plummet into the trees, walking fast, so unlike Della's usual slow and steady pace. "First off, the Bend's magic is going wrong, slipping out of our control. Every spell is a risk."

"What do you mean?" I ask, disentangling my fingers from hers.

"Sometimes the spells don't work, sometimes they do the wrong things, sometimes they are too strong and go too far. I don't know how to fix it. But I thought you should know."

So this is the thing she was keeping from me. Or at least one of them. This is what happened at the bar the night I put Della's brew in Jake's beer. The magic spread, went too far, infected a room full of innocent people.

"Remember I told you before, everyone has to find their own way into the magic. Like, for my momma, for her it was always music. She sang the magic out of the land the way Erin Lloyd sang magic into things."

"I can't sing," I hasten to say.

"I don't want you to. We've already seen your connection with the Bend's water systems, so that's what we're going to focus on. You use it when you're angry or when you're . . ." Della flushes. "Your magic is tied in with your emotions. It's instinctive. Anyway, I'm going to show you how to control it."

"Control the water?" I laugh. "To do what?"

"Like, I think maybe you can turn the magic into a weapon. Use it like a sword the way you do in fencing."

"Are you serious?" I ask. Turning magic into a weapon . . . imagine what I could do with that. Imagine how I could hurt those who have hurt me. Imagine how I could hurt Jake.

"If that's possible, why don't you do it?" I ask.

"Because I can't," Della says simply. "Or at least not easily. Maybe I could learn. But I'd never be as powerful that way as I am with—with my own thing. The Bend responds to each of us differently, to our own needs and desires and gifts. The Bend's magic demands that you know who you are and what you want. It has a way of whittling you down to your most essential self. And I have to warn you that you might not like what you find out, you might not like who you are."

She stops and looks me in the eyes. "Are you sure you want to become that person?"

"I already am her," I say, my tone steely.

"Okay," Della says, "then show me." I didn't realize it before, but we're standing by the creek. It is high and rushing, only this time I know I'm not to blame.

"What do you mean?" I ask.

"You've already done it twice. Once, when you made the water rise up here. And then when you—when you kissed me, you used the river to pull me toward you, didn't you? I felt it but wasn't sure. I think you'll work better with water than anything else." Della stares at me, waiting for me to do something, as if I have any idea what she's talking about.

"And how do I do that?"

"What did you do last time?"

I stop and think. Neither time was a conscious decision. The first time I didn't even know it was happening. And when I pulled her to me? There wasn't anything rational about it.

"Come on, princess," Della says, lacing her voice with impatience.

"Give me some help," I snap. "How do I start?"

Della shrugs and I want to hit her. She gives me a knowing smile. "Act on that anger you're feeling. Stop bottling it up and let it out."

I step toward her, but Della moves back. "Not with your fists, princess."

"Stop calling me that."

"Show me you're something different, then," she says, her voice taunting.

I hold out a hand over the water. "I don't know what I'm supposed to do. I feel stupid."

"Probably not as stupid as you look, though," Della says, smirking at me again.

I throw out a hand over the water, as if to make it spray her. Nothing happens, and Della laughs.

Her laughter wraps around me like a constricting snake. I need to break through it. Even though it makes me feel like an absolute moron, I pick up a long, slender stick from the bank and point it at her.

Della raises her eyebrows. "You gonna poke me with that?"

I lunge at her, jabbing the stick forward, hoping water will somehow follow. Della leaps backward, neatly avoiding my parry, and then laughs again. "What was that supposed to do? This isn't Harry Potter. Wands don't work here."

My cheeks burn so hot I know my face must be beet red. I let out a groan of frustration.

"You're thinking too hard. Listen to the water. Feel it. And then use it. Let your intention meet the magic."

I turn away from Della and look at the creek. I stare at its surface, watching leaves and twigs rush past. Maybe I need to touch it for this to work? I squat down at the water's edge, ignoring the surge of fear that being so near to it brings. The river sucked me down so easily yesterday and would probably have kept me if it weren't for Della.

I trail my fingers in the water, feeling again that surge of anger the water seems to hold, the anger so like my own. But I also feel the water's power, its irresistible tug. I look back at Della, who's staring at me, tense and waiting. But I don't want to hurt her. I don't want to turn the water into a weapon against her. I want to kiss her.

No, more than that, I want to prove myself to her. Show her what's inside me is so much more than the privileged exterior she seems to despise. I want to surprise her.

I wait until Della turns around and then I zip my hand over the water, arcing my arm out the way I would with a saber, drawing it across the backs of Della's knees. A thin line of water follows my movement, hitting her so hard she falls forward onto her hands and knees with a gasp.

Della looks at me over her shoulder, her eyes wide and shocked. Then she bursts into laughter.

I start to laugh too, shocked by what I've done. I didn't just use magic—I controlled it. I walk over and help her to her feet. She grins at me, her eyes filled with admiration, and the sight of it makes my chest feel like it's going to burst open. Without stopping to think about it, I reach for her and wrap my arms around her.

"Thank you," I whisper into her hair. Della's given me what no one else could—power, a sense of control in this brutal fucking world. And a weapon I can wield against it.

Della pulls back and grins at me, her eyes soft and playful. "I'll never call you princess again."

Before I can think too hard about it, I kiss her. This time, she doesn't pull away, doesn't change her mind. She melts into me, like she's been waiting too, like all she's wanted is my skin against hers. She kisses me like she's ravenous, like she hasn't touched another human in years. Like she doesn't just want me but needs me too.

I'm almost scared by the intensity of her want. I can feel her loneliness, all the words she's held locked behind her throat, the tears she's refused to cry. Somehow I have found the softness at the center of a girl who would have the world believe her heart is made of stone.

Della pulls her lips from mine and gasps. "There's more I have to tell you about the magic. About everything."

"Later," I say, pulling her gently to the bank of the creek. There will be time for secrets and revelations, time for magic and vengeance.

Right now I only want to make Della Lloyd go as soft as the water that laps at our feet.

TWENTY-THREE

DELLA

"Will you show me your magic?" Natasha whispers. Our limbs are still twined together, and the sun is going down. "The thing that's just yours?"

I hesitate. No one outside of my family has ever watched me do anything except make brews. It feels strangely intimate showing it to an outsider. Like showing them my very guts. But I promised Natasha I'd show her everything. And I want to. I want her to see this. After all, I tell myself, it will help her learn to control her own magic.

"Okay," I say.

She smiles. "It's not something gross, is it? Like, you can't rip a rabbit right out of its skin? Boil a man's blood in his veins?"

I throw back my head and laugh. "That'd come in useful, but no. I think you might be disappointed."

Natasha sits up, her eyes bright. "Not a chance. Show me."

I sit up too. "All right. Just stay over there. I have to focus."

And I can't focus with her smell in my nose, her still-hot skin against mine.

Natasha snorts and backs up a few feet.

I nod and close my eyes, rooting my fingers into the earth. I tune out Natasha's breathing, her nearness, all the millions of questions and confessions and concerns racing through my mind.

I focus on the endless, labyrinthine threads of life beneath us. I feel them drinking from the creek, passing nutrients through the soil. I let their life fill me too, until I feel as if I'm just another tree breathing in this forest.

This is what Natasha needs most, what I can give her: to teach her to tap into the magic in a way that's not only about anger and pain.

"Put your hand next to mine," I say without opening my eyes, and I feel her warm skin inches from my own. I reach out with my smallest finger and touch her. I've never tried to let someone into my magic like this before, but I want to, I want to.

I wish I could make the forest close around us, until it's only me and her and the growing world, without dead sisters or murderous mothers, without secrets or lies, without all the things that are sure to keep us apart: her family's money, my family's secrets, and the murder that binds us.

Natasha's skin makes my heart race. I can feel my magic tugging, wanting to leap outside my control and grow wild. But I rein it in, make myself its master. I'm here to listen. I focus on the infinite information passing underground, so constant it's like a song humming into my palms.

I go perfectly still, waiting for her to hear it too.

Natasha gasps. "What is that?"

I open my eyes and meet her startled gaze. "Magic," I say.

Natasha is staring at me, and instead of anger and suspicion, instead of pain, I see only wonder.

"This is how I tap into the magic, through the roots underground," I say. "Watch." I find a seed of lobelia beneath the earth and I make it grow. The green plant comes up through the soil and opens its leaves, then its delicate purple petals.

Natasha's eyes go wide. "Della," she whispers. "That's beautiful."

Stupidly, I find myself blushing. "Well, I can't exactly take credit for the beauty. I didn't make it, just encouraged it to grow," I say.

"Look at that, Della Lloyd being modest," Natasha says.

I blush again.

"What do you think I can do with my magic?" Natasha asks. "If I can learn to control it like you do?"

"I think . . . I think just about anything you want," I admit.

Natasha's eyes flash with desire, but it's not desire for me. Her look is hungry and anguished and a little wild. The bubble of peace my magic built around us bursts. I remember why we're here—because my mother killed her sister, because Natasha wants answers and revenge. Because, in a moment of despair, I decided to help her get them.

I freeze, my mind reeling. What am I going to do?

How do I get all of us out of this unscathed?

I don't think I can, no matter how hard I try. I'm not just caught between a rock and a hard place, like my manager said—I'm trapped like a fly in a web. And there's not a person in this world who can pluck me out.

TWENTY-FOUR
NATASHA

The woods have gone still around us. The only movement is a roly-poly crawling in the dirt between Della and me. Della looks lost in thought, her lips slightly pursed. She picks up a leaf from the ground and twirls it between her fingers. Then she looks up and catches me staring at her, and I swear her face breaks into ten different expressions at once. There's a vulnerability in her eyes I never expected to see there. Who knew this person existed under all of Della's layers of toughness and spite?

I'd like to lie here under the trees with her all day, listening to the creek gurgle and the leaves sway in the wind. Unwrapping her layers one by one. But there's a question I can't put off any longer.

"Della," I say carefully. "There's something I wanted to ask you about. A rumor I heard."

"A rumor?" Della's brows knit, her suspicions up that fast.

I reach out and curl a tendril of her hair around my finger.

"You know that story about the girl and the pack of dogs in the woods? I heard it was about you."

Della freezes.

I smile. "I'm not trying to accuse you of anything, I'm just worried about you. What really happened?"

She could deny all knowledge of this. She could laugh it off. But she doesn't. She holds her breath for a long time and then lets it out in a whoosh. She opens her mouth to speak and then closes it again.

"I won't be mad at you," I promise.

Della smiles regretfully. "You will, though."

"But you're going to tell me?"

Della nods. "Yeah, I guess it's finally time to tell the truth. But what you have to understand is that I wouldn't have done it if I didn't have to."

"Do what?" I ask, tension squeezing my insides.

"I wouldn't have lied about the dogs."

I let out a breath. "There were no dogs. You lied to the police."

She nods.

"So the police don't really have any reason to blame a pack of feral dogs on my sister's death?"

Shame washes over Della's features. "No."

She was right—I am mad. But even more than that, I'm vindicated. I was right. I was right to fight this feral dog story at every turn.

"Why did you lie about the dogs?" I ask.

"To hide something. Something no one can know about," Della says.

"But you're going to tell me?" I repeat.

Della's face twists with misery. I put my hand over hers. "I care about you," I say, and I mean it. I do care about Della. I want to help her almost as much as I want to get to the bottom of my sister's death. Maybe this is a chance to do both. "Let me help you."

"Do you remember how I told you the magic was going wrong, getting all twisted?" Della asks. "Well, it's done more than ruin a spell. It can . . . it can change us. It did change us, one of us."

"Who?" I ask. "You?" I lean toward her.

Della closes her eyes and her lips come together to form a word. "M—"

Her cell phone dings, its mechanical tone loud and wrong in the stillness. Della's word ends in a gasp. She pulls the phone from her pocket and looks at the screen, then jolts to her feet and steps away from me. Her face goes pale. She starts typing slowly, her hands shaking. You can tell she's not used to texting and it takes her ages.

"What is it?" I ask.

Finally, she looks up at me again and stows the phone away in her pocket. "Come on, we gotta go," she says, grabbing my arm and pulling me away from the creek.

"Della, what's wrong? What was that text?"

She shakes her head. "We've got to get you home, all right?"

"Della, what were you going to tell me? Whose name were you about to say?"

Della's eyes go wild. Dread gnaws my insides.

"Della," I say, unnerved. I've never seen her look so unsettled.

"It's a family matter," she says. "Nothing for you to worry about." But she won't look at me. "Let's just go."

I reach a hand toward her, but she flinches away.

We hike all the way back to Della's in silence, the tension between us so thick I feel like I'm choking. I try every few minutes to get her to talk, but she won't. She won't even stop walking, not until we reach my car.

"Sorry, Natasha, I—" Della moves toward me, but then she shakes her head. "I'll call you, all right?"

She jogs toward the house, and I watch her go. Her hair is lit flaming red with the fading sun. What the hell was that text? What could make a girl like Della lose her composure like that? And why was she so eager to get rid of me?

Most important, what was she about to tell me?

I pull out of the driveway and onto the road, my mind swimming with everything that happened today. I feel like I've lived through a week in the space of a few hours.

My cell phone rings and I answer it automatically, hoping it's Della. "Hello?"

"Where are you?" Georgia asks, not bothering with pleasantries.

"Driving," I say.

"Are you with *her*?" she asks.

"No." But I should be. I shouldn't have left when she asked. Something in my gut tells me Della's not okay, that something bad is happening.

"Good, because I've been doing some research."

"And?"

"And that guy Miles, Della's cousin, the one who was with you when you found Rochelle . . ."

"Yeah, I remember finding my sister's body pretty clearly," I say.

"Look, I just thought you should know that he works at Highland Rim as a janitor. I showed Margo his picture, and she recognized him."

"Lots of people work at the university, Georgia. So what?"

"Margo said he's always in the building where most of Rochelle's classes were. She saw him all the time when she met Rochelle after class. Don't you think it's weird that a guy who had daily access to Rochelle also happens to be cousins with the weirdo family that lives by the nature park where her body was found?"

Her words strike home exactly the way they were meant to. I don't want to believe it, but Miles is the one who made it possible for me to find Rochelle, whose spell led me straight to my sister's body. . . .

Della was about to name someone, a person whose name starts with the letter *M*.

I start to shake so hard I have to pull the car over onto the shoulder of the road. Miles is at Della's house right now. Is he the one who sent her a text that made her grow pale and shaky, that made her get me away as fast as she could?

"Tell me everything," I say.

Georgia starts talking, telling me about Miles's schedule,

how his coworkers described him, everything she could get her hands on. The picture she paints is glaringly similar to every portrait of mass murderers I've ever heard. Miles Lloyd is described as aloof, creepy, and resentful of the wealthy students. He doesn't socialize with his coworkers or smile at students or other staff. He disappears on his lunch breaks. He never talks about his family or hobbies. He's a shadow of a man at Highland Rim.

I said there was a serial killer. I thought it was Jake, but this makes more sense, doesn't it? Miles grew up right by the park and knows the land. He would have all the opportunity in the world.

But what if it really is a coincidence? What if all Georgia is describing is a lonely, quiet man with poor social skills?

"That's everything I've turned up so far. I moved the wildlife cameras to a better spot yesterday. I'm going to review the footage now. I'll call you back if I find anything."

"Okay," I say, my mind spinning.

"What do you want me to do with this information about Miles?" Georgia asks. "Should I keep it to myself, or . . . ?"

"Um," I say. I've seen so little of Miles, but what I have seen hasn't sent alarm bells off in my head. Miles seemed nicer than Della, respectful, almost gentle. But if he's truly innocent, it shouldn't be a problem, should it?

But what if I'm wrong? What if I'm wrong, and the police arrest him and he's innocent but can't prove it because he's poor? What if he spends the rest of his life in jail while the real killer walks free? I'm still not convinced Jake isn't involved.

Besides, I've seen how easily led the police are, how eager they are to take the simple solution.

But if Miles killed Rochelle and Samantha and Kaylee . . . it's a risk I have to take. Not only for me, but also for Della. Because he might hurt her too.

"Tell the police," I say. "Tell them everything you know."

TWENTY-FIVE
DELLA

I bang through the front door, my chest heaving. Miles looks up, relief spreading over his face. Momma lurches off the couch and staggers toward me. She's dirty and haggard, and even thinner than she'd been before. She found a dress somewhere, and it hangs off her gaunt frame in tatters.

I leap forward and catch her before she collapses. She's light as a feather and too exhausted to really fight me, so I move her easily back to the couch. Her lips are chapped and white around the edges, and dark smudges under her eyes make her look ghostly. I run to the kitchen and pour a glass of water at the sink. She tries to push it away, but I make her drink it and soon she's gulping it down thirstily.

"Where've you been, Momma?" I ask.

She can't answer, of course. She can never answer. But her eyes plead with me to understand. She seems more clearheaded than usual, despite her bad physical shape.

"Did you hurt anyone else?" I ask.

She stares at me.

"Why did you come back?" I wait for a response, but I see if I prod her much longer, she'll turn wild on me. I look at Miles, but he's staring at Momma with an unreadable expression that makes me nervous.

"Why don't you take a bath?" I suggest. "I'll run you some water." I pull Momma up off the couch and guide her to the bathroom. Miles stays where he is, his arms crossed.

I put the stopper in the tub and let the water flow. The rush of it mesmerizes her, and Momma soon sits on the toilet lid and watches the tub fill. She sways side to side to music I don't hear. When it's nearly full, I tell her to get in. She pulls the dress over her head and drops it to the floor, where it pools like silk. Then she climbs into the tub and lies back with her eyes closed while the water continues to churn around her. She seems almost normal.

Almost normal, and I almost gave her away to Natasha. I was so close. The terror of that grips me. Why did I do it? Because in that moment it felt like Natasha getting the truth was more important than anything. And maybe some small, pathetic part of me believed she would understand, that she would help me. That I wouldn't be alone with my burden anymore.

When I turn the water off, Momma begins to hum. I hand her a bar of soap and close the door behind me, taking the dress with me. I slide down the door and lean my head against it. Momma's high, clear voice comes through the wood, and tears rise to my eyes. She used to always hum while she bathed, while she worked, while she did anything. All those old mountain airs flowed out of her as natural as breathing.

But that's been twisted too, her songs turned into something dark, something dangerous, a thing the monster can use against me.

I remember the dress in my hands and unball it. It's made of expensive silk and doesn't have any tags inside, which means it must have been designed specifically for the owner. The color is a deep red, set with small gemstones along the single shoulder strap. It's much too big for Momma, maybe a size eight and made for someone tall. It probably cost more than my entire wardrobe. It's ruined now, marked with dirt and probably with blood, though the color of the dress hides it. There are tears in the fabric and the hemline has started to unravel. I recognize it, but I really wish I didn't.

After a few minutes, the front door opens, and Da's and Miles's voices drift down the hallway. Before long, Da is standing in front of me. I look up at him and forget to hide the tears in my eyes.

"Oh, Della, baby," he says, crouching down in front of me.

"She's in there," I say. "And she came home in this."

Da takes the fabric from my hands and holds it up to the weak hallway light. He studies it, turning it this way and that. "Is this the dress Rochelle Greymont was wearing in the photos on the news?"

I nod, misery unspooling in my belly. "Apparently she wore it to that party that she went to the night she disappeared."

"We'll get rid of it. Burn it," Da promises.

"First, can you go find some clothes for Momma to wear?" I don't want to risk leaving this door unattended, and Da can't be trusted as a guard.

He takes the dress with him, and I breathe a sigh of relief to have it out of my hands. But it only takes a second before guilt settles into my gut. That's Natasha's sister's dress, Natasha who I was just kissing, just revealing parts of myself to, parts I've never shown anyone else, Natasha who I almost told—

Da returns with one of Momma's own dresses, one of her old favorites—a black spaghetti-strap summer dress covered in cherry blossom prints, along with a pair of plain white underwear. The familiar fabrics ground me, remind me why I'm doing everything I am for her. Because I love her. Because we belong to one another. Because we are Lloyds.

I steel myself against what I feel for Natasha.

"Do you need help getting her to the prison?" Da asks. He doesn't bother asking if I plan to keep her here at home again. He knows better.

"No, I can manage. Miles might help me. And I'll stay the night with her, just to be safe," I add.

"I'll go find your sleeping bag and camping gear," Da says. He wants so badly to be helpful. But the one thing I really need from him, he can't do.

It's risky taking her back to the prison, but it feels even riskier to leave her here.

In her own clothes, with her skin clean and her hair washed and combed, Momma almost looks like her old self. I offer her

a pair of sandals, but she ignores them, preferring to stay barefoot.

Miles looks up when we walk into the living room together.
His expression is still hard to read. But I'm certain he won't do
anything to harm her now that he's seen her, especially since he
sat by her side while waiting for me to get home. Maybe he'll
actually try to help me now. Help me figure out what to do. At
the very least, he'll want to make sure Momma actually makes
it to the prison.

"You want to come with me?" I ask him.

He nods, his eyes on Momma's face. I wonder if he sees a
shadow of Aunt Sage there. Sage was light where Momma is
dark, but the shape of their faces was the same, the slope of
their noses, the slight dimple in their chins.

Miles puts the supplies and sleeping bag Da prepared for
me in the back of the truck, and I usher Momma onto the front
seat. She scoots close to me when Miles climbs inside. She's
strangely quiet and placid, like a cat that's already eaten its fill
and can't be bothered to hunt. But it could be a ruse, so I keep
one eye on her and one on the road as I drive. The sun is just
beginning to dip below the horizon when I pull into my usual
spot. I need to hurry.

"Come on, please," I say, careful not to touch Momma as I
try to herd her toward the prison. She keeps stopping to listen,
her head cocked to one side. A few times a sly smile comes over
her face. But finally we make it inside. The cool darkness that
must have felt suffocating to so many prisoners feels like salvation to me.

I set up her bed and lock her carefully in the cell. "Try to get some sleep," I say gently, but she only wanders in aimless circles around the small space, humming again.

"What happened? How did you find her?" I finally ask Miles.

He shrugs. "I looked out the front window and she was there, sitting in the middle of the yard, singing as loud as anything. She looked sort of lost and dazed. I went out and got her, and she just came inside."

"Did she say anything?" I ask.

Miles shakes his head. "She sang 'The Bloody Miller,' but that's it. I tried to talk to her, but she kept turning her face away from me. I think she was waiting for you to come home."

"The Bloody Miller" again. The same song she sang at the prison that one morning. Is it a message?

"Why do you think she came back?" I ask instead. "You've been looking for her for over a week. Why now?"

"Maybe it's surrender," he says quietly.

"Surrender?"

Miles's face hardens. "It's time for a long-term solution, Della. This cat-and-mouse tactic isn't working anymore. Next time you might not find her."

I look away. I thought Miles was going to change his mind after he saw her. He's always been the more tenderhearted of the two of us. But I know exactly what he's saying.

"You mean it's time to exterminate the mouse," I say coldly.

"You know I love Aunt Ruby too, Dee," Miles says, his voice dropping an octave. He glances back at her and pain flits across his face. "Even after all she's done."

"Not like I do," I whisper. "She's my mother."

Miles stares fixedly at me now. "Don't you think she came home because she knows it's time, deep down? Deep down, she wants this all to be over?"

"That doesn't sound like her at all, actually," I say. "Momma was never one to give up. I've never seen her surrender to anything."

"Maybe she's ready to surrender to this." Miles tries to take my hand, but I snatch it from his grasp. "And anyway, she's not your mother anymore, not really. She's practically all river siren now."

I ignore him. "Or maybe she's still trying to get us to understand something." She's tried, over and over again with me, but I haven't known what she meant. But there have been clues—her songs, that bloody braid of hair, a look of pleading on her face. None of them felt like her asking me to put her out of her misery.

"Please tell me you're not still thinking someone else could possibly be to blame for this," Miles says, exasperated. "There's only one killer on the Bend, and it's Aunt Ruby."

I shake my head. "I think there might be more. Maybe she's not the only one the magic has changed. I've been seeing signs of something else—heard it in the woods. There were tracks I couldn't place. And there are these strange birds that move in the treetops like shadows. I found Momma singing to them once. And one time they ran me out of the woods when I was trying to find her. I'm telling you—there's something more going on."

"Now you're acting like Uncle Lawrence," Miles says,

practically sneering. "Looking for any excuse. Never thought I'd see a true-born Lloyd so weak."

Before I can think about it, I've drawn back my hand and slapped him. "Get out," I say, breathing hard. "Get out now, or I'll find a way to curse you to within an inch of your life."

"We're not done here," Miles says, but he leaves all the same. I was going to let him take my truck for the night, but now he'll have a long walk back to Da's.

Alone again, I slump to the floor. I let myself crouch for five deep breaths, arms wrapped around my knees. And then I get up and start to prepare for the night.

I check again to be sure Momma's cell is secure, then I unroll my sleeping bag and set up a camping lantern. The yellow light floods the dark for a moment but then seems to recede, as if the darkness is too much for it. But it's enough for me to read by. I lie on my belly on my sleeping bag and pull out a well-worn copy of *Tennessee Native Plants*, which is about as close to a spell book as this family has. I memorized the contents a long time ago, but it's comforting to thumb through the soft-edged pages.

When my eyelids start to get heavy, I decide I may as well try to get some sleep before Momma's rages begin. I don't need to worry about rats or other animals; they seem to sense the predator inside Momma long before darkness falls. I switch off the lantern.

I curl up in my sleeping bag, eager for dreams to sweep me away from this prison, this burden, this horrible choice I have to make. But my mind is all twisted in knots—Natasha versus

Momma versus Miles—everyone wanting something different from me. And I don't know who to choose. I feel small and helpless and utterly alone.

As though my mother knows, as though that last bit of human inside her knows, she begins to sing.

The song is called "Tam Lin," a Scottish ballad she used to sing for me at bedtime. It's about a woman, Janet, who must rescue her true love, Tam Lin, from the Queen of the Fairies. When the fairies ride on Halloween, Janet must pull Tam Lin down from his white horse. Tam Lin warns her that the fairies will transform him into any number of hideous beasts—a snake, a lion—to try to make Janet let him go, but she must hold on until he becomes her beloved knight again. She does as he says and wins her true love back from the Queen, who admits defeat.

With every verse Momma sings, my heart opens to her a little bit more. Miles looks at her and sees a beast, a monster. But I look at her with a daughter's eyes. If I hang on long enough, if I refuse to let her go, maybe she'll transform into my momma again. And then I'll snatch her back from the magic before it carries her off into the unreachable night.

TWENTY-SIX
NATASHA

I stand trembling in the dusky prison, gripping my pocketknife, listening hard. I don't hear anything. But I know Miles and Della are in here somewhere. Or at least they were. It took me so long to gather up my courage to come inside; for all I know, they left through another exit.

I still can't believe I followed them in here. I sat by the side of the road after hanging up with Georgia for a long time, stunned by what she'd told me about Miles. But the second I saw Della's truck flying by with Miles in the passenger seat, I knew I was going to follow them.

I don't know where I thought they might go, but it sure as hell wasn't here. I could have called the police, could have kept driving. But I didn't. Instead, I watched them slip into the prison with an older, long-haired woman. And then I followed them inside, with Dad's pocketknife and my pepper spray gripped tight in my fists.

I don't know how much time has passed since then. I don't know how long I've been in this dark, musty prison, moving painfully slowly through the rubble, straining to hear the slightest sound.

I'm scared, but my anger is bigger than my fear. All this time I've been focused on Jake Carr, convinced he was the one to take my sister's life. But it was Miles. The guy who pretended to help me find Rochelle. Who pretended to care. He probably laughed at me while I kneeled over my sister's ruined body, my world being torn in two.

And Della? I'm not even ready to face up to what her part in all this might be.

So now I'm here, in an abandoned prison with at least two witches inside. I slide the knife into my pocket and pull out my cell phone. I want so badly to use its flashlight to find my way, but I don't want to risk being spotted. I'll have to rely on the weak, blue-tinged twilight coming in from the filthy windows near the ceiling.

Before I can put the phone back in my pocket, the screen lights up with a call. Georgia. Thank God I remembered to put it in silent mode or I'd be busted. With a sigh, I press the icon to send the call to voicemail. Whatever Georgia knows will have to wait. I keep moving.

The sound of someone singing draws me down a more open wing of the prison. The voice is low and lonesome-sounding yet filled with unmistakable love. Love that hurts, that bites, that devours.

I follow the voice until I find a woman in a cell. She is small and slight. Her long, dark hair falls to her waist. She stands against the bars of the cell in a sundress, singing for an empty room.

No, not empty. There's someone in a sleeping bag on the floor outside the cell. Just one person. Is it Miles, or is it Della? I grip my knife even more tightly and creep toward the slumbering body.

Della's face is illuminated by the dim light of a lantern. She's asleep.

I stand still a moment, deciding what to do. Finally, I nudge Della with my foot and she bolts awake, sitting up fast. She raises her hands defensively, as if expecting someone to strike her.

But then she recognizes me. "Natasha?" she asks, squinting up at me.

I point at the woman in the cell, and all my calm leaves me. "What the fuck is this? What kind of creepy shit are you up to?"

Della rises to her knees and raises her hands. "Look, you need to get out of here. You really don't understand what's going on."

"Let her out. Right now," I say. "This is totally fucked." I look back at the woman, who has stopped singing. "Ma'am, are you all right? I'm going to help you." If she understands, she gives no indication, staring back at me curiously.

"What did you do to her? Is she drugged?" I stride over and pull at the padlock.

Della sighs. "She's not drugged. That's my mother. And I

promise you, you really don't wanna do that." She turns up the lamplight, illuminating the despicable conditions of the prison cell.

"Why? Is this—did Miles do this? Is he coming back?" I grip my pocketknife and wonder if I'd be able to use it, if I needed to.

"What? No, he doesn't have anything to do with it." Della's on her feet now, walking toward me.

I try to make my voice gentle. "You don't have to protect him anymore, Della. I can help you. I can make sure he never hurts you or anyone else ever again."

For some reason, Della's mother throws back her head and laughs.

"Natasha, you really need to get out of here," Della says. "You don't want to be here when the sun finishes setting."

"Is that when he's coming back?"

Now Della's the one whose voice gentles. "No one's trying to hurt anyone. I promise. My mother is dangerous at night, and we're keeping it a secret because we don't want anyone to take her away from us. So we handle it ourselves."

"This isn't humane," I say, gesturing around the prison. "Why don't you keep her at home?"

"It's complicated," Della says.

I laugh. Complicated. As if that's enough to explain all this. "God, I knew there was something going on with you all. I knew it. If you don't let her out right now, I'm going to call the police." I take out my phone.

Della starts toward me, as if to snatch the phone from my

grasp. I back away until the cool bars of the cell press into my shoulders. I try to unlock the phone, but my fingers are shaking and I keep mistyping my password.

"Get away from there," Della yells, and then someone grabs me from behind and yanks me hard against the metal of the bars, making me drop my phone. Bony fingers catch in my hair, pulling back my head. A skinny arm snakes around my stomach.

"Momma, let her go," Della says, her voice wavering. The woman makes some movement I can't see.

"I'm not letting you out," Della says. "I don't care what you do to her."

I go perfectly still, my eyes locked on Della. Is she bluffing? I can't tell. Her face is impassive, her posture relaxed.

The woman's fingers clench convulsively in my hair, and I try not to, but I cry out. Then she lets go of me, and I stumble forward. I dash away from the cell and turn to look inside. Della's mother has doubled over, as if in terrible pain.

"What did you do? What's wrong with her?" I ask.

"Just watch," Della says, her voice suddenly resigned.

And before my eyes, the woman begins to change.

First, her hair grows longer and turns a muddy green color. Inexplicably, water begins to drip off the tips, as though she's been standing in the rain. Then her skin takes on a green-gray tint, and webs grow between her fingers, which lengthen into claws. She hides the rest of her transformation behind her long fall of hair. But I can feel the very air change around her, the threat of violence looming.

"Della, what is this?" I hiss. I take one step toward the cell, but Della pulls me back.

"Don't," she says.

I keep hold of Della's hand, gripping hard. She's the only thing in this room that feels safe or makes sense.

Her ghastly metamorphosis apparently complete, the woman crouches on the cell floor, surrounded by a curtain of dripping-wet hair. She begins to hum. Her voice isn't the same one I heard when I arrived. Now it is deep and full as the bottom of the river, moving with a soft rocking. There's a teasing, lapping quality that makes everything inside me want to float toward her.

I let go of Della's hand again and take a few steps toward the cell. Della tries to yank me back, but I fight her, pushing her hard enough to make her trip over a pile of bricks. I have to get to this strange, wild creature. I *have* to.

By the time Della steadies herself, I'm already standing at the bars of the cage, my hands gripping the metal.

The creature's song stops a half second before she lunges. She moves like lightning, roaring up with a mouth of teeth, her claws extended.

I scream. Della grabs the back of my shirt and yanks me to the ground with her. We lie together in a heap for one startled second and then I'm moving again. This time, I'm desperate to get away from the monster. Della tries to keep hold of me, but she can't. I push away from her, slip over something and fall, and then get up and run into the darkness.

I barely look where I'm placing my feet, my entire being focused on getting out of this prison, away from that creature.

Della might know the terrain, but she's no match for my years of running track. The sound of her breathing fades into the distance. I hurdle over an old chair and nearly topple into a brick wall. Then I'm down another hallway, running toward the door I entered. In my panic, it takes a while to find it, but then I'm outside in the fresh, clean air and racing for my car.

Just before I reach it, I realize a man is leaning up against it, his shape hardly more than a silhouette. But I recognize him. A long, lanky body, tousled hair. The tip of his cigarette burns red.

He spots me and yells my name, but I've already turned and raced away. I fumble in my pockets for my cell phone, but it's gone. I must have dropped it when Della's mother grabbed me. My pocketknife is gone too, not that I really knew how to use it. I don't even have my pepper spray.

Shit.

I run until my breath comes short, until I've exhausted the panic that drove me out of that prison. My mind is a muddled swampland of questions and doubts, with a big dose of self-recriminations.

If I hadn't let my anger get the best of me. If I'd called the police. If I'd had the presence of mind to keep my phone. If I hadn't trusted Della.

If if if.

But now it's nighttime and I'm stuck out here in Hicksville with a monster, two witches, and zero fucking clue what to do next.

I pause by the road to catch my breath. A huge diesel truck

comes roaring toward me, its headlights so bright I have to put my hand in front of my eyes. Taking what might be my only chance at help tonight, I stick out my thumb as the truck races past, blaring heavy metal music.

The truck stops with a squeal of brakes and reverses. That's when I notice a huge Confederate flag on the back. The window rolls down and a truck full of drunk teenage boys leer at me.

Oh, absolutely fucking not.

I flee toward the tree line, and the truck drives away, filled with the sound of raucous laughter. Forget hitchhiking—I'd rather take my chances with Della and her monster. And Miles. Miles is the one I really need to worry about, I remind myself.

Because even if she lied to me, I don't think any of this is Della's fault. And even if it is, I don't think she's the dangerous one. I think she's just caught up in something too big for her. Georgia thinks Della's a con artist or something worse, but she hasn't gotten to know Della the way I have, hasn't seen her moments of vulnerability, hasn't seen her magic.

Then again, Georgia would say that's exactly why I'm being fooled—because Della has wrapped me up in her influence.

I'm not so blinded, though, that I can't recognize Miles for a threat. I look around again to see if he's following me. There's no sign of him.

The only places around here besides the prison and a bunch of abandoned warehouses are Della's house and the nature park. If I can get to the nature center, maybe someone will still be there. At worst, I can break a window and use a phone.

My mind made up, I start what's probably going to be a

two-hour walk. In the dark. On my own.

I'm terrified—that something is going to happen to me before I can find out what happened to my sister, that my parents are going to lose another daughter. But I'm also terrified for myself. Raw, aching terror rips through me with every step.

I hesitate when I reach the bridge that leads over the river. The one place on earth where I have magic. It's paltry and untrained, but it's something. I stare down into the rushing water and hope it will rise up to meet me when I need it.

As soon as I cross over the bridge and onto the nature park, I hear something moving in the high brush. The smell of blood wafts toward me on the wind, raising every hair at the back of my neck.

This world would have me believe that my life is nothing, that my body is mere fuel for the fire. But it's mine and I want to keep it.

I *will* keep it.

I will.

When the monster leaps from its hiding place, I'm already running.

TWENTY-SEVEN
DELLA

I hesitated for only a second before I set off after her. But that was all it took for Natasha to gain a lead I'd never catch up to. I only wish I knew what she's planning to do—call the cops, pretend she never saw this, check herself into a psychiatric hospital? Miles promised to go looking for her, and he's much more likely to track her than I am. I'm sure she's long gone, though—probably called someone to pick her up.

So I go back into the prison, back to Momma's cell. The monster is raging now, pacing and skittering back and forth. She shakes the bars and grinds them with her teeth. She lets out a miserable, heart-wrenching cry that sounds both human and animal at once.

"Shit!" I yell, slumping down onto my sleeping bag. The monster stops making noise and watches me.

If Natasha brings the police here tonight . . . there's nothing I can do. I can't move Momma. I can't let her free. I can't leave her here alone. There's nothing I can do but sit here and wait for whatever comes. Miles said if he found her, he would try to talk Natasha down. That's the most I can hope for.

I won't be sleeping tonight. The monster purrs and chatters, slithering around her cage. No matter which way she turns, I feel her eyes on me. I climb inside the sleeping bag and pull it over my head so she can't see me. She stays strangely quiet for hours, often putting her ear to the ground for long minutes at a time, like she's listening to the earth.

Around what I think must be midnight, she snaps into terrifying life. She doesn't try any of her usual sly tactics. She's wild, roaring and throwing herself at the bars of her cell. I've never seen her try so hard to escape before. She puts so much pressure on the bars that bits of ceiling plaster float down. But the cell does what it was made for—it keeps the monster inside.

I watch her all night, somehow nodding off every few minutes and then lurching back into watchfulness. All night the river siren bellows and rails, shakes the iron bars and beats the concrete walls. I think she must be tired out by the time the birds begin to sing outside, but she rages right up until the moment she changes.

Then her human body slumps to the floor. She doesn't move or speak. She lies there, blinking into the far distance, like she's still seeing through the monster's eyes.

TWENTY-EIGHT
NATASHA

The world narrows to the ground in front of me and the panting breath of the monster at my back. I keep trying to gather my thoughts and do something besides react, but I can't think, can't plan. All I can do is run, terror wrapping around my heart so tight I feel every beat of my pulse in my eardrums.

My body knows it's in danger, knows how close death is. Is this how Rochelle felt right before she died?

Whatever's after me lets out a low moan of desire, its voice like a wolf's but deeper, more ragged. I risk a glance over my shoulder and make out the shadow of an enormous, loping creature several yards behind me. I stumble over a root and careen into a tree.

Just like that, I've lost my lead. The creature is going to catch me. I glance up into the tree overhead, some sort of evergreen. It has lots of low-growing branches, perfect for climbing.

My only hope is that the monster at my back can't climb.

I launch myself up, moving from branch to branch as quickly as I can. The bark is rough and sticky with sap, and needles graze my skin, pricking me in places. I've never climbed a tree before, but I've done indoor rock climbing with Georgia and Odette enough times to know how.

The creature circles the tree below me, moaning and scratching at the trunk. It can't climb. I'm at least twenty feet up, and it can't get me.

Relief floods me and I let my muscles relax.

Just then, the branch under my foot cracks and I instinctively reach for the one over my head, but my fingers only graze it as I fall.

I crash into the branches beneath me, bark and needles scratching my face and hands. I keep reaching out for branches and missing them. Finally, ten feet above the ground, I hit a sturdy branch and manage to hang on, stopping my descent. The sudden weight of my own body wrenches my shoulder, and I cry out in pain.

The creature below me responds with a pleased-sounding snarl and leaps.

I yank my feet up and brace them against the trunk of the tree just in time to avoid the creature's teeth, which snap closed on empty air. Its weight hits the ground with a thud that shakes the tree. Its breath washes over me, the stench of garbage and carrion and something worse. The smell seems to get inside me, making me feel weak, making fighting seem useless.

It snarls, resuming its pacing.

And I snarl at myself, "Move!" Whatever that hideous creature is, I'm no baby deer, no helpless mouse.

I start climbing the tree again, more carefully this time, always keeping a firm hold when I take a step. Once I'm twenty feet or so up again, I look down into the gloom.

The beast is only a shadow against the darkness. It moves fitfully, as though angry, starting up a whining, moaning complaint, clearly frustrated.

I cling tightly to the trunk of the tree, my heart still beating in my ears. But I'm safe. As long as I stay in this tree, I'm safe. I lower myself to a thick branch and test its strength before settling down, pressed into the crook of the limb, letting the trunk take most of my weight.

I lay my face against the rough bark, blessing Georgia for every time she dragged me to the climbing wall.

Georgia.

She's the only person who might know where I am, who might be able to send help. She knows about Miles, has certainly told the police about him by now. Surely, they'll figure it out and come find me.

Suddenly, I remember she called me earlier, before I found Della and her mother in the prison. I let the call go to voicemail. I wonder what she was calling to say. I wonder if she knows anything more about Miles. Or if her wildlife cameras showed something.

The creature stops pacing and the woods go silent. Did it leave? Or is it trying to trick me? I peer down and make out the barest outline of its shadow sitting beneath the tree. As if it senses I'm looking at it, the creature tilts its head up to gaze at me. Its eyes are startlingly yellow in the darkness. I have to bite back a scream.

Weren't Della's mother's eyes green, even after she changed? Green like Della's.

This isn't the same monster.

There's more than one.

The knowledge fills me with inexplicable rage. The truth is that anyone could have killed Rochelle—Jake, Miles, Della's mother, whatever—or whoever—this beast is. The world is just bursting at the seams with monsters.

"Fuck you," I yell at the creature. "Fuck you, fuck you, fuck you!" I scream so loud that something in my throat wrenches and I start coughing.

The creature below lets out a low, rumbling growl. I reach up and break off a weakened branch and hurl it down at the beast, striking it. "Fuck you," I croak one last time. Its eyes watch me from the darkness, malicious and patient. It's going to wait me out.

I rest my face against the rough bark of the tree, close my eyes, and weep. Some part of me wants to just fall out of this tree and let the beast have me.

I'm so tired. Tired of fighting. Tired of Rochelle being dead. Tired.

But I have to stay alive, stay safe, for as long as I can. I owe her that much. And I owe myself.

* * *

I spend the night slumped against the tree trunk, occasionally nodding off, coming awake with a horrible jerk of fear. The last time this happens, I nearly tumble out of the tree but catch myself just in time, gritting my teeth at the pain in my injured shoulder. I peer down at the forest floor, but the monster's gone. It must have found easier prey.

When dawn begins to break, I start to prepare myself for the climb down. My shoulder is on fire, though I think it's only sprained. But my neck and back ache too, and my legs feel numb. I gently stretch all my muscles, grateful I'm in good shape from years of track and fencing. Otherwise, I'd never get back down this tree with a sprained shoulder. I scan the horizon until I find the nature center.

All that matters is getting there and calling for help. Slowly, slowly, I begin to climb down. It's harder than going up, and several times I nearly slip down the tree trunk when I misjudge the distance to the next limb.

Finally, I reach the lowest limb, which is perhaps four feet off the ground. I cling to it, staring around for any signs of the beast who treed me. But it's gone.

I drop to the ground, cursing the loud thud my feet make. I stay in a crouch for a moment, waiting. But nothing happens.

So I stand upright and stretch again, working the pain and stiffness from my muscles. I'm so tired, the thought of hiking all the way to the nature center is exhausting. I set off in that direction anyway, walking quickly but warily, watching all around me for the beast. I snatch up a big stick from the ground as I walk. I grip it tightly, drawing some comfort from its weight.

After twenty minutes of walking, I start to worry I might be going the wrong way. It should be easy to walk in a straight line, but in the woods, it's not. I keep having to go around trees and brambles, snake around small creeks. I haven't seen any sign of the hiking trail yet.

I'm beginning to think about climbing a tree to see where I am when I hear footsteps, heavy ones, as if the person is wearing boots. They crunch over fallen leaves and sticks, not troubling to hide their presence. I go absolutely still, waiting, clutching my stick.

I'm too tired to run, too weak to fight.

A man strides out of the trees ahead of me, his eyes shaded by a large brimmed hat. He's dressed in a tan shirt and pants and carrying a large thermos. He doesn't notice me, his eyes trained on the trees above.

It's a forest ranger.

"Sir," I say, but my voice is hardly more than a croak. I clear my throat and try again. "Excuse me, sir," I say. Jesus, only a Greymont would be this polite in an emergency. "Hey!" I yell.

The ranger's head snaps toward me. "Good morning," he calls, his voice cheerful. He's oblivious to my distress.

"Can you—can you help me?" I ask, suddenly feeling all the weakness in my limbs.

The ranger begins to move in my direction. "Are you lost? Did you mean to leave the hiking trail? The park is closed, you know."

When he gets closer, I recognize him. This is the ranger who first picked Georgia, Margo, and me up the night of the search party. And he's the one who warned me about Della's family.

I should have listened.

He seems to recognize me too. "Miss Greymont, isn't it? What are you doing out here so early?" He cocks his head at me, concerned. "I thought we agreed you would stay out of the park."

Tears suddenly fill my eyes, clog my throat. I try to speak but can't get any words out. All I can do is stand here, trembling in every limb.

The ranger's face softens. He unscrews the thermos and pours coffee into the lid. "Here, this will warm you up."

I take the cup and drink gratefully. The coffee is cheap-tasting, bitter, but it pushes the lump back down my throat.

"Thank you, Mr.—" I rasp. "I'm so sorry, I can't remember your name."

He smiles. "Grange. Robert Grange."

I nod. "Can I use your phone?"

"Of course," he says, reaching for his belt automatically. "Well, damn. Must have left it charging on my bedside table," he says regretfully.

"Oh, well, can you show me to the nature center?"

"They haven't opened up for the day yet, but my cabin is just up here. You can use my phone there," he says.

I nod, and he puts a gentle hand on my shoulder, steering me. "You want to tell me what's going on?" he asks. "Is this—did you have a run-in with those Lloyd people?"

I nod, fresh tears gathering in my eyes.

He sighs. "Did they—did they hurt you?"

I shake my head. "They tried. I think—I think they're what happened to my sister."

"What do you mean?"

I don't know how to begin explaining what I've seen in the last twelve hours. Della's mother in the cell. Her transformation. The beast in the woods. "They—they're not normal," I say. "They're monsters."

Grange is quiet, as if unsure what to say.

It must be the exhaustion, the shock wearing off maybe, but I'm starting to feel a little dizzy. A little out of it. We must be near the road because I can hear the distant noise of a car. I've never loved the sound so much.

"Here we are," Grange says as we break out of the woods. I look up and see the back of a small cabin, lined with chopped wood. An ax is buried in a stump in the yard. Grange unlocks the door and flips on the lights.

We emerge into the kitchen. It's all very rustic, very mountain man–ish. But clean, neat, orderly, nothing out of place. That's all I can really notice before the room dips. I stagger, struggling to keep my balance.

Grange puts a steadying hand under my arm. "Whoa there. You all right?"

I nod, and that simple movement makes the room turn upside down. My knees buckle.

"Here, here," Grange says, half carrying me to the couch. "Sit down. I'll get you some water. You're probably dehydrated."

"Thank you," I say, struggling to make the room right itself. I'm here for a reason, but I can't remember what it is. Why did I come here? What's happening?

Grange returns with a glass of water. I take a few measured sips before I have to set it down on the coffee table in front of me to avoid dropping it. Even so, some of the water splashes onto the table. "S-sorry," I say, hearing how slurred my voice sounds. What's wrong with me?

"Just lean back there, darlin', and rest a spell. You'll be all right," Grange says, and his voice is so soothing, I do as he says. I close my eyes, let my hands drop onto the sofa on either side of my lap.

I feel a weight settle onto the couch. I turn my head, open my eyes. Grange is sitting next to me, his body turned toward me. His eyes study me. They're a strange brown-gold color that reminds me of autumn and full moons and apple cider. He smiles, and it's a gentle thing, all soft lips and crinkling eyes. But he's too close to me.

He takes my hand in his, runs his thumb over the back of my hand. My skin prickles a warning.

I move my hand, casually, and pretend I need to scratch my nose. Then I wedge it into the space between the cushions. My fingers touch something cold and solid. It's a ring with a setting, the smoothness of a large gemstone.

"I don't normally do things this way," Grange says, pushing a lock of hair off my forehead with infinite tenderness.

"Do what?" I ask, letting my eyes flit down to my hand.

Rochelle's sapphire ring lies in my palm.

Tears spring to my eyes. One begins to course down my cheek. Grange wipes it away with the pad of his thumb. He puts his thumb into his mouth and lets out a soft *mmm*.

He sees the ring but shows no surprise. He left it for me.

The state of this house shows me he's meticulous. He'd notice a ring wedged between cushions. He wanted me to find it. He wanted me to know.

Rage and terror leap into my chest and up my throat so fast I almost choke. I make myself take in one rattling breath.

Grange sighs. "Drugging a girl—it's not really my thing. But I'm short on time this morning."

"What are you going to do to me?" I ask, hating the fear in my voice.

Grange smiles again, but this time, I see the softness for the lie it is. His hand that was trailing gently through my hair tightens into a fist, pulling at the base of my skull.

I'm struggling to keep my eyes open, blackness threatening at the edges of my vision. But I squeeze Rochelle's ring, and the setting digs into my palm, a sharp, cold pain that keeps me here, keeps me conscious.

"Everything I did to her," he whispers.

I clench my fist around the ring.

Help me, I pray. *Help me.* But I don't pray to God. I pray to this piece of godforsaken wilderness that Della Lloyd calls the Bend. I pray to the magic of Della's great-grandmother. And maybe, maybe a little bit, I pray to Della too. *Help me.*

A cell phone rings. Grange ignores it at first, but then he groans and pulls it from his pocket. So he had it all along. "Grange," he grunts.

He listens for a moment. "On my way," he says. His voice is calm, but I see the anger in his eyes, the frustration. He stands and walks into another room.

I take my chance. My limbs are heavy, my head spinning,

but somehow I climb off the couch. I stagger through the room toward the kitchen and reach for the back door.

My hand closes on the knob just as I'm yanked backward by my hair.

"Oh no, you don't," Grange says. And then he strikes me, hard, in the side of my head.

I crash to the floor and the room goes black.

TWENTY-NINE
DELLA

I fall asleep near dawn, and when I wake it's completely bright outside. It must be nine already, judging by the play of light on the high prison walls. Natasha could have done anything by now. I might find police at my door. But if she told them about the prison, they'd have already come here. So if she blabbed, she left the prison out of it. Cast blame on us another way.

I hurry to pack up my things and stow them against the wall. I push fresh water and food into Momma's cell. She lies with her back to me, and I don't try to speak to her. Miles is nowhere to be seen, but I can't waste time looking for him. I need to get home and see what the next crisis is.

I run to my truck and drive home as fast as I dare. When I pull up the driveway, my body goes cold. Five police vehicles are parked across the yard, and men mill around with gloves on, taking pictures, collecting samples. Da sits by the ruined column on the front porch with his head in his hands. I go up to him, touch his shoulder, and when he looks up, I can see he's hungover. But his face fills with relief when he sees me.

"What's going on?" I ask.

"Miles got arrested," Da says.

Shit. "What happened?" I ask, rubbing my tired, burning eyes.

Da shakes his head. "They came in with a warrant to search the place about half an hour ago. Miles was here spending the night, and they put him in cuffs right off the bat. They asked a lot of questions about you."

Nothing about Momma, then. "But why? What reason did they give?"

"Those missing girls. Some anonymous tip about us being involved somehow. The police got a judge on the phone last night, I guess. Worked fast. You have any idea why?"

"It's a long story, but Rochelle Greymont's sister saw Momma change last night."

Da's face drains of color. "How the hell—"

I shake my head. "Not now. Not here. Let's just sit tight and wait to see what happens." My mind starts spinning through everything Natasha might have told the police. It must have been something about Miles, but what could she have told them? And why didn't she give up Momma? Or me?

"We've got something," a woman yells from inside the house. I bolt inside before the uniformed officer at the door can grab me. I run into Da's room and see the blond cop from the other day. Her blue-gloved hands hold a dress up to the light.

Oh, fuck.

Fuck.

We are 100 percent fucked.

I sink onto Da's bed. Detective Long bustles in. "What is it?"

"I think this dress belongs to one of the missing women—Rochelle Greymont. Isn't this the one she was wearing in those photos?"

"Bag it," the detective says.

"That's mine," I say desperately. "It was my homecoming dress."

He turns. "Outside, please, Miss Lloyd. I think we've heard quite enough of your tales."

I walk slowly back through the house and return to Da's side. "You were supposed to get rid of the dress," I say in a furious whisper. "Now it's in our house, covered in all of our DNA or whatever. It was in your *bedroom*. Do you know what that looks like?"

"I'm sorry," he groans. But he doesn't give an excuse—we both know he got drunk and forgot to burn the dress.

I'm going to have to choose. I see that now—Da or Momma. She came home wearing the dress. She's violent and unstable, even when she's not in monster form. There won't be any other evidence to tie Da to the missing girls. I either give her up or I lose Da. Those are my choices. And that's if I'm lucky.

I put my head in my hands. Da and I sit side by side like that for a long time while men and machinery move around us. Hours pass. Any moment now they are going to haul Da into jail and interrogate him, maybe me too. Or they'll turn me over to social services.

Detective Long comes outside and begins to move toward us when a uniformed officer stops him with a hand on his arm. He tries to keep his voice down, but I hear him. "Sir, Natasha Greymont—the younger sister—was reported missing last night. One of her friends said she knew Natasha was spending a lot of time here, that she was most likely here last night."

The detective's eyes flit lightning fast to Da and me. He pulls the officer to one side and begins to ask him rapid-fire questions I can't hear the answers to.

Natasha's missing. But Momma was locked up all night. The river siren couldn't have hurt her. Couldn't have killed her. She must have gotten lost running away. It couldn't have been Momma. But if anything has happened to Natasha, it's still my fault. I'm still to blame. There's plenty on the Bend that could hurt her. What if she's—

An image of her dead like Rochelle flashes through my mind—the twisted, bloody body, the open staring eyes—

The force of it makes my head spin. Sweat breaks out all over my body.

I watch to make sure no one is looking at me, and then I slip quietly away, around the side of the house and then down the hill. It's going to be a long walk without my truck, but I don't see a way around it. I start running toward the prison.

After an hour of half running and half walking, I am skirting inside the crumbling walls. There are still no police here. The prison is as quiet as when I left it. First, I need to make sure Natasha isn't here. I start at Momma's cell, in case Natasha came back for another look. Momma's asleep, or pretending to be. I leave her alone.

I step on something that gives an ominous-sounding crack. Natasha's cell phone.

Jesus, she didn't even have her phone last night. She couldn't have called for help unless she found someone to help her. And clearly she didn't.

The battery is nearly dead. There are dozens of notifications on the screen. Texts and calls from her parents, from Margo, from Georgia. I enter the simple passcode I saw her use a few times when we were together, and the phone unlocks. It feels wrong to violate Natasha's privacy, but I read the texts, hoping for a clue to help me find her. Then I listen to the voice mails, and one from Georgia stops me in my tracks.

"Nat, I found something else you should know about. On the cameras. There was a dude, I think maybe a park ranger from the way he was dressed, but the video quality's not great. Anyway, he was at the place where you found Rochelle's—where you found her. And he sort of bent down and, like, caressed the ground. I thought he was just doing ranger-y stuff like tracking an animal or something, but then the motherfucker lay down and, like, wallowed around. It was so bizarre. Call me back and let me know what you want me to do. I already put in that tip about your creepy friends. Love you."

Miles and I are undoubtedly the creepy friends. Georgia must be the reason the cops are swarming my house right now. The reason Miles is in jail. I'd be pissed if I didn't have enough to worry about already.

I look at the time stamp. This came before Natasha showed up at the prison last night. I don't know what Georgia means about the cameras, but Natasha must have. But she didn't get this message. She doesn't know about the forest ranger. Is he the reason she's missing, or is she just lost out on the Bend? Either way, she's in trouble and it's my fault.

I hurry back outside, run across the bridge over the river, and plunge into the trees.

The bright sunlight of this morning has faded, replaced by clouds. Rain is on the way, and the woods are dim and moist. I stay away from the trails and keep to the deer tracks, watching for any sign of Natasha or anyone else. But the woods are empty, except an occasional shadow moving overhead. I hike in the direction of the oak grove. Maybe Natasha will be at the locust tree, where we found Rochelle. It seems as good a place to look as any.

I walk for ten minutes without seeing or hearing anything. Rain begins to fall, pooling in the leaves and then dripping onto my shoulders and head in big plops. The sky grows darker and thunder begins to rumble in the distance, but it stays far away, a distant threat. The rain picks up, filling the trees with a steady sound and making the smell of earth rise up strong and sharp in the heavy air. Every animal must have sought shelter by now, yet there are still blurred shapes in the treetops, fluttering their wings.

Then the whistling begins. It's almost drowned out by the rain at first, but it grows louder, echoing from tree to tree. At first I think it must be a kind of birdsong I've never heard before, but then the melody emerges, unmistakably. Whatever is up there, it's whistling "The Bloody Miller," Momma's recent favorite. I shiver and hurry forward.

The rain beats against my skin, sharp as needles. A wind comes up over the river, buffeting me, as if it's trying to throw me off track. It catches the very breath from my lungs.

My hair is plastered to my face, and my clothes hang heavy on me. At least the rain will help confuse my tracks if the police come looking for me. I walk steadily until I reach the locust tree. It sits quietly alone in the rain, its blossoms spread like soaked trash around it. There's no sign of Natasha or anyone else. I slump against the tree, next to the place where the big slashes rent its bark. Those are already beginning to heal over, no longer so fresh and garish-looking.

I push my wet hair off my forehead and tip my face up, letting the rain wash over it, trying to think of what to do next.

Then the whistling starts back up. It's coming from directly overhead, and the fluttering of wings is back. I look up, blinking hard against the drops of water that fall into my eyes. Blurred gray shapes flit in the branches above me, whistling "The Bloody Miller" back and forth to one another.

The creatures' voices sound like birds, but not any one I can identify. It's hard even to say if they sound high or low, throaty or shrill. The song they're making is more emotion than notes, more feeling than sound, like it's reverberating in my chest instead of my ears. "The Bloody Miller" is only a container for grief and rage and hopelessness. It's like the river's song.

I shift to my knees and then sink to the ground, holding on to the rough bark of the locust and peering up into the branches, straining to make out the source of the whistling. If this were any other tree, I'd climb it, but wicked thorns protrude from the bark in clusters. Maybe that's why the birds have chosen it—they're protected.

I do the only thing I can think to: I hum back a verse. My voice is poor, nothing like Momma's, but it seems to be what they were waiting for. They sing louder and beat their wings, as if pleased I understand.

"What is it?" I say. "What are you trying to tell me?" The shapes begin to swoop and dive among the branches, as if they're frustrated. They are each about the size of a barred owl, but their shapes shift and mutate like shadows playing along a wall. One swoops by my head and I catch a glimpse of wicked, curled talons, each as long as my pinkie finger.

Next time the bird thing comes close, I reach out a hand to touch its feathers, but they are like a cold mist. It's not that my hand goes through, but that there is simply a sense of nothingness there. The creature turns its neck and looks at me over its wing, and I nearly yelp. There are human eyes set there among the beak and feathers.

Eyes that look a lot like Rochelle Greymont's.

Then with a voice almost human, she—not an it, I see now, but a she—begins to sing the words of the song, picking up after the miller has gruesomely murdered the girl and lies in bed fearing judgment.

There I lay trembling all the night,
For I could take no rest,
And perfect flames of hell did flash,
Like lightning in my face.

But instead of moving on to the killer's arrest and his moralistic promise that anyone who commits a crime like his will end up hanging on the gallows tree, she sings verses I've never heard before.

> Then the wraith flew to my bedside
> A girl she was no more,
> She slashed at me with burning claws
> And knocked me to the floor.

> The girl did beat and gash and tear
> Until the room shone with my gore
> "And you shall pay for all you've done
> Your hell I will be evermore."

I stand openmouthed, listening to the owl girl continue to sing. Momma told me once that these old murder ballads used to have different endings, before they were brought to the New World. In those endings, the women murdered in the songs got supernatural revenge on their killers. She said that's how a murder ballad ought to end. They should end bloody, just like they started.

But why is a bird with human eyes singing the same murder ballad Momma sang to me the morning after Rochelle disappeared? What is she trying to say to me?

As I watch and listen to the flitting ghost birds, I realize why they seem so familiar, despite their strangeness. They are a part of the Bend, part of its beating heart, yet they don't belong here either. There's something jarring about them—they are a sign of illness, a sign of wrongness. Like the river siren, they are the product of the Bend's wayward magic.

I was wrong about them before; they clearly don't want to hurt me. They want me to hear them, to see them. Like the river. Like the very earth I walk on. They are trying to make me understand.

But I can't communicate with birds the way Momma does or command butterflies and moths like Miles. I'm grounded—bound to the earth, the plants, and the insects that move beneath my feet. These insubstantial ghosts are about as far from my natural affinities as it's possible to be. I don't have a brew for this, don't know a spell to enable me to understand these unearthly creatures.

There's absolutely nothing rooted about them. They are winged and weightless, practically formless. They are wind and I am rock.

Yet there must be something that binds them to the Bend, some tangible thing that holds them here. Maybe I can be a conduit between the birds and the Bend's magic, like I was for Natasha? Maybe the Bend can translate? It's possible.

I sit on the damp earth and place my hands palms down and close my eyes. I wait, holding my attention on the movement of wings far above my head. Then I sense them, floating down toward me, settling like mist on my shoulders, in my hair, all around me, their weightless feathers brushing against my skin.

I let myself sink down into the soil, into the roots of the honey locust. Pain runs up through my fingertips, unimaginable pain. I have to grit my teeth to keep my skin in contact with the cool, wet earth.

A series of images begin to flash through my mind—terrible, bloody images. With them come emotions that don't belong to me. Terror mostly, and anger. A horrible helplessness. Silent tears bead in my eyes and flow down my cheeks.

At first the images and feelings are too overwhelming to make sense of—they are a jumble of human misery.

But then individual stories start to emerge. Some of the girls I recognize, but some I don't.

A girl who was hitchhiking. The trucker who'd given her a ride kept trying to put his hand down her pants. She demanded he let her out, and he did, on the side of the road, at the edge of the nature park. She never saw the sun again, and no one ever came looking for her.

A homeless woman who pitched a tent in the woods.

Rochelle Greymont, running from someone through the forest.

Samantha Parsons, who'd lagged behind her boyfriend on the hiking trail.

A teenager, with a sweet round face, stumbling behind a tree to pee while her friends smoked weed in a clearing. Kaylee Robins.

A middle-aged woman, with lanky limbs and dirty-blond hair falling like a sheet down her back, turning—

Aunt Sage. That's my aunt, Miles's mother. She's one of the birds.

My heart stops. Momma's first victim.

"What happened to you?" I whisper, feeling her new mist-cool wings brush my face, just as she used to pat my cheek in life.

She lets out a shriek. A flood of new images rolls out, jerkily, like an old-timey movie. Momma and Sage out working a spell on the Bend under a sky full of stars, Momma kneeling by the river, Aunt Sage squatting at the edge of the trees. They look every inch witches with their long hair, their skin washed pale by moonlight.

Momma is humming, that low, eerie hum she used to use when she was trying to work a particularly difficult spell. Aunt Sage is doing a complicated motion with her hands, like sewing. One of her healing spells for wounds.

A train's whistle roars far off in the distance. Tension builds in the air, an unbearable sense of approaching danger. This is when it happens—this is when Momma's magic goes wrong and she kills her sister.

I hold my breath.

A creature leaps out of the tree line and topples Aunt Sage to the ground. She screams, and Momma's head jerks up. Her knife comes out. She runs to her sister.

The beast is a blur of teeth and claws, bristling fur, rippling muscles. It bites Aunt Sage anywhere it can reach. Momma tries to fight it off, but her knife is knocked from her hand, and the beast clamps its jaws around Aunt Sage's throat.

Momma lets out a howl of anguish, a wail that's almost music. The Bend responds. The river rises from its bank and rushes toward them, tsunami-powerful. I expect her to use it to throw the beast back into the forest it came from, but when the water hits her, it stops, forming a wall behind her.

Momma begins to change. Her hair turns to its seaweed green, her nails lengthen into claws, her teeth turn sharp and deadly. Finally, she drops to all fours and, with a rush of river water, launches herself at the beast, who has been standing motionless watching the scene unfold.

This is the moment Momma became the river siren.

The two creatures fight, tooth and nail, slashing and biting. But Momma is stronger, and the creature must realize it is beaten. With a yelp, it escapes into the trees, trailing dark blood. Momma hisses at it but lets it go. She turns back to her sister, who is blinking up at her as the life leaves her eyes. Sage looks into Momma's face and sees not a monster, not a beast. She sees terrible love in her sister's jade-green eyes, terrible love in the glint of her sharp and bloodied teeth.

The vision goes dark. Aunt Sage is dead. That was the end of her part of the story.

But I know what happens next. Momma will drag Aunt Sage's body to the river, just in time for Da and me to arrive. I'll watch Aunt Sage's battered, bleeding corpse slip under the tea-colored water. And then Momma will let out a horrible, life-shattering, inhuman cry and bound away into the trees.

The next morning, Da and I will find her. We'll take her home. We'll lock her in the basement. We'll realize how much we've lost.

I slump to the earth, the weight of this new knowledge crashing down on me. Momma didn't kill Aunt Sage. It wasn't her.

And if she didn't kill Sage, then she didn't kill any of these girls.

Momma is innocent.

She's a creature of teeth and claws, the very embodiment of the river's power, but she's innocent.

Relief wells up in me, powerful and freeing. My mother's not a murderer. My family's not to blame for the deaths of all these women. Not to blame for Natasha's pain.

I reach into my pocket for the cell phone Miles gave me. I want to tell him. I want to let him know. But it's not there. I haven't gotten used to the habit of always pocketing it the way other people do. It's at home somewhere, probably wedged between couch cushions or sitting on my dresser. I try Natasha's, but it's out of battery and won't even power on. Then I remember Miles is in jail and can't answer his phone anyway.

Rochelle flies in front of me, recalling my attention. It's as if she can tell I've gotten sidetracked. Natasha. Natasha is what matters most now. She's missing.

She's missing and there's a monster on the Bend.

"Do you know where she is?" I ask.

Rochelle lets out a shriek of rage.

"I'll follow you," I promise. "Just show me where to go."

THIRTY
NATASHA

Don't panic. You can't panic.

This is what I've been whispering to myself for the last ten minutes, ever since I woke up in a dark room that smells like old leather boots that have gotten wet over and over again. I can't remember where I am or what happened to me. My hands are tied behind my back, my shoulder is screaming, and my head is one big, throbbing ache. Blood drips down my neck and cheek onto the floor. The metallic smell of it makes me nauseous, and I'm grateful to be lying down on my side.

My breath keeps coming in huge gulps that threaten to make me faint. I will my chest to stop heaving. I can't pass out. I can't panic. I can't let my fear override my mind. That's the one thing my childhood taught me. If I control my fear, I can stay alert and I can live. And fuck it all, I'm going to live.

Once my breathing steadies, I train all my senses on figuring out where I am. I'm blindfolded, but I think the room is completely dark too, so there aren't any windows here. The floor is cool and hard and slightly rough, like old wood. There's grit under my cheek.

The room smells musty and unused, and when I reach out with my feet, it feels like I'm kicking cardboard boxes. That's sight, smell, and touch. What's left? Hearing and tasting.

All I taste is the dry, sour inside of my mouth. Nothing helpful there.

I hold my breath a moment so I don't miss a single sound. My heartbeat in my ears. Nothing else. No footsteps, no electronics, no voices. No sounds of traffic. I'm somewhere isolated.

But how did I get here? Where was I last? I rack my brain, trying to remember.

The prison.

I was at the prison. And there was Della and a woman in a cell and then, and then . . . the woman changed, turned into a horror movie. I ran, Della chased me. I made it out of the prison and to my car, didn't I?

No, Miles was blocking my car. I had to run.

But where did I run to?

I'm hyperventilating again, struggling to pull breath into my lungs. This is like the time my biological dad locked me and Rochelle in a closet because he wanted to get high and didn't want us to bother him. We sang songs and told each other stories. Every time I started to cry, Rochelle thought of a new knock-knock joke I hadn't heard yet.

If Rochelle were here . . .

But Rochelle is dead. The knowledge falls on me with a

weight so great I want to be dead too. Rochelle is dead. The one person in this world who belonged wholly to me, who was a part of me, is dead. And apparently, I'm about to join her.

I lie limp against the hard, cold floor for a long time, the rope around my wrists cutting into my skin. Hours pass. I don't know what my captors are waiting for.

A doorknob rattles somewhere across the room. I struggle to sit up. "Damnit," someone whispers. Then there's a loud crack, and the door swings open with a groan and slams into the wall. I try to push as far away from the sound as I can, and my back comes up snugly against a wall.

"Natasha," a girl's voice says into the darkness. "Are you in here?"

It's Della. Did Miles send her? Is he here too? I stay silent, thinking hard about what to do. But her footsteps come closer and then she must spot me. "Oh, Jesus Christ," she swears, and crouches in front of me.

The sound of her voice is a relief from the dark nothingness of this room, but I don't know whose side she's on. Mine or Miles's? "Why are you here?" I ask, my voice weak and pathetic-sounding in my ears. "What do you want from me?"

"I'm trying to help you," Della says. She pulls the covering from my eyes, and I blink against the sudden light coming in from the open door across the room. "I promise."

I don't have any reason to believe her, but I do.

"Where am I?" I ask. This doesn't look like the prison. It's just a musty old storage room.

Della reaches toward me, and I flinch away, as if human

touch can only bring pain. Her brow knits. "You're on the nature park, in a cabin. It belongs to the caretaker. He's a park ranger who lives here year-round to watch for poachers. How did you get here?"

If I could see her expression, maybe I could tell if she's lying. But she's only a dark silhouette against the light behind her. "I'm not sure. Someone chased me, I think."

"You ran away last night from the prison and I heard today that you were missing. I came looking for you."

I want so badly to believe her, to trust her, but something's not adding up. "And you just happened to find me here? I'm not stupid, Della."

"Turn around so I can get the rope off your wrists," she says. "I'll explain everything, but first we need to go."

I hesitate, strangely afraid to turn my back to her. Some buried memory seems to tell me turning your back on anyone is a bad idea.

"Oh, for Christ's sake," she murmurs. She pulls out a pocketknife. "Hold still. I'm going to cut you free." She comes closer and kneels over me, reaching her arms around behind me. That wild smell of hers fills my nose, and even though I'm not sure whose side she's on, even though I'm not sure if I should trust her, the smell is comforting somehow. As she leans over me, sawing at my bonds, my heart rate begins to slow and my breaths come more evenly. It goes against all common sense, against all reason. But my body believes it's safe with Della Lloyd.

As soon as my hands are free, she backs away and puts the knife in her pocket. "We need to get you out of here."

"Did you call the police?" I ask.

"I don't have a cell phone. I found yours, but it's completely dead now." Della holds out my iPhone, its screen blank and cracked. I take it from her, if only for the familiar and comforting weight of it.

"Maybe there's a landline here," I say, pushing toward the door. I want to get out of this room, out of this darkness. All I can think about is the light.

Della grabs my wrist. "Please don't turn her in."

I yank my arm from her grip and clench my teeth at the pain in my shoulder. "Turn in who?"

"My mother."

"How can you even ask me that?" I say, making my way out of the room and straight into a kitchen. There are maroon curtains over the kitchen window, and weak gray light leaks in at the edges. I pull them open, but all I see outside are sodden trees. Della wasn't lying—we're somewhere on the park.

"She's my mother, Natasha."

I spin to face her and almost lose my balance. I grip the back of my head, but immediately pull my hands away because it stings. My hands come away bloody. "Did she kill my sister?"

"Oh, shit," Della says. "Let me find a towel for your head. You're bleeding really bad." Della takes a dish towel from a drawer and hands it to me. I snatch it from her grasp and press it to the back of my head, gasping from the pain.

"We need to get you to the hospital," Della says, looking around for a phone.

"Don't change the fucking subject. Tell me."

Della clenches her jaw and tries to glare at me, but tears fill her eyes. "No," she finally says. "I thought she had—for a long time, that's what I thought. But now I know it wasn't her."

"You thought—all this time you were with me, when you were making out with me, you thought your mom was roaming the nature park killing girls? And you didn't do anything?" I snatch up a cast iron pan. I want so badly to hit her with it.

"I'm sorry. I'm so sorry. I tried so hard to watch her, to keep her locked up. But she kept getting out. I've tried so hard, I swear. But she's my mother. She's my blood."

Everything clicks into place. Della's bruises and cuts, her secrecy. It wasn't Miles hurting her. It was her mother. Yet she kept protecting her, taking care of her. No matter how monstrous her mother became, she covered for her.

That's a story I know.

"Blood isn't everything," I say, lowering the pan.

"But it wasn't her who attacked you. I swear she was locked up all night. I stayed with her."

"What about Miles?"

"What about him?" Della asks, scrunching up her brow.

"How do you know it wasn't him?"

"Look where you are," Della says. "Why would Miles bring you here?"

"Fuck," I whisper. Finally, I look around the cabin, really look around. It's rustic and seems like a man lives alone here. A man with no taste and few needs. Whoever he is, whoever brought me here and attacked me, he could come back at any moment. "We have to get out of here."

"Finally," Della mutters. "Let's go."

We run into the next room, which is a basic living room with an empty fireplace and more rustic furniture. I'm about to run for the door when I spot a ring sitting on the coffee table.

It's white gold, with a big sapphire and little diamonds. Rochelle's ring.

With it come flashes of memory. Running into that ranger Grange out on the park, drinking his coffee. Coming here and sitting on his couch.

Squeezing Rochelle's ring in my palm so hard it cut me. I look down at my palm. That's where the ring's setting sliced into my skin.

"It was Grange," I say. "He drugged me. He hit me."

"Let's just go," Della says. She's standing at the front door with her hand on the knob.

I snatch up the ring and move toward her. But then the door opens, pushing Della back. I trip over the coffee table and fall. By the time I rise to my knees, a rifle is pointing at my face.

"Back, back," a man says. "Go back inside." All I can see is the black barrel of the rifle, but I recognize the voice.

Della raises her hands and nearly trips over me in her haste to get away from the gun. I finally tear my eyes away from the weapon and study the man who holds it. His broad shoulders, the barest outline of his biceps. Even without the gun, I couldn't fight him off.

"Woke up, did you?" Grange asks.

"If you touch her again, I swear—" Della starts to say.

Grange smiles, shakes his head with a light laugh. "This ain't nothing to do with you, Della Lloyd."

"I'm not your type, I guess," Della says.

"No offense," the ranger says.

"Wouldn't have thought she was either," Della adds, nodding toward me. "You only seem to go for blondes."

He smiles again. "Well, not usually, but you know us collectors. Can't resist a complete set."

The world falls out from underneath me. I might be slow from the drugs and the blows to my head, but even I can figure it out. "You killed Rochelle," I say, my voice hoarse.

He only smiles, but every hair on my body stands on end.

"What I can't figure out," Della says conversationally, "is where you've been hiding the bodies. My cousin Miles is a tracker, and he never found his mother's after she went into the river."

"Don't be nosy, Della," the man says reprovingly. "That's not neighborly."

"You're going to kill me anyway," Della says.

He laughs. "Well, that's true. But where are my manners? You ladies have a seat." He motions to an old vinyl couch. Della plops down on it like she's here to watch a football game. She even throws her booted feet up on the coffee table. When I don't move, the ranger raises his eyebrows at me.

I'm looking at the man who murdered my sister. A bright, hard anger builds in me.

"I said to sit down," Grange says, a mean edge to his voice now.

"Go fuck yourself, you sick bastard," I say, lifting my chin defiantly. Like Della said, he's going to kill us anyway.

Before I can blink, he has slapped me, hard, right across the face. I stumble back against the coffee table.

"Sit," Grange says, but I keep staring him down.

"Please," Della says. "Come here."

Her voice is soft, shaky. She's afraid for me. I step backward, not taking my eyes off Grange. I settle next to Della, who throws an arm around my shoulder. It takes all my strength not to curl into her side, hide my face against her neck. But that won't do. It won't do at all. I won't even allow myself to raise a hand to my bleeding lip.

Della, as if wanting to take Grange's attention off me, starts talking. I'm not looking at her, but I can hear the smirk in her voice. "Robert Grange, a humble park ranger and caretaker of the Wood Thrush Nature Park. A lover of nature. A man's man. Who likes to kill defenseless girls in his free time." There's so much mockery in her voice, so much disdain.

"Shut your mouth, Lloyd, and all you'll get is a bullet in your head. I'm not interested in you." Grange eyes me appreciatively. "Your friend, however . . ."

Now I do shrink against Della's side. Her heart is beating so hard I can feel it against my rib cage, and she's trembling. You'd never know it without touching her, though. She has learned to hide her emotions better than any person I've met before.

Grange reads my fear easily and it makes him happy. He's

getting off on my cowering, my bleeding, my crying.

I try to make my face go blank, will my heart not to race. I'll be like Della and give him as little satisfaction as possible.

"So, Robert, tell me, exactly how many women have you killed?" Della asks.

Grange laughs. "I like you, Della. I'll let you in on my secret, since I'm going to kill you anyway. This beauty right here"—he points to me—"will be my eighth. You don't count, of course."

"Of course," Della agrees. "I wouldn't think of it."

"What did you do to my sister?" I ask, hating how my voice shakes.

Grange sighs and closes his eyes like he's getting nostalgic over a childhood memory. "Oh, but if I tell you, it will take all the fun out of it for you. There won't be any surprises."

A chill runs down my body. "I don't like surprises."

Grange appraises me. "Well, all right. I suppose you deserve that much. I'll tell you the story. She was driving out to the witches' house for some spell work—"

Della and I exchange a glance. I can see she's as surprised as I am.

"—only her boyfriend ran her off the road right by the nature park. Threatened her, chased her. She got out of her car and ran into the woods, straight into me. She thought I was going to save her."

Jake, that bastard. I knew his "rock-solid" alibi was a lie. He was right when he said it was all his fault. He didn't kill Rochelle, but he drove her straight into Grange's path.

"So I took her to the honey locust tree. That's where I take all my girls. I think they deserve to die somewhere pretty, don't you?"

Hot tears burn my eyes, but I refuse to let them fall. "And then what?" I swallow hard, pushing down the sob that wants to rise up my throat.

"Well, I took my hiking stick and hit her in the back of the head. She went down so quick. I'll admit I like girls like that, who don't put up too much fight, who recognize when they're beat."

"You raped her," I say, horror in my voice.

Grange's face twists. "I would never. I don't go in for that sort of thing." He's honestly outraged by the accusation.

"Then why?" I ask.

"Pain is a beautiful thing," he says with a smile, a gleam in his eyes, like a religious fanatic's.

"What did you do to her?" I steel myself.

"Well, first I got out my knife and slit—"

"Stop," Della says. "She doesn't need to hear. Anyway, I already know what you did. You're the Bloody Miller." She says it like a title: Bloody Miller, capital B, capital M.

Grange's eyes light up. "And here I thought you young people only listened to pop music."

"What're you talking about?" I ask, suddenly grateful she made him stop talking. I don't want to know any more. I don't want to know how he hurt my sister. It's enough to know he hurt her and killed her, snuffed out her life and took her away from everyone who loves her.

"It's an old murder ballad, a folk song. It's called 'The

Bloody Miller.' He's acting it out. Over and over again." She turns to Grange. "But you forgot that the killer hangs in the end. There's always judgment at the end of murder ballads."

Grange shrugs. "They haven't caught me yet."

Della's wheels seem to be turning. "In the song, the girl the bloody miller killed was his fiancé. Was that your first kill too?"

A muscle in Grange's cheek ticks. "That was back in Florida, before I came here." His brow furrows as if with a painful memory.

"And then you got a taste for it?" Della asks.

When Grange doesn't answer, she laughs. "Pathetic. You think you're some special genius mastermind killing women out here in the woods. But you're just like every other man who gets cheated on or dumped or whatever and decides to take it out on the rest of us."

Grange puts a boot on the table and leans forward. "You know, maybe you are my type after all, Della. Maybe you are," he says threateningly.

She stops talking and stares at him, trembling harder than ever. I press closer against her side. Maybe it's my turn to be brave. But how? He's got a gun pointed at us and he's blocking the door. All I can think to do is keep him talking. Maybe if I keep him talking, help will come. But I can't stand to hear what else he did to Rochelle. It's too much.

"Who was the second girl you killed?" I ask. "After your fiancé?"

"Oh, her name was Teresa. She was a beauty. Long curly blond hair, legs for days. The cutest little nose. She'd come all the way from Kentucky, trying to get away from her folks. No one even thought to look for her here. Or maybe her folks wouldn't bother, I suppose. They'd cast her off."

"Why?"

Grange shakes his finger at me. "You're trying to keep me talking so I won't kill you. That's clever. Man lives alone here for a long while, he likes to talk when he gets the chance."

"Why'd you leave Rochelle's body out? Why didn't you bury her?" Della asks.

Grange's face darkens. "That's a long story, but it worked out nicely thanks to your harrowing tale of escaping a pack of feral dogs. Why was that now? I couldn't figure out why you'd spin such a yarn."

Della smiles at him cryptically, like she knows something he doesn't.

Grange seems to think it's a huge joke. "Oh, I do like you, Della. You've got so much more to you than most of these girls." He winks at me.

"I'm guessing you don't usually bring your victims to your house," Della says, conversational again.

"Oh no. Never. But this one was a special case. Had to work things out just so." He smiles at me. "Speaking of which, I think it's time we move along. Got to get things back on track." He motions at me with the gun. "Now, both of you are going to walk in front of me, real slow like. If you run or try anything funny, I'll shoot you before you make it two feet."

He marches us outside into the misty gray world. I can't even tell what time it is—it could be ten in the morning or five

in the afternoon. There are only gray skies and gloomy, dripping trees. As if we're already dead, marching through the
underworld.

Grange prods me in the back with the barrel of his gun and
I cry out, though the sound is muffled in the mist. "In there," he
says, pushing me toward the woods. Della walks calmly beside
me. I reach out and clasp her hand. It's sweating slightly, but
she grips my fingers tightly in hers, and strength seems to run
from her to me.

"Now, none of that," Grange says, and Della drops my
hand and looks me in the eye. Her expression seems to say that
it's going to be all right, that we'll make it out of this. But I can't
see how we are going to stand against a serial murderer with a
rifle in his hands. Even if one of us is a well-trained witch.

I won't beg. I won't get on my knees and beg for my life.
That's the one thing I'm not going to do. I'm not going to cower
any more than I have to. I'm going to take what comes. I'm
going to fight like hell if I get the chance, but if I don't, I'm
going to die without begging this piece of shit to spare my life.

The woods are dim and quiet, and even at gunpoint Della
walks in them as surely as a wildcat. She barely makes a sound
as she steps over the fallen leaf litter. Grange's boots sound loud
and wrong in the quiet. I remember what I felt when I fell into
the river—that an intruder walked the Bend. All along, it was
Grange.

After we have walked for ten minutes or so, up over hills
and then back down, the tree where I found Rochelle's body
appears in the dimness, its blossoms faintly glowing.

Something seems to flutter in the branches, among the leaves, like birds. It's the only sign of life I've seen here since we started walking. Grange doesn't seem to notice, but Della studies the treetops, as if waiting for something. Terror rises up in me. This is the place he killed Rochelle, where he intends to kill me. This is where he will hit me and cut me and do God only knows what else.

Georgia set up cameras here, I remember. If Della and I die, it will be on film. Grange will be caught. He'll go to jail. He won't be able to kill any more girls. Georgia will make sure of it. But oh God, I hope it doesn't come to that.

"What do you think those are—owls?" Della asks him. Grange glances up into the branches of the locust tree, and Della draws back her fist and hits him, hard. Blood gushes from his nose. Right then I decide my best friend isn't going to watch me get cut up and killed on camera. I grab Della's hand and bolt. It's a foolish move, maybe, but I'd rather be shot in the back running away from him than whatever else he has planned. Della hesitates for only a moment before she runs with me, guiding me toward the cover of the oak trees.

We make it a few yards before Grange fires his gun. Pain erupts in my calf and I fall. Della pulls me back up and somehow I run, with her half dragging me. The bird shapes above seem to follow us, flittering and chattering over our heads. Grange takes another shot, which whistles by my ear. I trip over a tree root and tumble to the ground. Della tries to yank me up, but my leg has gone numb and I fall again.

"Goddamnit," she snarls. She looks over her shoulder, and

I see exactly what she does: Grange advancing toward us, his rifle raised.

"Leave me," I say. "Just go." I'm sobbing from the pain and the terror, but I have enough mind to know there's no reason for both of us to die. "Go get help," I add.

"I'm not leaving you, and there's no help to get," Della says. "There's only you and me."

"No, go!" I scream. I push her away, as hard as I can manage. "Figure something out, but just go—now! If you stay, he's going to shoot you."

Della curses again. "I'll be right back. I won't leave you for long." Then she sprints away into the trees, leaving me alone with Grange. He could probably shoot her, but he's got eyes only for me.

He walks slowly toward me now, his face bloody but his eyes steady, sure of his prey. I wrap myself around my injured leg. I can feel that there's a chunk of flesh missing at the edge of my calf. Blood oozes from the wound.

Grange grabs me by the hair and drags me back toward the tree. I scream and he cuffs me on the side of the head. But then he seems to think better of it and lifts me into his arms and carries me instead. He props me against the honey locust tree. Black spots edge around my vision. I tip back my head and see thorns and green leaves, yellow blossoms. And then my sister's eyes. They shine out at me, her wide, blue eyes in the face of a—did Della call them owls? Shadows move among the leaves. More eyes peer out at me. Human eyes—brown and green and blue. But I keep mine on Rochelle's.

"Ro," I whisper. I must be hallucinating. Maybe it's the blood loss. But I've seen those eyes before—right before I crashed into this tree on the day I found her body.

Grange comes closer, and I feel the cold press of a knife against my cheek. "We'll have to make this quick," he says.

The shadows in the trees begin to move again, restless and angry, stirring the leaves with their movement. Grange notices them and steps back to watch them. His face goes slack with shock. He must have noticed their eyes. Must have recognized at least some of them. Because I'm pretty sure there are six. Six ghost birds with six pairs of human eyes. Six creatures for the six women he said he killed here. They watch him, transfixed with hate. He must feel it too because he shudders.

But then he looks down at me again and raises his knife. He starts to kneel, and I know what he's going to do. I can already feel the cold blade against my skin.

He means to make me the seventh.

I scream.

I scream out my terror and my pain, I scream out my grief and my endless loss. Most of all I scream out the white-hot, searing rage that has been growing inside me for weeks.

And it seems impossible because I'm sitting on dry land, and I can't even see the river, but I feel it inside me. I feel its coursing, rushing movement, its hungry biting mouth. I feel it moving inside me. I think I even feel it dripping from my hair.

The river's power explodes from my screaming throat.

Grange stumbles back, his eyes wide with shock and fear. Then his expression turns to anger, frustration in every line of his face. He moves toward me again, but he can't come near. It's like there's an invisible river rushing between us, holding him back.

Those golden eyes of his begin to turn yellow, and his face seems to pale, an ugly corpse-like color creeping up his skin. He lets out a snarl, and I recognize him: the monster who chased me through the woods and up a tree. It wasn't Miles. It was Grange.

Sure enough, a sulfurous, filthy smell begins to waft off him. It chokes me, and I stop screaming. I cough. He moves toward me, half human and half beast. Claws begin to extend from his fingers, and he drops the knife. He doesn't need it anymore.

Fear wraps around my chest and tightens, strangling my diaphragm, my vocal cords. I scoot back and back again.

I open my mouth to scream, but only a weak, hoarse sound comes out.

Grange laughs, the sound animal and cruel.

And then Della comes tearing out of the trees, her face desperate with fear. Grange hears her and turns just in time for her to snatch up his abandoned rifle from the ground, swing it as hard as she can, and smash it into his hideous, leering face.

He goes down, hard. Before he can get back up, Della points the rifle right at his face and pulls the trigger. There's a click, and then nothing. The gun is out of ammo.

Della doesn't miss a beat. She flips the gun back around and raises it in the air. She drives it as hard as she can into Grange's head, and he goes out like a light, his monstrous features melting away. Della just stands there, staring down at him.

But when an involuntary moan escapes my lips, Della leaves him and hurries toward me.

I have one shining clear moment of relief before the world goes black.

THIRTY-ONE
DELLA

It was Grange. The monster who killed Aunt Sage and all the others. The monster Momma battled and injured. The reason my whole life has gone to shit.

Earlier, when he came back to his cabin with that rifle, I thought he must be the monster Aunt Sage showed me in my vision. But I wasn't sure. Now I am. I've seen both of his faces.

I stand over his human body, considering what to do to him, but then Natasha lets out a terrible sound and all I can think about is that she might be dying. Grange will have to wait. I sling his rifle as far as I can into the trees and bolt toward her.

I don't think I'll ever be able to do anything but run toward this girl. She made me leave her earlier, but I couldn't do it. I wanted to run for help, but I couldn't leave her behind. I only made it a few yards into the trees before I stopped, knowing I'd never get help in time, knowing that she would die alone. I stood there, watching them, just out of sight, as Natasha unleashed her magic and as Grange began to transform. When I realized he was going to win—there was nothing to do but run back in and fight for her.

When I reach her now, Natasha is slumped on the ground, her eyes closed. She's breathing, but still as death. The ghost birds flit and cry above her.

"Natasha," I say, shaking her shoulder. She doesn't respond. I think she passed out. From blood loss probably. Her gunshot wound is bad, filling the air with a metallic tang. I yank off my flannel shirt and wrap it tightly around her calf, hoping it's enough to save what's left of her blood. "Please wake up," I say. "Please."

Desperation laces my voice. She can't die. Not now, not after everything.

I shake Natasha's shoulder again, and she finally groans awake. She opens her eyes blearily, as if it's painful. "You can't sleep yet," I say, making my voice rough and commanding. "You have to stay awake. Stay with me."

"You're such an asshole," she croaks. I laugh, and my relief echoes through the trees.

"So are you," I say. "We need to go. I'm sorry, but we can't stay here. We need to move. Grange could wake up any second."

"I—I don't think I can." Natasha is shaking, from blood loss and fear and probably from shock. It feels so cruel to do it, but I have to make her move.

"Come on, princess, show me some of that fighting spirit. Show me what you got," I tease. "We need to move." I try to sound strong and steady, but I can feel tears in my eyes, choking my voice.

"You promised never to call me that again," Natasha says through gritted teeth. She tries to sit up, tries harder than anyone should ever have to—but she can't. She slumps back down, trembling from the effort.

I'm going to have to try to use my magic. I've never attempted something like this before, but what choice do I have? I have to do something to help Natasha.

I grip her tightly with one hand and press my other to the earth. I feel my way underground, into the life and nourishment that runs beneath our feet. Somehow, I must convince it to pass through me and into Natasha. Can I make health and life pass from a plant to a girl? Surely if I could communicate with the ghost birds, I can do this.

I *will* do this. There's no other choice.

I scoop up a handful of wet soil and press it over her wrapped leg. I don't know what the magic will do, especially since it's so bent out of shape. I hold the soil to her leg and concentrate hard on pulling not just nourishment but life itself from the roots that twine beneath us.

From the honey locust, Grange's killing tree.

"Please," I whisper to the tree, to the magic, to Natasha. "Please."

At first nothing happens, and I'm afraid my heart will hammer right out of my chest. I'm afraid that Natasha will die. I'm afraid that Grange will wake up and start attacking us again. I'm afraid of so many, many things.

But then I feel it, life and health and goodness passing through my palm from the earth. It travels through me, and into my dirty hand pressed against Natasha's bleeding leg. A smell like rotting flowers surrounds us, and then dead, brown leaves begin to drift down from the honey locust, gently covering us. A tree branch overhead cracks ominously, as if the tree has gone dry and is about to start dropping limbs.

I glance over at Grange and see him beginning to stir. He gets to his knees, and his eyes catch on me. He starts to rise to his feet. He's in his human form, but the monster can't be far off.

We need to move, but I'm stuck in the trance my magic always puts me in, slow and twined into the earth so tight I may as well be bound with ropes. Natasha blinks and struggles beneath my hands as strength returns to her. My magic worked.

"Come on. We have to go," she yells. Small limbs begin to rain down around us.

Natasha scrambles to her feet. Whatever injuries she has, visible and not, don't seem to matter anymore. She's ready to run. She yanks me to my feet and begins to drag me out of range of the falling limbs. Away from Grange, who has managed to find the rifle, despite how far away I threw it.

I finally get my feet under me properly, so she doesn't have to carry so much of my weight. "You okay?" Natasha asks. "Are you snapping out of it now?"

I nod, feeling the earth's hold on me loosening. We move fast through the trees, putting distance between us and Grange. But I can hear him shuffling through the leaves behind us, coming back to himself. Maybe reloading that rifle too. I should have kept it.

"Where do we go? What do we do?" Natasha asks.

There's only one thing to do.

It's time for Grange to die. The Bend made him, so the Bend will have to deal with him. There's no other way. The police would never be a match for him. In his beast form, he's a creature of magic, more powerful than their guns. And in his human form, he's a man the police trust and respect. There's only one way to stop him. The river siren. Momma.

In fact, I think it's why the river siren exists. I think Momma made herself into a monster to stop Grange, only the magic was so damaged that she couldn't change herself back. If she kills him, if she makes things right . . . maybe everything else will go back to normal.

I turn to Natasha. "I'm going to go let my mother out of the prison. I'm going to let her kill him."

Natasha's eyes flash. "I'm going with you. I want to see the bastard die."

I consider arguing with her, but there's no time. And I can see there's no point. Natasha might be injured and exhausted, but she's not weak. She's not going to rest easy until the man who killed her sister is dead.

"Come on," I say. "Grange's truck."

We dash back to the cabin and leap into the unlocked forestry truck.

"He left the keys in?" Natasha scoffs.

"Who's going to steal it out here? I leave the keys in mine too." I put the truck into gear and back out as fast as I can.

Once we're on the road, the horrible fear in my gut loosens. For the moment, we're safe. For the moment, Natasha is safe. I glance at her. She's covered in blood, her clothes are ripped, and she's never looked less like the girl I first saw a few weeks ago. And yet her eyes are still blazing.

"I've got some things to tell you," I say, gunning the engine as we pass over the river. "I've lied to you a lot. I know you've got no reason to trust me, but I was doing what I had to— to protect my family. I was doing everything I could, trying to keep my momma safe, trying to keep other people safe. For a while I thought she really had killed Rochelle, and I know I should have told you, but—"

"I wouldn't have told me either, if it were me," Natasha interrupts. "She's your mom. And now we know she had nothing to do with it. You'd have been ousting an innocent person anyway."

"I felt like shit lying to you," I say. "Not at first maybe, but after I got to know you."

Natasha nods. "I believe you." She doesn't sound like she forgives me exactly, but at least she understands.

"I found out how it happened," I say. "How she became the river siren." And then I relay the contents of my vision of Aunt Sage's death—how Grange killed Aunt Sage, how Momma drew the river into herself until it took over.

"I realized it too—that Grange was the monster that was chasing me last night, not Miles. I thought it was Miles," she adds, half laughing. "I'm an idiot. But it was Grange all along. I hope Miles is okay."

"He'll be fine," I say, deciding not to tell her about his arrest right now. We'll deal with it later, like so many other things.

"And you're not an idiot," I add as we pull right in front of the prison. No time for sneakiness today. "We all suspected the wrong person. This whole time I thought my own mother was killing these girls. I locked her in a prison cell." Guilt floods me. I've done nothing but make mistakes.

But Natasha's got no time for guilt. She only cares about vengeance.

"If it's the river she's got inside of her," Natasha says as we run toward the prison, "all that rage and pain and power— when she finally lets it out, it's going to wash that motherfucker right out to sea."

THIRTY-TWO
NATASHA

Della unlocks the door to her mother's cell with a key she had strung around her neck. The sight of her pulling it out from under her shirt and fitting it into the lock breaks my heart a little. Imagine being responsible for something like that. Imagine the weight of that key.

That's enough to push away the last of my anger at her. Yeah, she lied to me. Yeah, what she did was wrong. But I'd have done it too. If it were Rochelle in that cell, I'd do it a thousand times over and never say I was sorry.

Della eases open the door to the cell. Her mother is way back in the corner, on the floor, arms around her knees, rocking herself. I wonder if she can sense what's happening on the nature park. I wonder how much she knows.

"Momma," Della says, her voice soft. She kneels a few feet away from her mother. "I want to let you out. And I'm not going to put you back in."

The woman looks up warily, regarding her daughter with suspicion.

"Momma, I know it wasn't you." Della's voice breaks. "I know you didn't hurt those girls. I know you didn't kill Aunt Sage either."

The woman lets go of her knees and sinks into a kneeling position like Della's. She looks at her daughter questioningly.

"I know there's a monster on the Bend. A killer. His name is Robert Grange. That's—that's who you've been after, isn't it? You've been trying to stop him. That's who that hair belonged to—that braid of hair you gave me. You were trying to tell me it was his. He's the Bloody Miller."

The woman crawls on her hands and knees toward Della, never taking her eyes off Della's face.

But Della hangs her head. "I'm sorry, Momma. I'm so sorry I kept you here. I'm sorry I thought you—" Now her voice cuts out altogether.

Ruby—I remember now, that's her name—reaches a frail, bony hand toward her daughter's face. Della flinches when her mother's skin meets hers. But then Della looks up. I can't see Della's face, but I imagine there's hope in her eyes. Hope for a different life.

Then Ruby raises her head and meets my eyes. I'm drawn toward her without thinking. Only this time it's not the magic of the river siren doing it—it's recognition. She and I—we're the same. We both lost a sister to Grange. We both want more than anything to see him dead.

"Will you help us?" I ask, kneeling next to Della, staring into Ruby's green, green eyes. "Will you help us kill him?"

Ruby's face breaks into a terrifying smile, but I'm not repulsed by it—it's like an echo of my own heart. Like seeing my bloodlust reflected in a mirror.

Della glances at me. "Let's go, then. Let's find him and end it."

The three of us walk out of the prison together, climb into Grange's truck, and drive back to the Bend.

We leave the truck by the side of the road and slip into the trees like three shadows. The rain has finally, completely stopped, but the overcast sky has brought twilight nearer. The woods are dim and silent, except for the drips of leftover rainwater. The angry energy that gripped the land earlier has settled into a simmering feeling of ill will.

I try to mimic how Della and her mother walk. A few things I can emulate: how they step with their heels, how they avoid sticks. But their lightness seems like magic to me. I still make twice as much noise as they do. Ruby is in the lead, moving like a breath of wind through the trees, pausing now and then to cock her head, listening.

I think the sun will go down soon. And when it does she'll change, she'll become as wild as the rest of this land, completely untethered to humanity. That's what her grief and rage has made her: a feral thing, single-minded and deadly. I'm surprised to find I envy her.

I try to keep up with Ruby and Della, but they're soon a few yards ahead of me. Suddenly, Ruby stops and whips her head around toward me. Her eyes widen as she looks at me.

I turn in time to see a beast hurtling in my direction, but it goes right past me. Grange—in his hideous, most monstrous form—hurls Della to the ground, and then he's a blur of claws and teeth. He snatches her up and drags her away by her pant leg. It happened so fast she barely had time to react. But as the loping beast charges off into the trees with her, she starts to struggle. She starts to scream.

THIRTY-THREE
DELLA

Grange drags me fast and mercilessly through the forest, and the world is a blur of sky and ground and trees. It's all I can do to keep my arms around my head, to keep from bashing it into a rock.

If he meant to kill me, he would have done it already. He wants Momma to chase him.

And chase him she does—for ten minutes at least, Natasha on her heels.

Soon, Grange starts to slow and Momma catches up. I catch glimpses now and then of her angry, frightened eyes. But twilight seems to be taking forever, and Momma's in that in-between place, that restless wild state she enters before she changes. The monster inside her is champing at its bit, longing to break free of its cumbersome human body and run.

Finally, Grange stops and lets me go. I scuttle away from him, the world spinning so hard I want to puke. I feel every scrape and bruise on my skin. But I'm not seriously injured. I was only bait.

With a cry of pain or pleasure, Grange transforms back into his human form. "I'm tired of running from you, Ruby Lloyd," he yells. "Tired of you tracking my steps. Tired of you getting in the way of my kills."

So the nights Momma has been running free on the Bend, has she actually saved lives rather than taken them? Has she fought with him over the bodies of girls he's killed? I bet she's the reason Grange wasn't able to bury Rochelle.

All along, she's been trying to stop him from killing. All along, she's been trying to save us. That's what made her wild, what made her violent—an urgent, desperate need to stop this man.

Before Momma can launch herself at him, Grange reaches out a muscular arm and grabs me by my shirt. I go still, waiting to see what will happen.

"I think it's time we finished what we started, don't you?" Grange asks, holding up his hand with its two missing fingers. So that was Momma too—maybe the injury she gave him the night he killed Aunt Sage.

Momma bares her teeth at Grange. She's still human, but you can see the monster trying to get out. It's rattling the bars of its cage.

He laughs. "Well, you're just a woman now, aren't you? A weak, disgusting woman like all the rest. It's disappointing really. Too weak to even control your changes like I do. Your body is just a slave to instinct, to the movement of the moon in the sky, like every other woman who bleeds. Pitiful."

Natasha snorts. "If that's true, why didn't you climb the tree last night and get me? Instead, you sat on the ground like a dog and howled. Maybe you're not as in control as you think." Anger laces every word.

Grange lets out a low, warning growl.

"I bet you didn't mean to become a beast in the beginning, did you?" I ask, drawing his attention back to me. "You're no witch. You didn't perform a spell. This just happened to you."

"Nothing ever just happens to me," Grange snarls. "I killed before I came here, and I'll kill when I leave."

"How long did it take before you realized what was happening to you?" I ask. "How many times did you wake up naked in the woods, covered in blood? Did you think you were a werewolf?" I laugh.

But then he puts a hand around my throat and flexes his fingers, and I stop laughing. Natasha makes a convulsive movement toward us, but Momma throws out an arm to hold her back.

"I've always made the world the way I wanted it. I've always bent things to my will. I've always taken what I wanted, done what I wanted. Whatever magic is here saw that about me, and it helped me." Grange is smiling, gloating.

"The magic doesn't admire you, you asshole," I say. "It recognized your intentions and turned you into a truer, purer form of yourself. With every kill you made, you transformed a little more into what you really are."

Grange smiles. "The ultimate predator."

I shake my head. "A monster. A beast."

"Isn't that the same thing?" Grange laughs.

I look at Momma, and I can't believe I ever thought that she is what Grange is. She looks back at me, and I see love in her eyes, love and anger and purpose.

"No, it isn't," I say.

The Bend has always seen what was good in us—Da's cleverness, Momma's depth of feeling, Miles's intuition, Aunt Sage's gentleness. But there was nothing good in Grange for it to respond to. The magic latched on to his essence, which was beastly, remorseless, and bloody.

And Grange infected the magic somehow, contaminated it. That's why our spells started going wrong, slipping from our control. That's why they've become more dangerous, unpredictable, and nasty. That's why Momma became the river siren when she tried to fight him. It's as if he turns the magic against us, simply by existing here as himself.

The Bend can't be healed as long as he walks here, kills here. It's too great a burden for the magic to bear.

As if they hear my thoughts, the ghost birds begin to make a commotion in the trees above us, flapping their wings and screaming.

Momma tips her head back and looks up at them. She begins to sing. I can hear the magic in her voice, the spell she's weaving.

I didn't think she could still work magic like this, but clearly I was wrong. Grange lets go of me and begins to move irresistibly toward Momma. He tries to fight it, tries to drag his feet, but he keeps moving forward. Natasha moves toward her too and I have to leap up and grab her arm, pull her to stand beside me. I cling tightly to her hand.

"Wait," I say. "She's about to change."

Sure enough, Momma buckles and a shudder runs through her, stopping her song and Grange's movement. The three of us stare at her, frozen, as she transforms. Momma throws back her head and lets out a songlike cry of pain and rage, water pouring off her hair. Grange seems to come back to himself and takes one step toward her.

That's when she pounces, throwing him to the ground. He rolls a little ways and then gets to his feet and runs. Momma chases him into the trees.

"Why doesn't he change into the beast?" Natasha asks as we hurry to follow them.

"I don't know. I think Momma bound him somehow with her magic. It probably won't hold now that she's back in siren form."

"What will happen to her—after she kills him?" Natasha asks. "Will she turn back to normal?"

"I hope so," I say. That hope catches in my chest. We could go back to normal—Momma singing her mountain songs, not to kill but just for the pleasure of singing them. Momma foraging in the woods again, Momma singing over the brew work. Momma loving Da again. Things can go on just as they were— us Lloyds against the world.

Then I glance over at Natasha, whose hair is fanned out behind her as she runs. Maybe I don't want things to go back to normal. Maybe I don't want to be a Lloyd against the world.

"I'm glad you're not dead," Natasha says.

"For now," I yell back, with a wild gesture at the woods. The trees have begun to shudder again, and leaves fall like a snowstorm, all those June-green leaves pouring down. Limbs snap off the trees and fall, crashing around us. The ghost birds follow overhead, breaking up the shadows of the interlacing branches.

Natasha runs more swiftly than me, her long legs propelling her along, hurdling over fallen trees. A branch strikes me in the back and I stumble to my knees, but Natasha yanks me up and practically carries me until I get the ground under my feet again.

In no time, we break into the meadow. The high brush whips in the wind with a ghostly moaning. Beyond it, I can hear the river. It's roaring, angry and unstable, threatening to drown everything for miles.

We arrive at the riverbank in time to see Momma drag Grange into the water. They both go under and they don't come back up. The current is moving so fast, even with Momma's unnatural strength, she wouldn't be able to fight it for long.

"Come on," I say, pulling Natasha with me. We run along the riverbank, watching for some sign of them. The river curves around a steep bit of rock thrust out over the water, and we slow down to maneuver around it.

I have to watch my feet on the last bit so I don't trip on some vines and pitch into the water. When I look up, what I see makes me stop so fast that Natasha crashes into me, nearly knocking me over.

Two monsters battle at the edge of the river, gray skin and green skin, claws and teeth and blood. They're nearly evenly matched.

I fight free from Natasha's limbs and from the vines and rocks, stumbling forward.

The river siren looks up and sees me, and in her single moment of distraction, the beast pounces, slashing her chest with one enormous clawed paw. Momma falls backward into the river and is quickly swept under and away in the raging current.

A roar goes through me. "No!" I scream and scramble toward the river, ready to leap in after her. Natasha grips me by the waist and holds me back with a strength that doesn't belong to her.

Grange's hideous yellow eyes stare back at me from the creature's face. He crouches low, his body gray and dead-looking like rotted flesh. He grins. He isn't a creature of the river like Momma. He's not even doglike, the way I thought before. He's something else, something made of death and rot.

The ghost birds fly overhead, cawing and crying and screaming. One starts up a song and another catches it like a ball. The monster begins to creep toward us. And Momma's not here to help us. We're on our own. For all I know, she's dead and floating down the river.

I will kill him. With my bare hands, my own teeth. I will rip this monster limb from limb. I put my hand to the earth and begin to draw out death. I will cup it in my hands and shove it down his throat. It might cost my life, but I'll give it gladly.

But Natasha pushes me to one side, breaking my connection to the soil.

She strides forward, her face fearless now, every limb of her body fluid and powerful as the river. I know better than to get in her way.

Whatever anger I have inside me, whatever rage Grange has drawn out of me, it's nothing compared to hers. That power in Natasha that I feared and admired and maybe even envied, we're about to see what she can do with it.

We're about to see exactly what kind of witch Natasha Greymont is.

THIRTY-FOUR
NATASHA

Della's mother careens backward into the river and then she's lost. She was our only hope of rescue, and now she's gone. Grange's eyes turn to Della, and my insides begin to churn. But not with fear. They churn the way this river does, dashing along with the force of a team of galloping horses, like a steam engine barreling down the tracks.

That magic I tapped into by the thorny tree, when I screamed and made Grange fall back—that was only a taste of what I can do. This close to the river, with the smell of it in my nose, the sound of it in my ears—here I am a match for him, in whatever form he chooses.

I stride forward, feeling the pulse of the river in every limb. Tapping into this magic doesn't make me slow like Della is when she grows things—it makes me feel wild, unbridled, hovering just on the edge of chaos. Infinitely powerful.

I raise my arms, and the river rises up, up, up over its banks.

It rises like water in a pot, boiling and frothing. I draw up a wave and smash it into Grange with such force that he is knocked off his feet and into the river.

Before I can exult, the monster is climbing back out. So I hit him again, hard. Hard enough to break bones. Hard enough to knock the very breath from his chest. The very life from his body.

I thought Ruby would be the one to wash this vile, evil creature out to sea. But instead it will be me. I let the river's rage and its power take over, until my own personal grief is just a pebble tumbling in its wake, until I cannot separate myself from the river.

Until I am the river.

My thoughts scatter and surge, and I watch the scene before me unfold as if through a prism. I am everywhere and nowhere, enormous yet weightless. I cannot remember a time when I was solid, land-bound. Haven't I always been a rush of water roaring in the night?

Grange crawls out of the water, and I become a wave, lapping, leaping toward him.

I will end him. For Rochelle, for Della, for Ruby, for every woman whose life he took. For every person left to grieve them. For the Bend and its magic and all of its creatures. For the river, for myself.

I raise my hand and feel all the power of the Bend clenched in my fist. I am death, I am vengeance, I am the river rising up to swallow the world.

THIRTY-FIVE
DELLA

I stand still, struck with awe, as Natasha battles Grange. Though can it be called a battle if only one person lands the blows? It's more like an execution. Natasha moves fluidly, powerfully, her face ecstatic, like those old pictures of saints you see in Catholic churches. Grange keeps climbing out of the water, persistent as black mold, but he can never reach her.

I don't think the Bend has ever seen power like this.

Then Natasha's image begins to waver, like the reflection of moonlight on a moving river. And a piercing, keening cry leaves her mouth, magnified and terrible, inhuman. Only it's a song. As she raises her arms, I see that her hands end in magnificent claws. She's drawing the river into herself, just the way Momma did a year ago.

Is Natasha becoming a river siren? Does that mean my mother is dead, and Natasha is taking her place?

Panic freezes me, and I stand paralyzed, watching the chaos

that surrounds me. I'm going to lose them both. I finally felt like I was getting Momma back, and now I've lost her. And Natasha—she's getting further away from me by the moment, as if she's being borne away on a current too. She only has eyes for Grange and wants nothing but his death.

"Della," someone yells with a hoarse voice that makes every hair on my body stand on end. I rip my eyes from Natasha and my knees nearly give out. A few yards down the riverbank, my mother staggers toward me, holding her chest and coughing. Her long, dark hair drips river water and her face is filled with anger, but it's her own anger. She's human again. Human hands and a human voice, calling my name.

A human body that's weak and bleeding and hurt. She needs me.

The thought releases my frozen feet and I run to her. Just before I reach her, she slumps into the mud, wrapped up in her own hair like a dolphin caught in a net. I fall at her side, checking for wounds. There are scrapes and bruises all over her, a huge bleeding slash across her chest. But she's alive.

"Don't—let her change—into—that," Momma rasps. "Stop her." Momma's skinny arms shudder to hold up her weight.

"Are you all right?" I ask, cupping her face. Tears roll down my cheeks and for once I let them. My mother is alive and human and speaking to me.

"Don't worry about me," Momma says. "My wounds aren't fatal. They'll keep. But your friend won't—go help her."

All I've done for the last year is worry about Momma. I thought there would never be room in my heart again for anything else. But Natasha—

"Are you sure? I can heal you," I say, torn between them.

"Later, Della. Go now, or it'll be too late," Momma says, gazing in horror over my shoulder, at whatever Natasha is becoming.

I scramble to my feet and turn, and my stomach drops down a hundred-foot well.

Natasha is wrapped in a current of the river like a shawl, her image wavering in the grip of the Bend's magic. Water sluices down from her hair, and her skin is already beginning to turn gray-green.

I move toward her with careful, reverent steps. The ghost birds fly around her, screaming and wailing and singing. The earth is shaking, trees are falling in the forest. It feels like the world is coming undone.

And what will be left in its place?

Natasha is barely recognizable, but neither are the ghost birds. They've grown huge and powerful, their forms no longer like mist. Natasha must have somehow channeled the Bend's magic to give them substance, weight, and strength. They are vengeance incarnate, like the harpies from those old classics we read in school.

The beast that was once Grange is pacing, restless and uncertain, trying to find a means of attack, a way into the fortress of river between him and Natasha. Natasha flicks her hands toward him and the winged creatures dive. No longer insubstantial shadows, their claws find purchase. They slash at the beast, drawing his blood.

Grange lets out a horrific roar of pain and rage. He begins snapping at the birds, trying to pull them from the air. But they are too fast, too angry. They slice into his skin, batter him with their wings.

I use the moment to get close to Natasha. She turns her hauntingly beautiful face to me, and the grief and fury I see there is almost too much to take in. I think if I look too long, it will annihilate me.

"Stop," I say, kneeling beneath her, my hands knotted in the hem of her shirt. "Please, Natasha, please stop."

Her eyes are wide and uncomprehending. She's lost in the Bend's magic, lost in the anger and trauma of the girls Grange killed.

I push up through the water that surrounds her, letting it drench me to the skin. I push through until I am nose-to-nose with Natasha. I slide my hands behind her head to cradle her neck, lace all ten fingers in the hair at her nape, and stare into her eyes. At least those are still her own, a tawny golden brown. And her lips are hers too, even if the teeth behind them aren't.

I push my mouth against hers, tasting river water. I kiss her, hard. "Come back to me," I whisper. "Come back."

Natasha jolts, and her body begins to shake.

"Don't let him take you from me too," I say. "I need you." I feel the truth of my own words. I do need her. I need her worse than I could have imagined needing anyone.

Natasha grips my upper arms, her claws digging into my skin. Her dark eyes are wild and lost. For a moment I think she will sink her teeth into my neck.

"If you let him do this, he wins," I say. "And all the rest of us lose."

I kiss her again, pressing my heat, my warmth, my human-
ness into her cold lips.

Natasha looks at me fiercely, possessively. When she reaches
a hand toward my face, I see it's human again. The green-gray
color of the river leaches from her skin.

I risk a glance at Grange. The birds are taunting him now,
drawing out his death. He's a wreck of bloody tatters.

Natasha shudders in my arms. When I look at her again,
she's fully human, only soaked and shivering and pale, transfixed by Grange's gruesome end.

Together, we watch as the birds circle the monster, diving
and pecking at him. He throws back his head and roars, and I
see one of his eyes is missing.

He swipes at the creatures, but he can't touch them. They
dive and swoop, slashing. He screams in agony. The birds
laugh, the sound high and chilling. They begin to take bites
out of his skin with their sharp beaks. Finally, the monster realizes he can't touch them, that his victims are going to exact
their revenge one scratch, one bite at a time. He will die slowly,
agonizingly. He turns and lopes back toward the river, maybe
thinking he can hide underneath the water.

But the birds give chase, stopping him at the shore, where
he falls. Natasha pulls me with them, eager to see every drop
of Grange's blood. There is only death and vengeance and pain
here. Natasha is high on it.

Suddenly I'm sick of it all. Our magic. The spells we sell to
angry, vengeful people. I'm sick of the darkness and the anger,
sick of the desperate people at our door. I'm sick of the Bend.

Natasha seems to sense the shift in me. She turns from the carnage and gazes into my face. Her eyes glitter in the moonlight, tears pouring down her cheeks. She is so beautiful and so strong and so good, and all I want is to find out what my life could be like with her in it.

Momma staggers up to us, still clutching the wound in her chest. She surveys the ruined pile of flesh that was Robert Grange. He looks human again, his monstrous form shed. "Let's put an end to it," she says. "Let's end it all."

"How?" I ask.

She nods at the ghost birds. "Let's set them free."

I look back at the swooping, diving ghosts, screaming like banshees as they rip Grange apart. He's hardly more than bone now, yet he's still moving, still feebly trying to beat them off. I catch a glimpse of his human hand in the moonlight, bone and blood glinting from his entreating fingers. Then he collapses and doesn't move again.

The women he killed have had their vengeance, but they aren't satisfied. They still circle him, wailing and screaming. Killing Grange was their right and their due, but it hasn't saved them. It hasn't released them from their bonds. They are still chained to their deaths, to their suffering.

"You two can help me," Momma says. It's so strange to hear her speaking. I'd forgotten what her voice sounds like when it's not lifted in song. It's steely. "Come down here," she says.

I kneel, pressing my hands to the wet soil of the meadow. I can feel the river's rage, a fury so vast it can't ever be sated. It will swallow the world and still not be full. Because there is no justice for what Grange has done. There is no punishment that can undo the pain and the suffering he's inflicted on seven women, on their families and everyone who loves them. The scars he's made run like fault lines through the Bend, threatening to break it apart.

I breathe deep. Natasha can't get her sister back, and neither can Momma. We can't give these women back their lives. No magic could. But maybe we can set them free, like Momma said. Maybe we can release them.

Natasha is still standing, gazing at the wreckage of her sister's killer with an unreadable expression. I tug her hand, pulling her down with me.

"Between the three of us, I think we can manage it," Momma says.

"How?" Natasha asks.

"The Bend will transform them, if we direct its magic."

"They—they can be human? Alive?" Natasha asks, her voice tremulous. The raw hope in her voice draws tears to my eyes.

Momma shakes her head. "No, not human. But more than wraiths. We'll give them what's left of that bastard's life. It will be enough to make them whole."

I put my hands to the ground and I sense it. Grange's blood is seeping into the wet earth, a powerful source of life that threatens to twist its magic into a hideous shape forever.

"Tell us what to do," I say.

"Draw his blood out," Momma says. "His life force with it. We need to separate it from the land, or it will change things, the way Erin Lloyd's life offering did. I don't want to think about what his essence could do to our magic if left unchecked."

Following Momma's movements, I help her draw it up and out of the ground, let it pool around us until the metallic smell of it pervades the air and we're kneeling in a pool of Grange's spent life.

"Now offer it to the ghosts," Momma says.

Natasha cups some of it in her hands and holds it up.

One of the ghosts begins to move away from Grange, toward us, blinking its human eyes. It lands on Natasha's outstretched arms and sings. It's an agonizing sound, filled with loss. We can see the moment the ghost begins to take in Grange's life, and I can feel the creature's hold on the Bend lessen.

Another bird lands and bends to drink from my cupped hands. The Bend's twisted magic was sustaining the creatures in their ghostly shapes, but as we feed Grange's life to them, they begin to change. Their shadows become brown-and-white feathers, and their human eyes turn black. They blink at us for a moment or two and then they fly away, now a pair of barred owls. They will have the freedom of the skies, the power of their beaks and their claws, without the burden of their human deaths.

More of the ghosts come and drink Grange's life from our hands. One becomes a great horned owl, and another a barn owl, beautiful and ethereal. As the ghosts transform, the anger of the river dies down until it simmers instead of rages. The broken feeling inside me softens.

One ghost lingers for a long time, staring into Momma's face. It's Aunt Sage. Tears pour down Momma's cheeks as the ghost begins to transform, its misty grayness softening into tawny, blond-brown features. Wise, yellow-ringed eyes peer out at us. It makes a high sound like a whinnying horse. A screech owl.

Then it flies away. Momma bows down to the earth, sobs wracking her body. Her sister is finally gone.

I take the last handful of Grange's life and hold it up to one remaining ghost. Rochelle's lovely blue eyes blink back at me in the air. The others took their freedom easily, grateful for a reprieve from their rage. But Rochelle hangs on to hers, grips it in her claws.

Natasha kneels beside me, gazing at her sister. "Can't you make her human again? Can't you bring her back?" she asks, her voice cracking.

I shake my head. If I could give Natasha back her sister, I would. I would do anything to give her back.

"Ro," Natasha whispers. "I love you."

The ghost beats her wings and sings.

"I don't think she wants to go free," Natasha says. "She doesn't want to forget."

I meet Rochelle's eyes. They blaze with anger.

"She wants to stay and protect you," I say.

"Ro, I'm safe now. You can go free," Natasha says, smiling through her tears.

Rochelle screams and beats her wings.

"Please," Natasha says. "I couldn't bear for you to stay like this. It would hurt me worse than anything. I love you so much. Please let Della help you."

"It's yours," I say, lifting my cupped hands to her once more. "You can choose whatever you want." Rochelle stares at me for a long moment, as if weighing me, deciding whether she can trust Natasha to me. Then she dips her beak and drinks, and I watch the Bend make one last transformation. Or rather, Rochelle makes her own.

She transforms into a snowy owl, her feathers so white in the darkness that she glows.

Natasha's breath catches. She laughs. "You would choose the most dramatic option," she says. She reaches out a trembling hand and strokes the owl's feathers. "I love you, Ro."

The owl takes off into the sky, winging away into the night. We watch it until it disappears into the unreachable distance.

The Bend goes quiet under us. That current of rage is still there, a deep vein in the earth and the water, but it has lost its destructive edge. In time, I think it will heal.

Relief washes over me. Grange is dead. The girls he killed are free. Momma is human again. It's over.

Natasha's surge of energy from all our spell work leaves her and she collapses beside me again, only a bruised and battered girl. I'm exhausted too, the thrum of the magic's energy leaving me depleted. But there's one thing left to do.

Grange's body lies nearby, torn and ruined, his crimes avenged. He did all the damage one man could, and yet the river goes on running, spreading my ancestor's magic through the Bend.

I stand over the dead and worthless corpse for a long moment, considering. There's nothing left of him but bones and sinew—a little food for the river's fish. He can sink to the bottom and be forgotten, which is more than he deserves.

I kick his body into the river, a final offering.

Satisfied, I go and lie down on the wet earth between Momma and Natasha. I gaze up into the bruised sky, listening to the rush of the water as the river dies down, listening to the brush in the meadow sway in the wind. I lie still, waiting for someone to find us, waiting to see what the world will make of the Bend's idea of justice.

The clouds part, and a hazy sickle moon shines down, sharp as one of the river siren's claws. I look over at Natasha, who gazes up into the sky, tears glinting on her cheeks. I take her hand and she laces her fingers in mine.

On my other side, Momma begins to sing.

EPILOGUE
NATASHA

Winter is here. Frost glitters on the grass in the morning and the river moves slow and sluggish, heavy with ice. I sit on a huge, smooth stone by the water's edge, my breath steaming in the air. I feel so at home on the Bend now that sometimes it's strange to remember it's the place my sister died, the place I almost died too. Somehow there's even more power in my connection to this place because of that. Because Grange is dead and Rochelle is alive, in her own way, even if it's not in the way I wanted. And I'm still here.

As awful and painful as it has been to uncover Grange's crimes, there's relief in it too, a sense of laying things to rest. The bones of five women were found buried under Grange's cabin. They were returned to the women's families for burial, except for one of the girls, who is still a Jane Doe. It hurts me to know she was never identified, that either there's a family out there somewhere wondering what's happened to their girl, or there's no one to miss her, which might be worse.

Georgia's wildlife cameras captured enough of Grange assaulting Della and me to make it easy for the police to believe the rest of our story. Della and I weren't sure how much to tell the cops about what happened. But between seeing what Grange did to me and finding the bones under his house, no one was sad to hear he drowned during a struggle with us and Ruby. It took some convincing to get the police to let them out of jail, but Miles and Della's dad weren't charged with any crimes.

The only thing the police didn't want to listen to was what Grange had told us about Jake chasing Rochelle onto the nature park. But Detective Ocampo believed every word. I don't know how she did it, but she got Jake to confess to his part in Rochelle's death, including his false alibi. Maybe Ocampo is a better detective than I gave her credit for, or maybe Jake's guilt had finally gotten too heavy for him. Either way, he was sentenced to six months in jail for lying to the police and obstructing justice. Six months isn't enough to pay for the loss of my sister's life, but at least his career was ruined. Della and I are still cooking up a spell to make sure Jake can't ever do to another woman what he did to Rochelle.

Georgia is using her own sort of magic to seek justice. After being so instrumental in figuring out what happened to Rochelle, she decided she was ready to do the same for Lena. She dropped her nightclub idea and instead made a film about Lena's disappearance, tying it to the thousands of unsolved disappearances of Black women and girls in the US. Margo and I helped her with research and promotion and anything else she needed. It was hard to face all those missing girls and their families, but it was empowering too because we were together in our grief and our need to fight.

The documentary is brilliant and beautiful and absolutely enraging. It even changed Georgia's parents' minds about helping pay for film school. Highland Rim hosted a screening of the film last week, and I talked Della into going with me. She and Georgia are still wary of one another, but if I leave it to Margo, I think she'll have them learning to like one another before too much longer.

Della, along with the rest of her family, has had her hands full trying to soothe the Bend back to normal after the damage Grange did. Now that I'm on winter break, I come here every day, and I can tell how much progress they've made. Today the Bend feels almost whole. I stretch out on my rock and listen to the river, trying to feel its movements in my muscles, the way Ruby has been teaching me to do.

Della sits down beside me so quietly I don't notice her for a moment. It's only her smell that lets me know she's here, the lingering scent of herbs in her hair, the last vestiges of plants on her hands.

"Hey," she says, and I open my eyes and smile. She kisses me softly and then leans back on her elbows to study me. It's hard to believe she's the same girl I met last June. She's still arrogant and rough around the edges, still contemptuous of everyone. There's still something slightly bloody about her smile.

But there's a lightness in her now, like a flower opening up to the sun. Not that I'd ever let her hear me say that.

"You want to learn old spells or make new ones today?" she asks.

Excitement rises up in me. "New, definitely new," I say. Spell work has been our courtship, to use an old-fashioned word. We go out with Georgia or Margo sometimes, but we're more comfortable together here, in a world we can share. Della taught me all the spells I wanted to learn, taught me how to walk softly through the woods, to identify plants and harvest them, to speak the right words as I stir a brew.

But I taught her too: to think of new spells meant for something other than vengeance, spells for protection and healing, spells for working good. We figured them out together.

The magic flows up through me now too, and it feels old and complex, tinged with pain and loss. But I feel like we're making it new, helping it grow soft new blossoms to match its thorns. The thorns are still there, though, and I'm grateful for them. I'm grateful to have some small measure of magic to wield against a world that thinks women's bodies are disposable, that their wills are weak.

Men's voices echo across the meadow, and my body tenses. Della puts a protective arm around me and turns, looking for the source. "Probably just some hikers," she says.

I let my muscles relax as the voices float downriver. There will always be men in the world who want to control and hurt and kill us. Men who drug us and drive us off roads and hit us with their fists. Men who take girls and make them their toys. Men who gain pleasure from our pain. Men like Jake and Grange.

They will walk through this world until it comes unraveled. They will keep on doing what they've been doing for thousands and thousands of years until the earth has had enough and ends us all.

But today I refuse to fear them, not a single one. They have strength and cruelty and endless complicity. They walk tall and almost always win. But not here, not on the Bend, where owls that were once girls fly free. Not here, where magic rises up to meet my will.

Here, we are witches and men are nothing.

Here, the river has teeth.

ACKNOWLEDGMENTS

A handful of kind and brilliant people made *The River Has Teeth* possible. The first is my spouse, John, who was there every step of the way, listening to my ideas, talking me through my magic system and plot problems, and assuring me that this book was absolutely better than my last one. John, thank you for your love, support, and all the scrambled eggs you made me. I did good when I picked you.

My editors, Alice Jerman and Clare Vaughn, have been amazing to work with, as always. Alice, thank you for helping me find the soft center of this sharp-toothed story. Thank you to my literary agent, Lauren Spieller: You are the fiercest of fierce advocates, and I would be totally lost without you. Enormous thanks to everyone else on my team at Triada US Literary Agency and HarperTeen, who all do such excellent work.

The first fellow writer who told me they loved this book was Ash Van Otterloo. Ash, thank you for getting my book better than anyone else ever could. I can't fully express how much it means to be seen and recognized and to have your words loved by someone who feels like a fellow traveler in the world. You're a star.

I've got to shout-out my pal Cayla Keenan, who listens to me whine in her Twitter DMs more than anyone should be subjected to. Cayla, thanks for always being ready to knock out someone's teeth for me. You are the ALL-CAPS queen of my heart.

In addition to those mentioned above, lots of generous people have given me feedback on various drafts of this book. I'd especially like to thank Brian Kennedy, Lauri Sellers, Lisa Amowitz, Em Shotwell, Wendy Heard, Hannah Whitten, Julie Patton, and Candice Conner. Thank you to my sensitivity readers for your insight, and to Penelope Gerosa for helping with my fencing references. Any mistakes I made are my own.

Fellow writers are immense comforts, and I'd like to thank Logan Malone, Rajani LaRocca, Kit Rosewater, Courtney Gould, Cat Scully, and Dante Medema for always being there to commiserate and uplift me.

I'd also like to thank my mother-in-law, Kathy, who might actually be my biggest cheerleader. She reads nearly everything I write, and even when it's way too strange and scary for her, she tells me how good it is. Kathy, thank you for always being excited about even the most piddly of my publishing news. You're the coolest.

Thank you to my family for loving and supporting me, especially my sister, Melinda, who always makes me laugh, and my father-in-law, Bill, who keeps me well stocked with weird books and outdoor survival gear. And finally, thanks to my momma, Sheliah, who is without a doubt the wildest, fiercest, mostly truly witchy woman I've ever met.